THREE FAE MONTE

RISE OF MAGIC
BOOK 4

STEFON MEARS

Also by Stefon Mears

The Rise of Magic Series
Magician's Choice
Sleight of Mind
Lunar Alchemy
Three Fae Monte
The Sphinx Principle
Double Backed Magic
Mercury Fold (forthcoming)

Cavan Oltblood Series
Half a Wizard
The Ice Dagger
Spells of Undeath

Power City Tales
Not Quite Bulletproof
No Money in Heroism

Standalones
The Hireling
The Captain's Cat
Save Whiskers!
The Ogre of Threepeaks
Between the Cracks
Sects and the City
Prince of a Thousand Worlds
Devil's Night
Portal-Land, Oregon
Stealing from Pirates
Fade to Gold
With a Broken Sword
Twice Against the Dragon
The House on Cedar Street
Sudden Death
On the Edge of Faerie

Short Story Collections
Spell Slingers
Twisted Timelines
Longhairs and Short Tales: A Collection of Cat Stories
Dangerous Space
Confronting Legends (Spells & Swords Vol. 1)
The Patreon Collection, Vol. 1-8 (Vol. 9, coming soon)

Nonfiction
The 30-Day Novel and Beyond!

Spells for Hire Series
Devil's Shoestring
Zombie Powder
Spirit Trap
Dragon's Blood

The Telepath Trilogy
Surviving Telepathy
Immoral Telepathy
Targeting Telepathy

Edge of Humanity Series
Caught Between Monsters
Hunting Monsters

Jumpstart Duchy Series
Into the Torn Kingdoms
The Dragon's Gold
The Gift Castle
The Deadly Feast
The King's Test
Triumph in the Torn Kingdoms

Published by Thousand Faces Publishing, Portland, Oregon

http://1kfaces.com

Starfield image © Ashestosky | Dreamstime.com (File ID: 11418999)

Jupiter illustration © Olga Kurbatova | Dreamstime.com (File ID: 145496119)

ISBN: 978-1-948490-07-8

The year is 2027
Six decades after the Rise of Magic

1

"You're doomed," Fionn said.

Rough words for Donal Cuthbert to hear from the lips of his own *cú sidhe* familiar, a meter-tall emerald green deerhound, sitting on the grass beside him. That only Donal could understand those words did little for their sting. And that those words carried an accent somewhere between Irish and Scottish only made them worse. As though his whole family tree was pronouncing doom upon his head.

"*Fuist*," Donal hushed his familiar in Gaelic. He kept his attention where it belonged — on his wards. They would fall. He had no doubt of that, especially since he could do nothing more to improve them. The only question was when.

The mere thought of time was enough to let that ticking sound back into Donal's thoughts. He banished it, as he banished the rest of the summer day around him.

Right now, only his wards mattered.

A sphere of blues and reds, half in and half above the gray, granite table before him. Wards designed to repel magical intrusion. A swirling ball of magic, the threads of its art shifting and sliding in their efforts to safeguard the secret Donal had concealed within them.

Across the table, his foe worked just as hard to breach those wards as Donal had worked to cast them. He could hear the tones of her efforts in his mind. The sound of her attention brushing against the threads of his magic as though strumming the strings of a harp.

She had the advantage. She already knew his signature. Could account for that element as she sought the barest flaws, the tiniest loopholes in the framework of Donal's spell. Or even just the frays where his attention might have been less than crystal-perfect while he was casting.

But Donal's focus was better than it had been a year ago, the last time his spells had faced a serious contest. Though that had been a battle for his life, and this—

"Ha!" said his foe.

His wards collapsed.

The timer dinged.

Donal sighed and sat back, aware of the day around him now. The grassy park with its gentle swells and its ash and alder trees. The warm sunshine of a June day here on the campus of CalThaum San Luis Obispo. The beads of sweat under the collar of his short-sleeved green airsilk shirt. The cool granite stool he sat on. The scent of the fresh-cut grass, smile-inducing on its own, for the recollections of his older brother having to mow the lawn back in Santa Cruz. Whenever Donal was angry at Bran, he'd sip lemonade while watching Bran mow.

Other students around the park lounged on blankets or participated in a massive game of touch football, that seemed to involve at least twenty players to a side.

And across the table designed for outdoor games of chess, sat Esmeralda. Pretty even at the worst of times, with her smooth dusky skin and waves of curly black hair, but right now she all but glowed in her red and yellow sundress. Her brown eyes flashed with the triumph of her smile.

And she cocked an eyebrow at Donal.

"Not much of a secret," she said.

"Hey, most of our classmates conjured their familiars in their first year of college. How many of them would give me shit for waiting until after not only getting my B.T., but passing my Journeyman's tests before even *trying* for one?"

"I prefer to think," Fionn said, pitching its words so that anyone could hear them, "that you waited until the perfect familiar became available."

Esmeralda glanced at Fionn, but narrowed her eyes at Donal, unconvinced.

"Oh," Donal said, "and I suppose your being jealous of your older sister was some big secret? Come on, Esme, she *teaches* here. Pretty sure the whole cohort has seen the way you look at her."

Esmeralda laughed, a rough, but honest, nasal sound. "Fair enough."

"Still," Donal said, as he stood. "You beat my time, so lunch is on me. Where do you want to go?"

But Esmeralda was looking past Donal, behind him to his right. Her mouth hung open in shock. "Isn't that…"

She let the words trail off, and Donal spun to his right.

Leaning against an alder tree stood a tall, handsome man with flowing brown hair and finely tailored airsilk clothes that ended in knee-high calfskin boots. A man nearly as slender as the rapier at his side.

But the most impressive aspect of the man was his palpable aura of power. Even after a year of studying with a half-dozen Hierophants at the finest university of Thaumaturgy on the West Coast — perhaps in the whole of the United North American States — this man's aura of power was beyond anything Donal had ever felt.

Three times before Donal had met this man, and each time he had felt humbled.

"Yes," Donal said, in answer to Esmeralda's unfinished question. "That's Hierophant Nicholas Mason."

"Good afternoon," Hierophant Mason said. "Good to see that the grad students still play the same games as the undergrads."

"Well, to be fair," Donal said, fighting down the heat he could feel rising in his neck, "we do play a more advanced version."

Hierophant Mason laughed. "I wasn't hiding an insult. Ward-breaking is a valuable skill, but I worry sometimes that newer magicians are too quick to abandon the basics."

"I'd challenge you to a game," Donal said, making Esmeralda gasp, "but I don't think I'd prove much opposition for you."

"Do you *know* him?" Esmeralda whispered to Donal.

"Oh, forgive me," Donal said. "Hierophant Mason, this is Journeyman Esmeralda Villaseñor, currently the top doctoral student in our cohort."

"We're tied, actually," Esmeralda said, losing her fight not to blush. "It's an honor, Hierophant."

"The honor is mine. I look forward to numbering you among my peers." Hierophant Mason gave Esmeralda a slight bow. "But now, alas, I must apologize for interrupting your lunch. I need to borrow Donal here for a while for a very important task. As some small recompense, name any restaurant you like, and my familiar shall make sure your lunch will be billed to me."

"I, well…" Esmeralda blushed even harder and looked away, as though Hierophant Mason had personally invited her to lunch.

Donal stifled a sigh. It seemed his lot in life to be shown up by more advanced magicians. Usually it was his brother Bran. He was as used to that as he'd ever get. But now Hierophant Mason too?

Competing with any Hierophant would have been bad enough. As Doctors of Thaumaturgy, Hierophants represented the pinnacle of modern magical skill and knowledge. But this particular Hierophant, well, even Bran couldn't compete with him.

Not only had Hierophant Mason cracked no fewer than *sixteen* secrets of that ancient grimoire *The Picatrix* and codified *three new types* of kinetic spells, but he had worked as a *licensed champion* for over a decade before retiring, unbeaten with either sword or spell. And that named only a few of his accomplishments.

The man was practically a folk hero, perhaps the first since Lloyd Bird restored magic to the world, some sixty years ago.

Finally Esmeralda managed to say, shyly, "Well, I've always wanted to try The Cormorant."

Of course she picked the most expensive restaurant in town. The one Donal had been hoping to use as a first-real-date treat, if lunch had gone well.

"Done and done," Hierophant Mason said. "I suggest their veal. Exquisite."

"Thank you!" And then Esmeralda actually giggled as she turned away and sped off with her head ducked and her strides exactly even across the thick grass.

"Oh, dear," Hierophant Mason said, looking back at Donal, who must not have been hiding his disappointment as well as he thought. "I just stepped in something, didn't I?"

Donal sighed and shook his head. "Nothing, most likely. What's going on? You and Hierophant MacDougall said I could finish grad school before—"

"This has nothing to do with investigating criminal magicians." Hierophant Mason frowned. "Well, probably not, anyway. But it's important, and you're the best man for the job. We should go somewhere private to talk."

Donal agreed, and as they walked across the park, Fionn commented once more in words that only Donal could understand.

"I told you you were doomed. Did you think I was talking about your game?"

IF DONAL HAD TO PLAY HOST TO A HIEROPHANT, AT LEAST HE HAD A good apartment for the job. Far better than he would have been able to afford on his old courier's salary, even with all the off-world jobs he'd taken, and the surprisingly high percentage of them that activated the combat-pay provision.

Of course, it was courier work that had put Donal in the right place at the right time to save the life — and the very mind — of Donatello Mancuso, the head of 4M, a major interplanetary corporation. Mr. Mancuso had been grateful enough to practically give Donal a blank check for education, living expenses, and broadly defined "incidentals."

And Mr. Mancuso had insisted that Donal not "skimp."

So the apartment Donal escorted his guest to that fine June day sat at the top of the three-story red brick apartment just off the edge of the CalThaum campus, at the foot of a picturesque hill, with a small river running past.

The sitting area of Donal's current apartment was bigger than any of the three apartments Donal had kept during his undergraduate studies in Berkeley or, after graduation, in San Francisco. To reflect that, Donal had abandoned his old mishmash of college furnishings.

These days he decorated in simple browns and greens, with several rubber plants to make the feel of his apartment suit the cool, Mediterranean climate of San Luis Obispo. Big comfortable couches and chairs, but a small dining set near the kitchen. Some kind of worn, dark wood for the hardwood flooring.

All kept fresh and dust-free through the ministrations of an air elemental named Uulians, conjured and bound by Donal.

"Very nice," Hierophant Mason said, looking around. "Is that a dedicated laboratory I see?"

Hierophant Mason was looking to the left side of the sitting room, where Donal had converted the second bedroom into his personal library/laboratory, with a permanent magic circle etched in the center of the floor, an alchemy table set to one side, and shelves of books along the walls.

Donal only smiled in answer to the obvious question.

"So Mancuso did right by you." Hierophant Mason smiled. "Glad to know it. You certainly did enough for him."

"I was just doing what was right," Donal said. "Coffee? Tea?"

"Nothing, thanks," Hierophant Mason said, "except a place to sit."

And with that the Hierophant eased comfortably into a brown recliner, his sword somehow finding the perfect alignment down his leg without appearing to cause the least discomfort. Might have helped that it didn't have a fancy basket hilt. Just a simple steel handle with tightly wrapped black cloth on the grip, and a faceted, teardrop-shaped gem of dark purple at the join of the crossbars.

If Donal had tried to sit in that chair wearing a sword, well, the results would have been awkward at best.

Just one of the reasons Donal didn't wear a sword.

Donal sat in the recliner's match, across the wide coffee table from his guest. Fionn sat on the floor beside Donal, apparently as interested in what the Hierophant had to say as Donal was.

Donal's stomach rumbled, as though to spite him. Or maybe just to remind Donal that he'd been looking forward to lunch almost as much for the food as for the chance to get to know Esmeralda better. He hadn't eaten anything since dawn but two slices of toast and a half a cantaloupe.

Hierophant Mason raised an eyebrow, but Donal shook his head and shunted aside his hunger. He'd need food soon enough, but right now he wanted to demonstrate a little control for the Hierophant.

Hierophant Mason smiled.

"You don't need to impress me, Donal. Fix something to eat if you like."

"After you're done. What's going on? Is this about Li Hua?"

Tai Shi Li Hua. Journeyman magician, interplanetary expert in combat and security, Donal's ex-girlfriend — and the woman who had subtly developed iron-clad control over the mind of her boss, Donatello Mancuso, and through him tried to set up her own inter-planetary shadow government.

"Tai Shi? No." Hierophant Mason sat forward in his chair, satisfied urgency in his tone as he continued. "She's appealing her case, of course, both the conviction and the sentence. But I don't think she's got a chance. You and Magister Machado, not to mention Mancuso's excellent assistants, gathered too much evidence for her lawyers to find a seam."

Donal's mouth tasted dry. No surprise. The subject alone was more than enough to quell his desire for food. He'd been falling in love with Li Hua when he found out what kind of person she really was. The closest he'd come to dating in the year since then would have been today's lunch with Esmeralda…

"What will be done with her?"

"Fair question. I'm pretty sure they gave her life, under full magical suppression. If there's anywhere her appeal might find a crack, it's the sentence. First conviction of its type. And with so little adjudicated case law on the books involving anything close to this scale of magical crime, they've had to lean heavily on precedents like conspiracy, racketeering, extortion and the like." He shook his head. "And, of course, her licenses have been revoked, and I'm pretty sure the U.N.A.S. Thaum Board severed her connection to her familiar."

Donal shivered at the mere thought of it. He remembered her familiar. Pinyin-Lung, a spirit dragon that was every bit as much a part of her as Fionn was of Donal.

"But I'm not here about Tai Shi," Hierophant Mason said, waving a dismissive hand. "I'm here about Ganymede."

"Oh. Ganymede." Donal sighed. "Which of Bran's great accomplishments did you want to ask about? The work he did leading that first scouting voyage? The way he saved Ganymede's entire first ship of settlers? I hear they're commissioning a statue of him for that one. Or maybe—"

"Donal."

"I can introduce you, if you like. It's no trouble. In fact—"

"*Journeyman!*" Hierophant Mason snapped that word out, and as he did he snapped his open hand into a fist.

Donal jumped as shock jolted through his aura. As though he'd been slapped, hard, everywhere at once. The sting of the aftermath made every hair on his body stand up.

The Jenkins Flash. The basis for Thaumaboxing, and without the spells establishing a boxing ring, a very difficult technique to pull off. Especially with such sharp force.

"I'm sorry, Hierophant," Donal said.

"I hate power games," Hierophant Mason said, sitting forward on the edge of his seat now, and his eyes blazing. "I hate the fact that the climate has changed enough that we're not all just *magicians* when we're among ourselves. That even when only surrounded by other magicians we must play the bureaucrat's game of Initiate, Journeyman, Magister and Hierophant. That was never what Lloyd Bird intended for us. But as all the gods stand witness, if I must accept the state of things, then *I will use it* when I must."

Hierophant Mason stood. Paced sharply back and forth in front of the recliner.

"So now, Journeyman, I will speak and you will listen, until such time as I ask you to respond."

He glared at Donal, as though daring him to speak even a confirmation aloud.

Donal said nothing.

"Good. Now." Hierophant Mason stopped pacing, one hand resting on the hilt of his sword, and faced Donal. "Had I wanted to talk to Magister Bran Cuthbert, I would be in Mazatlán right now, where he keeps his small estate. Tell me, Journeyman, am I in Mazatlán right now?"

Donal blinked. "No, Hierophant."

"No, I am not. So I trust it's evident that I have come to talk to you, not your brother." Hierophant Mason drew a deep breath then, and smoothed his voice as he continued. "I know what it is to walk in someone's shadow. I trained as a champion under Angus McElroy. Never saw a finer swordsman. For at least two years my name might as well have been 'McElroy's Apprentice.' But I made my own way, and so have you."

Donal raised an eyebrow and Hierophant Mason nodded.

"That's right, I said 'have,' not 'will.' Don't undervalue your accomplishments just because they haven't brought you fame. You've accomplished more in a year than most Journeymen will in twenty. You've saved lives, Donal. And if what we suspect about Tai Shi's ultimate plans is true, you may have prevented the relegation of all non-magicians to nothing more than second-class citizens at best, a *servant class* at worst."

Hierophant Mason shook his head slowly.

"Never forget, Donal. The core of a magician's power lies in his confidence. Don't you *dare* sublimate yours to the achievements of others."

"I've told him the same thing," Fionn said, "at least a dozen times."

"Then as long as I'm lecturing you," Hierophant Mason added with a smile, *"listen to your familiar."*

"I like him," Fionn said.

Donal fought not to squirm in his seat.

"Now," Hierophant Mason said as he resumed his seat. "Enough lecture. Let's try to resume something like a conversation, shall we?"

Donal nodded.

Hierophant Mason chuckled, then his face got serious.

"Now. I need you to go to Ganymede. There's … a situation developing. I need you to check it out. Handle it, if necessary. I'd go myself, but I've got to get back to Luna. Today. I presume you know what's been discovered, on Luna?"

"Of course."

Donal knew, all right. It was all anyone at school had talked about for months. A new class of spirit — they called themselves the Rhian people — that could self-incarnate using alchemically modified lunar soil. A new form of sapient life, complete with bodies. Donal didn't know exactly what Hierophant Mason had to do with the discovery, but no doubt it was something big and important, that would get written up in the history texts.

"Well, if the rumor I'm hearing is true," Hierophant Mason said, "the settlers may have discovered something similar on Ganymede. And I need you to check it out. Think of it as a summer internship."

"But—"

"Donal," Hierophant Mason said in a flat tone, "you're clever, inventive, and have been developing a foundation in Enochian theory, which I suspect will help. I wouldn't tell you you're the right man for the job if I had any doubts."

"No," Donal said, with a slightly abashed smile, "it's not that. It's just, there's no commercial traffic allowed to fly to Ganymede. Strictly military right now."

"I know. So I've arranged private transport for you."

Donal's next question almost lodged in his throat, but he managed to cough it out in a rush.

"It's not Starchaser Spacelines, is it? Because every time I set foot on one of their ships, someone tries to kill me."

"No," Hierophant Mason said, laughing. "I confess I did try to get their Captain John Jacobs to come out of retirement for this. No civilian captain in history has handled more uncertain routes than he has. Thought the lure of Ganymede might have been enough. But alas he was no more eager to transport you again than you are to ride in one of his ships. But that's all right. A cruiser would be too big for this anyway. Guaranteed to draw attention. No." Hierophant Mason rubbed his hands together. "I've found the perfect captain for you."

***

EDIK BARSHAI HELD THE SWORD IN A LOOSE GRIP. IT WASN'T *HIS* SABER, but at least it was *a* saber. Still. Balance wasn't quite right.

No excuses though. Goodness knew the rest of the setting was as good as he would get for a swordfight. The smooth, blue-white stone of his own ship's landing bay, here in Kennedy Spaceport, was free of any grooves or flaws that might catch his boots. All local stone, hewn from the moon herself, but kept flawless — though not slippery — through steady applications of thaumaturgy and alchemy by the Port Authority.

His helioship sat two dozen paces behind him. All around him, the walls of the open-topped cylinder that formed his landing bay, at least that far from where he stood. No crates or cargo to impede the fight. They had the room to move around all they wanted.

Even Dola, Edik's feline familiar, stood at least a half-dozen paces behind him. No way the meter-tall, shaggy, translucent gray cat could impede Edik's footwork.

The air was cool for a June day, and dry, tasting a little less of licorice than it usually did in Kennedy, where the first attempts to make the moon's surface habitable had left … marks. The air tasted of licorice, the water of lemons, and the grass outside the spaceport looked more dark blue than green, while the sky above looked more pale green than blue.

Still. Not too hot or too cold. Regular terrain. Plenty of room to maneuver. Everything was as perfect as it could get.

Unfortunately, that included his opponent.

Facing Edik, at a distance of seven paces, stood Carl Jones. Taller even than Edik, and muscled, with the little scars on his hands that came from a life of action. Jones had the kind of ebon black skin that picked up highlights from his muted purple work shirt, worn with black slacks and loafers.

Was that how all licensed champions dressed? Edik didn't know. He'd only met the one, as far as he knew. Maybe it was a kind of uniform, like suits for businesspeople.

"Ready?" Jones asked, and to the man's credit he let the word sound simple. No condescension. No mockery. Jones might have fought a thousand more swordfights than Edik, but he seemed to be giving this no less focus.

Jones held his own saber in a casual grip, point down.

Edik nodded. Raised his saber in salute. Was saluted in return.

"Begin," Jones said.

Edik swallowed against the sudden lump in his throat as he advanced a slow pace. His eyes flicked to Jones' sword, to his easy posture, his casual steps. Edik's heart had lurched to ramming speed, but Jones looked as though he were merely out for a walk, with his sword.

Five paces distant now.

Three.

Edik cut at his opponent's face. Tried to catch Jones between steps.

Jones parried as though he had all the time in the world. Shook his head.

Edik spun his wrist. Tried to turn that cut into a feint. Thrust at Jones' chest.

Another lazy parry. Another head shake.

Edik feinted high, then low, then attacked low. A quick jab at Jones' right hip.

The parry came fast and hard. Beat Edik's sword out wide without ever turning the point of Jones' saber away from Edik's torso.

Jones thrust.

Jones' blunted saber *thunked* into Edik's padded coverlet, right over the heart.

Edik's face burned with shame. He ripped off the training coverlet and threw it down.

"Enough of that," Jones said in a warning tone. "It's your emotions that are giving you away."

"A month we've been at this. And it's not like I'd never picked up a sword before. But I feel like I'm not getting anywhere."

"Your wrist is better. Your attacks. Your stance. But you're still broadcasting." Jones lowered his practice sword. "Not much, I admit. Probably ninety-nine out of a hundred opponents won't catch it. But if a great family comes after you, you can't broadcast anything. Because a great family won't send the ninety-nine after you. They'll send the one."

Edik took a deep breath. He felt more comfortable without the padding anyway. Not that the coverlet was too hot or constricting, only that he preferred his loose, red, button-up shirt, and his black slacks with the silver stripe down the side.

Style mattered.

Edik re-fought their brief bout in his head, looking for his own tell but finding nothing.

"If it's not my stance, and it's not my wrist—"

"Your eyes," Jones said with a nod. "Your emotions bleed into your eyes and tell me everything, even before your hand knows what to do."

"It's about focus," Dola said as he strolled up. The spirit cat spoke in a Russian accent as heavy as Edik's own father had had. "Think of a swordfight as a spell. In much the same way, your emotions must serve your goal."

"Exactly," Jones said.

Edik tugged at his blonde Van Dyke beard, as much for the

distracting sting as anything else. But before he could gather any words, Jones spoke again.

"Every real duel has consequences for losing. When those consequences are yours, when they really matter to you, of course your emotions will press in on you. But you're letting that happen even in a training bout. Why?"

It was a good question, and one Edik didn't have a quick and easy answer for. But he barely had time to look for one before North came roaring into the landing bay like a short, gruff hurricane.

"What's this I saw on your schedule?"

"Calm down, Roger." Edik pointedly dropped his practice sword and raised his hands. "I was going to tell you all about it later at the daily."

North might have been short, but he made up for it in muscled breadth. Scruffy, short black hair and beard, North might have looked like a craggy pirate, but he still insisted on wearing that crisp, navy blue faux-uniform, complete with gold clusters at the collar.

And he looked mad enough to draw the cutlass he wore.

Wouldn't be the first time Edik crossed swords with North. They were enemies for a lot longer than they'd been partners.

"Don't tell me to calm down." North punched his palm. "What the hell do you think you're doing? Leaving Kennedy at a time like this?"

"Well," Jones said, his deep voice loud enough to carry. "I'll just be running along then. See you later, Edik."

"You wait right there," North said, pointing to the spot where Jones was standing.

That wasn't good. North had to have been even angrier than he looked, if he was willing to risk Jones' wrath.

Jones cocked an eyebrow and slowly crossed his arms, but if North caught the implied threat in those brown eyes, Edik couldn't tell. North turned right back to Edik.

"Well?"

"I know we have a lot going on, but—"

"A lot going on?" North gnashed his teeth. "You'll be skipping close

to a month's worth of tours, *and* leaving me to support Anna on my own."

That last was the only part Edik really felt guilty about. North was a partner, but Anna Lukyanova was a friend. And this friend was acting as diplomat and intermediary for the Rhian. Anna was more than capable, and had the resources and contacts she'd accumulated growing up in one of the great families, but right now she needed all the people in her corner she could get.

Pressure was coming at her from all sides: the universities, the governments of Earth *and* Luna — including Kennedy's own governor — and worst of all, every one of the great families of Luna was trying get a piece of the Rhian people.

Including her own father.

Edik hated the idea of abandoning her now.

Jones cleared his throat. True, he was supporting Anna too. And true, Jones was a licensed champion. But he wasn't licensed as a magician, he wasn't a local, and he wasn't part of the Lunar business community.

Even North had more standing in this mess than Jones.

Anna had Edmund on her side too, though neither North nor Jones had mentioned him. Probably took Edmund for granted now that he and Anna were dating. That was a mistake. Edmund had better business instincts, and a better head for organization, than the rest of them combined.

Unfortunately, Edmund was still young enough to be naïve, and inexperienced enough that no one would take him seriously until he gave them no choice.

"Can't be helped," Edik said with a shake of his head. "We said we wanted to expand our charter business? Well, this is a charter for a *Hierophant*, Roger. Nicholas Mason himself."

"Piss on Hierophants, and piss on Mason. We need you and your ship here."

Dola hissed in a pained-sounding breath at North's words, while Jones scoffed.

North whirled on Jones. "What?"

"I dare you to say that in front of Mason."

"Piss. On. Mason." North turned to Dola. "And knock off your commentary. No one asked you."

"Back the fuck up, North," Edik said. Fire burned in his belly now, and he could taste it in his words. "I get that you're angry and you've got reason. But Dola is *my* familiar, and *my* familiar gets to say what he wants, when he wants. You have a problem with that, you bring it to me."

"Thank you, Edik," Dola said with a head-bow.

"Now," Edik said sharply, before North could respond. "I know the timing sucks, but use your head, Roger. My *Third Son* may be a helioship, but it's one of the smallest on the market. We're never going to get big charters. *But*, if we become known as the liner to *Hierophants*, we'll get all the high-end trade. Better rates for pretty much the same expenses."

"That does mean higher profits," Dola added, singsong style.

"What about Anna?" North spat. "What about those Rhian? Gonna leave 'em with just me and Jones here for support?"

"Don't forget Edmund. Plus Mason's coming back, and he swore he's giving her his full backing."

"He's coming back?" North's eyes narrowed until they just looked like more grooves in his cragged face. "Then who are you flying out to fucking Ganymede?"

"Some Journeyman. Name's Cuthbert, I think."

"Any relation to Bran Cuthbert?" Jones asked.

"Don't know. I'll ask him. Have to have something to talk about on a flight that long."

"Fuck Cuthbert," North said, "And fuck Mason too. We don't know what his agenda is. Anna doesn't need him. She needs you."

"Please," Edik said. "Mason's *name* is enough to get Anna some breathing room. Maybe even delay any further meetings until I get back. And with the profits from this trip—"

"Profits don't spend if you get shot out of the sky." North grinned an angry grin. "Navy hasn't given the all-clear to commercial Ganymede flights."

"I asked Mason about that." Edik sighed a deep breath and wished he felt as confident as he sounded. "With Mars declaring its independence, and Venus already making noises that direction, Earth's claim to control of space past Luna is legally dubious at best."

"Big comfort when they're slinging fireballs at you. Ones bigger than your ship."

"Mason says Earth's pressing its claim on Mars. That should keep the Navy too busy to have much of a force watching Ganymede. Especially with the number of ships they're supposed to have committed to whatever they're up to in that no-fly zone near Venus. And a ship my size doesn't need a big gap to fly through."

"No solid charts for that trip. Think you're up to facing down zuglodons?"

Zuglodons. Giant, wild spirits that roamed between planets and could rip ships apart to feed on their lacunas, the space elementals that powered interplanetary flight.

If Edik had any worries about this voyage, it was the risk of a zuglodon attack. However...

"Mason says this Cuthbert's got space combat experience, and has personally handled zuglodons."

"Are you *sure* you're not talking about *Bran* Cuthbert?" Jones asked. "I mean, he's a Magister, not a Journeyman, but—"

"I'd've remembered if it were Bran Cuthbert," Edik said.

"This is a damn fool mission," North said, "and you're a damn fool for taking it. And you're a stupid damn fool for not discussing it with your *partner* first."

"I'm sorry about that part," Edik said, quietly. "It was an opportunity that fell into my lap, and if I delayed I might've missed it."

"You get Mason to pay up front?"

"Half. The rest waits until we get back. The total will more than quadruple what we lose in tours over that time."

"Good luck collecting it when you're dead."

And with that, North whirled and stomped away.

"I better get moving too," Jones said. "Have to coordinate some things with North, if you're not going to be around for a few weeks. Anything special you want me to tell Anna?"

Edik sighed. "Tell her I'm just doing what I think Ivan Tsarevich would do. She'll understand."

Then Jones was gone too.

Edik turned to Dola. The shaggy gray cat blinked up at him.

"This *is* what Ivan Tsarevich would do, isn't it?"

"Tough to say," Dola said. "None of the old Russian folktales included helioships."

Edik thought about that as he stared down the passageway that led to the port. He turned back to Dola. Lowered his voice.

"I'm doing the right thing," Edik said. "Aren't I?"

"Absolutely," Dola said. "If we survive it."

"I'M DOING THE RIGHT THING, AREN'T I?" DONAL SAID TO FIONN.

Currently the emerald deerhound lay on its belly, head resting on its crossed forepaws. Fionn had been watching Donal move back and forth across Donal's bedroom, packing.

For a solid hour, ever since Donal finally devoured a couple of sandwiches for his lunch after Hierophant Mason left, Fionn had done little else but watch Donal.

Truth was, it had gotten a little disconcerting. Fionn usually ambled about whenever Donal packed, offering reminders or opinions about what Donal was packing and what he wasn't.

But Fionn had stayed silent. And here in Donal's big bedroom, Fionn had even stopped ambling about.

And it wasn't for lack of room.

Biggest bedroom Donal had ever been able to call his own. Big enough for a king-size bed. Two mahogany nightstands. A small shelf above the bed, with a dozen refillable books (currently histories about John Dee and Edward Kelly, founders of the Enochian system of magic). One modest chest of drawers between the two windows, which were open to let in the cool June breeze and the scent of the sycamore trees outside.

Most of all, plenty of floor space to wander around in.

And yet Fionn lay on the floor, between the doorways into the living room and the walk-in closet, and had said nothing for so long that Donal had finally felt that question burst out of him.

Fionn twitched its floppy ears. Tilted its head to one side.

"What do you mean by, 'the right thing?'" Fionn asked, in that thick Celtic accent. "Morally? Ethically? In terms of your studies? Or in terms of your own internal struggle against your brother's shadow, which I have consistently admonished you to forget about?"

"Well," Donal started, but Fionn wasn't finished.

"If you mean in terms of moving on from your relationship with Tai Shi Li Hua, then this is definitely the wrong thing to do. Go to space again now and you will think about her, remember past voyages and perhaps how you got together in the first place. Instead, in those terms, you should stay here and pursue Esmeralda Villaseñor."

Donal sank down to sit cross-legged on the scuffed wooden floor. Fionn sat up, so the two would be at eye level, perhaps a meter between them.

"Forget Li Hua—"

"I wish *you* would," Fionn said.

"I get it. I'm not talking about her. In fact, I think you only mentioned her to distract me. You've been quiet since Hierophant Mason left. What's going on?"

"Why did you say yes? You could have refused him. Taken the time for your studies. Your social life. And yet you did not hesitate. Why?"

"You don't like that I'm risking my neck. Is that it?"

"Hierophant Mason proposed a long, dangerous, possibly illegal voyage. He offered precious little in the way of information about what you will find at the other end."

"I got the impression he didn't want to bias me, in terms of what I'll find."

"Perhaps. That doesn't answer my question."

Nothing but patience in those glowing eyes. As though Fionn could sit there forever, if Donal didn't answer the question. Even though, ostensibly, Donal was the master in this relationship. Donal knew magicians who refused to answer to their familiars. Who didn't ask questions, but gave orders. Demanded obedience.

But that just wasn't how Donal did things.

"There may be a new kind of sapient lifeform waiting for us on Ganymede, Fionn. How could I possibly pass that up?"

"Adventure, then?" Fionn said. "Excitement? Is that why?"

"I don't hate it," Donal admitted with a sigh, "but … no. That's not it. If there's one thing I've seen too much of, it's corporate power plays. And not just the ones Li Hua was forcing 4M into. Anytime a corporation gets that big, you almost have to assume it's going to have the same kind of politics and backstabbing you'd find in a government."

Donal rolled his neck around. Shifted his position slightly so he was more comfortable: back straight and hands palm-up on the backs of his thighs. Just the pose he used for most meditation these days.

Fionn waited patiently for Donal to continue.

"But look at Rowan MacPherson and Red Sun. Ready to kill everyone aboard a ship over corporate politics. And that assassin who came after me in San Francisco. All over corporate interests."

Fionn didn't need to give voice to the question Donal could read in his familiar's eyes.

"I know, I know. What do those things have to do with new life on Ganymede?" Donal shook his head. "Everything. If what Hierophant Mason said about the Terran Navy being busy with Mars is true, that means the discovery of this new form of life might be happening in the center of a power struggle. Possibly involving yet more corporations."

"And?" Fionn said.

"And, well, *someone's* got to look out for the new kid on the block."

"Because it's the right thing to do?"

"It is. Isn't it?"

"For that reason? Yes. It is. But tell me. Is that your whole reason?"

"As clearly as I can know it right now."

"I suppose that will have to do then. But, master, I don't think you're being completely honest with yourself."

"Noted," Donal said as he spun upward to his feet. "Remind me of that when it's time for my next meditation. Maybe we can work something out."

"You should cast a memory circle," Fionn said.

"Good idea," Donal said, as he dug out a half-dozen airsilk shirts in assorted colors. One lasting benefit from his time with Li Hua — even Donal had to admit he dressed better these days. "I may get some spell ideas if I study during the flight."

"Yes, that," Fionn said. "But also, you might need to leave a record of your experiences, should this venture prove fatal."

Donal turned and looked as his familiar. No mirth in those eyes, no playful perk to the ears.

Fionn plainly believed this trip might Donal's last.

A wave of cold sluiced through his system, knotting up his guts. Two soothing breaths eased out the fear. Left Donal a touch more rational as he considered the implications.

"You're right," Donal said. "And maybe I better link Mom and Dad before we go. Just in case."

2

For the first six months after Edik had bought the ship he named the *Third Son*, it was the only home he could afford. So while most runabout-class helioships had little in the way of a galley and less in the way of sleeping quarters or creature comforts like laundry facilities, the *Third Son* was something of an exception.

It didn't have much. But thanks to Edik's devoted study of conjuration during his Associate's studies in Thaumaturgy, he was capable of conjuring his own elementals and doing most of his own ship's maintenance.

And the morning he left for Earth, Edik got out to his ship early to make sure every one of those systems was up and running the way it was supposed to be. He wanted to get as early a start as he could. The trip to Earth was fast enough, but he'd have to check in at the spaceport in San Francisco before he could fly down to … San Luis Obispo was it? He'd have to check the log to be sure.

Everything had looked good on the bridge, and now he was belowdecks, in the part of the ship passengers were never supposed to see.

No carpeting down here. No fancy paint on the dull white of the hull ceramics, lit by the moderate glow of a light strip down the center of the ceiling. A ceiling barely a dozen centimeters over Edik's head. A comforting closeness. Just three small rooms down here, connected by an even smaller passage.

He stopped first in the cargo area, surrounded on both sides by stacks of crates, leaving just enough room for him to walk through. He counted the crates, and tried to ignore the waft of dirty socks from down the passage.

"Count's right," Edik said. "Did you double-check the contents?"

"Of course," Dola said. "Magom's cleared it too."

Good old Magom. Originally Edik had only bound the earth elemental to help with the hull and simple needs, but Magom had proven helpful in more ways than Edik could count.

"Perfect. Even if things get delayed on Ganymede, we should be fine for at least an extra week."

"Hope our guest likes Russian cooking."

"He better," Edik said as he started down the passage, his boots loud on the ceramics of the deck. "If not, he's more than welcome to demonstrate his displeasure with a hunger strike."

On most runabout-class helioships, a little widening of the passage came next, which would have served as more storage. Or it might have been kept clear, because in the center of the deck here was the access hatch to the engine below.

On the *Third Son* it served as the laundry room, and the odor of Edik's dirty clothes was almost overpowering here.

"Couldn't you have brought clean clothes?" Dola said, wrinkling his nose. "If this odor wafts up—"

"You know it won't." Edik counted out the changes of shirts, pants and underwear he'd brought, all currently in piles on the deck. He nodded satisfaction. Once clean, Magom would compress the clothes — while maintaining their creases — for storage in Edik's narrow chest of drawers along the port side bulkhead. "Varia would never allow an odor to go that far."

Varia, the air elemental who kept the atmosphere fresh aboard the *Third Son*. She also orchestrated cleaning the laundry. Dola's advice. On his own, Edik would have left it to a water elemental.

Finally, Edik double-checked his own "quarters." Grandiose term for enough space to hang a hammock above a footlocker. Edik could still smell traces of borscht from the last time he'd slept in the hammock. Old, old habit of eating in bed.

"Everything looks ready down here." Edik looked back at Dola, who stood in the doorway. "Did you double-check our alchemical supplies?"

"Of course. And I had Magom verify them. It's all in the log, if you'd ever check it."

"The log is there for when I *need* it," Edik said, shaking his head. "I'd rather ask you."

A ripple of amusement washed along Dola's gray fur, up from the tail to end at his cerulean eyes. He twitched his whiskers.

"Systems check ought to be finished by now."

"Nixia," Edik called out.

Almost that same instant, she arrived.

Nixia formed from the vapor of the air before Edik, into swirls of lemon-yellow that looked like a beautiful meter-tall woman in a skirt and blouse that matched her skin. Her eyes were on the orange side of yellow, and her waist-length hair never stopped moving.

"Yes, Edik?" Nixia asked in a breathy voice.

Edik sat on the hammock, because the little room was starting to feel crowded.

"Have you finished the systems check?"

"I have, Edik," she said. "All systems report fully functional."

"Good. And the modification I made to the links. Did it check out?"

"That is difficult to judge for certain, but I believe you should be able to link back to the office from at least as far away as Mars."

"You're not sure it'll reach from Ganymede?"

"I can't be certain."

"Good enough. Thank you."

"Also, there's someone knocking at the hatch."

Edik blinked. "Port Authority?"

"No. He does not wear the uniform, and he is heavier and older than any agents of Port Authority I have perceived."

"That rules out Hierophant Mason," Edik muttered. Then, louder, he said, "All right, I'll come check it out. Dola, scout it quick. Nixia, thank you. That will be all."

Nixia vanished in a puff of air that threw back Edik's short blonde hair, while Dola turned and slipped straight out through the bulkhead.

Edik made his way back down the hall, up the access ladder, through the galley, past the head, and on into the main cabin.

The main cabin was geared toward the public eye.

Here the hull was painted gold, above a long, golden carpet that ran down the center aisle.

On either side of the carpet, four large, comfortable seats of actual Terran brown cow leather. Each padded and molded and tall enough for even Edik's comfort, and each could rotate three-hundred-sixty-degrees.

Along the walls, meter-long portholes trimmed in fiery red — one for each chair — each with a small shelf where passengers could keep snacks and drinks without fear of them spilling.

And above it all, a cabin-long ceiling mural of a mythical firebird's tail feather, red and blazing against the gold background. The tail feather lit the cabin with a fiery golden light.

Edik stopped forward of the seats, where Dola was waiting.

"Anna's father," Dola said.

Edik tugged at his Van Dyke. Why would Alexei Lukyanov be here?

"Alone?"

Dola nodded, then added, "Though I think he has people waiting back by the hangar entrance."

Edik drew a deep breath, then placed his hand in the right spot on the hull and said, "*Sezam otkroysya.*"

A seam appeared in the hull ceramics, then a curved rectangle of a door swung outwards.

Sure enough, there stood Alexei Lukyanov.

"Heavy" might have been Nixia's word for Alexei Lukyanov, but it wasn't the word Edik would have chosen. "Big." That was more like it. Lukyanov had the kind of weight that gave his body *bearing*. The same as his charisma did for his personality. The same as his family name did for his social and political interactions. All of them, just ... big.

A touch ironic, since Lukyanov stood just short enough that Edik could see the bald spot under the man's thinning hair. Still, the big man had vibrancy that many men half his age lacked.

He wore no sword at his side today. Which meant he definitely had people with him. The head of a great family couldn't risk running around in public defenseless.

"Mr. Lukyanov." Edik grimaced. "I wish you'd made an appointment. I don't really have time to talk."

"Odd thing," Lukyanov said, in an accent almost as thick as Dola's. "When a local tour ship logs a flight plan for Earth. Odder still when it logs no planned return flight."

Edik felt his mouth open, but no words came out.

"A *curious* thing, I might call it." Lukyanov smiled, and Edik could see no element of humor or reassurance in that smile. "Curious enough that my friends in the Port Authority — of course you realize I have such friends, and they have become most concerned about you since you began associating with my daughter. If I were to put a word in their ear about your ship doing something ... *curious*, especially after you met with someone like that Nicholas Mason. Well."

Lukyanov let the word fall, but Edik saw where it would land. There was nothing illegal about Edik flying to Earth, but if an investigation delayed him, Edik might lose this sensitive commission.

"Please, do come in, Mr. Lukyanov." Edik stood aside and gestured for the prominent man to enter. He spoke through gritted teeth. "Can I offer you anything?"

"*Nyet.* Just a ... moment of your time."

Lukyanov looked about as he slowly made his way to a seat in the center of the cabin. Edik followed, leaving the cabin door open so as to avoid giving any of the rest of Lukyanov's waiting group any reason to worry.

Lukyanov smiled as he pointed to the great red feather decorating the ceiling. This smile almost looked as though it contained real goodwill.

"The tail feather of the Firebird. Very good. Important that we remember our shared heritage, so far from Mother Russia."

"I was raised on the stories of Ivan Tsarevich," Edik said as he sat opposite Lukyanov.

"Good. Good. I knew that if my Anya put her trust in you, you must be a good *russkiy chelovek*. This is important."

"What can I do for you, *Gospodin* Lukyanov?"

Lukyanov smiled again. Leaned forward.

"You and I, we are worldly men. We know how things … *truly* work."

"Threaten me all you like, I won't betray Anna."

"Threats? Who speaks of threats?" Lukyanov widened his eyes and spread his hands as though astonished. "Someone threatens you, you tell me. I take care of it. For my Anya. And betray Anya? The last thing I would ask."

"We both know you don't agree with—"

"*Da,*" Lukyanov said, waving away Edik's concerns. "My Anya is confused right now. But she is a Lukyanova. She will remember her family, and she will do the right thing."

Edik had no doubt that Anna would do the right thing. He did, however, have a great deal of doubt that her idea of the right thing matched her father's.

"Then what can I do for you?" Edik said.

"You are having secret meetings with Hierophants, and then, poof, you fly away from Luna." Lukyanov shook one finger, and added a singsong tone to his words. "You are going someplace important."

"I'm just providing a ride for someone—"

"*Nyet,* let us not lie to each other. I will not ask you where you are going, and I will not ask you what you are doing."

"Then what—"

"But when you do what you do, and you find what you find. *Then* I want you to come back and tell me and only me. You are friend to my

Anya. You must know that what is good for her family is good for her, *da?*"

"I was hired for this by a *Hierophant.* I'm not going to risk his wrath for—"

"Wrath? Do not speak to me of wrath here. This is Luna. Mason's wrath is not what you should fear here. The wrath of Natalia Romanova, *da,* that I would understand. But apart from her wrath, it is *mine* that should concern you."

All the humor leached out of Lukyanov's icy blue eyes.

"You have friends here. You have business. All of these things and more can be taken away from you. A Hierophant, yes, he can hurt you. I can *ruin* you. And if you give me reason, I can stretch forth my hand to my friends on Earth. They will find the rest of your family and ruin *them.*"

Edik's hand leapt to his saber.

Dola hissed a warning.

Edik felt his grip tighten until the hilt of his sword dug into his hand.

But he did not draw.

"All these things and more I can do. But I do not *want* to do them. I want us to be—"

"Do you know what a *geas* is?" Edik said through clenched teeth.

"*Da.* Magical compulsion to do something or not do it." Lukyanov's eyes widened. "This Mason, he did this to you? Guaranteed your silence? Oh." Lukyanov clucked his tongue. "You make the wrong friends. That is against Lunar law. I will see about—"

"Oh, no," Edik said with a vindictive smile. "Nothing illegal about it when the recipient of the spell agrees. See, what Mason wants me to do, it *is* important. Too important to risk the likes of you finding out about it."

"Oh," Lukyanov said, and he made the word sound as though it punctured him. "That you would speak such a way to me. It shows how little you understand. I wish to help *you,* almost as much as I wish to help my Anya. I wish to see us all friends, working together happily."

"Obviously that can't happen," Edik said, "thanks to the *geas*."

"Pah," Lukyanov said. "There is always a way." He leaned back and yelled out, *"Dimi!"* Then in a more normal tone he said to Edik, "You remember my son Dmitri, of course. A Magister. Very talented young man. Don't worry. He will find a way for us to help one another."

Edik could hear the echo of footsteps crossing the blue-white stone of the hangar toward his ship's open hatch.

***

By Donal's standards, the San Luis Obispo terminal wasn't much to look at.

When Donal was working as a courier, he flew out of the largest and most lavish spaceports. Most often San Francisco, but also the even larger spaceports in Toronto and Durango, here in the United North American States. Not to mention airports all over Earth, some of which doubled as spaceports, like oh-so-busy Kyoto. Others were just large, impressive airports, like Greater Auckland and Abuja. And off-world, Donal had flown through Kennedy and King on Luna, New Leningrad on Mars, and even Gilgamesh on Venus.

Though, admittedly, Gilgamesh had consisted mostly of temporary constructions and few amenities because it was just that new. So new that Donal had arrived on the first commercial flight allowed to land. For certain values of "allowed," anyway. The Dagda knew it hadn't been an easy flight.

Still, Gilgamesh was the only and biggest port on Venus, and Donal had been there.

Yet even compared to that new construction, the San Luis Obispo terminal didn't look like much.

The landing area consisted of open fields of grass, with no shelter from inclement weather and only a few dedicated alchemy stations. Well, Donal supposed there was some small amount of shelter from the tree covered hills in the area surrounding the port, but they did more for wind than they ever would for rain.

The landing field formed a half-circle, and the terminal itself sat in the center of the straight edge. A broad, squat, round building of treated brown adobe, only one story tall. On the opposite side of the terminal from the landing field were a half-empty series of stables, for horses and runners.

Beside the main terminal sat a second building, connected by a covered walkway. The second building, also adobe, was smaller, and square. It didn't look like part of the port proper. Probably some kind of administrative facility, or maybe a military adjunct. Something added by the Terran Navy, perhaps, for reasons Donal couldn't guess at.

Donal arrived by runnercab. A four-legged model, barely two meters tall, with green lizard-like skin and entirely too talkative a man at the reins. The man had loudly proclaimed heritage going back to the Aztecs — it felt as though he'd recited half his family tree — and pontificated at length about the weather, baseball, and worst of all, politics. The last thing Donal wanted before heading off to space again was some cabbie's analysis of the recent senate race.

If Fionn weren't tucked away in the silver faun pendant around Donal's neck, the familiar probably would have prompted Donal to correct the man's fundamental misunderstanding of modern election rules and their relationship with elected offices. Fionn always seemed to think that it was Donal's responsibility as a magician to correct each and every layman's mistake about either magic itself, or the strictures placed on it by modern society.

But Donal had no time nor inclination to explain why oaths of office weren't, and shouldn't be, magically binding. Much less to try to get a cabbie to accept that the re-elected senator from California shouldn't lose his seat for refusing to magically bind his oath of office, the way his opponent had promised to.

So the moment the cab stopped, Donal tossed money onto the front seat — enough to include a decent tip — grabbed his duffel bag and took off before the cabbie could say another word.

Pretty June day, with that fresh, early summer scent to the air. A little warmer than back in Santa Cruz or San Francisco, but Donal liked the change. Kept his mind coming back to the elemental factors at play in life. Just another way to continue absorbing the complex elemental structure of Enochian magic.

Not that his mind could stay on his studies right now. Not when he was about to leave Earth for Ganymede on a questionably legal — not to mention questionably safe — mission.

Every time he thought about that he got a tremor of excitement in his gut. He hadn't done anything adventurous since that trip to Venus last year. This time, though, that excitement was moderated by the memory of his parents' worried expressions when he'd talked to them over the link.

So, for right now, he let his mind fix on whatever it could, even if it flitted to another subject only moments later.

Like the people ahead of him in the short line to enter the terminal. A group of suited men and women who looked to be flying up or down the coast on business. They threw jargon back and forth as fast as inside jokes. Their lingo so alien it was almost like listening to familiars talk among themselves.

Clear blue sky above Donal, with only a few incoming ships. All of them the latest style, resembling large natural birds. Right now he could see a stellar jay leaving, and a swallow and a robin coming in. And unless Donal was mistaken, he could see a variation approaching from the east. A gray flying squirrel, by the look of it.

Suddenly Donal was at the front of the line. A man in a sloppy uniform checked Donal's name off a list. Didn't even wave a sniffer to make sure Donal wasn't carrying anything he wasn't supposed to. But then, few things were actively barred from Earth-only travel these days, and no one had any reason to suspect Donal was leaving Earth from this port.

Just the first questionably legal thing Donal was doing on this trip. And he was pretty sure it wouldn't be the last.

Inside, the terminal looked like one big room. The "gates" were arrayed around the center like spokes around a hub, where passengers sat on hard wooden chairs in open lounges while they waited for runners to take them to their ships.

How hard would they be, those chairs? Earth-of-water hard, or earth-of-earth hard? Maybe even fire-aspected earth-of-earth. Wouldn't know 'til he sat.

All right. Truth was, Donal wouldn't know for certain unless he took the time and effort to set a circle, get deep into a meditative state, and work with Fionn to analyze the chair. Next semester he was supposed to start working with spirits that could speed such analysis, but his professors insisted on first assigning enough personal analysis to form a solid foundation of understanding.

Donal half-suspected that was a delaying tactic. It was common knowledge the modern understanding of the Enochian system went only so far, even at CalThaum SLO, widely acknowledged as the best school for Enochian studies. Even surpassing Oxford, and Dublin's Trinity College.

Donal shook his head to clear the reverie. Squeezed his toes inside his brown leather loafers to bring his mind back to the present.

Thin, beige carpeting on the floor under those loafers. Flooring solid as stone underneath the carpet.

A snack bar in the center of the terminal, surrounded by support pillars, where maybe three or four teenagers in uniforms served simple fare to maybe a half-dozen patrons at the moment, most of whom looked to be after coffee.

Next to the snack bar floated one — *one* — illusion-based travel board, listing all incoming and outgoing flights.

One. Donal couldn't believe that. Stood there, right inside the entryway and craned his neck back and forth. Surely there had to be smaller ones by each of the "gates."

Nope. From what he could tell, the "gates" were only differentiated by engraved signage with their "gate number." And under each such engraved placard, an actual chalkboard with flight data. As in, somebody had to be going around and updating them.

By hand.

In this day and age.

No way that was cheaper than maintaining small, illusory signs…

No. Not cheaper than *maintaining* the signs. Cheaper than paying at least a Journeyman's rate to cast — Donal ran a quick count — twenty such illusions?

Probably.

Donal grimaced.

Only about half the lounges were in use today, and most of those only had crowds of six-to-ten. Donal wandered one lap, just for a look. All right, maybe because on a deeper level he still liked the field-work game he'd cobbled together with Fionn, and that game required him to check all potential exits. Twenty one — one at each gate, plus the main door. Twenty-three, if Donal included the two private bathrooms beside the snack counter. But those last two weren't real exits.

The game also required Donal to keep an eye on potential threats. Even the cute ones, of which Donal had spotted at least eight. Donal briefly considered trying to engage a pretty blonde woman in conversation. Not so much to find a date — he still had hopes that something might click with Esmeralda — but just to have something to do.

Otherwise, unless Donal wanted to get in some reading, there wasn't much else to occupy him while he waited. Sitting alone at Gate 6 might have drawn attention. He'd already breakfasted on two bagels, cheese, and a half a cantaloupe, so he didn't want anything from the snack bar. And those were about all his options. No shadow plays to watch. No news feed. Meditating would have been as bad as waving a sign saying, "Look! Magician waiting for a flight *where he's the only passenger.*"

Not exactly inobvious.

Few choices, though. Apparently, travelers through the San Luis Obispo airport were expected to entertain themselves.

Donal sighed. Found a seat at "gate" 18. Not too hard a chair. Maybe water-aspected earth-of-water. Dug a refillable book out of his duffel, and started re-reading about how Edward Kelley dictated the Enochian alphabet to John Dee, based on what the "angels" were telling him.

Personally, Donal doubted the Enochian spirits were angels of the Christian god. His personal theory was that Dee and Kelley only understood them that way because they were both devout Christians.

Still, Donal wanted to understand the process of that language's development as much as he could. He suspected that it contained the truest secrets of the system.

"Excuse me," a silken female voice said, before Donal could even get through half a page. "May I sit, Donal? I brought a peace offering."

Donal knew that voice.

Rowan MacPherson.

DONAL CLOSED HIS EYES AND SIGHED. DETECTED THE FAINT SCENT OF lilacs under the stronger aroma of rich coffee.

So much for his peaceful wait at the tiny little San Luis Obispo airport terminal.

He opened his eyes and there she still stood. Rowan MacPherson, once again. A staggeringly beautiful woman with pale skin and flowing, fiery red hair, wearing a green airsilk dress and holding two cups of coffee. A woman with the kind of poise, genetics, and Celtic ancestry that would have made Donal's mother weep with joy to see Donal even talking to her.

Only because Donal's mother didn't know Rowan MacPherson.

"I made a complete circuit of the public areas here," Donal said. "I noted everyone. Why didn't I see you?"

"Perhaps I was in the restroom."

Donal said nothing.

"All right, I didn't want you to see me until I had a peace offering, so I stayed to your blind spots. May I sit?"

"Oh, why not?" Donal said through a sigh, sliding his book back into his duffel. His hand reflexively reached for the messenger bag he no longer carried while he shifted consciousness enough to verify that the coffee was as free of magic as Rowan MacPherson herself.

He accepted his cup of coffee as she sat — leaving an empty seat between them.

"So," he said, "murder any innocents lately?"

"Donal," she said, with the patience of Brigid herself, "why do you insist on saying things like that, when the people around us wouldn't understand that you're joking?"

Donal wasn't joking. True, she'd been nowhere near the New Leningrad spaceport when that garbage can blew up. And she hadn't been on the *Horizon Cusp* when business tycoon Hassan al Rashid was murdered. And she was already on Venus when that ship full of mercenaries tried to intercept Donal's flight and murder at least one of the passengers.

And Donal had no *hard evidence* that she even had ties to any of those events.

But he was sure Rowan MacPherson was behind them. Each one a bit of corporate espionage attempting to benefit Red Sun, a big and growing corporation on Mars.

He was equally sure she'd never even come close to admitting to any of that. Not around Donal. Heck, she even denied responsibility for most or all of it.

And yet, here she was again.

So Donal said nothing. Just tried to match her patience. Sipped his coffee, which was a strong Moroccan blend, tasty enough to make him blink.

"That's right," she said with a sincere-looking smile. "I remembered that you loved that little Moroccan restaurant in San Francisco. I was there yesterday, by the way. Mr. Mohatar sends his regards."

"You spoke to him about me?" Donal's tone came out flat, and he hoped it carried enough threat to make her think.

"Just making conversation," she said, raising her free hand as though surrendering. "Can we start over?"

"I think it's more than a little late for us to start over."

Her nostrils flared in a sigh that made a passing man in a jumpsuit trip over his cheap shoes.

"Please, Donal. You didn't hear me out on Mars. You didn't hear me out on Venus. Please. Hear me out this time."

"And if I say no?"

"I'm not threatening you, Donal. I've never threatened you."

"You've threatened plenty of other people though, haven't you?"

"Donal," Rowan MacPherson said slowly, "if you won't listen to what I have to say, I have no reason to listen to your accusations."

"Then let me thank you for the coffee before you leave."

Rowan MacPherson sipped her coffee as though she had all the time in the world.

"So don't let me keep you," Donal added, trying to make her stand up and leave through the tone of his words alone.

"Your flight's been delayed at least an hour, you know." She smiled. "Are you sure you wouldn't prefer having someone to talk to?"

The taste of that excellent coffee turned bitter on Donal's tongue.

"What did you do?"

"Me?" she said innocently. "Nothing." She pointed to the chalkboard timetable below the "Gate 18" sign. Instead of two p.m., it now read three. "All I did was read the sign."

"You've already admitted you were in San Francisco yesterday. And here you just happen to approach me as the port gets word that my flight *from San Francisco* has been delayed by an hour? And you expect me to interpret that as coincidence?"

"I flew in through San Francisco because it's the nearest major spaceport. I approached you now because you just got here. As for the flight delay, well, perhaps you should ask yourself what I would gain by delaying your flight."

"A captive audience?"

She laughed, a damnably musical sound.

"Oh, Donal, you credit me with so much more power than I have."

"Enough power to know I was flying out of this port today, when I didn't know myself until yesterday. But then, I imagine running Red Sun affords you a lot. Or at least, all you corporate types seem to have—"

"Oh," she said, laughing even harder, "I don't run Red Sun."

That made Donal stop.

"But... You've spoken as though you do."

"No. Not at all." Her laughter had stopped, but her eyes and lips showed that laughter was no more than a heartbeat away. "I represent some of their interests, that's all. I'm ... a consultant of sorts."

"What are you, some kind of corporate spymaster?"

"I like that," she said. "Makes it all sound very cloak-and-dagger. Believe me, Donal, I would love to sit and tell you all about what it is I do. And get the chance to listen to you talk about your studies. But we both know you think I'm the devil, so—"

"I don't think you're the devil."

"No?" She fluttered her eyelashes, making her green eyes look even brighter.

"No, if you're anything supernatural, you're most likely one of the *Daoine Sidhe.* You're that careful with your words and your offers, and the Dagda knows you're beautiful enough. Not to mention dangerous enough."

Rowan MacPherson smiled, and Donal got the impression she felt sincerely complimented. More than a little disturbing.

"Donal," she said, quietly, "in the interests of building goodwill with you, I will tell you that you're closer to the truth than you think. Someday I'll tell you more about that, if you'll actually listen."

Donal called Fionn out of the silver faun pendant around his neck. The deerhound appeared in a flash of emerald light, standing beside its master. Fionn, after all, was a *cú sidhe*, a fae hound, and the best person around to ask what Donal needed to ask.

"Is she *sidhe?*"

Rowan MacPherson said a dozen quick words that Donal couldn't understand. They sounded vaguely like Gaelic, but not quite.

They also sounded a little like the language familiars spoke among themselves.

Whatever she said, Fionn answered her back the same way before turning to Donal.

"Yes, and no," Fionn said in English, words quick, as though it had been waiting for Donal to ask that question. "I believe the word you would choose for her is 'changeling.'"

Rowan MacPherson tilted her head back and forth, which made her fiery hair dance. Not agreeing with that characterization, but not quite denying it either.

Changelings. Fae babies left behind when the fae stole human children. That was how Donal's grandmothers had explained the term, anyway. Donal had thought changelings were nothing more than myth. Or perhaps an explanation for people born with more magical ability than others.

But that would make Rowan MacPherson a full *sidhe*, raised by humans. That just seemed too impossible to believe. More likely she was a half-breed, born to a human mother and a *sidhe* father, and raised among humans.

If changelings were real, then it seemed more likely to Donal that the story about them was a cover for infidelity with the *sidhe* — and few could resist their beauty — than that the fae were willing to leave one of their own behind as a price for stealing a human child.

If changelings were real…

"There are changelings?" Donal asked. "I mean, they're real?"

"Obviously," Fionn said.

"And you never told me this because…"

"It isn't something I can talk about unless asked."

"Are there other things you can't talk about unless asked?"

"Of course. But I can't tell you what unless—"

"Unless I ask directly and specifically." Donal sighed. "I've been studying magic since high school. Why have I never heard about this before?"

"I suspect that those who know," Rowan MacPherson said, "see the benefits of keeping their silence."

This was too much, too suddenly. Donal tried to re-cast every conversation he'd had with this woman, trying to understand her in terms of this new information, but it was just too much. He wasn't sure where to begin.

To her credit, Rowan MacPherson merely sat there, giving Donal time to absorb this new information.

"Wait," Donal said, holding up his free hand. "Before you say anything else." Donal cleared his throat. Looked straight into those so-green eyes. "Person known to me as Rowan MacPherson, have you ever, directly or indirectly, cast any kind of glamour, charm, enchantment, or other magical effect on me or affecting me?"

"One moment." Rowan MacPherson wrinkled her nose while she thought, and as the Dagda bore witness, even that was attractive. She met Donal's eyes again. "No. Never."

"She's telling the truth," Fionn confirmed.

"Wait," Donal said, as his thoughts backed up even further. To Fionn he said, "I've never detected even a hint of magic about her. But she can cast spells?"

"I can," Rowan MacPherson confirmed.

"Then why can't I—"

"Because I hide what I am," she said. "It's my nature." She nodded her head from side to side a moment, then added, "Plus, I don't like the structures of your organized magic, so why would I want magicians to notice me?"

"You said you never cast anything that affects me."

"And I haven't," she said emphatically. "The little bit of glamour that makes me appear normal requires nothing you think of as 'casting,' and it affects only me."

Donal sighed. Of course she'd found a way around his phrasing. She was half-fae, and obviously one of her parents was *Daoine Sidhe*, perhaps even a high court noble.

"She has never enchanted you in any way though," Fionn said. "I'm certain of it."

Donal nodded. "All right then. What is it you want from me, Ms. MacPherson?"

"Rowan, Donal, please."

Fionn nodded, encouraging. The *cú sidhe* seemed happier now that Donal knew what Rowan MacPherson was.

"What is it you want from me, Rowan?"

"Well," she said, leaning forward just a little. "I *was* just going to ask you to meet with me when you get back, and tell me about the spirits you find on Ganymede. But since you know what I am anyway…"

She smiled. "How would you feel about being an emissary?"

EDIK SAT IN THE MOST COMFORTABLE CHAIR ON HIS SHIP, BUT TENSION sang through every muscle of his body.

The chair was his captain's chair. Padded. Able to recline. A chair he spent more time in than any other.

Everything around that chair was designed to make him as comfortable and happy as possible, here on the little bridge of his helioship. The chair sat at the vertex of twin white ceramic counters, where all the important controls of his ship were at his fingertips.

Two hallucinatory scanner displays of the area around the *Third Son*, that right now showed the pale blue sky and rolling hills outside San Luis Obispo. Pretty much the same view as Edik got out his front viewing porthole. Would have been a nice day, without the damned bureaucracy.

Golden illusory hand grips for pitch, roll, yaw, and a big red lever for speed. Even a miniature rendering of the ship itself, for quick access to readouts of all systems.

Not that he used those readouts much. He preferred just asking Nixia.

If only Nixia could handle this task for him.

No. This was something Edik had to do for himself, while Nixia kept the ship flying that stupid looping hold pattern.

Edik sat, his chair swiveled hard to port. His fingers pinched one particular strand of the floating, glowing blue spaghetti mess that was his communications station. As though, if he pinched hard enough, he could do physical damage to what had to be a teenage idiot on the other end.

Of course, Edik would *know* if she was just some teenage idiot, if the link had included a proper rendering of her head. As almost every professional link did. But no. Apparently here in scenic San Luis Obispo, off-world pilots like Edik didn't rate that much common courtesy. All he got was audio.

Dola, sitting on the floor just to his left, twitched a warning with his whiskers. Edik was not to lose his cool. That would only cost them more time.

So Edik drew another deep breath, flaring his nostrils just as wide as he could to draw at least a little comfort from the borscht and herb scents that lingered perpetually on his bridge.

And he tried again.

"I know I'm late." Edik tried to keep the exasperation out of his voice, but he knew that was a losing battle. "And believe me, I'm very, very sorry I'm late. I flew all the way from Kennedy today. I would have been exactly on time, except that your comrades up in San Francisco knocked me to the back of the line. Twice. Then they demanded an inspection of my 'cargo,' and they didn't even give me a reason for any of that."

"There's concern about contamination from Lunar goods," said the Port Control Officer, who sounded like she was just out of high school. Or maybe she was still a student, and here on Earth, port control was just a summer job. Nothing important.

That would have explained so very much.

"I understand that," Edik said, before she launched into her pat recitation of the excuses she called reasons for that pointless inspection. "And if any of these goods were to be off-loaded here on Earth, I'd be all for your inspection. Truly. I promise. Just like I promise that every one of those goods would have had an Earth destination listed on my cargo manifest. Which, as you can see from your copy, they do not. And they do not because none of that cargo is to be off-loaded here on this big blue bureaucratic nightmare of a world. Not so much as a single crate."

"I understand," she said, and she must have, because she had the audacity to sound bored by the whole conversation. Probably took her away from some important summer homework, or maybe the chance to paint her nails. "However you *did* set down on the planet carrying those goods. And you did set foot outside your ship, so the hatch was opened, which activated Terran Port Code section three-cee-point—"

"*I get that,*" Edik insisted. "Really. Of course, I wouldn't have had to open the hatch, if your comrades hadn't insisted on an inspection."

"Which they had to do under—"

"*The point is,*" Edik said, "I know I'm late. I'm sorry I'm late. If I'd known what SF was going to put me through, I'd have planned for it and I would've been here hours ago. But none of that matters anymore. I'm here. Now. And my poor passenger is waiting for me. Has been waiting a long time now, due to circumstances beyond my control. So could we please speed this along?"

"I'll see what I can do."

"Thank you," Edik said, putting more feeling into those words than the twit on the other end of the link deserved.

She cut the link.

Edik blinked.

"No. She did not just cut on me. She didn't. She couldn't be that stupid. She—"

"Steady, Edik," Dola said.

Edik leapt to his feet. Dola didn't even blink. Edik grabbed the handle of his saber. Didn't draw it. Let go. Sat back down. Puffed out a hard breath.

"I swear," he said. "If we ever try to do more with Earth than the occasional—"

The link pulsed pale blue, accompanied by a soft chime that in no way suited Edik's current mental state.

"She's probably going to tell me it'll be another hour."

"Want me to answer?" Dola asked.

Edik reached out and pinched the link.

This time an image accompanied the voice, forming in three dimensions above the communications web. And to Edik's shock, the woman was sixty if she was a day. Steel gray hair, even more wrinkles than hairs on her head. Most insulting of all, she had a kind, patient expression, as though she really did understand everything Edik was going through today, and really, honestly did want to help.

Which, given the day Edik had been having, just made him want to punch her.

"Please proceed to landing bay six, whenever you are ready. And thank you so much for choosing San Luis Obispo as your destination. On behalf of the whole Port Authority staff, I hope you have a pleasant stay here and come visit us again soon."

"Thank you," Edik grumbled, but before she could cut the link he said, "Wait!"

She blinked at him, apparently unsurprised.

"Obviously I missed my original departure window, when my arrival ran late. But my passenger might be in a hurry. Any chance you can get me in the queue starting—"

"I'm sorry," she said in that deceptively young voice, and her blue eyes looked ready to cry on his behalf, "but I can't put any ships into the departure queue until they've completed all landing procedures and filled out any required forms."

"You already have my forms," Edik said with his best salesman smile. "Sent 'em to you while I was on my way down. So maybe we could—"

"I'm sorry. Rules are rules."

She cut the link then.

Edik swore liberally in Russian as he landed the *Third Son* himself. As he touched down on the green, green grass, he added a few extra curse words in Gaelic, because he was feeling a little rebellious against his Russian heritage after dealing with those damnable Lukyanovs.

But finally — *finally* — his ship was down on the ground of San Luis Obispo at last. Only maybe six hours after he finally got out of Kennedy, which meant only about three hours late, all told.

"Nixia," he said, then waited for the air elemental to take lemony form in the air before him. "Double check the port codes here, if you would. I don't want any surprises."

"Of course, Edik. Shall I keep an ear on the local communications as well?"

"Please."

Edik turned to Dola.

"What do you think? Is he going to come out to the ship, or do we have to go get him?"

"He's a Journeyman, is he not?"

"Right." Edik sighed. "We go get him." Edik stood. Stretched. "Tell me again why I want to get more commissions from Hierophants?"

"Profit margins."

"Right."

"Mind you, your calculations neglected to include certain, shall we say, nuisance factors?"

"Right again." Edik chuckled and shook his head. "Let's go get our meal ticket, shall we?"

Edik strolled through into the main cabin, opened the hatch, and stepped down onto that green, green grass. Terraforming spells on Luna had never quite gotten things right, but Edik had gotten so used to them, that he all but forgot just how green terran grass got.

Here in San Luis Obispo it grew a dark green, and it smelled like childhood. That little house his father had, just outside Moscow. Where Edik had pushed so hard to get to help his father mow the grass. Back when things were good.

Edik pulled a blade from the field at his feet. Tucked it between his teeth. A little taste of childhood to soothe a bad day.

He looked around. Most of the fields were empty, so the port couldn't have been doing that much traffic. Was it a good sign for their economy that they didn't need that much traffic? Or a bad sign?

No way to judge. Not here in California, where elemental trains still ran up and down the coast, and horses were as popular as runners. Maybe more so. Edik didn't exactly follow the current Earth trends.

But the ships in port here were all new designs. Those silly looking giant versions of actual birds. Like the sparrow North flew. People could make a ship look like anything, but nowadays they didn't push themselves harder than looking out their windows.

Hadn't been all that long ago that more ships were designed with myths in mind, like Edik's. Or to mimic the old rocket ships that people seventy years ago had *thought* would be what brought them to space. Back before technology fell.

More magic nowadays, but less creativity.

Dola cleared his throat.

Edik glanced down at the huge gray cat, then followed those cerulean eyes to see ... a magician. Short, with pale skin and black hair. This kid looked about as Celtic as anybody Edik had seen in three or four years. Green shirt looked like airsilk, which made the short sleeves redundant. Brown slacks looked like cotton. What was the point of wearing an airsilk shirt with cotton slacks?

Waste of money.

"Think that's our passenger?" Edik said.

"Got the aura of a Journeyman, even if I don't see a familiar." Dola nodded. "And he does look the part. I mean, have you ever seen such a stereotypical magician?"

"Seriously," Edik said, laughter in his voice. "Half expect he just walked out of class, and is bursting with questions about some fine point of thaumaturgic theory."

Edik raised his hand and waved. The kid waved back.

"This is the guy who beat *zuglodons*?" Edik said, trying to keep his astonishment off his face. "Plural?"

"Maybe he's one of those secret agent types," Dola said. "Looks like a thaumageek, but he's actually the deadliest man you'd ever meet, with a knife."

Edik looked down at Dola. The shaggy gray spirit cat twitched his whiskers and ears in a shrug.

"At least he carries his own bags," Edik said. And then he raised his voice. "Donal Cuthbert?"

"That's me." The kid had a nice smile, at least. Not condescending, the way a lot of Journeymen were to Initiates. And he picked up his pace. "I take it you're Captain Barshai?"

"Call me Edik. We're going to be in close quarters for a while. No point in being formal."

They shook hands. Up close now, Edik could see trouble in those blue eyes of Cuthbert's.

Looked as though Edik wasn't the only one who'd been having a hell of a day.

"Let's go ahead and get you squared away," Edik said, taking the kid's duffel bag. "Sooner I can formally get you aboard, the sooner they let us leave."

"Good," Cuthbert said. "I'll feel more comfortable about this once Earth is behind us."

"You and me both," Edik said, then jerked his thumb at his familiar. "Oh, and this is Dola."

"Pleased to meet you, Dola. I'll introduce you both to my familiar, Fionn, after I've settled in."

"Forgive the impertinence, Journeyman Donal Cuthbert," Dola said, "but I trust there will be no question of demesne on this flight?"

Edik blinked. Hadn't even thought about that. True, if this kid was a Journeyman — and Dola hadn't been kidding about the kid's aura — he could challenge for the right to be senior magician on the voyage. Could make Edik's life very difficult.

"Of course not," Cuthbert said, and bless him, the kid sounded as though the notion never even occurred to him. "This is your ship, Edik, and your rules. And please, both of you, call me Donal."

Edik smiled. "I think we'll get along just fine, Donal."

They boarded the ship.

THE BRIDGE OF THIS LITTLE HELIOSHIP WAS A STUDY OF THE PILOT'S mind. Edik Barshai. Donal almost felt he knew the man better, just sitting in here during takeoff. And not just because the bridge smelled like a blend of alchemy with boiled meat and potatoes.

He'd gotten some small feel of Edik when they met. Decent aura for an Initiate, but more impressive was that he had a familiar. Donal had only known a few Initiates who mastered the familiar spells. Most of them either had trouble with the conjuration or the alchemy or both.

Donal wasn't exactly top of his class in alchemy himself. Still, the fact remained that he was competent. And this Edik Barshai seemed to be at least passable himself. Probably handled all his own ship maintenance. Made good business sense, as well as good magic.

And the familiar he had. Dola. A gray cat. Donal had the feeling that the choice was significant. Mythically. In much the same way that he himself had a *cú sidhe*. But Donal didn't know Russian mythology well enough to even hazard a guess.

Still. No way an Initiate could have built this helioship. And yet the feel of Edik's magic was all around Donal. As though he'd personally reinforced every spell himself, and perhaps added a few of his own, personal modifications.

Donal hadn't been sure how he felt about that part. On the one hand, Nicholas Mason himself had hired Edik for this flight. But on the other, Donal didn't relish the notion of having to help with emergency repairs at high space because it turned out that Edik wasn't quite as good as he thought he was.

The bridge helped Donal feel a little better. The way Edik organized the ship's systems around a single seat, right there at the fore of the ship. Donal could tell that the little white counter he sat at, at the rear right side — er, starboard aft side? — of the pilot's station originally housed some of those systems. At least the communications or navigation. Something like that. And yet, now it was nothing more than a guest chair, with each of its systems routed through the pilot's station.

Practical. And clearly functional. An encouraging sign.

But even more than that, Edik used his ship's elemental spirits like crew. He'd spoken with two sylphs and a gnome, just since Donal had come aboard. Issued orders and taken reports, with perfect confidence and perfect ease. Routine.

And each one of those spirits seemed content and happy in its relationship. In fact, the main air elemental — Nixia, if Donal had heard correctly — seemed to almost have taken a fancy to Edik. And any magician who got along that well with his bound spirits was a magician Donal was happy to know.

"Please," Edik implored the old woman on the link. "We're behind schedule enough already, and I have three more pickups to make before dinner. And you know how these muckety-muck magicians are about eating dinner on time."

"Dola," Donal whispered to the shaggy gray cat, sitting just behind Edik on the floor. When the cat turned those cerulean eyes on Donal, he continued, in Gaelic. *I am the only passenger. Yes?*

"You are," Dola said, in the same language. *"But it sounds better Edik's way."*

Donal chuckled.

And the cat must have known something. Because now Edik and the woman were laughing, and the ship was leaving the ground.

"Throwing your own kind under the train," Donal said when Edik cut the link, trying for teasing. "Shameful."

"I'm a pilot first, magician second," Edik said, one hand working three golden controls while the red lever that looked as though it controlled speed remained at "All Stop."

Despite this, the ship lifted off, tilted beak up, and began speeding through the atmosphere…

…only to level off again after only a maybe a hundred meters.

Heading … south?

"Where exactly are we going?" Donal said.

"Far enough from San Luis Obispo that no one will notice when I bank us out over the Pacific. And from there, far enough that no one is *likely* to notice when we go nose up and head for deep space."

"Likely?"

"We're a tiny ship. No reason anyone on this rock should give a used tea bag about our destination." Edik smiled over his shoulder at Donal. "Me, I don't trust things like likelihood or reason."

"We've had something of a day," Dola said. "Please forgive Edik if he seems a touch paranoid."

"I'm only a touch paranoid because the universe keeps reminding me that everyone's out to get me."

"I know the feeling," Donal said.

That got him another glance over Edik's shoulder.

"This trip's already more complicated than I bargained for."

"What do you mean?" Edik said, and he made the question sound as though Donal had pronounced his doom.

"Nothing. Not really." Donal tried to laugh away his words.

The silence that followed told him the attempt hadn't worked.

"Really," Donal said.

Edik shook his head and turned back around.

Dola looked up at Donal with those big, dark blue eyes. Clearly Edik's familiar didn't believe Donal's dismissal any more than Edik did.

Well, if they were lucky, they'd never have to know what Donal was talking about. Acting as emissary from a fae court wasn't exactly a safe occupation.

Donal looked back through the forward view porthole at the clear blue skies, and the deep blue ocean below them now.

Edik adjusted one of his golden controls, and that view became sky and clouds, and a hint of golden sun. Not that Donal could tell the change in direction from his seat. The earth elementals that handled local gravity aboard the ship were good. Smooth. Donal had ridden in ships twice this big that didn't handle those kind of sharp movements without … certain undesirable kinetic sensations. But here his seat held him snugly, without making him feel confined.

Maybe there was a reason Hierophant Mason chose this ship for the flight to Ganymede.

"Tell me, Donal," Edik said, and there was a warning tone in his voice, "do the complications of your day involve some kind of flying saucer?"

"Some kind of what?"

Edik pointed at the hallucinatory scanner display to his left, a three-dimensional rendering of the region around the *Third Son*. In the distance was a dot. No. Not quite a dot. It was round like a dot, though. Like a discus, or maybe a dinner plate.

And it was coming their way.

DONAL STARED AT THE SMALL DOT DISPLAYED THE *THIRD SON'S* PORT side scanners, from his seat to the rear of the bridge.

That dot was definitely coming their way.

Donal's stomach soured, and the alchemy, meat and potatoes smell of the bridge seemed less comforting that it had only moments before.

"That's a ship?" Donal said.

"That's a ship," Edik confirmed from the pilot's seat. "Not much bigger than we are. Probably an airship. Maybe bound for Japan. Quite a coincidence, though, that they came so close to the flight path I had planned out."

"Edik drew up this flight plan," Dola added, "specifically to avoid all major travel routes."

From its spot near the door to the main cabin, the gray cat familiar exchanged a quick glance with its master.

"Which means this is a private ship," Edik said, his attention back on flying. "Not public. And as I said, I don't believe in coincidence."

"Could be bound for the Hawaiian Republic," Donal said.

"Could be." Edik shook his head. "Nixia, rouse Xincapph, would you? We'll need his services a little sooner than expected."

"Of course, Edik," Nixia's voice said, though Donal noted she hadn't bothered manifesting.

"Xincapph?" Donal said.

"Our lacuna. Xincapph will be handling both scanners and transit for the major part of our flight. Hate to wake him while still in a major sylph zone, but—"

"You aren't planning to—"

"Don't tell me how to do my job, Donal, and we'll get along just fine."

Donal was about to object — flying by space elemental in a region tightly controlled by air elementals was on Donal's top ten list of most dangerous things to try — but he glanced over at the port side scanner again and noted that the dot in the distance wasn't quite so distant as it had been a moment before.

And Edik *had* been hired by Nicholas Mason himself...

"Xincapph has handled atmospheric flight before," Dola said. "The risk isn't as great as you think."

Donal noted the word choice there, and didn't find it all that comforting.

"Xincapph is ready," Nixia's voice said.

"Donal," Edik said, "you have your belts on?"

Donal didn't. He'd assumed the five point safety harness attached to his chair had been a relic of its prior use. Especially with the gnomes doing such solid gravitational work, even inside Earth's pull. True, Edik had his belts on, but that might just have been habit. Or regulations.

"Trust me," Dola said. "You'll want those belts."

Suddenly the five-point harness felt like it had at least two dozen points. Donal couldn't find them fast enough. Couldn't find the places they hooked together.

"Ready?" Edik said, hand on that red lever.

Donal wasn't. He had two points clicked shut. Two more would not cooperate. And for the life of him, Donal couldn't figure out what to do with the fifth.

But Edik didn't wait for an answer.

He shoved that red lever from "All Stop" to "Ahead One Quarter."

Belts cut into Donal in two places on his left side. One yanked down hard across his clavicle, and that other tightened in just under his rib cage. Air felt like a memory to his lungs. There wasn't any. Only that squeezing tightness.

And the blue ahead of him? That blue sky filled with smearing clouds and a hint of sun? That was gone now. All straight to black.

Donal coughed. Choked. Couldn't get any air. Why couldn't he get any air? That pressure at his clavicle and gut squeezed him like he might burst any moment. Just pop. His heart was pounding like it was trying to breathe too. And he couldn't swallow. Sweat broke out on his forehead. Under his pits.

Was this it? Was Donal just going to die in this chair because he didn't have his safety belts fastened before that maniac at the controls activated his *lacuna* inside a planet's atmosphere?

Suddenly an angel appeared before Donal. A tiny yellow angel, in a flowing sundress the color of ripe lemons. It had sweet orange eyes that looked infinitely patient. It leaned in and pressed tiny, disturbingly feminine lips to Donal's.

Air. Sweet, pure, wonderful air flowed into Donal's lungs. A single deep breath. Then another. Then another.

Just as suddenly as the appearance of that sylph — not an angel after all, although in the moment the difference was moot — a green, rocky humanoid form took hold of Donal and righted him in his seat.

The remaining three belts were clicked on his behalf. No longer were any belts cutting into his flesh. Trying to squeeze him to bursting.

Just like that, Donal sat properly in his seat again. Air flowing into his lungs with each breath, even without the yellow intermediary. The sylph was gone, and the gnome too. Both back to whatever their normal duties were, when they weren't saving the life of a passenger.

"Better?" said a soft voice in a thick, Russian accent. Dola. Right next to Donal. Concern in those deep blue eyes.

"Much," Donal said, already getting his heart rate under control, and rubbing away the lingering pains in his stomach and collarbone.

"Good," Edik said from the pilot's seat, without turning around. "Do me a favor, if you would. From now on, when you're sitting on a seat that has safety belts, *put them on*. They're not there as a suggestion, and they're not there to be fashionable. I mean, you get that we're moving at some pretty serious speeds, even if you don't always feel them?"

"Of course. But you didn't say—"

"Didn't think I had to. From now on, please do us both the favor of assuming that space travel is a somewhat dangerous pastime, and that you might be expected to do your best to stay alive and uninjured."

Tension spiked through Donal's shoulders and jaw. It was one thing to be lectured like a novice when Donal had done something questionable. But this harness issue, that was something Edik could have mentioned before.

Donal opened his mouth to say a few choice words.

"Remember," Dola said softly, "you promised nothing that would challenge Edik's demesne."

Donal closed his mouth.

Technically — *technically* — Donal hadn't been about to challenge Edik's seniority in formal, thaumaturgic terms. But that was sticking to the letter of what Donal had promised. Not the spirit.

Donal sighed.

"Fine," Donal said. "But please, do what you can to make sure safety requirements are clear? I mean the flight to that point had been so smooth."

"Sure," Edik said. "Dola, please act as steward on this flight, if you would."

"Of course, Edik," Dola said. "Donal, in another decan or so you should be safe to move about the cabin. In the meantime, would you care for a beverage?"

Donal blinked. He had the sudden feeling that this flight was going to feel a lot longer than it actually was.

3

Edik glanced over the displays one more time. Nothing but normal space traffic. Thin streams heading for or away from San Francisco and Durango. Others more distant, just inside the atmosphere, heading for other airports or spaceports.

Nobody too close to the *Third Son*. Nobody acting like they'd noticed Edik's little firebird of a helioship leaving Earth.

Nobody but that one flying saucer.

Maybe.

That ship was gone now. Or at least, far enough away that Xincapph couldn't sense it over regular space traffic. Which meant as good as gone.

One other advantage of bringing the lacuna into play early — Xincapph now knew what the space around that little flying saucer felt like. Knew the taste of the gap it made in fabric of space. Well, that was as close as Edik could come to understanding how lacunas perceived the universe around them, as translated by Dola.

What mattered was that Xincapph would notice that flying saucer if it showed up again.

And Edik had that tight feeling low in his gut that said that saucer was going to show up again.

No reason for it. No way Mason told anyone his plans. No way Lukyanov could have anyone tailing them. If he could have done that, he wouldn't have had to bring his son into play. Wouldn't have needed Edik at all.

"Hey," Edik muttered to Dola. "Any chance our passenger can help us with … whatever it was exactly that Dimitri Lukyanov did?"

"I confess, I doubt it," Dola said, "but we can always try."

Edik hummed something noncommittal. After all, that flying saucer hadn't followed Edik from San Francisco, and it certainly hadn't tailed Edik all the way from Kennedy. Which meant the most likely answer was that it was following Donal.

Donal, who'd been having a bad day of his own. Donal, who had something he wasn't sure he wanted to talk about.

Donal, who even now was back in the main cabin, meditating.

"What do you think of this kid?" Edik said to Dola, while checking and double-checking his scanners. He'd want to swing out toward Venus for a few decans before swinging back onto course. He did that, especially if he angled right past where Luna ought to be at the time, and Edik should be able to establish once and for all if that flying saucer was tailing him.

"Troubled," Dola said. "Kid's got worries on top of worries. And he didn't have his familiar out. Only reason to walk around without his familiar is if he doesn't want to listen to whatever his familiar is going to say. That worries me a bit."

"Me too. Hope he's not one of those *magicians are the masters of the universe* types. This voyage would get pretty damned long."

"Or pretty damned short," Dola said.

They laughed together.

"No. If we killed him, we'd have to answer to Mason. Not sure that's a better option, even if Donal looks down on spirits."

"Doubt he does, to be honest," Dola said. "He thanked Nixia and Magom for saving his bacon back there."

"His bacon shouldn't have needed saving, but yeah. Fair enough."

"We'll need to talk to him, though. Need to find out what he's running from."

"You think he's running from something?" Edik glanced back over his shoulder at Dola. Watched a ripple work its way down that shaggy gray fur.

"Yes," Dola said slowly. "Not sure it's immediate trouble though. We'll need to play this cautiously."

"Especially since he *is* a Journeyman," Edik said with a sigh. "Odds are if I push too hard here, he'll pick up on some of our problems."

"I thought we were going to ask him to help with those." Dola twitched his whiskers. "Or am I getting lost in your plots?"

Edik chuckled. "No plots. Not of mine, anyway. Anna's, well…"

Edik and Dola locked eyes. As one they turned to look at the closed bridge door, and the main cabin beyond it.

"You think this has to do with Anna?" Dola asked. "With the Rhian people?"

"How could he possibly be involved with that?" Edik said, and even he thought he sounded like he was trying to convince himself. "Hasn't been to Luna since before we discovered them. You saw his passport."

"Doesn't mean anything," Dola said. "Did you stamp him for this trip away from Earth?"

Edik gave Dola a sour look. His familiar knew full well that only authorized customs agents could stamp a passport. But the point was well-made. The great families of Luna certainly had the resources to bring people to and from Luna without getting customs involved at all.

For all Edik knew, Donal was working for the Romanovs.

And that better not be true. Having one great family mucking about with this mission was bad enough. But if Donal was working for Natalia Romanova … if he was working for the most powerful woman on Luna … a woman who wanted, more than anything else, to seize control of everything she could get her hands on…

Well. Edik would just have to make his apologies to Hierophant Mason for killing him.

DEEP MEDITATION. THERE WAS NOTHING ELSE QUITE LIKE IT.

So much of magic involved moving energy around, or calling on elements, or dealing with spirits. And some of it even dealt with calling on gods — though that sort of magic was not officially sanctioned by any Thaumaturgic Board Donal knew of. So far as he knew, it was still going through a great deal of debate, in which the various religions of the world all wanted a hand in what was done and what was not done.

But sanctioned or not, people did it anyway. As some of them had in their family lines since before the last time magic fell. Even Donal and his brother called on the Dagda, Lugh and others freely, though never in any formal way.

But meditation. Proper, deep meditation. That wasn't like anything else.

Most magic was active. Meditation was passive. Contemplative, without contemplating anything specific. Most times, at least.

Right now, Donal sat in the other kind of deep meditation, blissfully unaware of the helioship around him.

Withdrawn, deep into the recesses of his own mind. Past the point that he held even awareness of his own heartbeat. His own breath. Or even his own thoughts.

Donal's whole awareness centered on a single fact.

The fae were awake and active.

What that meant, he couldn't be sure. No way to be sure. Surety in this matter wasn't the point. Not now.

It was this one fact that mattered. This one fact Donal had to be certain he truly understood. Truly absorbed, to the deepest parts of his mind.

The fae were not merely content to wait within the worlds of their mounds. To wait, and dream, until magicians like Donal projected parts of themselves among those dreams to tempt a sleeper into awakening. Into taking up the familiar bond, and participating in the new, modern world.

No.

The fae were awake. And active.

All on their own.

They were watching. And more than that, if there were changelings — if Rowan MacPherson could be believed, and Fionn insisted she could — then there were fae out there having sex with humans.

And no one seemed to know they were there.

This … this was bigger than anything Donal had ever run across. So big, he wasn't sure how to process it. What it truly meant.

It was one thing to look on the old stories, those still told by his grandparents, as parables of a sort. Tales told to convey the truths of magic even during the reign of technology. Ways of keeping the magic alive, and maybe hint at things that actually happened.

But there were changelings. Real, honest (more or less) offspring of fae and humans. That meant that going under the fae mounds was a real thing. Participating in their parties. Possibly even going missing for decades…

Possibly without aging *a day*, though the world continued as it would.

Incredible.

And what did it mean?

What did it mean that the fae had watched magic rise again, and not come forward? What did it mean that they watched humans establish their magic, reach even beyond the planet that bore them for the other worlds of this solar system?

And yet did nothing.

If they did nothing.

Could they have been active all this time? Could some of them have been hiding with Lloyd Bird's people on that island off the coast of Ireland, concealed by magic all those years?

And most of all, what did it mean now that the fae approached Donal, through Rowan MacPherson? Wished him to represent them to spirits on a moon of Jupiter. Spirits Donal might not even encounter. Even if the whole point of his going there was to "scout the place and do what needs doing" on behalf of a Hierophant.

Too many questions. Too many thoughts. Too many to begin to try to work his way through, even if he had unlimited time to sit around and talk with Fionn about it all.

And so Donal did the only thing he could.

He meditated.

He stilled every part of his being and focused on that single thought. Let it permeate him. Work its way through his consciousness so that it could properly inform him. Properly adjust the way he saw the world, the way he considered events and news and ... everything.

He focused on that one thought, and let it settle within his mind.

The fae were awake and active.

Donal wasn't sure how long he'd been at it. Truth was that without setting a mental alarm, Donal would never have known how long he spent in meditation. But at some point, he felt a sensation he thought of as a mental knock.

It was a brush of power. A vague sweep across the edges of his senses. He recognized it immediately as the presence of Dola, Edik's familiar. A shaggy gray cat, semi-translucent as Fionn was when present, and just as big.

And such a brush of power to a meditating magician was tantamount to a request for his return.

Of course, such an act was more than a real "request." Because the fact that Donal noticed it meant his mind was already easing out of the deeper channels of meditation. It might have been irritating under other circumstances, but in this case it was just as well.

He needed to talk to Edik.

So Donal eased his consciousness slowly back to present.

First he reached for his magical senses. Always there, of course, just as his physical senses were, but beginning awareness along those lines was always a more gentle return.

No threats. No build-up of power. No sensation of urgency.

All to the good.

Donal regained his sense of his body before he considered opening his eyes. He could tell his body was right where he'd left it — sitting in the front, port-side passenger seat in the main cabin — which was always comforting. Sometimes back in his undergrad studies, students would move the bodies of meditating classmates, just as pranks.

Donal had woken up naked on the quad, in a toga at a football game, and one time, well, he didn't want to think about that one…

But even though Fionn wasn't currently guarding Donal's body, it seemed that Edik and Dola were above such petty pranks. Donal could feel the harness of that chair across his chest, feel the deep comfort of its padding all the way up to cradle his head. He could have fallen asleep in this chair, were he tired enough.

Donal could smell only fresh, clean air, though unless he was mistaken it carried a hint of licorice. Odd. He hadn't noticed that earlier. Perhaps Dola took this steward job too seriously, and was bringing snacks?

Donal opened his eyes. Dola did indeed stand before him in shaggy gray splendor on the rich gold carpet, but Donal saw no snack tray.

His stomach rumbled a modest protest. But food wasn't on Donal's mind.

"What did you mean," Donal asked, "when you'd said you two had had something of a day?"

"Luna," Dola said, "isn't like Earth. It's run as much by its great families as by its bureaucracy—"

"Tell me about it," Donal said. "The Romanovs tried to kill me once, claiming a moral crime. All I'd done was deliver a package."

"What package?" Dola asked, tilting its head in much the same way Fionn might have.

"Can't answer that," Donal said. "Nondisclosure agreements. Suffice to say it cut into their business, and Natalia Romanova sent a hit squad after me."

"You eluded a Romanov hit squad?"

Edik's question, coming from the open door to the bridge, where he now stood. He sounded entirely too surprised by that question, but then, Donal had no right to feel affronted.

He hadn't fought his way past those Romanov guards. He'd run. Flat out. Through the spaceport. And even that hadn't been enough. In the end…

"Well," Donal admitted, "it wasn't so much that I eluded them, as I led them on a merry chase to my ship, where … Hierophant Mason saved me."

Donal didn't like the flush he felt creep up his neck, much less the ripple that went through Dola's fur or the way Edik cleared his throat.

"I fought a duel with Natalia Romanova once," Edik said, easing himself into the chair opposite Donal. "Just a few months ago. In rain and mud. Rough bit of fighting."

"Did you win?"

"I was about to when it got interrupted." Edik smirked. "Second time that day I'd fought a duel, only to have it interrupted. Terrible luck, sometimes."

"What are you running from?" Donal asked.

"You first," Edik replied.

Donal locked eyes with this helioship captain, this Initiate, and shared a smile. In just that moment, he felt more kinship with this man than he had so far. Two men, over their heads, no matter what Hierophant Mason was thinking when he gave them this job.

Enough kinship that Donal was willing to let pass that little incident with the lacuna and those cutting straps.

"First things first," Donal said, and called Fionn forth from the silver faun pendant tucked under his green airsilk shirt.

The emerald deerhound formed in a flash of brilliant light that same color, and Donal was slightly disturbed to realize that Fionn and Dola really were the same size. Yes they were spirits, not animals, but Donal was used to thinking of the *cú sidhe* as so *big*, and to see what might have been a housecat the same size was just wrong.

"Fionn," Donal said, "These are Initiate Captain Edik Barshai and his familiar, Dola. Edik, Dola, this is my familiar, Fionn."

Quick greetings all around, including several quick back-and-forth comments between Fionn and Dola, in that language that only familiars could understand.

"I hate when they do that," Edik said.

"I try not to take it personally," Donal said, "but they don't always make it easy."

"Cost of doing business," Dola said.

"I must admit," Fionn said, to Donal, "I'd think you were accustomed to it by now."

"In any event," Donal said, "Fionn, Edik here was about to enlighten us about what it is he's running from."

"No," Edik said slowly, "I believe *you* agreed to go first."

Donal smiled. "Worth a shot."

"We're running from something?" Fionn asked, in words pitched only for Donal's ears. "Just what exactly did you do while I was housed?"

"Nothing," Donal said the same way. "Well, I did almost get killed when Edik called on his helioship's lacuna while still in Earth's sky."

But Donal didn't give Fionn a chance to respond to that. Instead, in English, he continued.

"All right. I'm not quite sure where to start."

"Edik." Nixia formed in mid-air, a vision in tiny yellow, her voice as breathy as a breeze. "You asked to be informed if that saucer returned."

"Right," Edik said, standing. "Looks like later for that story."

<hr>

EDIK GRUMBLED HIS WAY BACK TO HIS CAPTAIN'S CHAIR, DOLA HOT ON his heels. Edik dropped into his seat and strapped in, and was gratified at least a little to hear Donal strapping into the bridge's one passenger seat.

Edik called up the scanner displays, one to his left and one to his right. Stretched the port side scanner larger, for a better view.

Sure enough, it was that same saucer.

No. Wait. It was *a* saucer. Quicksilver in color, an oval ball — too symmetrical to be an egg — surrounded by a wide brim in pale green. Odd, that. The brim made the overall shape perfectly round, but the body of the ship was stretched a bit in each direction, from the center swelling. Odd design choice.

Had the saucer on Earth been slightly off in shape? He hadn't had a good enough view to make sure.

"Nixia," Edik said, "is Xincapph sure that's the same ship?"

"It was Xincapph who brought it to my attention as such. It's outside the reach of our sylphs."

Edik reached into the holographic projection of the ship. Grabbed it with his hands. A weird sensation, and warmer than he always expected it to be, but functional enough. Just his way to ask for more details from his lacuna.

And Xincapph responded, quick as always.

"Earth origin," Edik recited aloud as his lacuna supplied data. "Made in San Jose, California. Is that usual for small helioships?"

Edik soldiered on before Donal tried to answer that question. It was for Dola to remember and check on later.

"Can't get the registration. That's fairly typical though. Does transmit its transponder, though. Apparently this is called the *Silver Streak*."

Edik glanced over at Dola. Both of them blinked.

"What?" Donal asked.

"Well, it's an odd name for a ship, is all. *Silver Streak*. Sounds like a comic character."

"Perhaps it is," Dola said. "Perhaps it's an homage?"

"More likely a name that won't show up on any ship registries." Edik shook his head, went back to the readout. "Rated for deep space travel. Up to six passengers. Four crew…"

Edik glanced back at Dola. Dola didn't speak, but he didn't have to. Didn't matter anyway, because Donal asked.

"Is that odd?"

"For a ship this size? Yes. Most require a crew of two. The only reason to have four—"

"Is if it's armed," Dola finished.

"Civilian ship, though," Donal said, "right?"

"No military codes to its transponder. And nothing like that shape I've ever heard of in a military ship. Still." Edik shook his head. "Tell me. Anyone in the U.N.A.S. government paranoid enough to have started a secret police?"

Donal didn't say anything, which gave Edik that sinking feeling in his gut. Edik glanced back. Donal had both eyebrows down and his mouth stretched in a line.

"Out with it," Edik said.

"It's not anything certain," Donal said slowly. "It's just … this last senatorial race got pretty ugly. Some of the senators have started expressing concerns about magicians and magical training. Wondering if some of us have … secret agendas."

"Lovely," Edik said. "Just lovely. And here we are, two magicians, flying a secret mission for a Hierophant, to a world officially off-limits to civilian travel, without so much as a thread of official clearance from any kind of government agency."

"Perhaps," Dola said, "this mission is a bad idea?"

"Lovely," Edik said again. "Just lovely. And if you were thinking that, my dear Dola, why didn't you share it with the class sooner?"

"I did. You said," — and Dola repeated Edik's words back in Edik's own voice — "I know, I know, but Hierophants are the future. They shit more money than a guy like me will see in his lifetime. That's worth a little risk."

"You didn't have to quote me in front of our guest," Edik said, quirking one eyebrow.

"Edik," Donal said, in a tone sharp enough that Edik almost gave himself whiplash looking where his passenger pointed, back at the display.

Sure enough, the saucer had picked up speed.

And if it was armed, it might be coming into firing range any moment.

As Donal stared at the scanner display and the growing image of the saucer, he wondered what it would be like to enjoy one long flight, just one, where no one was trying to kill him. When he was a courier, it seemed as though anytime he flew farther than the moon, that pretty much guaranteed that someone wanted to stop his delivery. Someone who wouldn't let a little thing like Donal's life get in his way.

Or her way. Murderers came pretty evenly distributed among the sexes, in Donal's experience.

Sitting here on the bridge of the *Third Son*, Donal couldn't help but think about how this job was supposed to be different. About how he actually expected to at least reach Ganymede in one piece.

Sure, he had never felt all that certain that he would *leave* Ganymede in one piece, but still. This just seemed unfair.

It was thoughts like these that left Donal sitting there, gripping the straps that bound him to his passenger seat, while Edik and Dola leapt into action.

And Edik and Dola seemed to have a system down for this sort of situation.

Dola dove into the holographic display of the ship, quite literally getting into the system.

Edik, though, wasted no time slamming that red lever from "ahead half" to "ahead full." And seemingly the same instant had both hands dancing among the three golden controls that dove his ship from its current course and steered it through a series of loops.

"Should—" Donal cleared his throat. "Shouldn't we try to talk to them first? What if—"

"That," Edik said, nodding toward the port side scanner display, "is a ship on an intercept course. Believe me when I tell you there's absolutely no other reason for it to hold that bearing."

"And these loops?"

Donal's answer came from the saucer — a great big ball of orange fire, speeding on a direct line at where the *Third Son* would have been without that latest loop.

"Further questions?" Edik asked.

"N—" Donal started to say, then finished, "Yes. what can I do?"

Edik glanced back, while continuing to send his ship through a series of rolls and twists, narrowly avoiding a second ball of fire. One that came close enough that Donal could swear he felt the heat of it.

"Don't know," Edik said, his full attention back on his controls.

"What *can* you do? You're supposed to be a Journeyman, right?"

Donal didn't answer that with words.

Instead, he pulled back into himself. Not his awareness, so much. That he needed keeping track of the outside world. No, what he pulled back in were his emotions. His fear at this sudden assault. His worries that he might never see his family again.

All the little bits of feeling that were locking down most of the muscles in his body, for want of some physical outlet. If he couldn't run and he couldn't throw punches or kicks, his body chose to express itself by tightening everything it could tighten.

But tension was bad. Tension inhibited the flow of power.

So Donal drew three quick, deep breaths. Each bleeding away his body's tension until he felt loose and relaxed. Still very much aware of how close those fireballs were coming. Still very much aware of his danger. And yet now Donal was in control, not the situation.

That was the greatest power of the magician — to maintain awareness of all threats, while in a state of mind that not only allowed useful assessment, but encouraged action.

Donal could see the situation clearly now.

Edik was a damned good pilot. He was executing maneuvers *in anticipation* of how and when the saucer would fire. He was managing to stay one step ahead of their gunners.

However, the saucer was faster than the *Third Son*. Or … perhaps it was merely that the saucer's pilot only had to worry about closing the distance, since the *Third Son* could not counterattack.

Donal smiled. Rubbed his hands together. He called Fionn back out of the silver faun pendant, and Fionn immediately took up position in front of Donal and connected with him, adding the *cú sidhe's* magic to his own.

Donal eased his attention into the web of spells that comprised the outer layers of the *Third Son*, those woven tightest into the ceramics of the hull, just inside the civilian-grade wards that wouldn't do nearly enough to stop those fireballs. Skimmed his mind along the surface of the various spells and enchantments of the ship, seeking the right kind of pattern. The right kind of...

There. The tail. Of course. The tail of the firebird. It had the right kind of angle, and a vaguely tunnel shape to its spells.

Perfect.

Donal began weaving together bits of deception magic, one of his two specialties. He started first in the web of the hull's spells, adding little bits that would look to an observer as though they shunted power without appearing to shunt power. The way a ship that wasn't supposed to have weapons might try to hide its weaponry.

Tricky, but for what Donal had in mind, necessary.

Check that. Not *necessary*, but more effective, depending on how good the saucer's magician was. And better to assume competence.

"Any time now, Mr. Journeyman," Edik said from the pilot's seat. "Hard to stay one step ahead when they can keep…"

Edik let his words trail off as Donal cast his first spell.

A ball of fire appeared to shoot out of the tail of the *Third Son*, dead straight at the oncoming saucer. A bright orange ball, tinged with green, with which Donal implied acid in the alchemy of the assault.

The saucer banked hard to port and dove aside.

Donal "fired" again. Twice more in quick succession. Each time near where he guessed the saucer was going. Each time adding just a little more heat to the effect. Just in case he came close enough to scare them.

Donal could only hope he didn't guess too well. The deception wouldn't hold if the fireball hit the saucer and failed to do any damage.

Fortunately, the saucer's pilot didn't seem to want to take the risk. He kept their ship ducking and weaving now under Donal's steady stream of shots. That slowed the saucer down. Not much, but maybe enough for…

Edik let out a whoop so sharp and loud it almost broke Donal's concentration, which was no easy feat. Donal was about to ask why…

…then realized he could no longer see the saucer on the scanners. And he checked both, to be sure.

Before Donal could ask what happened, Edik was out of his chair and gripping Donal by the shoulders.

"Brilliant! Absolutely brilliant!" Edik's smile was so wide Donal wondered if he'd see a second row of teeth behind the first. But Edik was still raving. "Never saw anything like that before. Your illusions were even showing up on *my* scanners! How'd you do that?"

"Simple," Donal said, grinning now despite himself, and trying not to hear Magister Machado's chiding about maintaining an aura of mystery. "Well, not *simple*, but all part of doing the job right. Fireballs wouldn't distract a pilot who could tell at a glance that they weren't there. So it's all about adding dimension to them along all elemental lines, especially spirit or space—"

"Donal, you can fly with me *anytime!*" Edik danced around in a circle right there in the tight space of the bridge, while Dola came back out of the holographic display.

"Was that your work, Donal?" Dola asked, sounding more impressed than Donal liked. He *was* a Journeyman, after all, and studying to become a Hierophant himself.

Donal only nodded, and started undoing his safety straps. If Edik could dance, then surely Donal didn't need to be strapped in like a child in a runner.

"How did we get away so quickly?" Donal asked, finally free to stand now that Edik was dropping back into his pilot's seat.

"Best part about having a good relationship with my lacuna." Edik smiled, then winked. "If you ever get your own ship, I can't recommend that enough. The better terms you're on with your lacuna, the better it can do for you in times of trouble."

"But its speed is its speed," Donal said. He'd studied some of the magic of space after his first trip to Mars, and all accounts indicated that the power of lacunas responded linearly to most thaumaturgic controls, with only moderate allowances for change under the newer Deception Drives. But this ship was too small to afford something that expensive.

Edik only grinned even wider. "That's what everyone says, but don't you believe it. Lacunas, they *are* space in a way we'll never truly understand. Space both is and isn't there for them, if you understand what I mean."

"I don't," Donal said quickly, "but I'd like to."

"Maybe I'll introduce you later." Edik tilted his head back and forth, as though he wasn't willing to promise that. As though he might have thought it wasn't a good idea, for reasons he didn't seem to want to go into. But what he said next was, "Suffice for now to say that what we think of as speed isn't what *they* think of as speed. And when we're pressed, for short periods of time, I can ask Xincapph to fly us at speeds *he* thinks are fast."

Donal blinked rapidly as he absorbed that.

"That would play hell on the wards. Not to mention—"

"The spells that hold the ship together." Edik blew out a quick breath. "I know. Believe me. But Xincapph and I have done this more than a few times, and trust me, I have a strong sense of how often and how long I can do that, without risking any serious damage to the ship."

"Serious damage?" Donal asked.

"Speaking of," Edik said, standing. "Dola, keep an eye on things while I handle maintenance?"

"Of course, Edik."

Edik started into the main cabin. Donal stopped him with a hand on the shoulder.

"Serious damage?" Donal asked again.

Edik smiled. "Let's just say that some of my spells now need their alchemical support a little ahead of schedule."

Edik pushed past into the main cabin, heading for the back of the ship.

"Let's not just say that," Donal said, following, with Fionn hot on his heels. "Let's talk detail, here."

"Come along then," Edik said, chuckling. "I'll let you give me a hand. I'm entirely too happy with you right now to feel insulted that *you're questioning my ability to maintain my ship.*"

Donal stopped asking questions. But he did follow along.

EDIK WAS THOROUGH. DONAL WAS SURE OF THAT MUCH.

The two of them had spent a good hour going over various spells and enchantments, checking and re-checking them before applying the right combinations of alchemical formulae to support those spells.

Spells, by their nature, were of limited duration. A few hours, usually, or until the sun next rose or set, in some cases. Some could even last for days at a time, if the magician was well-used to casting them and if they didn't contain elements that grew too complex.

But the structure of spells appeared to be subject to what was officially called "entropy." Donal had come to question that term, here in his graduate studies, because "entropy" was an older term for something to do with physics. And magic, of course, had little to do with physics.

"Entropy," as Donal understood the term from his studies, would have implied that all spells naturally decay because spell structures, by their nature, were artificial and could not hold. But that wasn't why spells decayed. Spells decayed because the power invested in them slowly ebbed away with use.

The better the magician, the more efficient the spell. The better the magician knew and used that spell, the more efficient it grew beyond even that.

And yet, no one had yet discovered a way to shunt enough power into a well-enough structured spell that it could be maintained indefinitely through a single casting. Repeated castings were still necessary, or another power source had to be applied. Elementals and other spirits could supply the power, but where spirits weren't used, the answer was alchemy.

The formulae of alchemy lent an endurance to the structure of spells beyond anything that a casting alone could provide.

And though Edik was not a good enough alchemist to have made his living inventing and refining formulae, he could handle his own maintenance with quick, quiet efficiency. He knew his blends, handled his mortar and pestle with aplomb, and had a good instinct for how much his spells needed when and where.

Donal probably learned more about ship maintenance in that hour than he had in a whole semester dedicated to the magic of space travel.

Truth was, Edik didn't need Donal along for maintenance at all. So Donal kept his mouth shut except to ask questions — that is, to gather information rather than question what Edik was doing — and help grind when he could.

By the time they were finished, Donal felt a good deal better about flying all the way to Ganymede in this ship. Yes, every spell in it had been touched up and tweaked by an Initiate, even though it had originally been cast by at least a Journeyman, but in this case the Initiate really knew his ship and its spells.

And that wasn't all.

Donal had always thought of himself as good with spirits. He never failed to be polite and respectful to the spirits he worked with, and had even developed a fairly cordial relationship with Fionn. Certainly a more cordial relationship than Donal had seen from almost any other magician. At school, most of the other students — and the faculty — kept a more distant relationship, some even a clear master-servant vibe.

But with Edik, Donal saw a magician who made him look downright formal.

Edik seemed to have developed an actual friendship with every one of the spirits of his ship. Donal had never seen anything like it. Never *heard* of anything like it, much less read about it in the trade magazines.

Edik laughed and joked with his spirits as he worked (though the spirits didn't tell any jokes themselves, they seemed to enjoy Edik's). He didn't utter commands, he asked for favors. He addressed them often by name, not just for designation but for familiarity, and Donal had even heard Edik use gender-based pronouns for his spirits, based on how they appeared.

Bizarre. Nixia was a "she" to Edik, and Dola a "he." Even though they were spirits, and had nothing like gender in the human sense…

But then, Donal had thought the same of the fae. Despite the tales he'd grown up with from the lips of both grandmothers, Donal had assumed that the fae — the actual fae — would have been genderless in the same way elementals were.

Now, Donal wasn't so sure. After all, Rowan MacPherson was a changeling. And the fae, they weren't just sleeping in their mounds. They were awake and active in the world, and apparently having sex with humans.

Perhaps that meant that elementals had more gender to them than Donal had believed. Certainly Nixia acted female, even appeared to have something of a crush on Edik. Though such appearances could be deceiving.

Still, Donal certainly couldn't deny that Edik got more out of his spirits than any other Initiate Donal had ever met. Heck, even more than some Journeymen.

Possibly even more than Donal himself, though it was a bit early to say that for certain.

So as Donal reclined in the forward, starboard side chair of the eight in the main cabin, resting after that hour of intense study, learning, and thinking, he wondered whether he had been laboring under basic misunderstandings about the nature of spirits in the first place.

He glanced over at Fionn, who was currently lying down with its — his? — head on its forepaws. Donal glanced up toward the bridge, where Edik was checking on their situation. Perhaps making sure that the saucer wasn't following them, despite his assurances that this would be impossible.

"Fionn," Donal said quietly, in tones pitched only for his familiar's ears. When Fionn's ears perked up, Donal asked, "do you … have … a gender?"

"Yes," Fionn said. "I am male."

"Why didn't you ever mention that before?"

The moment those words were out of Donal's mouth, he knew the answer. And he said it along with Fionn, "Because you had to be asked directly."

Donal sighed, and wondered what else he needed to think to ask his familiar.

4

Edik sat at his captain's station and checked and re-checked his charts. A holographic representation of space in three dimensions, floating above the white ceramic counter of his captain's station. Might as well have been an old timey yellowed map, for all the good it did him. There just wasn't enough detail. Most of what he'd been able to cull together made it look as though the space between Earth and Ganymede was almost entirely clear.

No way Edik could be that lucky.

Part of problem, of course, was that the military wasn't releasing their official charts past Mars, and the Mars routes were so well flown that they might as well have been clear.

Edik didn't really want to go toward Mars — too many potential witnesses, and the fewer ships that spotted the *Third Son*, the happier Edik would be — but this time of year it was just too much more efficient to follow a Mars route two-thirds of the way, before leaving the established routes and venturing into space that looked all too dark.

Too dark indeed.

There should at least have been listings for the nebula formations. The navy could have given him that much.

Hell, even a "here there be dragons" would have been *something*.

Frankly, this little information was just insulting to good, established pilots like Edik. Sure, maybe men like Donal, who spent most of their days with their feet on one planet or another and not nearly as many aboard ships in the air or at space, maybe those men believed that most of space was truly empty.

Proper helioship captains like Edik, though, knew better. Space was only maybe half-full of actual space.

Beyond the wild lacunas and occasional zuglodons and other strangeness, there were the nebulae. Vast swaths of color in the darkness, reds and greens and blues. Those nebulae were the subject of intense study and debate by magicians way beyond Edik's pay grade, who all had different theories about what they were, how they worked, and most importantly, to them, how they could be used magically.

Edik mostly wanted to avoid flying through them.

And with Dola down checking on things belowdecks, Edik could admit to himself that his desire was little more than a superstition. So far as he knew.

Edik had never flown a ship through one of those nebulae. Had done his best to avoid flying near them. Too many stories the spacers told. Most of them probably lies, but why take the chance?

Maybe the blue nebulae really did break the bonds of lacunas.

Maybe the red nebulae really did hide something bigger and more dangerous than zuglodons.

And the green ones, well, Edik didn't think it was likely that they truly led into whole other universes, but that was just a risk he was not willing to take.

He had way too much to do in this universe to worry about any others.

And without those nebulae properly marked and noted on Edik's charts, plotting his true course to Ganymede was proving more difficult than he wanted to believe.

So Edik settled for doing the only thing he could trust himself to do right now. The only thing he'd really done in plotting this course, even if he would never have admitted it to Jones, or North, and certainly not to Donal.

Edik drew his course once more to the point on the Mars run where he would leave the established routes. Then he pulled his tiny image of the *Third Son* along the holographic depiction of space, across one other Mars-Earth passenger-liner route, then across two Mars-Earth cargo routes, and then…

…then he just held the image there. If he did nothing else before the ship got to that point, Xincapph would bring it to a halt right at those coordinates, and the *Third Son* would not move a klick without Edik taking over manual controls.

Dola chose that moment to stroll through the closed door to the main cabin.

Edik said, "Xincapph, update," and closed the charts.

"Any progress?" Dola asked.

"We're more than a day ahead of schedule, thanks to our escape from that '*Silver Streak.*' Apart from that…"

Edik looked into Dola's trusting blue eyes, and sighed.

"…no. I tweaked the course a little to account for the changes, and to try to confuse that saucer if it's still on our tail, but otherwise, no."

"Any chance of us getting better chart data between here and there?"

Edik cocked an eyebrow. He hadn't mentioned any of his chart concerns to Dola, but apparently he didn't have to.

"I know you pretty well by now," Dola said, and a pleased ripple wandered down his fur to his tail, which twitched only a little before standing straight up.

"No," Edik said with another sigh. Then nodded toward the main cabin with his chin. "He still meditating?"

"At this rate he'll spend more time in meditation today than you do in a week."

"Well," Edik said slowly, "you always say I need to spend more time in meditation."

"You do. Carl says so too."

Edik bit down a rejoinder at that. Carl Jones was more than an

Initiate, though not a Journeyman. At least, not officially. He certainly denied being one. Still. He felt like a Journeyman, and had a Journeyman's sense of magic, but no official paperwork listing himself as anything more than an Initiate.

Probably meant he had the training and experience of a Journeyman, even if he never took the licensing tests that would let him carry the title and charge the higher rates for any spellwork.

Edik suspected it all had something to do with Jones' old work for the Navy. Work Jones didn't like to talk about, and Edik didn't feel inclined to ask.

Either way, Jones was experienced enough a magician to have a right to critique Edik's practices.

Not that Edik would admit that either.

"So…" Dola said, letting the thought trail off, even though Edik could see where it would land.

"No, I haven't called home yet."

"You want to." Curiosity rippled across the cat's cheek fur. "Why not?"

Edik sighed.

"So," Dola said again, this time sitting up straight with his long gray tail curled around his feet. "Are you more worried about how Anna's doing in your absence, or whether Carl has killed North?"

"Hadn't thought about that second part," Edik said, tugging on his blonde Van Dyke.

"Yes, you had," Dola casually corrected Edik to the truth, as the cat so often did. "But it makes you feel better to emphasize Anna."

"Ha!" Edik said, pointing at his familiar and smiling. "You missed, for once. Yes, I'd thought about it, but both are *really* worries about Anna, aren't they?"

"Why?" Dola blinked pretended innocence. "Because you're worried about what would happen to Anna if Carl hurts his credibility on Luna by harming a local businessman in a petty dispute, and you're worried that North will, well…"

"…make a jackass of himself, as usual, and hurt Anna that way." Edik grimaced. "Do I have *any* secrets from you?"

"Would you want to?"

Edik sighed. "No, I suppose not."

"Didn't think so. Secrets from your familiar are a bad policy. The kind of thing the academics do, because they're worried about letting spirits know them too well."

"You're going way out of your way to not tell me to call home."

"And yet you get the message anyway," Dola said, twitching his whiskers. "Seems you know me pretty well too."

"Fine," Edik said. He turned to the snarl of glowing blue strands above the far port corner of his captain's station. Reached for the bottommost strand. Pinched it and gave it a twist.

A moment later, the pleased, well-formed face of Edmund appeared in the air above the snarl. His tight black curls well-trimmed, as always, and he had a red tie just visible at the collar, that worked well with the reddish shades in his dark brown complexion.

"Edik!" Edmund said, his face splitting in a wide, honest smile. Just the sort of smile that gave away how young he was, and gave no hint about how competent he was. "Anna will be so glad you called."

"Is she there? With the time difference—"

"No. Sorry. She was here an hour ago, but Hierophant Mason wanted her to meet him over at the courthouse—"

"COURTHOUSE?" Edik jumped to his feet.

Edmund's hands appeared, waving as though they could dismiss whatever Edik was thinking. But Edik was too afraid of the possibilities to be sure *what* he was thinking.

"It's all right," Edmund said quickly. "This is a good thing. It's—"

"That Barshai?" North's voice, from somewhere behind Edmund.

Then Edmund's holographic head got shoved aside, replaced by North's blocky, scraggly head.

"Still alive, huh?"

"Try not to sound too disappointed," Edik said, one eyebrow high.

"Enh," North said with a shrug of his massive shoulders. "Wasn't sure if it was time to collect the insurance money."

"Might not qualify for it, you buzzard. Not if they prove I was doing something illegal."

"Big difference between not legal and illegal," North said, one thick finger raised. "They'd have to prove a crime was involved to claim illegality, and if I know you, you're on routes that look innocent at this point."

Edik wanted to say a bunch of things. Mostly, he wanted to swear at North. Or talk to Edmund, or Jones. Hell, even Hierophant Mason would be better to talk to right now than North. But he knew North wouldn't give up the link.

"How's Anna?"

"Fine," North grumbled. "Over the stars that an actual Hie-ro-phant is here to help her out. Treats him like a shadow play star."

Edik chuckled, then said, "Bugging him with a bunch of alchemy questions, is she?"

"Not yet, but it's just a matter of time. Makin' those moon eyes that gotta be making our Edmund jealous."

"What are they doing over at the courthouse?"

"Not sure I should tell you," North said, sly smile on his face. "Supposed to be a secret and all. And this is too open a link to really trust…"

"They're suing the Lunar government for interference." Edmund's voice, from out of view.

"Fine!" North spat that word out like it tasted bad. Edik could almost smell the old pirate's rank breath through the link. "Yeah, they're suing the government, the universities, Earth, and I think the Romanovs before they're done. Something about breach of first contact protocols."

North shrugged, then got a pensive look Edik wasn't used to seeing on that cragged face.

"Didn't even know we had first contact protocols."

"That's because you're just a skipper," Edik said with a smile so pleased it probably looked lustful. "If you were a proper *helioship captain* like me, you'd know that part of the licensing involves—"

"Dropping to your knees for Earth?" North looked angry enough to try to punch Edik through the link. "Don't wave your creds in my face. I'll hit 'em where you're most vulnerable."

"Just saying," Edik said, smiling even wider. "In fact—"

"Well, Mr. *Helioship Captain*, if you're so smart, why didn't *you* think of the first contact protocol thing?"

Edik sat back, blinking. "Wasn't sure it applied," he said quickly, while trying to get his mind moving faster than his tongue. Truth was, now that he thought about it, he probably should have been the one to think of first contact protocols. "Usually it's about contact while at space or in an uninhabited territory. Luna doesn't qualify for either, so—"

"Hah," North said, grinning wide now like he'd caught Edik in a major error. "Jones said something similar when Mason first brought it up. The two of you think you're so all-fired smart, but neither one of you thought of it, did you?"

"All right, North," Edik said with a sigh. "You're right. I didn't."

"Better." North nodded hard enough to shake his shaggy black beard. "Way you two talk to me, like I'm a dunce and you're both smarter than geniuses. Ought to treat me with more respect."

"Well," Edik said in as close to a reasonable tone as he could muster, "if you'd try being less of an ass yourself—"

"Gentlemen," Edmund said, his face only just becoming visible.

It was an effect Edik had seen a few times in his days, and he always found it disquieting. To see a third of a head, or even half of one, floating in the air there. As though it should be leaking something, which did not help the image.

"One at a time, please," Edik said. "I have to eat soon."

"Weak guts, eh Barshai?" North said with a laugh. "Guess I'll let the boy tell you what's what."

North's head vanished, and Edmund's came fully into view. Edmund straightened his tie.

"Captain Barshai," Edmund said, "Anna asked me to tell you that she understands what you're doing. And she wants you to call in as often as possible. Partially because she's worried about you—"

Great. Anna was in the middle of the kind of fight that could ruin her life if she wasn't careful, and she was worrying about *Edik*?

"—but also because, if you find..."

"What?"

"Well," Edmund said, his trim brows furrowed, "she wouldn't tell me what you were up to, and Mr. Jones only said something about a flight to Ganymede, but I think it's more than that. And I think Anna knows what."

Edik tugged his Van Dyke while he thought about that. Could Lukyanov have told his daughter? Maybe let something slip when he was trying to get her to let something slip?

Edik shook his head. "Better you don't know, Edmund. But what did she say?"

"She said that if you find what you think you'll find, then what she and Hierophant Mason do might have a direct bearing on your course. Sir, did that make any sense to you?"

"Yes," Edik said, with a slow nod of his head.

"Would you care to explain any of it to me? Are you really going into a potential first contact situation?"

"Can't answer that. For you, as much as for me." Edik grimaced. "Sorry, Edmund. Really, you *are* better off not knowing."

Edmund sighed. "Every time I've been told that, it's always turned out to be wrong." He shook his head. "Oh, well. I trust you, Captain Barshai, and I trust Anna. So I hope you're right."

"Me too, Edmund. Me too."

Edik signed off the link then, and turned to Dola.

"First contact protocols?" He said. "Think that's why Hierophant Mason told me I'd be doing more than just flying the ship?"

"Hierophants are like the old time wizards," Dola said. "They know more than they admit to, and they never tell you everything you need to know."

"Kind of like familiars, eh?" Edik smiled. "Just teasing. Let's go wake our guest and see about some dinner."

Edik knew he had to eat. Knew he hadn't touched anything since that ham sandwich way too many hours ago.

But finding out he might be expected to handle organizing first contact protocols in his capacity as a helioship captain, and maybe hold those protocols on a distant planet, against the Terran Navy and the local settlers, well, that was the kind of news that made him not want to eat.

Maybe he could find some way to shift that responsibility to Donal? The man did seem to like responsibility…

THE BOWL WAS BROWN CERAMIC, AND IT SUITED ITS CONTENTS. DONAL had never eaten borscht before, but it reminded him of a couple of types of Irish stew his mother made from time to time. Lots of beef and potatoes, plus leeks, garlic, and other spices.

The borscht seemed to be heavier on beets than Donal expected, but then he wasn't used to beets in his stews.

He and Edik sat in the forward two seats of the main cabin as they ate, their familiars by their sides. A breeze almost too slight to notice maintained a moderate temperature.

Donal had long since realized he'd be spending the greatest part of this long voyage in this simple room with its eight large portholes. Truth was, only the portholes and the comfort of the large, brown leather seats made the idea at all appealing.

He had comfort in here, and he had a good view of space. Too much to ask, he supposed, for a ship this small to have on-flight entertainment. From his days as a courier, Donal was used to ships large enough to offer shadow plays, and massages, and multiple restaurants.

But this mission was more important than its creature comforts. And if Donal had only one other human for company on the flight, he could do worse than Captain Edik Barshai.

Even now, Edik smiled at Donal from his seat.

"Good?" Edik asked.

"Quite," Donal said. "Reminds me of some of my mother's stews."

"Irish? Really?"

"Beef and potatoes." Donal shrugged. "Probably only so many ways to prepare them."

"So," Edik said a spoonful later. "How do you feel about the Rhian situation?"

Donal had to chuckle at that.

"What?" Edik asked, one thin eyebrow raising just enough for Donal to notice.

"Nothing really," Donal said with a smile. "I just figured we were going to resume our conversation from earlier. What you think I'm running from. What you *are* running from, that sort of thing."

Dola said something to Edik then, in words Donal wasn't meant to understand. Edik nodded as he listened, but that eyebrow had yet to lower itself.

"We can cover either," Edik said at last, "but I think both are going to be important before all this is over."

"So you *do* think we're flying into the same kind of situation?"

"No," Edik said drawing out the word. "The Rhian people are back on Luna, with a firmly established society, a local socialite alchemist rallying people to their cause, and a freaking Hierophant by her side, helping out. We" — Edik pointed back and forth from Donal to himself, with his spoon — "are flying into little more than a border town, with no laws, no Hierophant, and quite probably the Terran Navy. I *wish* this was a Rhian situation."

"Fair enough," Donal said, then helped himself to another spoonful before continuing. "Well, to answer your questions in vague, reverse order, one, I am in favor of the Rhian people having self-determination, and full citizenship status. Even their own settlements if they want them, though that's really something for the Luna locals to decide."

"All right," Edik said, and now both eyebrows were up just that fraction of a millimeter. "Now." Edik sat forward in his chair. "What the hell are you running from?"

"From? Nothing," Donal said. "To? Probably a world of trouble. It's just that ... well..."

Fionn interrupted Donal then, in words Edik and Dola wouldn't be able to understand.

"Are you sure he can be trusted with this?"

Donal thought about that through another spoonful of borscht.

"Edik," Donal said at last, "I want to tell you what's going on with me. The Dagda knows we need to trust one another if we're going to survive this trek. Plus, I have to figure Hierophant Mason knows what he's doing."

"That is his reputation," Edik said, his tone noncommittal.

"But I need your word about something before I can come entirely clean." Donal let those words sink in for a moment, but if Edik felt any surprise, Donal couldn't tell.

Clearly not a man to play poker with. Not for Donal, anyway.

"What?" Edik said, tone still noncommittal.

"It involves spirits that most people … don't really know about. I need your word that you'll keep the secret I'd have to tell you. And I mean from anybody except Dola."

A wave of curiosity rippled down Dola's fur. Dola twitched its — *his* — ears, and said something to Fionn that Donal couldn't understand. And neither could Edik, from the curious way those eyebrows finally came down, which made Donal feel a little better.

Fionn responded in kind, and Dola turned and nodded at Edik.

"Well, clearly *they* think this is a good idea, so yes. I swear on my captain's license that I will keep all secrets revealed by you or your familiar during this voyage."

"Thank you, Edik," Donal said. "Now—"

"One moment," Edik said, spoon hand coming up. "I need you to make the same promise. Otherwise…"

"Fair enough," Donal said before Fionn even turned to nod. "I swear on my place at CalThaum San Luis Obispo that I will keep all secrets revealed by you or your familiar during this voyage."

"Thank you," Edik said with a nod. "Now go ahead."

Donal made it quick. Stuck to the basics about the fae, and his role because, truth to tell, he wasn't sure how much he was allowed to reveal himself.

Edik looked entirely too calm about this information for Donal's taste. Donal expected shock, or slack-jawed amazement. Something. But instead, Edik just sat there, working a bit of borscht around in his mouth.

Finally, he said, "This is a secret? I always just sort of assumed they were out there."

Fionn chuckled, his ears going back.

"I mean," Edik continued, "all these elemental spirits running around, and some of the odder types that I've heard Japanese and Chinese magicians talking about, why should faeries be any surprise?"

Donal hissed in a breath, but Fionn didn't seem offended by the term.

"So, you're an ambassador for them, huh?" Edik said, sipping from his cup of water. "Isn't that kind of thing on the bad ideas list?"

"Well," Donal admitted, imagining that his grandmothers would have said the same thing, albeit in different words. Hell, probably in Gaelic, to boot. "Might be, but I didn't see that I had a lot of choice."

"No," Edik said, his face suddenly very serious. "*You* had all the choice in the world. I mean, I get it, these are the spirits of your fore-fathers, and you feel a certain responsibility, or maybe you're inter-ested in what magics they can teach you, or maybe just because your familiar is one of them. I get all that. But *you* had a choice. *I did not.*"

"You're in league with the fae?" That *would* explain his blasé atti-tude to what Donal thought of as a shocking revelation.

"Not in the least," Edik said. "I'm talking about what *I'm* running from." Edik shook his head. "How much do you know about the great families of Luna? I mean, apart from the Romanovs trying to kill you. Which I respect you for, by the way."

"Not much more than that," Donal admitted. "I get the feeling they kind of run the show up there. Like each one is a cross between a government agency and a major corporation."

"Pretty much," Edik said. "They aren't *above* the law, per se, but catching them at anything illegal, much less proving it and getting a conviction, well, your chances would be better of flying home from here under your own power."

"And you're running from one of them?"

"The Lukyanovs. Second place in the most important family contest. Not far behind the Romanovs, and doing what they can to close that gap."

"What do they have on you?"

"It's not what they have on me," Edik said, shaking his head. "It's what they have on my ship."

Donal dropped his spoon into his empty bowl with a loud *clink*.

"Come on," Edik said, setting his own bowl down on the gold runner carpet.

EDIK HADN'T BEEN PLANNING TO SHOW HIS PASSENGER ANY MORE OF HIS ship than he had to, but Donal was right about one thing. They were only going to survive this trip if they trusted each other.

Besides, there was always a chance Donal could help. He wasn't a Magister, but he *was* a full Journeyman, and he *was* in school for his Th. D. Sure, more than ninety percent of Th. D. students washed out and settled for a Master's, but even so. Maybe he'd picked up a trick or two beyond his pay grade.

Edik led Donal into the back of the ship, their familiars trailing behind them, deep in a conversation of their own. This much Edik had already shown Donal. A small cabin at the back, beside the head, where Edik had let Donal help with the routine maintenance.

This time, though, Edik continued down the access ladder to the lower deck, where the supplies were stored, as well as Edik's own bunk. But Edik couldn't stop there.

He led Donal along the plain white ceramic deck, through the narrow space between the crates of supplies, to the access hatch to belowdecks. Known on larger ships as engineering.

Edik looked up at Donal for a moment, then popped open the hatch.

"Ever been in an engine room before?" Edik asked.

"Not while the ship was moving," Donal said. "Always wanted to see a lacuna in action though."

"Well," Edik said, as he took the short, ceramic ladder down into the engine room, "may not be too much to look at. I don't have a drive as fancy as any of those big ships you're used to."

And he didn't. He didn't have one of the big HK Drives, and certainly not one of the new, expensive Deception Drives. The *Third Son* wasn't much more than a runabout, in terms of helioships, and it didn't have room for more than a cast off Riverbend Drive.

The Riverbend Drive was invented by now-defunct Riverbend Thaumatics, and part of the reason they were out of business. The drive was supposed to be able to handle ships ten times the size of Edik's. Truth was, by the book it wasn't an efficient enough set of spells and bindings to trust with a ship the size of the *Third Son* for anything more than a jaunt to Earth and back.

But then, most engineers didn't really understand lacunas to save their lives. Half the bindings in the Riverbend Drive weren't necessary, and Xincapph was far more effective since Edik had gotten rid of them.

Not that he would admit any of this to Donal...

Edik dropped down into the small room. Entirely that same basic white ceramic of unpainted ship hull. Not much to see in this room. The real show was one room forward, on the other side of an open portal: the drive room.

Nevertheless Edik glanced around at the open space. He liked this room. Did most of his serious alchemy down here. He inhaled deep of the pungent scents of the herbs he used to keep his lacuna happy.

Vervain. Always more vervain than any of the books called for. Maybe that was just Xincapph's taste, or maybe it was a statement about all lacunas.

Or maybe it was just that this was one of the few ships where the lacuna felt comfortable enough to express his desires that way.

Edik didn't know for sure, but he knew which way he'd've bet.

This room might have been empty, but the drive room was full. The drive room was only maybe half the size of this room — wouldn't have been big enough for Donal, Edik and both familiars to stand in. Not unless they were far friendlier than Edik would have been comfortable with. And currently Xincapph was taking up the whole space.

Well, *almost* the whole space. The containment circle was drawn wide enough to touch the walls, but it didn't include the corners. And the walls of that room were all black and red and purple from the inks Edik used to maintain the spells of the main drive: binding the lacuna, keeping it happy, and tying it into the rest of the ship.

Another room, aft, behind the only other door out of this room — the only door on this deck that closed — contained the bindings of the rest of the ship's systems. Two dozen elementals bound into the engines that kept the ship flying, scanners running, gravity working and air flowing. And none of those counted the extra spirits bound in the back section of the main deck up above. The spirits Edik kept around for redundancy, for little extras, and just for company.

Truth was, spirits were better company than most people. In Edik's mind, at least.

Right now, Xincapph was visible, which was rare around a stranger. Usually the only people Edik brought down into the engine room were agents from customs or the ship bureau, verifying that everything on Edik's ship was up to standards, and not in violation of any laws regarding ward strength or weapons.

Around those types, Xincapph always stayed invisible.

But apparently Donal was on Xincapph's okay list, because there he floated. A lime green swirl, like a mobius strip that shifted colors along the green-blue spectrum, singing out three-tone tunes that must have served as a form of communication. At least, to judge by the way Dola often seemed to nod from time to time.

But if Dola understood, he wasn't talking.

Typical. Edik wasn't allowed to have secrets from his familiar, but his familiar had secrets from him.

At least Nixia didn't mind translating for Xincapph.

Donal's attention immediately went to the lacuna. His posture alert, in the slightly leaning forward posture taught to all freshmen to try to improve their ability to sense magic.

Edik cleared his throat.

"What's he saying?" Donal asked. "I feel like that song is saying something."

"Well," Edik said, keeping a straight face, "he's saying that he's pleased to meet you… No. Wait. I missed a note. He'd be pleased to *eat* you."

Donal's head whipped around so fast Edik expected it to pop right off his shoulders.

Edik chuckled. "Sorry. Couldn't resist."

Donal smacked his forehead, and started to laugh, which Edik thought was a decent way to handle it, if a bit oversold.

"Honestly," Edik said, "I have no idea what, if anything the songs mean. I suspect *he*" — Edik waved a hand toward Dola — "knows, but you know how hard it is to get a familiar to admit anything he doesn't want to admit to."

"If Xincapph had anything to tell you," Dola said while Donal smiled, "Nixia would let you know. She's always been very good about that."

"And what about you?" Edik said.

"*I*," Dola said, "am wondering when you're going to show our guest the reason we're down here."

That brought Donal's attention back to Edik, and Edik felt his lips go flat and wide in what only the unobservant would confuse for a grin.

"Yes, Dola," he said, "of course. You're right as usual."

Edik shook his head and grumbled, then went to the port bulk-head of the engineering room.

"Ever used pop-outs before?"

"Once," Donal said, "on Venus. Popular in the prefab stuff, aren't they?"

Edik nodded. Demonstrated by slapping a section of wall and making a work table pop out, complete with the circle he'd left from his last working. He tapped the right spot to pop the work table back in.

"A necessity on a ship like this, but most folks don't know we have them." Edik shook his head. "Most folks would just assume I work on the floor, or do my blending elsewhere, or—"

"Most folks," Donal prompted, "but not the Lukyanovs?"

"Not Alexei Lukyanov, no." Edik shook his head again. Just the thought of having Alexei Lukyanov and his son Dmitri traipsing around down here was enough to sour the lingering taste of good borscht. "Despite the fact that he probably spends more on his airships than I paid for this ship, he not only knew I'd have pop-out storage down here, he knew where to find it."

Donal seemed entirely too relaxed about this invasion of Edik's privacy. Edik settled for flaring his nostrils in a deep, calming breath. Still, his heart was beating faster in irritation at this whole situation.

Maybe Dola and Jones were right about Edik needing to meditate more.

Instead of delaying with more explanation, Edik crouched down, reached forward, and tapped a pop-out storage bin.

It slid out like a drawer. Deep enough, wide enough and long enough that Edik could barely reach the far side from the near side in any direction. Normally, it would be full of alchemical ingredients that he preferred to store down here, especially for a longer voyage like this one.

Right now, it only had—

"A memory circle?" Donal said, leaning over to look inside.

Edik leaned down to look as well, hoping against hope the Dmitri Lukyanov had gotten something wrong about the spell, or that it didn't survive deep space well, and that it had decayed.

But no, it just looked as solid, simple and black as it had when Lukyanov had drawn it with a combination of special inks and his own blood.

Also, a touch of Edik's blood. Just the thought of it was enough to make his skin crawl.

"You know what it is then," Edik said.

"Well, of course. I've used them before. Thought about setting one up for this trip, but, well, changed my mind at the last minute. I didn't want to risk anyone finding it if I didn't make it back. Still—"

"What exactly is it?" Edik said, hearing the fire of frustration in his own words. "Lukyanov said it would transmit my experiences back to them?"

"Something like that," Donal said. "This circle would be connected with another one somewhere else. The idea is that the travel circle sends the information, and the remote circle holds it for you, until you need it later. Good for traveling, and for spies, for that matter. But I don't know how anybody'd use one against you without your..."

Donal's eyes widened enough to rival the bowls they'd been eating dinner out of.

"Your blood is in there too. Yours, and the Magister who cast it."

"Yes," Edik said with a sigh. "They said they'd know whatever happened to me on this trip, and that would help them get around my geas."

Donal blinked at that. "You're under a *geas*?"

"Yeah. Did I forget to mention that?"

Donal actually laughed for a beat before answering. "Yeah. Kind of an important piece of information. How did the Lukyanovs get you to agree to a geas?"

"They didn't. I wouldn't. The geas is Mason's work."

"Oh," Donal said slowly. "Geas for your silence, and the Lukyanovs think a memory circle — or at least a variation on one — will get around it."

"Because I won't have a choice, and because I won't have to actually communicate anything. They said it would just happen automatically."

"More or less," Donal said, his voice growing distant as he looked closer at the spell. "No way it could be transmitting all the time though..."

He pulled out a tuning fork. Held it up.

"Do you mind?"

Edik shook his head.

Donal tapped the fork against his hand, and Edik felt the vibrations reverberate through his own nearby spells. Donal waved the tuning fork slowly above the memory circle, then around it in a circle. He looked like he was going to wave it at Xincapph next, but must have changed his mind because his slipped it back into a sleeve Edik hadn't noticed at the base of his shirt.

"What do you think?" Edik asked.

"Well," Donal said, still staring at the circle before turning to Edik. "It won't transmit all the time. Only at key moments. Moments of great stress or great revelation."

Fionn said something that Edik didn't catch, and Donal started laughing hard enough that he needed a moment to catch his breath.

"Fionn points out that sex would count. Which means either Lukyanov is a voyeur, or—"

"No," Edik said, voice flat, "it means he wants to find out if I'm having sex with his daughter. The pig."

Donal looked up at Edik, a swirl of questions in his eyes. He didn't ask any of them. Or perhaps, he asked only one.

"You live a complicated life, don't you?"

"Like yours is so simple, Mr. Ambassador?"

"Fair enough," Donal said with a nod. "I might be able to break this, but I'd want to examine it in detail before trying anything like that. Especially with your blood involved. They might have put in a safeguard, in case you break it."

"They did," Edik said, his words tasting even more sour as he remembered it. "Lukyanov took his time to explain it slowly, as though he needed to use simple words, the arrogant bastard."

"Let me guess, nastiness ensues if anything breaks the circle?"

Edik nodded.

"Well," Donal said with a small smile, "then we don't break it."

Edik felt one of his eyebrows slowly make its way up his forehead. "You have an idea?"

"No guarantee," Donal said. "This is the work of a Magister, and I might not be able to do more than thumb my nose at it." Donal smiled. "But yeah, I have an idea."

TEN MINUTES LATER, EDIK WAS SITTING ACROSS THE OPEN POP-DRAWER — or whatever exactly Edik had called it — from Donal. Both magicians sat cross-legged, with their familiars standing behind them, noses against the base of their skulls.

This variation on a memory circle was pretty complex. Not the most complex thing Donal had ever seen. Not even the most complex thing he'd seen in the past month. Still, he had to take it seriously. This wasn't some game with a classmate.

"You're certain," Donal said again, and Edik nodded.

"Trust me," he said. "I've had to go deep before, in-flight. Nixia and Xincapph can keep us out of trouble until we're done. And if worse comes to worst, since you're running the show down here, Dola could go handle things in my absence."

"All right then," Donal said.

Donal began to shift his awareness and smacked his tuning fork against the edge of the pop-drawer. The fork's pure, clean tone rang out, rocketing Donal into an even deeper state of mind than he could normally have achieved in the space of a breath.

And even that was so much deeper than he could have gone so quickly, only a year ago. Some of that was from his schoolwork, yes, but some of it still came back to the lessons he'd learned from Li Hua about field work. About the need to abandon the school-taught breathing patterns. About the need for speed of response time, and the ability to go without crutches.

Li Hua would have called the tuning fork a crutch.

But with Edik's — and his own — life on the line, Donal wasn't going to take any chances. He needed to shift his awareness as far as he could, give himself as much clarity of magical vision as he could manage.

Donal waved the tuning fork in a simple four-circle pattern in front of Edik, getting a stronger sense of what some would call the man's aura. That essential portion of Edik that filled his body to over-flowing, so it extended some centimeters beyond his body. Within that portion of Edik flowed his unique magical signature.

Only a year ago, Donal would have presumed that a magical signature was like a thumbprint, a fixed expression of the self over which one had no control. But scarcely more than one semester into his graduate studies, Donal was already coming to suspect that was not the whole truth. That the signature represented the inner self, whose nature might have been *largely* fixed from a young age, but was not altogether immutable…

The inclusion of Edik's blood in that variation on the memory circle spell would mean his aura and signature were all through it. Donal needed to understand Edik's signature well enough to isolate it, or he might have a tough time tracking down the true source of the spell.

If he couldn't accomplish that, the rest of this was pointless.

So Donal drew a series of quick, but deep breaths. Fast in, slow out, and each one getting slower on the exhalation.

Each breath took Donal deeper and deeper into a meditative state. Shifted that much more of his awareness. Made the energies of magic that much clearer to his sight. To his hearing.

And as he went deeper, Donal heard clearly the resonances echoing in harmony or discordance with his tuning fork. Usually Donal used the fork only for his own spellwork. Knew exactly how it would respond and resonate with not only his own spells, but those used by others to interfere or intrude on his magic.

But here, with his focus on the memory circle variation, Donal heard even more than normal.

Three points of harmony. Two of them from Edik's own signature, but one from the other magician. The Magister. This Dmitri Lukyanov that Edik spoke of. Apparently some element of Lukyanov's nature harmonized with his own. Interesting.

Four points of discordance. Two of those were Edik's, which did not necessarily bode well for the rest of the trip. But the other two belonged to the signature of the Magister.

One harmony, two discordances. Formed a triangle of its own. Perhaps a stable structure.

Perhaps even a key. Only time would tell.

"I detect no chicory," Fionn said.

"No?" Donal asked. "Are you sure?"

"I scent trace remainders of eryngo, eyebright, horehound, and star anise, but no chicory."

Fionn paused, but Donal knew to wait until his familiar spoke again for confirmation.

"Bergamont, marjoram, and coltsfoot, as well. Plus the blood, of course." Fionn shook his ears. "Odd choices. This is more than a memory circle."

"What do you mean?"

"Only what I said. Beyond that, I cannot yet be certain. Please, Master, proceed with caution."

Donal nodded, drew another deep breath, and began to study the memory circle variation again.

He had taken a brief look at it before. Seen the bones of its structure, so similar to the kinds he had used himself, either for class or on some courier mission or other. And yet so very different, from its core on out.

This spell looked like a crimson funnel web, extending up from the physical circle for perhaps a full meter before beginning to fade to invisibility. Strands of that spell would reach all the way back to Luna. Others would reach to Edik. Threads almost as tight as those that bound this circle to its twin back on Luna.

Its twin…

"Edik," Donal said, unconcerned at how distant he must have sounded as he kept most of his attention on the spell. "Did they take some of your blood with them?"

"Yes," Edik said, a slight shiver running between his shoulders. "Two vials."

"I was afraid of that," Donal said. "They only needed one for the second circle. It seems they want to keep a link to you, just in case."

"I wish I could say that surprised me."

"Don't worry. There are ways of dealing with that. But we'll have to get to that later."

"I agree," Edik said. "This thing comes first."

With his mind so deep into the magical awareness, Donal could hear something more under Edik's words there. Some deeper meaning. Some reason this circle bothered him, beyond all the obvious reasons.

But the man was entitled to some secrets.

Donal probed a little deeper then. Memory circles were generally a very personal kind of magic, so they didn't need the sorts of structures required to tie a separate individual. They could use shortcuts that this version could not afford.

All Donal needed to do, in theory, was find the places the spell structure had to expand to cover an individual who was not the caster, and fray them. They might unwind on their own, but even if not, the fraying would help Donal determine which connections were weakest.

A spell like this, Donal didn't need to break it from the ground up. He only needed one aspect of the connection to Edik to fail, and the spell would become useless. If it continued to transmit anything at all, it would be incomplete, inaccurate information.

It might even fail to trigger at all.

In fact, that would be the best place to start…

Donal extended his awareness inside that red funnel web of spellwork. Masterful bit of casting, even if Donal wouldn't want to admit that to Edik. Clearly this Magister Dmitri Lukyanov was a careful, cautious man, and solid in his foundation of theory.

Donal moved along the data sifting section of the spell, where it determined from what it gathered, whether the data was important enough to transmit. From there, he needed glide along only a short distance to find the key he needed. The junction where the spell's triggering mechanisms connected to its detection of Edik's mindset.

But there was something off about it. It should have been a fairly simple series of tests along the lines of Edik's state of mind. But there was something more underneath it.

Troubling, that. If it turned out to be a two-way connection, then Magister Lukyanov might be able to begin influencing Edik. And Donal had seen too much of people under magical influence.

Donal reached for the strand leading to the undercurrent of spellwork…

…and got kicked right out of the spell.

Suddenly Donal was no longer deep in the right frame of mind.

His awareness was still shifted, but no more than he could do himself within a breath or two. That deeper state was gone. He was fully aware of himself sitting cross-legged on the cool ceramic floor. The smell of alchemical herbs — especially verbena — in his nose. The troubled expression on Edik's face.

The jolt of concern from Fionn.

And at almost the same instant, a small red and yellow servitor appeared in the air above the memory circle variation.

Even with his advancing education, Donal could not explain how exactly he knew he was looking at a servitor — a manufactured spirit — instead of a natural but bound spirit. He considered it the difference between looking at an extremely realistic painting of an outdoor scene and actually looking out a window.

The servitor was no more than a half-meter across, and shaped like a red bear with yellow edging to its fur and claws. But it had power. More power than Donal had sensed inside the memory circle variation, which was more than a little concerning.

The servitor spoke directly to Donal's mind, with a voice heavily accented in Russian.

"Ah, ah, ah. There is to be no tinkering with the spellwork of Magister Dmitri Lukyanov. Admiring the work of your betters is one thing, but actually tinkering? *Nyet.* This we will not allow. Attempt it again, and you will feel my claws rend your soul."

The bear servitor spun back down inside the funnel web of the memory circle variation.

Donal sat back. Blinked at Edik.

"So," Edik said. "I presume you heard that too?"

Donal nodded.

"Couldn't actually rend our *souls*, though, right?"

"Well," Donal said slowly, "that's a matter of interpretation. Some believe that the essential part of ourselves that extends beyond our bodies—"

"Our auras."

"As good a word as any. Some believe it is a manifestation of the soul, and part of the reason that we suffer so when it gets hurt."

Donal shook his shoulders. Somewhere in there they'd tightened up.

"I hate servitors," Edik said, voice still conversational, as though complaining about some governmental fact of life that they could do nothing about. "They're like cheating. A way for poor magicians to make up for the fact that they have bad relationships with real spirits."

"Doesn't change the fact that that one could maybe fry me for messing with that spell."

Dola said something to Edik then, and though Donal didn't understand the words, he didn't really need to.

"I'm pretty sure Dola just said that at least I'd done my best."

"Something like that," Edik said, frustration all through his voice.

"Don't worry, though," Donal said with a grin. "We're not beaten yet."

***

AFTER CLOSING THAT POP-OUT DRAWER, AND STRETCHING FOR A FEW minutes, Donal was pretty sure his idea might work. If Edik could handle his end. And that was the real trick. Donal might have been in the middle of his graduate studies, but Edik, for all his competent alchemical work and good relationships with his elementals, was still only an Initiate.

And thaumaturgy was a demanding art form.

As Magister Machado had once told Donal, studying the higher levels of magic was about more than learning spells. It was about training the self to deeper levels. The ability to reach and use deeper states of mind. To channel greater and greater amounts of power.

And to do all of those things for longer than any lesser magician could possibly handle.

All the reasons Donal had gotten himself in so much trouble by overreaching in the past.

And if Donal's plan was going to work, he had to hope that Edik wasn't overreaching now. That he was an experienced enough Initiate to handle more than most magicians his grade could handle.

And it started here.

Donal stood in the … well, he didn't know what this room was properly called. Engineering, he supposed, though Edik hadn't named it that Donal had heard. This was the empty white room next to the drive room, where now the lacuna, Xincapph, was singing a haunting five-note harmony.

Donal stood to one side, allowing the primarily verbena scent of the lingering alchemical work help keep him in a ready frame of mind. Fionn stood beside him, pawing at the white ceramics of the deck as though wanting to pace. Or perhaps wanting to help.

But this first step, this had to be Edik's.

Edik sat in the middle of the room, cross-legged but not quite still. Not so still as he should have been, at least.

His eyes were closed, but moving. His nostrils flared with each slow breath, but his face looked too tense.

Dola slowly circled Edik, offering tips and advice, or maybe just making soothing sounds. Whatever Dola said, it was only for his master's ears, and Donal could not comprehend it.

Didn't matter. Edik needed to meditate. He needed to go as deep as he could. Deeper than any of his usual magics would require, which might be the problem.

If this was going to work, Edik needed to meditate so deeply that he lost, for a brief window, his sense of self. He needed to *become* his breathing, not just follow it.

That was a lot to ask of an Initiate.

Donal found himself falling into familiar meditative breathing patterns, in sympathy. Wanting to help. Wishing that he could somehow lead this Initiate to where Donal needed his mind to be, but that just wasn't how it worked.

Maybe it would one day. Donal had heard of Hierophants guiding the minds of others to alter their consciousness for them, but he didn't have any idea how to even begin.

And so he watched. His own breaths, slower that Edik's. Not a good sign.

Or at least, probably not a good sign. It could have been that this was slower than Edik's usual meditative breathing. Certainly the tension in his face was finally smoothing. His eyes moving less behind his eyelids.

It might have been that Edik was even now sinking into a deeper frame of mind than he had ever achieved before.

If so, Dola would know. But Dola was busy helping. Assisting in what ways he could, even though ultimately meditation was as personal a skill as could be.

Donal was good enough at meditation that Fionn could guide him, channel his thoughts. But that was a Journeyman trick. Beyond the skill of most Initiates. And likely beyond Edik's skill as well.

Though the man did have unusually good relations with his spirits…

Donal waited with all the patience he could muster, keeping his attention on Edik, and trying not to worry that something was happening in the space around them without anyone raising the alarm.

Finally, Dola turned to Donal and said, softly, "He is ready. Or, I should say, he is as ready as he will get."

"Is he empty?"

"No, but only the dregs remain. This is deeper than he has gone before." Then Dola let out a sigh that seemed to stretch from the tip of his tail all the way to his ears. "I've told him and told him that he needs to meditate more."

"Difficult," Fionn said, "persuading them of things they don't wish to believe."

Donal raised an eyebrow at Fionn, but the great emerald deerhound only regarded him back with that look Donal had come to think of as neutral to hide humor.

"Well," Donal said, "let's see what we can do."

Donal paced a circle around Edik then, trailing power with each step to turn his path into a fully cast circle. Not as good as an inscribed circle, but sufficient for this task.

Fionn and Dola then began to pace that circle, Dola connecting with Edik and Fionn with Donal.

Donal drew a deeper breath, and expelled out any worries and concerns. No time for them now. No time for anything but this spell.

Gazing deep past his own circle, Donal could see where the memory circle variation connected to Edik. But now that connection had to pass through a barrier of Donal's magic. It could do so, of course. Donal could not simply cut it off, not without harming Edik deeply (and possibly awakening the wrath of that servitor).

But if the connection flowed through Donal's magic, then so did the information it carried.

And this was the key to Donal's whole effort. Resonances of Donal's magic around the core of the connection would hide the deeper spell he needed to set into place.

But it would only work if Edik emptied enough of himself. He needed to not be Edik for a few minutes, so that Donal's spells could form a layer between the core of the memory circle variant's ties and Edik himself. This would allow Donal to taint or transform any information the memory circle variant transmitted.

Donal could completely undercut the spying spell, without tampering with its structure or alerting its protective servitor. Elegant. If he could pull it off.

If Edik could achieve a deep enough meditative state.

If any of Edik remained, then Magister Lukyanov's connection would be deeper than Donal's, and this would all be so much wasted effort.

Donal began to weave a slow spell of deception, sinking it into the circle through his connection with Fionn. This was only the first spell he needed to cast, and the easiest of the lot. This was a simple deception. Blah. Boring. Nothing happening. It was taking any information that the memory circle variant pulled out of Edik and overlaid it with a sense of pointlessness. As though this were not only nothing worth noticing, but that it was so dull that even taking the time to notice that it wasn't worth noticing felt like wasted time.

Redundancy there, but in this kind of spell, redundancy only helped. The more repetitive Donal's approach, the more likely the information carried by the memory circle variant might get missed by anyone watching from the other end.

And with any luck, missed by the bear servitor too.

Everything else on Donal's side hinged on this spell working. The theory was sound, but it wasn't until Donal finished building the dull, regular structure of this deception and released it to Fionn to ease into the circle that he would find out whether or not it worked.

Donal released the spell. Fionn eased it into place.

Donal counted his slow, meditative heartbeats.

One...

Five...

Twenty...

That meant that several minutes had passed, with no objection from the bear servitor. And no objection from the bear servitor meant that it should also fool anyone on the other end.

Stage one, complete. Donal had found a way to sneak a spell past the watcher. That meant his approach had merit.

This could work.

Next, Donal needed to work up a much more elaborate deception. This would settle into Edik at his core, and modify the information that the memory circle variant attempted to spirit away from him.

Donal had originally considered using a variation of the same "unworthy of notice" spell that he was using to hide this attempt from Lukyanov and his servitor. But that wouldn't be enough. The information would still flow, and all it would take would be for the wrong event to get noticed and the rest would fall apart.

No. Donal needed to go deeper for this one. He needed to get ornate. He needed a spell that would take information that Edik knew or learned, and modify all of it before it went out. Not a lot, just enough that it wouldn't be worth anything to the Lukyanovs. And not every bit of information either. The more times the spell functioned, the greater chance that something would go wrong. Get noticed.

That could have disastrous consequences.

And so Donal sank into a cross-legged sitting position and began to construct an elaborate spell. It would take any new information about spirits, whether incarnate or not, and shift it into political data about the colony on Ganymede.

The presence of any new type of spirit would become political divisions among the settlers.

Any new sense of magic or discovery would turn into shock at the way the Terran Navy was moving in and asserting direct control over the colony.

Donal had no way of knowing if that was actually happening, but for purposes of this spell the truth didn't matter.

Donal sank deeper and deeper into his own mind for this. He had to make the spell structures perfect. And he had to make them as clean as possible. As textbook as he could. He couldn't hide his signature, of course, but the closer he made the spell structures to generic, the more his deceptions could help hide his own presence in the magic.

Donal had no way of knowing how long he was at this before Fionn got his attention.

"We're done," Fionn said, and Donal could tell his familiar was trying not to sound dejected.

Donal held the structure of the spell in his head. Determined not to lose it. Determined not to give up, no matter what was happening around him.

Donal opened his eyes.

He saw Initiate Captain Edik Barshai, sound asleep on the deck in front of him. Above him, the shaggy gray cat Dola was shaking his head.

"I'm sorry," Dola said in his heavy Russian accent. "He's just not in practice enough for this."

"I'm not sure he was deep enough for it to work anyway," Fionn said.

"Probably not," Dola agreed, shaking his head enough that his whiskers shook. "Sorry, Donal. Thank you for trying."

Donal sighed and released the spell he was holding. He might have heard mocking, bearish laughter, but in that moment it might have been his imagination.

One thing he could hear, though, with certainty.

In the next room, the lacuna Xincapph was trilling out a three-toned piece that sounded too much like a lullaby for Donal's taste.

"Was he *trying* to put Edik to sleep?" Donal asked Dola.

"With Xincapph, it's hard to tell." Dola shook his head again. "I wish I could say no."

"Fine," Donal said. "Well, I guess I should go catch a nap myself."

He stood and started for the ladder.

"Will you want to try this again later?" Dola asked.

"Only if you think it'll have a better chance of success."

Dola didn't say anything as Donal climbed the ladder.

But then, Donal hadn't really expected a response.

"I blew it didn't I?"

Those were the first words out of Edik's mouth. He'd lain awake in his hammock for a good twenty minutes before voicing them. He'd been hoping he could fall asleep without having to utter them, but just lying there with his thoughts, there was no way to keep them quiet.

Dola, lying curled up on the footlocker underneath Edik's hammock, seemed to consider that for a few minutes. Or maybe it was only a few seconds. Either way, right then it felt like hours to Edik.

"Well," Dola said at last, "I'd be lying if I said you were able to go deep enough in meditation for Donal's spells to work. But I do have to admit, he was asking quite a bit from you. You're good, but you're only a ... what is the term for you again?"

"Initiate," Edik said. He drew a long breath through his nose, drawing some small comfort from the lingering scent of borscht from the last time he slept down here. "It means I'm good enough for the grunt work of magic."

"I'll never understand the terms you people come up with. What was wrong with wizard?"

Edik shrugged. He knew Dola was trying to distract him, and honestly he didn't want to be distracted.

"Did I even get close to the state Donal was asking for?"

"For you? Very close." Dola hesitated, but Edik waited until his familiar finished. "It's like pouring out a full glass of water. Most people would look at it and say it was empty, but the truth is that there'd still be drops here and there, clinging to the sides and bottom."

"And that was too much?"

"For what he had in mind, yes."

"What would it take for me to be able to truly empty the glass?"

"Tough to say," Dola said, and Edik could hear the ripple move down the cat's shaggy gray fur — not from the sound it made, which was barely any, but from the tone of his familiar's voice. "Donal goes that deep as a matter of course. Or at least he went that deep earlier today during one of his meditation sessions."

Dola's tone grew thoughtful. "Not during the other one though. That was more of a contemplative state of mind. I wonder what he was thinking about?"

"Stop trying to distract me."

"Sorry."

Edik looked over his shoulder, through the silk webbing of his hammock at Dola, who was looking right back at him.

"Would you like to work up a meditation plan for me? Maybe I could get that good at it?"

"If I did, would you follow it?"

Edik thought about that, then sighed.

"No, probably not. It always feels like wasted time to me."

Dola shook his head.

"Does sleep feel like wasted time, Edik?"

"No," Edik started to say, then chuckled and lay his head back down. He let his breaths fall into a regular pattern. He tried emptying his mind, but there was no chance of that working right now. Not when he was worried about that spell Lukyanov had attached to him. He half-wished Donal hadn't told him about the connection. It felt as though he had a parasite attached to him.

And Anna. Edmund had said she was worried about Edik, when

she should have been worried about herself. Yes, Edik was doing something dangerous, but so was she.

He hoped she understood exactly how much peril she was in back there. Two great families, at least three governments, and little Anna standing up to them all. Yes, she had a Hierophant on her side, plus whatever Jones really was, and even North might not be too much of a weight on her shoulders.

But in the end, Edik had the feeling that the fate of the Rhian people was in her hands, not theirs.

And now Edik was flying blind into a potential first contact situation. He wasn't just ferrying a greater magician out to the hinterlands. From the sound of things, he had a role to play when they got there.

And with all this going on, Edik was supposed to be able to just empty his mind? To just stop thinking entirely?

It just didn't seem possible.

Even sleep didn't seem all that likely. Though in the end, sleep arrived sooner than Edik expected.

Probably Dola's doing.

5

Days later, Edik sat in the comfortable chair of his captain's station as the *Third Son* came to a halt at the far edge of a cargo shipping lane, no more than two days out from Mars. Right exactly where he'd set his course. He sat there staring out at the stars and eating a ham-and-cheese sandwich, made from actual Earth-grown ham, Earth-harvested wheat grains, and Earth-churned cheddar cheese.

It even had spicy mustard, the kind Edik could never get on Luna. At least, not for a price *he* was willing to pay.

The days preceding had gone as well as they could have. Clear space and little traffic. Only a few hints at the edges of scanner range of anything that might have been the *Silver Streak*. Dola was convinced that the flying saucer continued to follow them, but Xincapph had not been able to verify that. So Edik tried not to think about it.

Not that he had much luck there. He still sometimes woke up from dreams where he couldn't quite evade those fireballs. And that was when he wasn't waking up from dreams about Dmitri Lukyanov reading his every thought and action. Maybe reaching out and controlling him, no matter how Donal, Fionn and even Dola assured

Edik that this was not possible. Not through that memory circle thing. Especially not with a Hierophant's geas on him.

That's right. The Magister couldn't control Edik, because the Hierophant had dibs.

Was it any wonder that Edik wasn't sleeping well?

Why did he accept this mission again?

Oh. Yes. Money. Opportunity. Expand the business.

Maybe small-time was a safer way to live…

Then he thought about Anna, and Jones, and North, and all the trouble he'd found himself in only a few months ago, when Edik *was* content to live the small-time life.

Maybe he was just cursed?

Now *there* was a line of reasoning he didn't want to pursue.

At least Donal had proven himself helpful. True, he couldn't seem to do anything about that memory circle, but that was as much Edik's fault as anything. Well, *more* Edik's fault than Donal's. Edik had begun trying to add daily meditation to his schedule, but he kept finding excuses to cut that time short or do other things instead.

Probably just as well. Edik had the feeling he'd need a lot more than a few days practice to get to the state that Donal kept talking about.

If Edik could even do it at all. He *was* only an Initiate, after all, and this sure sounded like more advanced magic.

But Donal didn't seem to hold it against him. He was more than happy to help with ship maintenance. And each time Edik thought he saw that *Silver Streak*, Donal had been eager enough to lay a false trail of illusions behind them. Just in case.

He'd even helped with the link back to Edik's office on Luna. Edik hadn't been in touch with anyone from home in days, and it was starting to wear on him. He needed to know how Anna was doing. Maybe even find a way to get some advice from Hierophant Mason without triggering the memory circle.

If that could be done.

But each time he tried the link, he got no answer. Donal had gone over that link, refining the spells Edik and Jones — well, mostly Jones

— had cast, and lending a little additional power to them. So the link was probably working.

Still. No answer.

And now the *Third Son* sat at the edge of that cargo lane. The end of the course Edik had been able to plot in advance. Not even much traffic near him right now. Just a giant cargo vessel shaped like a blue whale. Had to belong to some Terran company. No way a Mars company would use a ship that looked like that.

Apart from that ship, only the stars around Edik now. Hints of a red nebula ahead to starboard, but nowhere near where Edik would have to fly.

This was the edge of everything he could predict. This was the edge of where his charts were certain. Beyond this, all the way to Ganymede might as well have been unexplored space, for all the good his charts did him.

The Terran Navy kept that all data to themselves. No doubt to discourage exactly what Edik was doing right now.

Behind Edik, Dola paced. Edik felt sure that Dola wanted to say something, but held his words.

That was unusual in and of itself. The shaggy gray cat had no problem expressing himself. In fact, Edik had always encouraged Dola to speak his mind, ever since the initial binding. Edik wanted nothing to do with the master-servant kind of relationship that most magicians had with their familiars.

Even Donal, for all his politeness and interest in working *with* spirits instead of merely binding and commanding them. Even he still got called "master" by Fionn every so often.

Edik could never have tolerated that from Dola. Edik didn't want a slave. He wanted a partner.

Edik swallowed the last bite of sandwich. Washed it down with pure Earth water that didn't even taste a hint like lemon. Refreshing change from the water at Kennedy. Sat his empty mug down on the far starboard edge of his white ceramic captain's station.

"We've got this," Edik said, trying to reassure himself as much as Dola.

"You don't believe that any more than I do." Dola stepped up to where Edik could see him, shaking his whiskers. "This isn't like anything we've ever done before, Edik. We're not explorers. We have no idea what's between us and Ganymede."

"You agreed to this voyage too."

"Yes, but you were talking about hitting unofficial channels on Mars for better charts. Bribing corporation navigators. Now you say you don't want to do that."

"Donal made some good points about those Mars corps. We might get followed."

Dola narrowed his eyes. "You're worried about the *Silver Streak*. You think if we go to Mars it will catch us again."

Edik stared out at the stars, but nodded. Every time he thought about that little ship his stomach knotted itself up. He thought about those fireballs. About how Donal's trick to buy time for escape might not work twice.

"We're not explorers, Edik."

Edik smiled, wistfully.

"Not much choice, have we?" Edik sighed. "Is Donal meditating again?"

"Reading right now." A ripple passed down Dola's fur. "Though he focuses so deeply on that, he might as well be meditating. Do you want me to get him?"

"No," Edik said, voice distant. Meditation and reading. Were the two related? Where did they relate to piloting? Or dueling? Jones always said that Edik gave away too much with his eyes when he dueled. Was he thinking too much? And when Edik had been evading those fireballs, that was probably the most empty he had ever been…

Edik shook off that flow of thoughts. Something to discuss with Dola later.

"I guess," Edik said, reaching for the red lever that was currently set to All Stop, "it's time for us to become explorers."

"*Without a plan?*" Dola said and leapt onto the captain's station, between Edik and the lever.

"You said yourself we can't plan for this." Edik didn't try to keep the exasperation out of his voice, though he did ease his hand down to drum his fingers on the white ceramic of his station. "We don't know what's between us and Ganymede. We're not … *we're* not explorers…"

Edik could feel his brow creasing as he worked through the details of a potential plan. Madness. Certainly this was madness. But it might be their only chance…

"Edik?"

Dola sounded worried. Edik turned back to see his familiar's nose scant centimeters from his forehead, as though to take his temperature.

Edik smiled and scritched Dola's chin.

"I have an idea." He glanced back toward the main cabin. "Think we can slip past Donal without drawing his attention?"

"As long as we don't bring a jazz band," Dola said. "Why?"

"Come on." Edik hopped out of his captain's chair and hustled down through the main cabin, Dola hot on his heels. Sure enough, Donal was sitting in the foreword, port-side passenger chair in the main cabin, engrossed in a refillable book. Didn't even look up at Edik went past.

From there Edik went down to the storage deck, and then the access ladder to belowdecks.

"Edik," Dola said, as he followed down into the all-white room next to the drive room, where even now Xincapph was twirling like a ruby Mobius strip and singing out a five-note trill that Edik couldn't pretend was harmonious.

Edik held up a hand to still Dola's objections.

Dola wasn't having it.

"*Edik,*" he said, stepping between Edik and the drive room. "Talk to me."

"It's so simple," Edik said, broad grin on his face now. "*We're* not explorers, no. But lacunas are explorers by nature. Space is their natural habitat. Of course Xincapph can find us a route to Ganymede. And a safe one."

"Safe for *him,*" Dola said. "But what's safe for him might not be safe for us. Plus, in case you'd forgotten, Xincapph will be dragging a ship with him, which is not actually the natural state of a lacuna."

"So?" Edik said. "His senses are intact, more or less, and he's proven that he can carry us at speeds that other captains don't dare dream of."

"For a reason," Dola said. "Edik, do we have enough supplies along to handle maintenance if Xincapph flies us too fast for too long?"

"I won't let him. He only needs to set the course, not set his own speed."

"And suppose that speed is part of how he thinks of his course?" Dola shook his head. "We don't know enough about how he thinks. What he'll do."

Dola hitched himself up and put his forepaws on Edik's shoulders. Looked directly into Edik's eyes.

"Edik, this could be suicide. Is this really a risk you want to take?"

"What are our alternatives?" Edik reached out and stroked the ghostly fur of the cat's cheeks, softer than silk. "No, we need to do this. And I think Xincapph is ready to handle it. I think he'll want to help and not hurt. So if I can make clear what will hurt us—"

"That's still a gamble."

"So translate for me."

"I can't. Not really." Dola sighed and dropped back down. "I'm sorry, Edik. I try and I try with Xincapph, but every time I think I'm close to understanding how his mind works, he shifts off along a tangent I could never have seen coming. I'm not sure I could translate for him. Not for something this important."

"I could," Nixia said, her breathy tones confident as she eased to honey-golden appearance right in mid-air. "I've been communing with Xincapph since the day you summoned me, Edik. I cannot say I understand him as I would another sylph, but I'm confident that I could translate your desires to him, and his responses in turn. And I will keep the sylphs alert to his movements and decisions. We will keep you abreast of his every deed, and we will keep him within safe limits."

"Are you sure you can do this, Nixia?" Edik said. "If you managed to offend him, he could—"

"Do you trust me, Edik?"

"I do," Edik said, not needing to even think before he answered.

"Then trust that I can handle myself," Nixia said with a slow smile. "And that I will not let harm come to you, Edik, not when I could prevent it. Trust in me. Tell me what you want, and I will carry your desires to Xincapph."

Edik smiled, then glanced at Dola, eyebrows high.

Dola quirked a feline smile of his own, and bowed his head.

"Let's go back to the bridge then," Edik said. "And plan ourselves a route."

DONAL LOOKED UP FROM HIS BOOK AND ZEPHYRPAD, BLINKED AT THE sight of space passing, visible through the four huge portals along the starboard side, right in front of him. A good day's homework, even though he didn't properly have an assignment. With so much time to himself about the *Third Son*, he'd determined to get ahead on his understanding of elemental aspect work in Enochian magic, in preparation for the coming semester.

Enochian work split elements along finer and finer lines than any other system he had heard of. Any magician might call on the element of fire. But Enochian work expected the magician to see even fire as a whole, composed of earth-of-fire, air-of-fire, water-of-fire, spirit-of-fire, and fire-of-fire. Enochian work demanded that a magician learn to work with elements along those lines.

And then it went a layer deeper still. A magician had to understand the aspects of each division. Understanding, say, air-of-fire wasn't enough. He had to master water-aspected air-of-fire, as well as air-aspected air-of-fire, fire-aspected air-of fire, and so on.

The basics of the ideas had seemed simple enough, relatively speaking, but getting into how it all worked in practice, that was a depth unlike anything Donal had ever attempted before.

And all of that was only the foundational work of the system. Enochian magic had depths that no one had truly understood since John Dee and Edward Kelly first developed the system, before the last time magic fell.

The more Donal understood now, the better questions he'd be able to ask of his professors in the coming semester. The better his chances of making it all the way through his graduate studies.

Donal needed to graduate. He needed his Th. D. Only when he achieved that level of mastery could he devote his time and efforts to cracking the deeper secrets of Enochian magic. The thirty aethyrs, each rumored to be an astral realm unto itself. The hundreds of spirits named in the Tablet of Union.

If Donal could crack even one of the great secrets of this system, he could die knowing he had made a meaningful contribution to human thaumaturgy.

And as a happy side effect, he would free himself forever from the all-encompassing shadow of his brother, the great Bran Cuthbert.

First, Donal needed to become a Hierophant.

And that meant mastering his studies, beyond even what his fellow students achieved.

But he had done enough for today. This was a process of years, after all, and impatience was the surest way to be one of the majority who would eventually leave the program without the highest degree.

Donal set his book and zephyrpad down on another chair. He stood on the gold runner carpet of the main cabin of the *Third Son* and stretched, first his waist, then his legs, then his arms and neck. He ran through basic power exercises, taking power from his own core and moving it along the several energetic channels of his self. A simple exercise, but an important one. By repeating it multiple times per day, he prevented build-ups in his thoughts, and kept bad habits from forming in his practices.

Donal had gotten even more demanding of himself and his exercises over the last few days. Seeing Edik fail to achieve even a properly deep meditative state only served to remind Donal how fragile these skills could be, if not properly emphasized and maintained.

Donal called Fionn out of the silver faun pendant at his neck. The ghostly deerhound appeared in a flash of emerald light.

"A productive day," Donal said. "Shall we see how Edik's doing with our flight plan?"

Fionn agreed without wasting words, and fell into step as Donal entered the cockpit and strapped himself into the guest seat.

"How's it going?" he asked as he gazed out the front portal. They seemed to be moving at a good clip, which suited the red lever's position: Full Ahead.

"Pretty well," Edik said, but he sounded distracted. He was watching his charts, not the stars. The three dimensional representation of space, instead of space itself.

Donal almost chuckled about that, but then he looked at those charts.

Space seemed to be filling in.

That was the only way he could think of it. The charts seemed barren except for the position of distant stars and planets, but while Donal was watching, he could see a blue cloud formation appear on the chart, and some kind of moving satellite. Meteor, perhaps.

Donal angled for a better look out the forward portal.

Sure enough, he could see that dark blue nebula. He couldn't see the meteor though.

"Edik?" he asked, and got only a grunt in response.

"Edik," he tried again, and this time Edik glanced back at Donal.

"Edik," Donal said, "are your charts supposed to do that?"

"No," Edik said, with a slight shake of his head. He turned back to watch the charts. "They can't do it at all, actually. What you're seeing is Dola's handiwork."

"Edik?" Donal said, and this time he waited until the man looked back at him. "Would you care to tell me what's going on? This is the longest I've seen you in the pilot's chair without your hands on the … controls…"

As Donal said that, he noticed that the golden controls for pitch and yaw both turned as the ship pivoted.

He looked back at Edik.

Edik sighed.

"Look," he said. "I told you before. You don't question how I handle my ship, and I won't—"

"But you're *not* handling your ship. Are you?"

Edik met Donal's eyes, then smiled.

"I am indeed," he said with a chuckle. "I'm delegating. I'm giving orders to my crew, and they're handling the flying."

Donal said nothing for a moment while Edik went back to gazing at his charts.

"Edik," Donal said, a moment later. "You mean your spirits are handling everything right now? You're not doing anything?"

"Not a thing." He sounded distant again, like he was only paying half-attention to Donal.

"That's not normal, though, right?"

"Never done it before." Edik turned to Donal and was smiling now. "Not sure any other ship captain anywhere could do what I'm doing. Not without a whole web of spells trying desperately to maintain the illusion of control. None of them have the guts and heart necessary to have as good relations with the elemental members of their crew."

Edik blinked, then frowned. "In fact, you know when you were asking me earlier about crew counts?"

Donal didn't, and he knew it showed on his face.

"Back when we first encountered the *Silver Streak*. Register said they had a crew of four. But that only counts human crew. Doesn't include the elementals necessary to keep us alive and moving through space like this. That's not right."

The red lever shifted from Ahead Full to Ahead Three-Quarters. Edik's hand was nowhere near it at the time.

"All right," Donal said, trying to process all this. He'd talked with both Captain Jacobs and Magister Machado about ship's flight and elementals, and neither one had ever indicated any belief that it would be safe or practical to leave the flying to the spirits.

But here, Edik was doing just that.

"So," Donal said, his student voice coming out, "let me test my understanding here. Right now, this ship is entirely under the control of the lacuna, Xincapph?"

"Not remotely," Edik said. "That doesn't account for the sylphs, undines, gnomes and salamanders who keep us safe, alive and comfortable while Xincapph handles the flying. Taking us someplace we don't even have proper charts for."

Edik gave Donal a big smile. "This is the coolest thing I've ever been part of."

"So, Xincapph is handling the flying, as well as charting the course, and filling in the charts as we go?"

"Almost." And here Edik's grin got proud. "Dola's filling in the charts, with Nixia's help interpreting. He's getting all the scanner readings and updating the data as fast as it comes in." Edik clapped his hands once, loudly. "When we get back I could sell that chart data for a near fortune. No one else has it."

Donal started to say something, but Edik wasn't finished.

"Well, no one but the Navy anyway, and since they aren't sharing, too bad for them."

Edik laughed, but Donal saw a couple of small flaws in this plan.

"Doesn't this go beyond the boundaries of the bindings on Xincapph?"

"The out-of-the-box bindings, sure, but I stripped out a bunch of those a long time ago. Not necessary, you know?"

Donal felt his heart skip a beat at that. This lacuna was only bound by the bindings an *Initiate* felt were necessary? An Initiate who couldn't even meditate properly?

"You wouldn't mind if I double-checked those bindings, would you?" Donal smiled as he said it, but he doubted the smile looked sincere.

"I do mind," Edik said, his eyes back on the charts. "My ship, my demesne, my rules. You promised not to challenge me on that, right?"

"Right," Donal said, while his stomach tried its best to sink through the floor.

He looked over at Fionn, who had been strangely quiet through this whole exchange. Fionn looked back, his eyes as emerald green as everything else about him.

"A promise is a promise," Fionn said, in words pitched only for Donal's ears.

"We'll need that chart data to make sure we get home safe," Donal said to Fionn, in the same way. "Won't we?"

Fionn nodded, and Donal could tell the deerhound had reached the same conclusions Donal had.

"Then there's only one other thing," Donal said. And he waited until Edik looked back at him before he continued. "We're about a week out from Ganymede, right?"

"Probably a little less by my estimate, the way Xincapph is taking us. Why?"

"Because Dola won't be able to handle the charts that whole way. Not without breaks."

Edik tugged at his blonde Van Dyke, but Donal spoke without waiting for a suggestion.

"He can show Fionn how it's done. Then Dola and Fionn can rotate, so they get rest. No point in pushing either familiar too hard."

Edik smiled and reached his hand out to Donal.

"I knew there was a reason I liked you."

The two men shook hands.

***

For the better part of the next week, Edik barely left his captain's chair. In fact, only when he needed to hit the head, help Donal prep a meal, or at least stretch his legs. Still, he ate, slept and handled everything he could handle from that seat.

Part of it was that he wanted to keep an eye on the evolving charts, as translated by Dola and Fionn from the data provided by Xincapph. And they did an amazing job, just based on what he could tell from the scanners. These charts would end up as good as anything he could have bought from the navy, albeit not quite as complete.

After all, they were limited by what Xincapph could sense, and

Xincapph was only one lacuna and still responsible for transporting the ship. Larger ships like the navy had, they bound separate lacunas for scanners and for the main drive.

Edik could only wonder what he could accomplish, if he could have two lacunas in his small helioship.

But in the meantime, he watched his ship's progress through space. All too near a lacuna feeding ground at one point, and Donal had been called hurriedly to the bridge to erect illusions that would keep the wild lacunas from developing too much interest.

And there were zuglodons out here too. At least a half-dozen that Edik had spotted, though fortunately Xincapph was no more eager to approach them than Edik was. Twice the zuglodons pursued, but both times Edik took the reins off of Xincapph, letting him fly just as fast as Nixia would allow.

And Edik kept a strict eye on the wards and systems the entire time.

Truth was, those zuglodons could be a problem on the way back. They were easy enough to evade now, but Edik hadn't brought enough extra supplies along to maintain his spells against the strain needed to outrun them. Not as often as he'd had to allow for extra speed on this trip.

On the trip back, Edik might find out just how much Donal knew about fighting zuglodons.

In the meantime, Edik tried linking back to the office on Luna at least once a day, at different times.

No luck, which did nothing to ease the concerns in his mind or the disquiet in his guts.

Nevertheless, on the tenth day out from Earth Edik found himself on approach to Ganymede at last.

Dola stood beside him now, as the moons of Jupiter came up on the scanners. Fionn was in the system and updating the charts, but that wouldn't be necessary much longer.

Edik smiled down at Dola, whose whiskers had more droop than Edik liked. These twelve-hour shifts must have been rougher on the familiars than he'd thought.

"All right?" Edik asked.

"Could use more rest, but I imagine you won't need quite as much intensive work out of me once we land." His ears flicked back, then up. "Or will you?"

"No way to know for sure," Edik said through a sigh. But he pointed out through the front view port. "At least we're almost here."

"Yeah," Dola said, "now all we have to do is get past the picket line."

And Dola was too right about that.

Edik checked what he was seeing against the display on the charts.

Sure enough, there was Jupiter, huge and proud as its namesake. And spiraling around it, its moons, of which Ganymede was the farthest out. Also the slowest moving.

And also, the only thing in the area ringed by Terran Navy ships.

Destroyers, by the look of them. They had that old style design, as though they were built from steel and forged to sail the seas instead of the stars, but they were nimble enough by reputation.

They were also big enough. Easily six times the size of the *Third Son*.

In fact, that was Edik's only edge right now. The navy ships had better scanners, but not six times better, and the *Third Son* was a good six times smaller than those destroyers.

That meant Edik had spotted the navy, before the navy spotted Edik.

That meant Edik might survive this yet.

"Want to go get our guest?" Edik said. "I think we'll be needing his services."

Nixia manifested in the air in front of Edik, as Dola left the bridge.

"I've asked Xincapph to return control of the ship to you," she said with a coy smile.

"Good timing," Edik said. "Did he dispute the order?"

"I didn't phrase it that way. He looks forward to resting a bit."

Edik had little understanding of how lacunas reckoned time.

"How much rest will he need?"

"Uncertain," Nixia said. "Though if refreshed in your usual ways, he'll probably be fine. This is a long voyage for him though. At least, the longest since he was bound."

Edik sighed again. He had no idea how quickly they'd have to leave Ganymede, and if the lacuna were tired, no way to predict what kind of speed Edik could expect in an emergency.

"Does he have enough left to see us to the atmosphere?"

"Of course," she said. "I'd never see you dead in space." But then frown lines creased her brow for the first time that Edik could remember. "But land soon. Please."

Edik blinked at the implications of that as Donal took his seat at the aft, starboard part of the bridge. And he was good enough to strap himself in.

"What's the situation?" Donal said.

"We've got a picket line up ahead. A good dozen ships crisscrossing Ganymede, and you can bet they're at the optimal distance to cover each other's scanners. So we have—"

"—to figure out how to get past them. I thought Earth wasn't supposed to be paying that much attention to Ganymede right now."

"Apparently even Hierophants make mistakes."

"Not very comforting." Donal drew a slow, deep breath. "Right. How long do we have?"

"Ten minutes, by my estimate," Fionn said, emerging from the holographic charts and looking as bedraggled and exhausted as Donal could remember. Even Fionn's eyes had lost some of their luster.

Donal ordered him right into his silver faun pendant, to rest.

"So I'll be doing this without Fionn's help," Donal said. "Not ideal."

"What about this trip has been ideal?" Edik said with a snort.

"Fair enough."

"What do you need from me?"

Donal thought about that for a moment, staring at the charts. So Edik watched the charts too, as he waited to hear what Donal's plan was.

On his own, Edik would have wanted to wait for the perfect moment, when the angle of the sun, Jupiter, and the other two moons provided maximum noise, then try to fly down the spot that looked least guarded on the charts. Probably around the polar ice cap at the northern end.

But then, on his own Edik didn't figure he'd have a great chance of success. Especially not with Nixia pushing them to move.

"Why only ten minutes?" Donal asked. "Why not wait here for better conditions?"

"Xincapph is getting tired. I didn't even know he *got* tired. The sooner we can get into range for the sylphs to take over, the better."

"Is that going to be a problem on the way out?"

"Focus," Edik said, feeling entirely too pleased with himself to be able to say that to someone else for a change. "We need to get down to the surface or this has all been for nothing."

"Right." Donal smiled, and it was a wicked looking smile. Absolutely vicious.

Edik was starting to like this kid more and more.

"Right," Donal said again, then rubbed his hands together. "Just fly us in like we belong here. Don't stop. Don't answer any links. Just fly us right in and land us someplace like you have every right to be doing this and no one has any right to question you."

Edik narrowed his eyes, but Donal didn't look like he was joking.

"You're sure?"

"Sure as I've been about any of this."

Edik didn't like that answer, but he didn't have a better one. He looked at Dola, who twitched his whiskers in a shrug.

Edik sighed deeply, and started in on the controls the way he imagined he would if this were any other port of call. His course would take him right past the picket line, which meant this was going to be over soon, one way or the other.

And behind him, Donal began casting. Moving enough power that Edik could feel it crackle just off the edges of his skin.

Closer and closer the *Third Son* came to the picket line. Destroyers, that right now looked almost the size of moons themselves, moved to intercept. The link chimed. A red glow emanated from the slap pad, for immediate contact without hunting down the right strand of link.

Edik's hands twitched with the urge to answer. Not answering a call from the navy went against everything he'd ever been taught. Those guys weren't assholes, after all. They were just human beings. Just spacers like Edik, doing a job in a tough situation.

Of course, that wouldn't stop them from blowing Edik out of the sky…

The link stopped chiming. The red glow faded. Edik crossed his fingers, and kept his hands steady on the controls.

Four klicks from the picket line now.

Three.

Two.

Two destroyers on an intercept course.

Edik held his breath.

One klick distant now.

The ships veered off. Back to their places.

The *Third Son* passed unchallenged through the picket line.

"YES!" Edik whooped, throwing one fist in the air then getting his hands right back onto the controls.

Ahead of Edik, he could see the grayish-yellowish-greenish surface of Ganymede. He could tell where the colony was, because even from this distance he could see the pale yellow of their fresh-cast Barrier, creating a section of surface amenable to human life.

And it looked as though Edik would get to land down there after all.

"Don't head for the Barrier," Donal said, voice sharp and sudden as his words.

"What do you mean? Where else can we go?"

"Doesn't matter. Right now you need to land us someplace away from the Barrier, near the inside edge of a crater, maybe. That would be best."

"Donal—"

"Do it, Edik."

Edik didn't like that tone at all, but he had to admit these weren't normal circumstances.

So he picked a huge crater no more than a hundred klicks from the Barrier, and moved in for a landing.

DONAL WAS ONLY JUST STARTING TO RELAX WHEN EDIK SET THE helioship down on yellowish-greenish dirt just inside the lip of a huge crater. This crater alone looked to be bigger than the whole Santa Cruz area where Donal had grown up.

But Donal was smiling. His trick had worked, and they got past the picket lines. Now they only needed to—

"Donal," Edik said, spinning around in his pilot's seat, "would you care to tell me why you just gave me an order? Against all agreements?"

His tone was measured, but there was anger floating in the back of his eyes.

Donal stopped smiling.

"Hey," he said, hands coming up in surrender. "I didn't want to give you an order, but for the illusion to hold, we couldn't have any delays. If we did anything that didn't look as though we knew exactly what we were doing, the illusion might have collapsed and those fine navy personnel might have made us very dead."

That seemed to dampen down Edik's anger.

"Just what did you do?" he said.

"Gambled," Donal said, his smile returning, and seeing a match in Edik's eyes, even if Edik's face wasn't ready to yield to the camaraderie. "I figured you had a point about the *Silver Streak*. Showing up enough, despite your course changes, that maybe it knew where we were going. That meant it was likely a government ship of some kind, and that meant it probably had licenses and permits the like of which even the navy had to take seriously."

"So you *guessed?*"

"Not at all." Donal undid the straps that held him down as he spoke. "I figured that no government ship was going to come out here and get into a pissing contest about who had authorization and so forth. So whoever authorized the *Silver Streak* to stop us from getting here, probably told the navy to look out for it and let it pass. Just in case it had to fight us here."

"So you made us look like the *Silver Streak* and that was enough?"

"Not remotely," Donal said, though he didn't take offense. Edik was only an Initiate after all, and the deeper secrets of deception magic weren't all that easy for the layman to guess at. "Helped that I knew what the *Silver Streak* looked like, I admit. But *they* had to know what countersigns and passwords to expect, to prove that we were the right ship."

Donal rubbed his hands together.

"So yes, I had to fool their scanners, but that was the easy part. I've had plenty of practice with lacunas and zuglodons in the wild, after all, and their natural senses are better than the restrained version we get out of our scanners."

Donal stood. He couldn't sit still any longer. Edik didn't stand up though. He just stared at Donal, not quite slack-jawed.

"The rest," Donal continued, "I couldn't do until someone tried to link us. Then I had a magical link, through the communication link. Get it?"

Edik stared back in a way that said he very much did not get it, though at least Donal saw the light of recognition in Dola's tired eyes.

"Once they opened a link," Donal said, "I had a direct connection to someone who was in a position to know what passwords and countersigns to look for."

"What if their captain held that information close?"

"Then the captain would bring himself into the illusion, and it would fool *him* too." Donal shook his head. "Don't see why they would, though. On a long-range mission like this one? No reason to hide information like that. Wasn't as though they expect a lot of traffic."

"If they don't expect a lot of traffic, why all the ships?"

"No idea," Donal said, still smiling. "Not as though I actually spoke to them, after all. I just laid down an illusion that they got all the right passwords and countersigns, just the way they'd been told to expect them."

"And why did that mean we couldn't go straight to the colony?"

"Looks better if we have a clandestine destination that the navy didn't know about," Donal said. "Makes everyone a little more irritated with the people back home who set this up. Makes them wonder if someone back home is trying a power play or something."

"And guarantees that they'll continue to watch us."

Edik clearly lacked proper appreciation for the intricacies of deception.

"Of course they're watching us," Donal said. "They'd do that either way. Which is why we'll sit here for about half an hour. Then I'll lay down another deception, and *then* we go off to the colony."

Edik had a lost look. Clearly he wasn't following.

"Look," Donal said, slowly. "They can't mess with *us*, not if we've got authorization that comes from somewhere up the chain of command. But they'll be dying to know what we're up to. So when we lift off from here..."

"...they'll waste resources trying to figure out what we did here. What will it look like?"

"Like we transmitted information to a ground vehicle. A runner would be best. That then took off in the opposite direction. They'll likely lose sleep wondering what's going on down here that they don't know about."

"And thus worry about what's down here that they've missed. And maybe pay a little less attention to us."

"That's the plan," Donal said, trying another smile. "Once we get inside the Barrier, they'll only be able to do so much without pissing off the settlers."

"Of course," Edik said slowly, "they'll fail to find the runner, or the contact. And they'll figure out they've been duped."

"Maybe," Donal said with a shrug. "If I do it right, it'll look like they've found evidence that faded before they could analyze it. But there are no guarantees. That's always the risk with deception magic. But between you and me, they may not want to admit they were duped. And even if they come looking, by then we should have made contact with these local spirits and gotten things underway that are much bigger than one commercial vehicle getting past their picket line."

"Of course, they might still arrest us all the same."

"That was always a risk." Donal shrugged again. "Now, do you want to sit here all day and list all the things that could go wrong? Or shall we proceed?"

Edik gave Donal a long look, then glanced at Dola, then back at Donal.

"Nothing personal," Edik said, "but I think I'm glad you don't live on Luna."

"Why's that?" Donal said.

"Because with machinations like yours, you'd end up starting a new great family."

"Or just pulling down the ones that are there." Donal rubbed his hands together. "Now, let's start planning the illusions that will keep these guys guessing."

EDIK SAT ALONE ON THE BRIDGE.

Donal was back in the main cabin, working on his illusions. Or deceptions. Or hallucinations. Whatever he called them. Far as Edik could tell, "hallucinations" were illusions of a semi-permanent nature, like the controls systems of his ship, his workstation back at Kennedy, and so on.

The more temporary kinds of things, like the spells that had gotten them past the picket line, those were "illusions."

But to hear Donal talk, it was all more complicated than that. The categories had subcategories based on nuances that Edik didn't quite see, and that depending on those nuances, they could jump major categories.

Edik wasn't quite sure how all that worked.

He wasn't quite sure he cared, either.

But he was thinking about it, nonetheless.

Part of that, he knew, was that Dola was actually housed, for the first time in ages. Yes, Edik still had the tiny silver cat figure. Carried in his pocket day and night, and had for every day since he'd summoned Dola back in school.

But Edik never asked Dola to return to the silver figure, and Dola never seemed interested in going into it. He liked being out here, in the world, with Edik. And Edik liked the company.

But right now, Dola was in his house. Had asked to go there, whiskers and tail both drooping with exhaustion.

Apparently, Dola had ways of recuperating while housed that did not function while he was out in the world with Edik. And yet, Dola had never mentioned this before. It might have been covered in the classes, but those were years ago.

And Dola had been strained enough by updating the charts in twelve-hour stretches, that he finally felt the need to house himself for a time.

And so, Edik sat alone on the bridge. Thinking about thaumaturgy. Thinking about Dola. Thinking about anything except the reason he was on the bridge right now, instead of back in the main cabin with Donal.

Edik looked over at the blue spaghetti snarl of illusory — hallucinatory? — links that formed his communication station. Specifically, he looked at the one link tucked away down at the bottom.

The new link.

The link straight back to his office in Kennedy. All the way back on Luna.

The link that had failed to connect him for days now.

He might be outside its range. Donal had said something about even formal lines of communication needing relays from out here. Relays that were not yet permanently established. Relays that would keep even the naval destroyers from linking home about the arrival of the *"Silver Streak"* here on Ganymede.

Or at least, would delay them. Edik was pretty sure the Terran Navy would know about the need for relays, and have ships positioned to provide them.

Still, it was a delay.

Like Edik was delaying.

He sighed.

Usually the lingering scent of borscht on his bridge made Edik feel at home, no matter where his ship was. Right now, it just reminded him of all he was away from.

Not so long ago, Edik and Dola had been on their own. Responsible for no one else. Independent.

Now, Edik had real friends in Anna and Jones. Possibly in Edmund too, but since Edmund was an employee, that relationship might never be a true friendship. Edik even had a business partner, if not exactly a friend yet, in North.

And he was here. All the way out on Ganymede, at the very limit of human exploration.

So very far from home.

Edik reached out and tweaked the link, put out the sending to his office. To home.

Nothing.

Edik kept sending. Kept trying. He didn't have to fly right now. Didn't have to keep an eye on Xincapph, or take reports from Nixia, or even check on the charts, forming at Dola and Fionn received their updates.

He had nothing to do but link home and hope — *pray* — someone answered.

Minutes passed. Nothing was happening.

Edik stopped. Pulled his hand back.

He smirked at himself. If Dola were here, he knew what the shaggy gray cat would say.

"Focus, Edik."

And so Edik closed his eyes. Focused on his breathing. Slow and steady. In. Out.

Every time he worried about those navy ships, he brought his attention back to the flaring of his nostrils. The filling and emptying of his lungs.

In. Out.

Worrying about alchemical supplies. Worries about Xincapph. Worries about Anna, and Dola, and even himself, just a little.

In. Out.

Finally, Edik got to as deep a meditative state as he ever really reached. He was pretty sure he was empty, but had the feeling Dola would have told him otherwise.

He reached out and tweaked the link. Sent out his call home.

And for the first time in far too long, felt it connect.

The smiling face of Carl Jones tried to form above the spaghetti snarl, along with the rest of Jones' head, but wasn't quite as sharp and clear as he should have been.

It was a little disquieting, to see Jones' tight curls fade to nothingness, his strong jaw blend just a little with his throat.

"Edik?" Jones said, and even his voice sounded off. Distant, with a slight echo. "That *is* you, isn't it?"

"It's me, Carl," Edik said, and even though the link was weaker than he'd ever experienced before, just the sight of Jones' smiling face was enough to ease some of the tension in his shoulders and jaw. Tension he hadn't realized was there.

"Good to see you, man," Jones said. "Anna'll be so relieved. She's been worried sick about you."

"*She's* been worried about *me*?" Edik shook his head. "I've been worried about *her*. How is she? How's the court case going? How's—"

"Edik?" Jones' head faded for a moment, then came back slighter. "I think the link is fading. The court case side of things is doing okay. That Hierophant Mason knows his shit. The problem is her father—"

Jones' head vanished.

Edik thrust his hand back for the link strand, twisted and twisted it, his heart pounding like it was trying to *make* the link connect.

"Carl? Carl!" Edik kept twisting and twisting. Tried to force his thoughts through it. Force the link to connect.

But there was no answer.

"Okay, that's everything I can do for now," Donal said, poking his head through the doorway. Then he looked at Edik. "Everything all right?"

Edik tried to convey to Donal without words that he had just asked the stupidest question asked since the dawn of time.

Donal looked unashamed.

"You managed to get a link, but got cut off?"

Edik shook his head. Wasn't worth answering. But an idea made hope rise in his chest.

"We need to go back over the spells. Find a way to boost the power."

"I hate to say this," Donal said, slowly, "but I don't think it'll matter."

Edik opened his mouth to lay into Donal, who apparently, despite the number of times Edik had emphasized this, yet failed to understand just how important this link was.

But Donal spoke before Edik could.

"It's not the link. If you got it, you're magician enough to hold it, even if the connection was too thin for a non-magician to connect at all."

"But we got cut off. There must be something we can…"

Edik trailed off, because Donal pointed up.

"The picket line," Donal said. "They must have cut the moon off from all link communication."

The expression on Donal's face suggested that meant a great deal more than Edik's ability to link home.

"What?" Edik asked.

"I'm not sure," Donal said, "but we better get moving. I'm betting the navy is sending someone down right now."

6

E dik kept the *Third Son* low as he flew across the surface of Ganymede to the Barrier in the distance. Not more than a few klicks away, but Edik kept his speed down as well. Anything to make himself just a little less obvious to the Terran Navy ships up in the picket line above.

"I don't see anything on the scanners," Edik said, sparing a glance away from the forward viewport. "Are you sure a ship is coming down?"

"No," Donal said from the bridge's guest chair. "But if they're cutting off communication, the settlers will want answers. Easiest way to provide them, while looking for answers, is to come down and look around themselves."

Edik nodded. But still…

"Are you worried that they aren't on the scanners?"

"No," Donal said, and Edik had to admit the kid didn't sound worried. "They may even take extra time, to make the settlers sweat, if there's any question about who's in charge around here."

Edik nodded again.

He could have let Nixia handle this flight, but he did it himself all the same. Part of that was that he'd barely handled the controls himself in days now, what with most of the flying having been handled by Xincapph for the last week.

But Edik knew the real reason. He needed distraction from his worries about home.

"You need to put them out of your mind now," Donal said.

Edik had to glance back at him. "Didn't know Journeymen were mind readers."

"We're not," Donal said. "But I figure you know the ship well enough to fly steadier than you're doing right now."

Edik forced himself to take a deep breath, biting back a sarcastic response at the same time. Donal could have raised that point a number of ways. And he was right. Edik was a little less steady on the controls than normal right now.

"You going to be all right without Dola for a while?"

"No," Edik said, flying steadier now. "I'm not used to not having him around. How do you do it?"

"Conjured my familiar late. After graduation. So I miss him, but I'm at least as used to going it alone as having Fionn around."

Edik shook his head. "Don't know what I'd do without Dola."

"Well, if we're going to play this smart, you'll be without him for a few hours, at least, and we can't wait that long to start investigating. We're here now. The clock is running."

Edik flared a deep breath through his nostrils, and eased the *Third Son* through the pale yellow Barrier. Paler than the ones he was used to on Luna, where every city and most of the great family estates had dark, strong Barriers of their own.

"Why d'you think it's so pale?" Edik asked.

"Hmmm?" Donal said, his voice distracted. Distant. As though he were casting something right now. Edik couldn't feel any power moving, but that might not mean much. Not with the skill discrepancy between them.

"The Barrier," Edik said. "It's pale."

"The spells are new. It'll settle into its normal color over the next year or so, depending on local factors."

"What about this wild magic you were talking about?" Edik said, bringing the *Third Son* a little higher so he could get a look at the settlement.

So far as Edik could tell, the whole settlement was nothing but a collection of white ceramic cones. Yeah, maybe they were a couple of stories tall, but grouped into circles the way they were, with little paths between them, the whole thing looked like some giant massage tool.

"Oh, you'll notice that soon enough. The spells of the ship are keeping us from noticing it right now."

"They are?"

"Of course," Donal said, as though he couldn't believe he was teaching Edik anything about flying. And Edik was more than a little surprised to listen to him. "Why do you think you don't notice fluctuations as we move through the space between planets?"

"Never really thought about it."

His own voice was growing distracted. Edik knew that, but didn't care. He didn't really listen as Donal went into the thaumaturgy of it all. Something about the wards built into helioships that Edik had never had reason to notice before.

Most of Edik's attention was on the cone building he'd just noticed. Scarlet red, it was, and taller than the others. And it flew a red flag emblazoned with a gray-haired, muscled man with a full beard.

Edik could see people moving about the streets too. Well, not streets. Not really. More like the dirt paths between places. And they were all moving on foot. Not a runner or horse to look at.

"What's that flag?" Edik asked, interrupting the flow of Donal's lecture.

"Flag?"

Edik pointed.

"Zeus Industries? I didn't know they had any interests here. Must be the ones funding the expedition."

"Name makes sense," Edik said. "What do you think? Where should I set down?"

"Not near the red building," Donal said. "We don't want to be that close to even semi-official scrutiny. People will realize soon enough that we aren't actually the *Silver Streak*."

"We still look like that?"

"For now."

Edik flew another lap, figuring he might as well cement that image in the heads of the locals, then set down just off to the side of the main block of buildings. Probably closer to the Zeus Industries building than Donal would have liked, but if they had to run for it, Edik didn't want to have to cross the whole compound.

And Edik set the ship down.

"Just in time," Donal called from the main cabin. When had he jumped out of his seat? "Looks like the welcome wagon is here."

<hr>

Donal looked out the starboard side portals of the *Third Son's* main cabin, at the group approaching.

The first thing he noticed? No uniforms. About a half-dozen people were approaching, all fit-looking men and women, all likely in their thirties, to look at them. But not one of them was wearing any kind of military or corporate uniform.

True, not all the corporations used uniforms for most job titles, but many of them did for their official guards.

The second thing Donal noticed? Magicians. Three of them. Two of the women and one of the men. Without getting any closer, Donal figured them for Journeyman, all three.

That could be good or bad. Too soon to tell. Donal could certainly hold his own against most of the Journeymen out there, but against more than one? He wasn't sure he'd come that far in his studies.

Of course, he was hoping it wouldn't come to that.

With those primary observations out of the way, he scrutinized a little closer while he waited for Edik to join him. Sounded as though Edik were issuing orders to his elementals.

Donal almost lost time thinking about the amazing relationship Edik had with his elementals. Donal had never seen anything like it before. He'd heard of some modern ships that allowed their lacuna to handle the navigation and course-plotting, but actually letting the lacuna not only select its own course but also handle all the flying?

Donal shook his head, to focus on the approaching group. Magic could wait.

No weapons on them. Not even Pacifiers. That was good.

They all dressed in simple, practical clothes. Work boots. Work pants and shirts with lots of pockets. All muted primary colors...

Maybe they *were* in uniforms? After a fashion? They all kept their hair short, and the men were clean-shaven. Three of group — two men and one woman — were in taupe. Two men were in dark green. The other woman was in a dull tomato red.

No division based on training then. Two of the magicians were in taupe, and the other in red.

One other thing occurred to him then. They all appeared to have Hispanic or Latin American lineage. Donal tried to recall what country had sponsored Bran's expedition. He'd assumed it was the United North American States, but Mexico didn't usually play much of a role in space exploration. They were more focused on re-developing the lost magic of the Aztecs and Mayas to have much focus beyond the skies of Earth itself.

The welcoming committee got too close to see now, as they approached the side of the ship. No way Donal could continue to observe them without getting spotted.

They knocked on the side of the ship. Not where the exit hatch was. Could it not be seen when it was closed? Donal almost smacked himself on the forehead. Obviously this was the result of his illusion, disguising the ship.

Edik snickered as he entered the main cabin. He had his sword on his belt again, and Donal had almost not realized he hadn't worn it for the flight.

"They're not armed," Donal said.

"Don't care," Edik said. "There are more of them, than us."

Edik opened the hatch.

"Hi," he said, "I'm Captain Edik Barshai, and this is my associate Donal Cuthbert. Are you from the committee here to meet us?"

A couple members of the welcoming committee whispered something to each other. They looked more closely at Donal.

"Well," the woman in red said slowly, "that depends. What are you doing here? We weren't expecting any checkups for at least another two weeks."

"Well," Edik said, glancing back at Donal, "some of the folks back home are worried about the latest reports, and wanted us to check on things a little early."

"That's against protocol," she said, and Donal couldn't help admiring the fire in her eyes. There was something compelling about the woman. Her features were plain, and Donal's sense of her aura suggested that her magic wouldn't impress him, and yet when she spoke it was hard to look away from her. "You two stay aboard your ship until we can confirm that."

"Just so we're clear for the record," Donal said, "What's your name?"

"Rosita Gonzalez-Villarreal. Chief administrator here."

"Well I'm sorry, Rosita Gonzalez-Villarreal, but no can do," Donal said, trying desperately to imitate his recollection of the way security guards aboard the *Horizon Cusp* had sounded when not complying with requests from the passengers. Of all the ships he'd flown, that crew had the best, most professional security team. And they had the best bored but official tones. "We're here to check on developments that, shall we say, nobody planned on when the original protocols were established."

Gonzalez-Villarreal glanced back at her people, who all looked a little more grim. Her eyes flashed when she turned back, but before she could speak, Edik beat her to it.

"Look," he said, nodding back at Donal, "*he's* got all the magical authority the folks back home can give him, and I think you all know what that's worth." He let that sink in a moment before he continued. "But me, I think we don't have to come at it like that."

"What are you saying?"

"Well," Edik leaned a little closer. Gave his words a conspiratory tone. "Look, we both know you guys found something here that the boys back home weren't planning on. Now everybody's scrambling for a piece of the action. Heck, even the navy's cut off communications, just to keep anyone else from getting in on the act. Tell me I'm lying."

"It's true," a man in green said, quietly. "Off-moon communications went down around the time that this ship entered the atmosphere. Looks like the work of those navy ships up there."

All of them glanced skyward.

Edik smiled.

"See, that's what I'm talking about. The Terran Navy's going to make a power play, and I think we'd both rather that not happen."

One of the men in taupe leaned in and whispered something to Gonzalez-Villarreal.

"He did, didn't he?" she said, looking close at Donal. "What did you say your name was?"

Donal's stomach sank. He'd been asked that question far too many times in that tone, even just in the last few years. Each time, it was always for the same reason.

He should have known he'd be asked here too.

Here, of all places.

"Donal Cuthbert," he said.

Gonzalez-Villarreal glanced back at her companions, then smiled.

"I can't believe I missed that," she said. "You even look like your brother, especially through the eyes and cheekbones. Your brother talked a lot about you. He's very proud of you, you know."

"Yeah," Donal said, trying not to let his words sound dead. Trying not to sound as though he'd flown dozens and dozens of decans through space only to fly straight into his brother's shadow once more. "I'm really proud of him too. There's nothing Bran can't do."

He meant every word of that. But he still felt as though admitting it out loud was like telling the world he'd never live up to the standards his brother set.

Only now did what Donal and Gonzalez-Villarreal were saying

                STEFON MEARS

really seem to click for Edik. And Donal was glad that Gonzalez-Villarreal and her companions couldn't see Edik's eyes go so wide, or the way his jaw slackened.

"Well," Gonzalez-Villarreal said, her tone much friendlier now, "I think we can scrounge up some coffee and refreshments back in the cafeteria while Bran Cuthbert's brother tells us why he's flown so far from … where is it you're going to school?"

"CalThaum San Luis Obispo," the woman in taupe said, and her eyes were smiling at Donal like she knew a secret. "He's studying to be a Hierophant."

"One brother a Magister and an explorer," Gonzalez-Villarreal said, "and the other soon to be a Hierophant. What a family."

"But we told you," Edik began, but Gonzalez-Villarreal cut him off.

"We know what you told us," she said. "But I for one would like to hear the truth."

THE DISTANCE FROM EDIK'S SHIP TO THE CAFETERIA WASN'T MUCH MORE than a hundred meters, but it felt like the longest walk of Edik's life.

It was all just so strange.

Edik had thought of himself as being somewhat worldly. Or other-worldly. He'd been born on Earth, but lived most of his life on Luna. He'd flown to every major port on Luna and Earth, and had even been to New Leningrad on Mars. He hadn't thought there was much of anything he hadn't seen before.

Over the course of that hundred meters, Edik found out just how wrong he was.

First of all, there was the sky. It wasn't the blue of earth. It wasn't the pale green of Kennedy, either.

Instead, it was a dark blue, almost purple. Was that an effect of the Barrier's settling into place? Or a likely permanent sky? Because on the one hand, it would be weird to live under a sky that dark year-round. But on the other, he had to admit it was beautiful. Like some dark gemstone, lit from within by the distant sun.

And the sun did look more distant here. Might have been a trick of the time of day, but Edik thought it really did look smaller here in the sky above Ganymede.

And then there was the dirt. It wasn't quite the odd blends of grays, yellows and even greens that Edik saw outside the Barrier. But it wasn't the brown dirt of Earth, either.

It was an even darker gray than outside the Barrier. And it was uniform, not blended. Was this another part of the acclimation process? Would the turf be just as soil-dark and brown as the dirt of Earth in another year or two?

All of these questions flew into and out of Edik's head in quick succession. Within no more than the first dozen steps outside his ship.

Because something happened then that drove the rest of those concerns straight out of his head.

Edik didn't really have the words to describe what he experienced then.

It was as though a wind had blown through him. But it wasn't a wind composed of air. It was a wind composed of raw magic.

It blew straight through him. Edik began to feel it a few centimeters from his body, then it blew harder and went straight through his core.

Edik had to stop walking. Put his hands on his knees to steady himself.

Because as that wind of magic blew through him, it carried…

It carried power, but too wild and quick for Edik to touch. He reached for some of it, instinctively, but it seemed to slip through his grasp.

It carried an odd kinetic sensation. As though Edik were dropping and flying at the same time, and his gut couldn't tell which, or even which way was up. Might have made another man nauseous, but Edik had flown too long under too many conditions for any kind of motion sickness to hit him.

And more than either power or odd sensations, that not-wind carried … information.

That was the only way he could think of it. This wind of magic that blew through him held secrets. Secrets about Ganymede. Secrets about the settlers. Secrets even about magic itself. Things that Edik, maybe even Donal, could never have guessed at.

And they were all here for the taking. For the understanding. All he had to do was grasp them…

"Shh," the woman in taupe said. She had one hand toward Edik, but held short of touching him. Physically, anyway. She was a magician too. Edik could tell now. And she was moving power in a way that Edik had to admit he found soothing. Not quite a caress, but regular pulses past his … aura? Edik had never quite liked that word any more than his professors had, but most of them kept coming back to it.

The way this woman moved power felt smooth and regular. Comfortable and familiar. Even though he'd never met her before.

He had to admit, though, that whatever she was doing was working. Edik had his focus back.

The whole group had stopped moving. Only Donal seemed to join Edik in reacting to the wind of magic, but Donal wasn't leaning forward, hands on his knees. He had his eyes closed in an almost blissful expression.

"You'll get used to it," the woman in taupe whispered to Edik. "Takes a little, but you will. Helps if you meditate outside once a day for the first few days. You're more likely to get a better sense of it that way."

"Amazing," Donal said. "It's wilder here than on Venus. On Venus the currents are steadier, less like eddies, and they don't convey as much."

"Same thing his brother said," a man in green said, and the whole welcoming committee chuckled.

"Venus has had magicians on it for years longer than we've been here," Gonzalez-Villarreal said. "We're only now starting to get any kind of handle on it, and we can only do that much thanks to some of what your brother picked up." She smiled. "Maybe you can help us take it further?"

"I'll try," Donal said, "but that has to be second priority."

"We'll get to that. You ready to go on, Captain Barshai?"

Edik nodded.

They started walking again.

So Donal really was Bran Cuthbert's little brother, huh? Edik almost started to wonder why Donal hadn't said anything. But then he thought about the *little* part. Couldn't have been easy, growing up with a brother like Bran Cuthbert.

The group got about a dozen steps closer to the cafeteria when flashes of red and orange light lit up the sky.

"Firefight," a man in green said. "Someone's not supposed to be here."

Edik shared a look with Donal. Edik started to say something, but then another wind of magic hit him.

The whole world went away for a moment. The sky, the firefight, even Donal and the welcoming committee. All gone. Instead, Edik found himself standing on a high mountaintop.

The sky here was blue-black, and not at all purple. The sandy dirt under his feet was yellowish gray.

And Edik wasn't alone.

Standing beside him, a small creature.

It looked like a six-legged lizard, fashioned out of greenish brown rock. It had a smooth, scaled head and skin, and a crest behind its head. A slender tail extended at least its body length, which couldn't have been more than a half-meter.

"Save us," it said. "Please, Edik Barshai. We beg you. Find us. Save us."

And just like that, the mountaintop was gone. The sky was that dark purple-blue again, and the dirt that same dark, dark gray. And Donal and the welcoming committee were all standing there, staring at Edik as though he'd had a fit.

Edik rolled his shoulders, surprised at how tight they felt. How tight all his muscles felt, really, from his ankles on up.

Edik blinked, trying to understand exactly how he'd experienced what he had clearly experienced. But he didn't for a second question that it had been a real communication.

He laughed off his supposed fit though with a snide comment about the winds here, but he knew he needed to get Donal alone just as soon as possible. He needed to tell him.

Edik didn't know what that creature was, exactly, but knew a distress call when he heard it.

DONAL COULD TELL SOMETHING HAD CHANGED FOR EDIK. AFTER THAT second gust of raw magic, when he had locked up all through his body, his attitude had changed. Donal wasn't quite sure what it was that changed, but Edik looked … suspicious. As though expecting to get attacked at any moment.

But then, Edik had probably never felt a gust of wild magic before. Much less had so much magic pass through him at once that it locked him up that way. Arms, legs, back, neck. Looked like a whole-body seizure.

Poor guy. Only an Initiate, after all. He didn't have the training to handle more magic than he was accustomed to channeling on his own.

So Donal was glad when the welcoming committee got them indoors and behind wards. Yes, the wards on the cafeteria building were the same, simple wards that came on all of these temporary constructions. Simple, and not good for more than maintaining their integrity in the face of the unknown, but they were more than enough to keep any further gusts of magic from hitting poor Edik like that.

Donal, on the other hand, would have loved a little more time out in them. He'd gotten to spend so little time on Venus that he hadn't really gotten to explore such gusts at all. The two he'd already felt here had been fresher and more exciting, made the few he'd felt on Venus limp and predictable by comparison.

But from those two brief gusts, Donal had only gotten to take a small amount of that power into himself, and he hadn't had even a moment to analyze it.

He couldn't wait to learn more about this local magic.

But that would have to keep, for the time being.

First, the locals.

The cafeteria was typical for its design. The big, round bottom floor of a three-story conical building, maybe thirty meters across, with all the furniture built in. Running bars circled the ceiling, shining out light from simple fire enchantments. The kind supported by alchemy, rather than elementals.

In the center, the transparent bubble tube. Maybe three meters wide, the tube allowed water elementals to carry a warded cage and its bubble of air up to the upper levels and back.

The cafeteria design had long bench seating, with a pass-through window at one end leading into the kitchen, next to the flapping door that led into the same room. There was also a buffet setup near the kitchen. Empty right now.

And all of it that same, uniform white ceramic.

"Didn't bring any paint with you?" Donal asked as Gonzalez-Villarreal led them to the table nearest the kitchen, and the two guys in green continued on through the flapping doors. "I'd think all this white would get to you after a while."

"Your brother said pretty much the same thing," Gonzalez-Villarreal said with a smile. "But we couldn't spare the room in the cargo hold. We're developing some pigmentation here through alchemical means, that we should be able to spread."

"Maybe a little sympathetic approach to spread it?" Donal asked.

"Exactly."

They exchanged a smile. Edik didn't share their humor, though he did sit next to Donal. Edik was watching the others — all seated farther down the table, available but not intrusive — and checking the exits as though he expected a fight.

"It's okay, Edik," Donal said, putting a hand on his shoulder.

Edik forced a smile then, and Donal could tell he didn't mean it. Donal wondered if he was the only one who could tell, or if the fake smile was as obvious as it might be.

"Food will help," Gonzalez-Villarreal said. "Food always helps."

And just about then the two men in green returned with a pot of coffee and, unless Donal was very much mistaken, plates of scrambled eggs and bacon. They certainly looked like scrambled eggs and bacon.

The smell, though, was slightly off. Not quite salty enough for bacon. And Donal had traveled off-world enough to know what that meant.

"Those were never part of any chickens or pigs," Donal said, pointing at contents of the plates set in front of them. "Were they?"

"Alchemy and sympathy," Gonzalez-Villarreal said, taking a crisp bite of … whatever passed for bacon. "It's what's for breakfast."

Donal chuckled, and his stomach rumbled. Edik's followed a moment later, and the three of them tucked in.

For imitation bacon and eggs, Donal had to admit that it wasn't bad. Oh, the core stock of it was the same thing he could have found in any of the low-end restaurants on Mars or Luna, but whoever prepared it here was a magician. Literally. Had pulled off a few tricks to bring the tastes closer into alignment with the substances they imitated.

Good enough for Donal. Edik too, by the look of him. He devoured his even faster than Donal, and went through two cups of coffee before Donal finished the one.

Of course, Donal was savoring his coffee. This was better stuff than Edik had about the *Third Son*. Almost tasted like it was brewed from real Puerto Rican beans.

By the time the food was cleared away, and all three of them were on their second or third cups of coffee, Gonzalez-Villarreal started up the conversation again.

"Sorry, but we can't offer you any chocolate cake. We could only manage a little of that before the next six-month supply run, and we're saving it for a special occasion."

"Are you?" Donal asked, keeping his face as neutral as he could. "Or did you already have that special occasion?"

Gonzalez-Villarreal studied him for a moment, then Edik, then turned her gaze back to Donal. In a soft voice, she asked, "What brings you here, Journeyman Cuthbert?"

The formal phrasing of the question was not lost on Donal. She was acting as though the whole settlement were her demesne. Which it might very well have been.

Donal started to answer, but she cut him off.

"The truth," she said. "Not some so-called official story, because there's no way you're here officially."

"What makes you say so?" Edik asked, tone only a little belligerent, but more so than Donal would have liked.

"Simple," Gonzalez-Villarreal said with a shrug. "You're not military, and you have no political ranks. You're not here with guards, or alchemists, or any of the kind of official personnel we've seen with every kind of crew that has been out here since the navy moved in."

"Some missions have a more … clandestine nature," Donal said, matching her pitch, and trying to imply volumes with his delivery.

Gonzalez-Villarreal shook her head slowly.

"Try another one." Before Donal could speak though, she flared a sigh through her nostrils and added, "Look. Your brother's a big deal here, and the way he talked about you, you'd think you were the one who restored magic to the world, not Lloyd Bird. So talk straight with me. Maybe we can help each other."

Donal shared a glance with Edik. Edik managed to give the tiniest shake of his head, but Donal couldn't agree with him.

"Do you know what's going on on Luna?" Donal asked.

"The Rhian situation?" Gonzalez-Villarreal nodded. "Yeah, word about that has reached even us."

"I bet it reached you for a very, very good reason."

"What exactly do you know?"

Donal sipped his coffee, let the rich taste swirl in his mouth while he decided how to answer that.

"I'm not here for a politician. I'm not here for the military. I'm here for something even bigger." Donal frowned. "At least, it's bigger in my opinion, and I'm betting you'll agree with me."

"Who sent you?"

"Hierophant Nicholas Mason."

Gonzalez-Villarreal sighed. She shook her head.

"Why did it have to be him?" She glanced down the table, where the rest of her welcoming committee had been talking in low voices, very visibly trying not to listen in. She raised her voice and said, "Mason again."

"Damn it," said a man in taupe. One of the magicians.

"He's going to get us in trouble," Gonzalez-Villarreal said, then shook her head. To Donal she said, "Let me guess, he made this about organized magic?"

"No," Edik said, and the way Gonzalez-Villarreal turned to look at him, it was as though she'd forgotten he was there. Edik continued, "This isn't about organized *anything*. This is about doing what's right, and you damned well know it."

"What's right." Gonzalez-Villarreal sighed. "What's right? You tell me, Mr. Helioship Captain. Is it right that we bind spirits for our own use? For our own needs to fly about the skies? Hell, can you name me any way we *don't* bind spirits to make our lives easier?"

"Spirits we call from another plane of existence," Donal said. "Not spirits we find, inhabiting bodies in this one."

"Immaterial," she said, her eyes still on Edik. "Or are you going to tell me that your ship isn't chock full of bound slyphs and undines, gnomes and salamanders, not to mention at least one lacuna."

"Damn it." Edik slammed down his coffee cup hard enough that Donal was amazed it didn't crack. Edik stood. "Donal, let's go. These people are just bureaucrats."

Donal looked from Edik to Gonzalez-Villarreal, and saw fire in her eyes, burning bright enough that it might burn Edik at three paces.

"I am a *magician*," she said, voice low and angry, "not a damned bureaucrat. I'm also a *Journeyman*, so mind your manners, *Initiate*."

"You know," Donal said softly, "Hierophant Mason told me that, time was, we magicians never used titles when it was just us."

"Times change," Gonzalez-Villarreal said, eyes still on Edik. "And I'm not going to let some Initiate talk to me that way."

"Well," Donal said, "in case you've forgotten, *I'm* a Journeyman. And he's with me. He gets to say what he thinks."

Donal stood, Gonzalez-Villarreal's eyes on him now. "And right now, I think he's got a point."

Donal waited for her to draw breath, before speaking over her next words.

"If we can't be civil to one another, then maybe we should call it a day and try this again tomorrow."

Gonzalez-Villarreal raised an eyebrow. Looked back and forth from Edik to Donal. Donal tried not to smile. She still had that angry fire in her eyes, but she didn't want Edik and Donal to leave without finding out what they knew. She also didn't want to overplay her hand.

If Donal was reading her right, she and her people weren't on the same page as the navy, and maybe not as Zeus Industries. That meant she couldn't afford to strong-arm Donal yet. She might risk him running to one of the other local powers.

"Sit," she said at last. "Let's try this again."

Donal nodded at Edik. Edik shook his head.

"Come on," Donal said, sitting back down. "If she'll play nice, maybe we can get somewhere yet."

Edik shook his head again, mouth stretched as though the thought of this tasted bitter, but he sat.

"So," Donal said, "let's look at this another way. You've met Bran. Bran told you all about me, and Bran had no reason to lie. I don't think he's even met Hierophant Mason, and I guarantee you Bran didn't know I was coming."

"Your point?" Gonzalez-Villarreal said.

"My point is that you have the advantage here. You *know* I'm trust-worthy. *I* don't know how far I can trust *you*."

Donal had more to add there, but she cut in, pointing at Edik.

"I don't have any reason to trust *him*."

"You have the best reason I can give you," Donal said. "I vouch for him. I swear to his trustworthiness on my power."

Donal wasn't sure whose eyebrows shot higher, Gonzalez-Villarreal's or Edik's.

"All right," she said with a nod. "I'll accept that. But I need to know what you know already."

"No you don't," Donal said. "That's the point."

"My demesne," she said. "My rules. Unless you want to challenge me to the *Comórtas Draíocht*."

"I've twice faced death in the duel of magic," Donal said, expression as flat as his tone. "Including once against a combat specialist. And I'm still here."

Gonzalez-Villarreal shook her head.

"Challenge me then. Because I'm holding to my position. Tell me what you know or we have nothing more to say to each other."

Donal sighed.

"You're right, Edik," he said, standing up. "Time to go."

As though they'd been waiting for those words as a cue, the rest of the welcoming committee fanned out between Donal and Edik and the only exit Donal had seen.

The one they'd come through.

"No," Gonzalez-Villarreal said. "You're not going anywhere."

7

The moment Gonzalez-Villarreal issued her little proclamation, Edik did three things at once.

First, he leapt on top of the solid, white ceramic table. One of the nice things about these temporary buildings — much more solid than most people would have thought. But Edik had lived in one for six months during his early days on Luna, and he knew just exactly how solid they were.

Second, he called Dola out of the silver cat figure in his pocket. Dola immediately covered his back, without even bothering to ask a question. No doubt because Dola saw Edik do the third thing he did in that first instant.

Edik drew his saber and brought it straight to Gonzalez-Villarreal's neck.

Donal had barked a command word in that moment too, and Edik saw and felt Fionn rush out of his own house and immediately set a circle around them.

Two of Gonzalez-Villarreal's people were almost as fast. The men in green. They drew slingers and had them trained, one each, on Donal and Edik.

Edik hated slingers. One-handed weapons, like miniature crossbows without bows. They slung spells woven into small alchemical balls. Sometimes their shots might daze or put a target to sleep, sometimes they might make a target … malleable.

Sometimes they burned like acid.

In theory, they were only legal for the military or police to carry, and Edik had heard rumors that they were still experimental. Unreliable. But none of those details stopped the great families from arming their personal guards with slingers back on Luna.

That the settlers had slingers was definitely not a good sign.

"None of that now," Edik said. "Chances are pretty good I could cut her throat before either of you could sling me."

"He's quite quick," Dola said.

Gonzalez-Villarreal glared hatred at Edik. Probably never had a sword at her throat before, much less had one draw blood.

Only a trickle, yes, and an accident, true, but neither she nor her people knew that. And Edik wasn't inclined to enlighten them. These settlers were up to no good. He'd been sure of it since he got that distress call, and those slingers only confirmed Edik's suspicions.

"Don't kill her yet," Donal said, and Edik smiled. He could have blessed the kid for the offhand tone. As though they'd planned this. Louder, to the others, Donal said, "My familiar has already set a circle for me. And it's not just the kind of casual circle most of you could set on a moment's notice. I invite you to take a closer look and see what I mean."

Edik waited.

"As I'm sure you can tell," Donal said, after giving them a moment to check his work, "these wards are more involved than you guys could have erected in that frame of time. Possibly more so than you could do in an hour. Your slingers aren't powerful enough to break through them. Not before my familiar and I could mount a serious counterattack."

Edik opened his mouth to add something, but Donal spoke first.

"So why don't you set those slingers on the floor. Kick them off to your right. Wouldn't want them to go off in your hands and dump their spells on the group of you. Like, say, if someone hit their bindings just right with air-aspected air of fire."

Edik could hear the smile in Donal's voice. "Grad work does have its benefits."

Edik couldn't quite follow the thaumaturgy of what Donal had said, but either the other magicians could or they believed Donal's tone or expression. Or maybe they were just that impressed with his wards. Because the two magicians among the welcoming committee muttered something, and the men in green set down their slingers. Kicked them off to their right.

"So," Edik said, staring right back into Gonzalez-Villarreal's eyes, and he knew his own eyes were smiling. "I *was* just going to have you move your people aside and escort us back to our ship, but it occurs to me that we haven't found out anything yet."

"Too true," Donal said. "We've been trying to play nice, and here you guys had to get heavy-handed."

"Quite rude," Edik said. "Oh, and forget all that *Comórtas Draíocht* stuff. Maybe Donal here likes a good old fashioned magical duel, but me, I'll cut your throat if those words even threaten to pass your lips. So choose your words carefully."

That made Donal hesitate a little too long for Edik's comfort. Maybe the kid wasn't quite as comfortable with all this as Edik had hoped.

But then, Edik hadn't had a chance to tell Donal about the distress call.

"Look," Donal said. "There's a firefight going on above us. Whatever it is, that means someone thinks they can take on an entire picket line of navy ships."

Edik wasn't sure that was true, but he didn't interrupt as Donal continued.

"So whenever they finish killing each other, the winner is coming down to the surface, and they won't be in a good mood."

"Might even be in a worse mood than I am," Edik said. "I do so hate being threatened."

"It's true," Dola added. "If you guys hadn't threatened him, Edik wouldn't have gone for his sword. And those slingers…"

Dola clucked his tongue.

Three magicians among the enemies, and all of them would know that a familiar wouldn't volunteer that kind of information if it weren't true.

In that way, familiars were more trustworthy than magicians themselves.

"The point is," Donal said, "we might still be able to help each other. But you're going to have to come clean about the situation. I don't care how much trouble you're going to be in with the powers that be back on Earth. They don't mean much to me in this instance."

"So what does?" Gonzalez-Villarreal asked, looking past the sword tip and at Donal instead of Edik.

She still hadn't raised so much as a finger to that thin trickle of blood, and Edik respected the hell out of her for it. Showed real guts.

"No," Donal said, shaking his head slowly. "No more answers for free. I wanted this to be a conversation. You tried to turn it into an interrogation. Well, the tables have turned, but you're getting your wish."

"Edik," Dola said, and Edik spotted a man in taupe trying to move toward the front door. A magician.

He pressed the blade of his sword a little tighter against Gonzalez-Villarreal's throat. Not hard enough to draw more blood. Just hard enough to dent the skin and make a point.

"Ah, ah, ah," he said. "Nobody gets to leave the party until it's over."

"You kill her we'll overwhelm you," said a man in taupe. The one who hadn't moved. A non-magician.

"She'll still be dead," Edik said with a shrug of his free shoulder, "and between his magic and my sword, I'm betting we can take the rest of you down."

UNREST FILTERED THROUGH THE WELCOMING COMMITTEE. EDIK WAS sure he saw the two magicians in taupe mutter to each other. No doubt forging some kind of plan of attack.

Edik silently thanked Jones for teaching him to throw a knife, and for giving him one to keep in his boot. Edik had a reasonable chance of killing Gonzalez-Villarreal and still throwing that knife into the throat of a magician in taupe before things got out of hand.

"Let's everybody behave," Donal said, hands raised, a trickle of power dripping from his hands, as though in warning "I don't think any of us want anyone getting hurt today."

"I'm not so sure about that," Gonzalez-Villarreal grumbled, glaring at Edik.

"Be that as it may," Donal said. "Tell us what you found. And don't hold anything back, because I'm sure you know we were briefed for this."

"Why ask then?"

"Got to know how far I can trust you, even when you have a sword at your throat."

Gonzalez-Villarreal growled — actually growled — but the woman in taupe — one of their magicians — said something rapid-fire in Spanish that Edik had no hope of following.

"I caught the word 'enemies,'" Donal said. "If she's talking about outside this room, and I think she is, you might want to listen."

"*Fine,*" Gonzalez-Villarreal said. "Only the biggest discovery since Carterite, and we're not giving it up, or handing it over to Earth, or donating it to some charity or whatever the hell Mason wants us to do."

Biggest thing since Carterite? That was pretty damned big. Edik wasn't sure he could think of anything bigger, including the Rhian people (though he knew Donal might have disagreed). Carterite was what made travel between planets fast enough to shrink the whole solar system down to maybe two weeks' travel end to end. Even the *Third Son* had its share of Carterite, like all modern helioships did. Even if it was mixed into the ceramic in certain parts of the ship.

"Wait," she said, and now Gonzalez-Villarreal was smiling in a way

Edik didn't like at all. "If you think we couldn't fight off those navy ships, then you don't really know what we have, do you?"

"Knowing what you have," Donal said, "isn't the same as knowing how much of it you've mastered."

"Maybe," she said, but she didn't sound convinced.

Edik pressed the blade a little tighter. This time a second trickle joined the first.

"Fine," she said. "You brought up the Rhian people, so you must know about the locals we've found here. But what you may or may not know is that the locals here are like power amplifiers. Run a trickle of power through them and it comes out a current. Run a current … and you have enough to maybe shoot down a ship in orbit with spellcraft alone."

"Impossible," Donal said. "Even the spells of thaumaboxing wouldn't produce that kind of effect. Not even amplified the way you suggest."

"The spells of thaumaboxing don't involve direct channeling of the element of fire." She nodded, despite the sword at her throat. "The locals here can even amplify that and solidify it so that the flames become a thing of this world."

"That would be like shooting raw lava," Donal said, and Edik didn't like the wonder in his voice. Not one bit.

"Exactly. And that's only scratching the surface."

"We knew you'd made contact with local, native spirits," Donal said. "Spirits that naturally incarnate into bodies, the way … the way we humans do."

Edik was sure Donal had been about to say something else. Surely he hadn't been intending to mention the fae folk. Not here and now.

"Then you have no idea what you've wandered into," Gonzalez-Villarreal said, with a slight shake of her head. "What do you think you're here to do?"

"Wrong person to ask," Edik said, and he let his smile get lopsided as her angry eyes turned back to him. "See, I'm a helioship captain, as you so astutely observed earlier. And that means I'm fully trained and qualified to declare this a first contact situation."

Gonzalez-Villarreal sucked in her breath, but before she could speak, Edik got there first.

"And as a helioship captain licensed by Luna, Earth and Mars, I'm claiming the first contact position here. I'll be the one to meet with these locals, and you are now obligated to take me to them."

Gonzalez-Villarreal shook her head slowly, then started laughing like Edik had just told her the first joke she'd heard in five years.

"The guy from Zeus Industries tried to play it the same way." She sighed. "Rodriguez over there" — she pointed and the only non-magician in taupe waved back at them — "is a licensed helioship captain, and he's our official first contact man."

"That's as may be," Donal said, but Edik cut him off.

"Do you have three?" he said, over whatever Donal was trying to say. And just to be sure, when Donal stopped talking, Edik repeated himself. "Do you have three fully licensed helioship captains here?"

Gonzalez-Villarreal didn't answer, which was the same as saying no.

Edik smiled again. "Then in accordance with general protocol, I'm demanding oversight of your first contact, to make sure all the proper rules and regulations are being followed."

"You can't do that," Gonzalez-Villarreal said.

"Actually," Rodriguez said, "he can, because you already told him we have a financial stake in this. The guy from Zeus would have done it, if they hadn't had a financial stake of their own. I tried to warn you someone back home might think of this, once the navy stopped trying to—"

"Can it, Rodriguez," she said. Then spoke through clenched teeth. "All right, Barshai. We'll give you oversight. Just as soon as hell freezes over."

Edik blinked.

"Earth doesn't run things here. Neither does Luna. Neither does Mars. Fuck your license, your interplanetary law, and your first contact protocols. *I'm* in charge here, and I refuse to acknowledge your authority."

"Sounds as though we're at an impasse," Donal said. Then

shrugged. "Or Edik could kill you and we could see if the next in line is more reasonable."

"I won't be," the woman in taupe said. "Believe me. If I were in charge, you guys wouldn't have made it off your ship."

"Damn it all," Edik said. "Look. The navy is kicking ass up there. And maybe you can force the locals to help you shoot down their ships, but are you willing to bet you can fight off that whole picket line before they manage to take you down? How many of you have ever killed someone, much less shot down a ship?"

For a moment, Edik could hear nothing but the pounding of his own heart.

"Look," Donal tried again. "We're not here to jump your claim, and Hierophant Mason didn't ask us to seize anything from you. We're here to check out the situation and make sure the—"

"That's enough, Donal," Edik said. "They know we're here to check out the situation."

"Make sure of what?" Gonzalez-Villarreal asked, one eyebrow high in a way that made her look more attractive than Edik expected. Of course, he'd always had a thing for tough women.

"Doesn't matter," Donal said. "Now, are you going to work with us or not?"

Gonzalez-Villarreal flared her nostrils in a slow breath. Glanced down at her people, then up at the ceiling, and perhaps at the firefight going on up in the sky.

"Will you stand with us if the navy tries to take over?"

"Yes," Donal said, and Edik glared at him for it. But Donal muttered to Fionn, who muttered to Dola, who said to Edik in words only Edik could understand, "Easier to handle these people than the navy, and we don't know where Zeus Industries stands."

"All right," Edik said. "I support Donal in this. We'll stand with you against the navy."

"Swear it," Gonzalez-Villarreal said, but Donal shook his head.

"If you hadn't tried to strong-arm us," Donal said, "I'd've been happy to swear that. But right now I don't trust you. So you and your magicians — both of these two and any others you might have…"

"All the magicians of this settlement are in this room," she said.

"The three of you will each swear on your power that that's true, and also that no settler or ally of yours will make any move against Edik or I in any way while we're here."

"You're asking too much."

"I'm not sure I'm asking enough." Donal shook his head. "We don't know what you intended, if you'd managed to take us."

During that exchange, Edik looked a question at Dola, to see if his familiar thought Donal had left out any important points. Dola shook his shaggy gray head.

"All right," she said, and Edik very much liked the sound of defeat in her voice. "We'll swear. And we'll take you to the locals."

"No," Edik said quickly, and thinking even faster. "I plan on sticking to first contact protocols anyway, and I can't properly investigate your handling of this situation with you guys watching over my shoulder."

"No," Gonzalez-Villarreal said, shaking her head. "We'll let you see them on your own, but only if you forswear first contact protocols. We're not acknowledging outside authority, and that includes those protocols."

"The protocols are acknowledged, interplanetary space law," Edik said. "Refusing to honor them makes other planets *less* likely to acknowledge you when you declare independence, not more likely."

"Take it or leave it," she said. "Or start a fight you might be less able to win than you think."

Edik's gut twisted at the thought of this. All but demanded that he refuse.

But Donal had a point. They *were* at an impasse.

And this might be the only way forward.

But then Edik had an idea.

"All right," Edik said. "I forswear the rules of first contact protocol to any alien forms of life you introduce me to, while I'm here on this moon."

"Good enough," Gonzalez-Villarreal said.

Donal looked doubtful, but he held his tongue.

"Then let's get to your oaths," Donal said. "We have alien life forms to meet."

––––––

ONCE THE OATHS WERE SWORN, AND DONAL HAD CONFIRMED THEM magically, he felt a lot more comfortable about his situation. Edik had drawn that sword faster than Donal would have believed. And bringing it straight to Gonzalez-Villarreal's throat, well, that was almost too much.

Donal had to admit it was the right move though. Those two men in green had been carrying slingers. And their holders must have had a hold-out design, to keep Donal from sensing their presence.

Not a good sign that they were carrying the weapons at all, much less hold-out style. But then, they had no way of knowing who Donal and Edik were when they landed.

Donal looked forward to comparing notes with Bran about these people, the first chance he got.

For now, though, the rest of the welcoming committee had gone back to their normal jobs here at the settlement. Or perhaps they were spreading the word about Donal and Edik. No way to know for certain, not without sending Fionn out to investigate. And Fionn was still looking a little pale, instead of his usual vibrant self. His coloring not quite its normal emerald yet.

Donal would prefer to send Fionn back into his pendant, but under the circumstances it seemed like a bad idea.

So Gonzalez-Villarreal herself led Donal and Edik out of the cafeteria and across the compound, between the white temporary structures and notably away from the red Zeus Industries building.

"Where are their people anyway?" Donal said, waving a hand toward the large, red, conical building. "Why didn't they send anyone to meet us?"

"We don't let them," she said, and Donal heard real satisfaction in Gonzalez-Villarreal's voice. "They thought they could come here and throw their weight around. They thought wrong. The minute they set their building up, we put them under house arrest."

"And they let you?" Edik said. Edik still had his saber out, and Donal admired the way Edik and Dola reflexively kept a full-view watch going as they walked. Whenever one turned his head, the other turned the other way to keep an eye on things.

Donal wondered how well that would work if another wave of wild magic hit them now.

"Didn't have much choice," she said. "They have one Journeyman. We have three, only one of whom — me—was officially logged as a Journeyman."

Donal nodded, only mildly surprised. "The other two went through the apprentice system?"

"That's right," Gonzalez-Villarreal said, sounding impressed. "And they didn't take their license exams, because their jobs here, officially, are non-magical."

"Tricky," Edik said.

"Seemed like a good idea." She glanced at Donal and shook her head. "Not good enough, I guess."

"You're the one who set us on opposite sides," Donal said.

"No," Gonzalez-Villarreal started, then stopped herself. "Anyway, right about then the navy showed up, and communications home have been spotty. For all we know, that's a Zeus Industries ship that got into a firefight up above."

Donal glanced at the purple-blue sky above. Quiet up there now. Whatever that fight was, it was over.

"How long do they keep you guys gut off, when they do it?" Edik asked.

Cut off…

Something about that idea tickled at the back of Donal's head. Tickled hard enough that Fionn turned and looked at him, a hint of his normal sparkle in those emerald eyes.

Fionn nodded, as though agreeing with a conclusion Donal had not yet drawn.

"Usually not more than a day or so," Gonzalez-Villarreal said.

"Proving a point. But after a firefight." She spat on the dark gray dirt. "They may keep us cut off this time until they make their move. So you better be serious about helping us, because we're going to need it."

They were still a good two or three rings inside the outer perimeter when Gonzalez-Villarreal stopped outside a building that had no markings at all. Nothing but the pure white ceramics of a temporary building.

"They're inside." She stepped up and gave a complicated series of knocks. Donal thought it felt like the rhythm of a piece of classical music.

If she'd expected Donal not to catch and memorize the pattern, though, then she'd forgotten the importance of patterns in higher magic.

But then, it was more likely the pattern was because only three members of their settlement were magicians.

The door opened then, sliding to one side. Inside was a black, hanging curtain.

A man in green leaned out through the curtain, slinger in hand.

"It's all right," Gonzalez-Villarreal said. "These are Journeyman Donal Cuthbert and Captain Edik Barshai. I'm going to introduce them to the locals."

"No need," Edik said. "We've already met."

Gonzalez-Villarreal's jaw dropped so fast Donal thought he heard it *clunk* off of her collarbone.

"Impossible," she said.

Donal didn't say so, but he was thinking much the same thing. Edik had never been here before. He'd had no time outside his ship's wards to go wandering. He'd had no opportunity at all to meet the locals.

But then realization trickled up Donal's spine.

They'd walked from the cafeteria to this building — a good two hundred meters — outside any wards but the new Barrier, and there had been no gust of wild magic. But there had been *two* on the walk from the ship to the cafeteria. If there had been *one* during that first walk, then the lack of a gust now would make sense. Would have been consistent. But there had been *two*.

Which meant the second one might not have been random…

"Entirely possible," Edik said, smiling. "During that second wave of wild magic back there, one of them made contact with me. Addressed me by name."

"It's true," a voice said from somewhere on the other side of that curtain. A voice that didn't sound human. It had two native tones, one deep and one mid-range, and the tenor of the voice sounded almost wet. Like rain would sound, if it could talk, which only made Donal wish he'd taken the time to speak to an undine or two at some point.

That voice sounded very much like he believed a water elemental would sound.

"I was the one who made contact with Edik Barshai," the voice continued, while the man with the slinger looked back inside the curtain. "And I wish to continue our conversation."

"As you can see," Edik said, broad smile on his face, no doubt at the shocked anger of Gonzalez-Villarreal, "we need no introduction to the locals. Which means you aren't introducing us. Which means—"

"First contact protocols," she growled. Then poked her finger hard into Edik's chest as she said, "Don't get cute about it, Barshai. We have too much at stake here for games."

"And I'm not playing games," Edik said, enough anger in his tone now to match hers, and Donal didn't like the cold look in his eyes. "Now you and your men clear out so we can begin our assessment."

Gonzalez-Villarreal closed her eyes and flared three deep breaths through her nostrils before finally saying, "All right, Barshai. We'll play it your way for now." She held up one finger. "For now."

She snapped her fingers and two men in green, both with slingers drawn, came out from behind the curtain and fell into step as Gonzalez-Villarreal marched away.

Edik smiled at Donal. Nodded toward the inside.

"Come on," he said, "I'll introduce you. We have a lot of work to do."

THIS BUILDING WAS DESIGNED FOR PURE STORAGE. THE BOTTOM FLOOR of the cone had no permanent furniture, and no bubble tube in the center. High ceiling — twice as high as the cafeteria — and a doorway at the back that Donal knew led to a stairwell to a second floor, which would have a ceiling even higher, if more pointed.

The runner lights were dimmed, and the panel windows along the outer wall were all covered with black curtains, same as the doorway.

Apparently Gonzalez-Villarreal didn't want anyone even seeing the locals without permission.

And the locals were a sight to see.

Six-legged lizards, maybe a meter long in body, with another meter of tail. Sinuous necks, with arrow-shaped heads and crests behind them. Scaly bodies in the way shale was scaly, rather than the way lizards should have been scaly. No shine to their greenish brown scales. Each one was individuated not by colors, but by patterns. As though they'd had different geological patterns in the rocks they'd formed bodies from.

And Donal was pretty sure they'd formed their bodies from the native rock, rather than being born into them the way humans were. They had that look, and it would have been consistent with what he had heard about the Rhian people on Luna.

That one detail — shaping their own bodies rather than being born into them — seemed to be the whole basis for dismissing them as "just" spirits like any other, rather than self-incarnating entities the way humans were.

And even complicating the picture further, Donal was certain that the fae took both approaches. The *sidhe* were born, in much the way humans were, which was why they could interbreed with humans and produce offspring like Rowan MacPherson in the first place.

But others among the fae seemed to shape themselves out of natural elements. From the tales of his grandmothers, Donal had reason to believe that entire types of trolls pulled themselves bodily out of the native rock, in much the way the Rhian did, according to accounts.

And possibly much the way these locals here on Ganymede had done.

There were only four of them in the room.

And Donal was certain it was just the four of them. They had a solid, heavy feel, magically speaking. Donal barely had to shift any consciousness to bring the auras of their power into full view.

And they were powerful. Each and every one of them carried more power than even Hierophant Mason, and Hierophant Mason was the most impressive magician Donal had met.

If there were others in the building, Donal would be able to sense them. He didn't doubt it for a moment.

"Cinnamon," Edik said, and Donal stopped moving and looked at him.

And so did each of the locals. They were scattered about the room, three near the edges and one in the center. Edik appeared to have spoken to the one in the center. But Donal couldn't figure out why. They didn't smell like cinnamon. They smelled like…

Fresh cut grass on a summer afternoon. Yes. Very much the way backyard grass smelled at his parents' place when Donal had still been a teen, and loafing as he watched Bran mow the lawn with that old-fashioned push-mower. The one their father said "built character."

Donal blinked. Could they control their scent?

"Cinnamon is as good a name as any for me," the local in the middle said. Cinnamon, by his — his? — own decision. "But my people are the Du Mak."

"So this isn't your first home?" Edik said, and Donal had no idea why Edik said that. Yet he did, and as he said those words, he sank down cross-legged to the floor, putting him close to eye-height with Cinnamon.

Donal did likewise. The two familiars took up position just behind their magicians.

"No," Cinnamon said. "And we are only one clan, as are those you met on Luna. They are ours, of us, those Rhian people. It is they who spoke your name to the winds of space, for us to hear. For us to know. They speak to us of your efforts on their behalf. Yours and Anna Lukyanova, and Carl Jones and Nicholas Mason."

Edik snickered, but Donal wasn't sure why.

"Wait," Donal said, and Cinnamon turned to look at him. At least, Donal *assumed* Cinnamon was looking at him. Cinnamon didn't have any eyes that Donal could spot. "If you guys are connected to the Rhian, then Gonzalez-Villarreal and her people aren't the first to make contact with you."

"Yes," Cinnamon said. "And no. We are of the same, but we are not the same. Their focus, not our focus. The Rhian would not have taken bodies without your ... alchemy?"

Donal and Edik nodded.

"But we take bodies everywhere we go. From local stone. It ... comforts us against the rough nature of planetary bodies."

"Planets are rougher than space?" Donal asked, but Edik held up a hand to forestall the question.

"That doesn't matter right now. Would you and your people here consider the Rhian people—"

"They are kin, but not as you think of kin. Not as you humans seem to have kin. We have similar natures, but not—"

"I understand," Donal said suddenly, his eyes wide with the realization that it was true. "You're the same in that you share certain characteristics. Perhaps a similar place of origin. But you vary from other clans or types, for lack of a better word. And where you vary, you vary *widely.*"

"True." Cinnamon tilted its legs, and waved its tail up high in an odd pattern that drew the attention of the other locals in the room. They came closer.

"You're not actually native to this world, to this ... plane of existence," Donal continued, while Edik stared at him, eyebrows high. "You come from someplace else, and pass through in places where the barriers between worlds are thin."

"Just so," Cinnamon said. "You have met our like before? Perhaps others of us?"

"On Earth, back in the islands my forefathers came from," Donal said, his tone as formal as though he were presenting at a convention, "we have other people who come from another plane of existence. Who pass through in places where the barriers between worlds are thin, especially at certain times of year when those barriers are thinnest. We call these people many things. Good neighbors. Fair folk. Collectively they are known as the fae."

Donal drew a deep breath. "And I am here as their representative."

Edik was rapidly losing control of this situation, and he didn't like it. Donal had been going back and forth with Cinnamon for a good ten minutes, explaining about the fae of Earth and trying to persuade them to declare an alliance. Or maybe it was to declare themselves an offshoot of the Terran fae. Edik wasn't quite sure what Donal's goal was.

And Edik didn't really care. Not about that.

He was here to rescue these Du Mak. Get them out of their bondage to the settlers. And even Edik could tell they were bound here. Right now they were inside a magic circle, cast around the whole of the building...

"Donal," Edik said slowly.

"But the advantages of this outweigh the immediate concerns," Donal said, and from the passion in his voice, Edik could tell the kid wasn't listening. "If you declare even a temporary alliance with the fae—"

"*Donal,*" Edik said more urgently, this time putting one hand on Donal's shoulder.

Donal finally turned to look.

"We're inside a magic circle, you know."

"Of course," Donal said. "No way they'd leave them..."

Donal's eyes got wide. He spat a word at Fionn, who immediately rushed to the window.

"Surrounded," Fionn reported.

"Of course," Cinnamon said. "I thought that was part of your plan."

"Don't have much of a plan," Edik said, coming to his feet and drawing his saber. "And we're out of time to discuss alliances with the fae."

"But," Donal started, but Edik jumped in over him.

"Later for that. Right now I'm the closest thing to legitimate authority, and we're going to have to go with that."

"But if they accept an alliance—"

"Donal, there's no time."

"He's right," Dola said, and then Dola said something to Fionn that Edik couldn't understand. From his expression, Donal couldn't understand it either, which was at least some comfort.

"Fine," Donal said, coming to his feet.

"Know this," Cinnamon said. "We consider you here as our rescuers. I and mine pledge to aid you however we might while both you and we remain here on this place you call Ganymede."

"Good enough for me," Donal said.

Edik didn't bother saying anything.

"Situation?" Donal asked his familiar.

"Surrounded, as I said." Fionn tilted his head slightly. "Two of their magicians are absent. Only Rosita Gonzalez-Villarreal stands with those surrounding us. But others have joined her. They wear the scarlet jumpsuits of Zeus Industries personnel."

"No executives then," Donal said. "Executives don't wear jumpsuits."

"In this case," Fionn said, "one does."

"Must have another job on the side," Edik said, and he stepped over to peek out the window.

"I see three guys in green with slingers," Edik said, "but I'm betting there are more."

"Wait," Donal said, and he was smiling. He turned to Cinnamon. "The bindings that keep you here—"

"Yes," Cinnamon said. "While within this building, we cannot act against Rosita Gonzalez-Villarreal and her people."

"That doesn't include Zeus Industries," Donal said. "That's something."

"I'll focus on Gonzalez-Villarreal then," Edik said. "You take out the Zeus boys if you need to."

"Gonzalez-Villarreal won't risk attacking us."

"I doubt her word will—"

"Here word backed by magic," Donal said with a fierce smile. "Saw to it myself. I may not be able to impose a *geas* yet, but I could do that much, and I did. They move against us and all three of them lose their magic. Spirits turn on them too, possibly starting with their familiars."

"Depends," Fionn said, "on the relationship they have with their familiars."

"If they have familiars," Dola added. "We haven't seen them yet."

"Sorry, Donal," Edik said, "but I can't trust that she hadn't found a loophole, the way I did."

Edik stepped to the door. Reached for the handle. Turned to Donal.

"Wait," he said. "Do you want to put up a circle first?"

"Door first," Donal said.

Edik shrugged, tugged the curtain back, and threw open the door.

Donal issued a word to Fionn, who put up a circle just inside the walls of the building, making it inside the larger circle.

"Well," Gonzalez-Villarreal said in a mocking tone, "are you satisfied that we haven't harmed the locals?"

"Not at all," Edik said. "You've bound them here and constrained their actions without their consent. That's against Article 1, Section 2.2. You're in violation, and will be in big trouble if you don't break these wards right now."

"Aw," she said, "can't Cuthbert do it?"

"I could," Donal said, and it sounded like he had more to say, but Edik didn't let him.

"Of course he could," Edik said, raising his sword to his shoulder, casual-like. "But if *he* does it, then we're doing it as the authority. I'm trying to work with you people. Take it down yourself, as a gesture of goodwill, and we can write the whole incident off as a misunder-standing. Maybe call it frontier enthusiasm."

"Frontier enthusiasm," she said. "I like that. Not going to do it though. And Cuthbert," she said a little louder, "I'd be careful going after those wards. They're not simple things, the type even poor Journeymen like ourselves could construct over the course of an hour."

Donal started to say something, but Edik didn't want the conversation going that direction.

"What about you?" Edik said loudly, addressing the oldest man in a scarlet jumpsuit. He was mostly bald, and what hair he had was gray. Must have polished his reddish scalp, the way it gleamed.

In fact, it wasn't just natural pigmentation emphasized by his jumpsuit. This man's whole complexion was reddish, though he had the rough, blocky features of the less fortunate among the northern Europeans. That kind of complexion meant he was from Mars.

Combined with his belly, the complexion and shape of his head didn't do him any favors.

"Name's Nilson," the man said. "And I think this is just amusing as hell. Watching a bunch of civvies trying to play executive games."

"You're not military," Donal said.

"No," Nilson said, with a considering frown, "I'm not. It's true. Except that it's not quite true either." He smiled, and the smile made him even uglier, which Edik had not thought possible. "See, I'm ex-Terran Army, and now I'm loaned out to the Navy for this mission."

"What?" Gonzalez-Villarreal said, her head whipping around so fast Edik was surprised it didn't pop off.

"That's right," Nilson said. "The official call came in this afternoon, while the ships up above were on maneuvers."

"That wasn't maneuvers," Edik said, "That was a firefight. Seen one before."

"Yeah?" Nilson asked. "Seen any of the recent dogfighting have you? Up to speed on all the latest military magic and alchemy? Civvie like you?" He snorted. "'fraid you missed this one."

"So what?" Donal said. "Navy has to play by the first contact rules, just like everyone else. Don't they?"

"Yes, and no," Nilson said, and he looked to be enjoying this way too much for Edik's taste. "See, the military doesn't acknowledge civilian helioship captains as having any authority in first contact situations."

"This isn't one," Edik said, trying to make his tongue move as fast as his mind was whirling. "These locals are connected to the Rhian people on Luna, so—"

"Maybe they are," Nilson said, as though the idea weren't new to him, "and maybe they aren't. Either way, Gonzalez-Villarreal's people here already declared it a first contact situation, and declared their man Rodriguez in charge of it. So now the navy's going to send down three helioship captains — surely you folks realize they've got way more than three up there — to assess and control the situation, tribunal style."

"No," Gonzalez-Villarreal said.

"'fraid so," Nilson said.

Edik's hand twitched on his saber. He could see now that the other guys in red jumpsuits had Pacifiers and slingers, all held behind their back. This Nilson stood ready to make this a fight. The settlers might side with Edik and Donal, but that wouldn't matter. They'd never be able to fight off Pacifiers, let alone the slingers.

Donal was whispering something to Fionn though. Edik could barely even tell that words were leaving his mouth, but they were, and Edik could tell that only Fionn would understand them.

That meant Donal needed a delay for something.

"All right, hold on," Edik said, waving both hands and counting on the naked steel in his right hand to ensure that all eyes were on him. "I don't know about you, Gonzalez-Villarreal, but I'm not buying that on this guy's say-so. You bring down those captains, and maybe I'll believe it. Until then, I'm sitting tight right here, and making sure the Du Mak people don't suffer anything worse than—"

And then everyone outside the building froze in place, bodies locked and shaking. Edik could think of only one thing that might have caused it — a might gust of local magic. Mightier than even the one that had allowed Cinnamon to make contact with him.

Edik knew he certainly had to have locked up as hard as the people in front of him right now. All of their eyes wide, and eyeballs rolling. Their arms and legs locked rigid.

Edik almost wondered why he wasn't feeling the effects — apart from a sympathetic ache from his own limbs at the memory — except that he knew he stood inside not one, but two sets of wards.

And Donal was spitting our Gaelic like the worst hairball any cat had ever suffered. So fast and sharp that Edik couldn't follow it, and he spoke pretty good Gaelic, for an Initiate.

But Donal was doing something big.

***

DONAL CHANTED FAST AS HE EVER HAD BEFORE. AND AS HE DID HE reached out, guided by both Fionn and Cinnamon, and he gathered the flowing strength of the mighty gust of local magic — a gust called forth by Cinnamon at Donal's request — and used that raw power to shred the wards binding the Du Mak to this place.

Wasn't as hard as Gonzalez-Villarreal had made it sound. Her people were good all right. They knew their way around wards better than Donal had only six months ago.

But then Donal had started playing the wards game with his class-mates. Especially Esmeralda Villaseñor, who was better at wards than all of these people combined.

Donal had been able to spot the key flaw while Edik had them talking. It was a simple thing, really, and the kind of problem that tends to creep in when more than one caster works on a spell.

The wards were woven like a spider web of spellwork. Tailored to match the physical confines of a conical building. One person had handled the physical barrier keeping the Du Mak within, tying it into their nature in a nifty bit of thaumaturgy. Another hid this place and its contents from scrying attempts from without. A third had handled counterspell work, to resist unweaving the spell.

Not a bad effect, that one. Deception magic, such that every thread examined with a goal of penetrating or unweaving the spell appeared to be three threads, that led to three more, which continued on out from there. Gonzalez-Villarreal's work, from the feel of it, and not bad.

But Donal specialized in deception magic. And he hadn't been looking to penetrate the spell, or unweave it. Common mistake, to consider those the only viable options. To not recognize that a solid punch to the weakest link in the spell might be enough to rend the whole thing to its component power.

And with three casters, Donal needed only to examine the places where the spells wove together. Spells were idiosyncratic by nature, and involving more than one caster meant more than one set of idio-syncrasies.

Donal found the weakness at the place where Gonzalez-Villar-real's arrogance met the cautious uncertainty of the other two Jour-neymen. Perhaps less certain of the rightness of their cause.

Whatever the reason, it left a weak point.

Donal's whole spell to gather and channel the wild local energy couldn't have taken thirty seconds.

Thirty glorious seconds, full of vibrant, unchained power that whispered to Donal of secrets beyond secrets. Hinted at a layer of pure power that underlay even the disparate elements, that might have been a core even deeper than Dee and Kelly had found through their Enochian experiments, all those centuries ago.

And all the while, the people outside, caught up in the gust, had been held in place by the collective cry of the Du Mak people.

That was another little bit of Donal's brilliance, even if he did say so himself. And even if he did get the idea from what Edik had said about Cinnamon's earlier introduction.

Donal knew the Du Mak people could not harm the settlers. Not directly or indirectly.

But they could talk to them. No proscription against that. And if they talked all at once, on the most powerful gust of magic to flow through this settlement in a year, well, they couldn't help the outcome.

And a little seizure that failed to harm the body in any lasting way, well, that wasn't against the proscription. Especially in the act of communication. Might not even have been their fault. They might not have known it would happen.

But Donal had known. And it bought him the time he needed.

And then the wards were down.

Cinnamon and his people vanished before the settlers and Zeus Industries flunkies finished moving their limbs and moaning.

"Well," Donal said. "Guess that removes that immediate issue."

"What have you done?" Nilson yelled.

"Me?" Donal touched his chest with one hand, as though to as how he could possibly have done anything wrong. "I only did what Gonzalez-Villarreal suggested. I took a shot at those wards."

"They're gone," she said, and she looked pale. "How? How did you…"

"I told you," Donal said. "There are advantages to graduate study."

"Doesn't matter a bit," Edik said. "They've been freed of their bindings. As is proper." Edik gave Donal a nod. "And I still haven't seen any sign that the navy supports your claim…"

Edik let his words trail off as Nilson pointed up.

And Donal looked up to see two ships coming down out of orbit.

One of them, a little runabout. Looked like an old fashioned life boat, with canvas stretched across the top, even though Donal knew the whole thing had to have been made from ceramics, at the least.

And the other ship looked all too familiar.

Donal looked over at Edik, who looked back at him with a grim expression.

The two of them looked back up at the silver flying saucer that could only be the *Silver Streak*.

And Donal had the feeling he wasn't going to like finding out who was in that ship.

GONZALEZ-VILLARREAL WHIRLED ON NILSON, FINGER JABBING AT HIM.

"This was never part of our arrangement."

"Is now," he said.

Meanwhile, Gonzalez-Villarreal's people gathered around her, looking uncertain, while the two other men in red jumpsuits — young, fit men who looked as though they'd seen their share of fights, just to judge from the scars on their faces — flanked Nilson and looked ready to defend him if need be.

Donal wondered about that. They weren't magicians. They weren't armed. And yet they didn't look worried in the least. He was tempted to shift awareness, to look for enchantments on their persons, but he didn't think he could spare the time.

"We have to talk about this," Gonzalez-Villarreal insisted. "You can't just step in and take things over. There are rules."

"Sure," Edik muttered, just loud enough for Donal to hear, "*now* she wants to play by the rules."

Donal smiled, though he didn't feel all too happy about the situation. Yes, the Du Mak were currently free. And yes, they were capable of traveling among the worlds by themselves, if Donal had understood them correctly. But still, Donal wondered how easy it would be for them to get past that picket line of ships. If they needed bodies. If they would show up on scanners the way lacunas did.

There was just too much Donal didn't know. And he *hated* that.

"All right," Nilson said, waving his hands in the most demeaning pacifying gesture Donal had seen, perhaps ever. "Tell you what. I and mine need to have a little confab about the sitch, and then we can all get together in, say, an hour?"

"You including us in that?" Edik asked, sword forward, probably to make sure he wasn't ignored.

"More the merrier," Nilson said with a condescending smile. "We'll all meet in the Zeus Industries building in an hour."

"No," Gonzalez-Villarreal said. "Our cafeteria."

"Our food is better."

"We don't trust you," Gonzalez-Villarreal said pointedly.

"Then *learn*," Nilson said, and all the humor was gone from his voice. "Look, you and your people can play house here all you want.

But you're damned fools if you think you can just *claim* a discovery like this. It belongs to big boys. Not to you."

"They belong to themselves," Donal and Edik said at the same time.

"Quaint notion," Nilson said. "We'll explain the truth of that to you soon enough." He smiled then. "Oh, and Edik, you really *should* make sure you attend. Someone's going to want a few words with you."

Nilson winked.

"Fine, fine," Edik said, but Donal thought he heard uncertainty under the bravado. "An hour then? Gives us time to take a nap. *Assuming* you guys don't object to us returning to our ship."

The ship. Something about the ship. And the Du Mak people…

"Not at all," Nilson said. "But if you try to lift off, they'll burn you down." He smiled again, a brief lift of the corners of his mouth as he said, "Oh, and don't try to link home. Picket line's still not letting links past them."

Linking home…

Of course!

"Fine, fine," Donal said, giving Edik a significant look. "Trust me, the *last thing* we want to do is link home right now."

Edik furrowed his brow. He didn't get it. Donal almost sighed, but he didn't want to be too obvious. Not here.

"Come on, then," Donal said, hustling out the door and across the dirt back toward the *Third Son*. Edik followed, and all around the compound, people were coming out of the conical buildings to see what was going on. Almost all of them had that same Latin look, as though the whole settlement had been assembled in Mexico and parts south, though Donal spotted a few darker complexions as well.

Donal led the way, trotting between buildings and not answering questions. Edik right behind him, and the two familiars watching the flanks to make sure no one approached who meant them harm.

Then they were back aboard the *Third Son*, safely seated in the main cabin.

"What?" Edik said. "What do you have in mind?"

"We're cut off from links," Donal said with a smile. "What do you want to bet that's driving Lukyanov's servitor *mad*."

Edik blinked in confusion.

"The memory circle variant's cut off," Donal said. "The spell can't work, and we know that if anything interferes with that spell, the servitor pops out to handle it. With extreme prejudice. But there's no one to hurt."

"And you think talking to it right now is a *good* thing?"

Donal nodded.

Edik sighed, and led the way.

8

Sure enough, Donal was right. That red bear servitor with the yellow edging to its fur and claws was floating in the air down belowdecks. And it looked angry enough to chew through the hull.

"Hi there," Edik said, leaning down through the hatch from the deck above. Donal lay next to him on the cold ceramic deck, both of them watching the servitor. Donal had his tuning fork in hand, clearly ready to act if the opportunity came.

What might have been less clear, Edik could only hope, was the deception spell that Donal wove right then. Donal had promised it would be too subtle for anyone, much less a servitor, to notice.

Their two familiars were down there with the bear. Flanking it.

The red bear servitor looked up at Edik and growled.

Edik smelled deep the herbs and borscht scents from below him and from down the hall behind him. Drew at least a little comfort from their familiarity. Despite his baser instincts telling him that fleeing is the only intelligent option in the face of such a thing.

"Not playing smart, Barshai," the bear said directly to Edik's mind, in a chiding voice heavily accented with Russian. Though Edik was certain that Donal could hear the servitor as well. "Better you restore contact. Better I don't have to shred you like fish."

"Don't think you can do that," Edik said. "After all, if you hurt me, Lukyanov doesn't get any information from me."

"Can hurt him though," the bear said, nodding toward Donal with its nose. "Am thinking that this would be most pleasant experience."

"Let's not be hasty there," Donal said, but Edik shushed him.

"Look," Edik said, hoping that Donal's plan was going to work. "Your problem is that all connections with home have been broken, yes?"

"*Da.* And you will be restoring them immediately, or this pretty ship of yours will pay the price."

"I thought you said *I* would," Donal said quickly.

"Am thinking, hurting ship would hurt Barshai more. And am thinking my master does not need Barshai to return, if there is no information to get from him."

The bear nodded.

"Well," Edik said, and he didn't like the way his heart rate jumped up at the overt threat to his ship. If what Donal said about this thing was true — and Donal had no reason to lie — it could probably chew its way through key bindings and wards. Spells that Edik didn't have the reagents to fix out here in the middle of nowhere.

He realized he'd lost his train of thought. Swallowed. And tried again.

"Well," he said, "it's not anything I can help, you see." Edik pointed up. "The Terran Navy has had its ships blockade Ganymede, and that includes cutting the whole moon off from link contact." Edik shook his head grimly. "Apparently that extends to memory circle contact."

"Am thinking you are trying to get me to explore this," the bear said in a considering voice. "Am thinking you hope that once I am outside this ship, you could break this spell before I could stop you. Perhaps you even hope this would dismiss me."

"That *would* dismiss you," Donal said, and Edik could have kicked him. "But that's not the point. We're not trying to do that."

"*Nyet?*"

"Nope," Edik said, refusing to fall back into the old Russian accent he'd had as a child. "We were hoping you could find a way to break through the lines and establish link connection for us."

"Is outside my province," the bear said. "This I cannot do."

"Well," Donal said slowly, as though considering his options. "There is another possibility."

"That being?"

"The locals here are the Du Mak people," Donal said, and Edik did kick him this time. What was that idiot thinking, giving the bear that information? The damage was done, though, so he didn't interrupt as Donal continued. "They have the power to amplify our efforts. If you let us connect one of them to the circle, together we could punch through the link ban and re-establish contact with your master on Luna."

"They have this power?"

"They do," Edik said, before Donal screwed up and told the bear any more about them.

"And why would you do this thing?"

"We've found only enemies here," Edik said with a sigh and more honesty in that sentence than he liked. "We need allies, and we need them badly. I'd prefer even the Lukyanovs to these people."

"Why?"

"Better the devil you know," Edik said. "At least, with the Lukyanovs taking power here, I'd have connections. Resources. This could become a good thing for us after all."

The bear seemed to consider this for a moment.

"Very well. You will bring one of these Du Mak people to me. If I sense such power in them, we will proceed." It raised a paw like it was going to shake a finger, but instead showed several razor-sharp claws. "But do not think to trick me, now."

"Perish the thought," Donal said.

Edik let Donal talk for a moment and reached out with his mind. Tried to find the same feelings, the same sensations, he'd had when he'd been in touch with Cinnamon earlier.

Contact came faster than Edik would have dreamed.

"Sought, I answer you, Edik Barshai."

"Yeah," Edik thought. Or, thought he thought. He wasn't quite sure how this worked, but he tried projecting his thoughts to the Du Mak leader in as coherent a fashion as possible, which for him meant speech.

Agreement with the plan came rapidly.

Almost as rapidly came a pulse at the wards. Not from a single spot on the wards, but all around the wards in a single instance. A pulse strong enough for Donal to raise his eyebrows at Edik, even while Donal was saying something about temporary alliances and no promise or commitment of future work for himself out of this.

Nixia barely showed her pretty face before Edik said, "Show him in."

"Happily, Edik," Nixia said.

A moment later, Cinnamon stood before Edik. One moment he hadn't been there, the next minute he simply … was. No clanging across the deck above. No wrestling a stone body down the access ladder. No signs of effort in any way.

One moment Edik was telling Nixia to admit Cinnamon.

The very next moment, Cinnamon stood right in front of Edik on the deck.

Edik couldn't help himself. He reached out and touched Cinnamon's leg. Solid and cold as shale.

Physically here. Without the hatch being opened. Without crossing the intervening space.

Physically here. Just like that.

That was too much for Edik. His head swirled. His guts roiled. He turned and vomited on the deck. Retched and retched until he was empty.

"Edik?" Donal said, but Dola was already there, nose pressed against Edik's forehead. Soothing him. Calming him.

"Teleportation," Edik muttered. "These Du Mak can actually teleport. Right through wards. Right through walls."

"Hush," Dola said, and Edik knew only he could understand his familiar's words. "Hush. It's all right. They're allies. They've put their trust in us, and they will do their best to aid and work with us. They are allies. We are safe."

Edik felt pale and shaky, and shuddered through a breath that tasted foul as his mouth did right then.

"Right down here," Donal said, gesturing for Cinnamon to take a place near the red-and-yellow bear servitor. "If you agree," he said to the servitor, "we'll pop out the memory circle variant and get to work."

The servitor narrowed its eyes at Cinnamon, then gave a considering nod.

"Much power has this one. Much focus. Am thinking it could do what you say. Could launch power where we focus it. Let us proceed."

Donal gave Edik a sympathetic look that made Edik feel even worse than he already did.

"We don't need Edik for this next part."

"We do," the red bear insisted. "For ensuring this is no trick. All parts of the spell must be present. Includes him."

Dola muttered, "I'll have the undines clean this up."

"Thanks," Edik said.

Donal had already dropped down through the access hatch.

Edik sighed, and dropped down to join him.

WHAT DONAL HADN'T TOLD EDIK, AS THEY'D PREPARED TO GO AFTER the memory circle variant, was that working deception magic on servitors wasn't quite the same as working it on living beings like humans. And it wasn't quite the same as working deception magic on natural spirits like elementals either.

Truth was, every servitor was different. Each had its own qualities, yes, but it had its own emphases as well. If this bear servitor of Magister Lukyanov's were focused on perception the way a true watcher servitor would be designed — or at least the way Donal would design one — then even Donal's best deception spells would probably fail against it.

So Donal hadn't admitted to Edik that he'd been gambling.

While Edik had been leaning down through the access hatch to that room off the drive room, talking to the servitor, Donal had cast three small deception spells.

Little nothings, really, but telling.

The first had been a change to the feel of the air on the deck where Donal and Edik lay down. A slight change to the apparent temperature and moisture level. Like it was almost, but not quite, going to form a mist. Too subtle for Edik to notice, with his focus on the servitor, but if the servitor were perceptive enough, it would spot the spell and wonder what was up.

The servitor did not notice that spell.

The second was almost as subtle, but more directly in the servitor's view. Donal cast an illusion to add subtle strawberry highlights to Edik's blonde hair. Not much, and not enough to draw Edik's attention. It *did* draw Dola's attention, being that it was a spell cast on Edik, but Dola didn't bother with more than a glance to determine what the spell was and whether or not it meant harm to Dola's master.

The servitor did not pay the spell even that much mind.

Donal almost let himself smile then. That the servitor failed to notice a spell cast on Edik was solid information. It was watching its own main target — the memory circle variant — and wasn't concerned about other spells cast on Edik.

Donal had been mostly certain that was the case. After all, the servitor had not bothered to interfere when Donal had tried to interpose a spell between Edik and the memory circle variant.

But that effort had been doomed to failure, what with Edik unable to empty his mind properly. And this time the servitor was out, active, already agitated at the lost connection, and had reason to be suspicious, because of the conversation it was having with Edik.

Still, the servitor did not notice. So much the better.

Finally, Donal cast one more subtle spell. This was an illusion on himself, to make himself appear, to the servitor, to be focused with his magic entirely on the servitor.

If the servitor noticed that this was an illusion and not Donal's true focus, then it should have said something. Should have chided or threatened Donal to keep his magical nose to himself. Or pierced Donal's true point of focus.

True, it might not have done anything, even if it penetrated the deception, because the servitor had already said that Donal was allowed to admire the work of his better — in this case Magister Lukyanov. But it was important for Donal to test this, because while the illusion of his focus had been on the bear servitor, his true focus had been on the threads of spellwork tying Edik to the memory circle variant. And Donal wanted as much study time as he could get before the moment of truth came.

Donal had been looking for the weak point. Hoping against hope that he could find a key spot even a third as vulnerable as he'd found in those wards earlier.

No such luck. The threads were tight, and the spellwork solid.

But then, Donal hadn't really expected this to be so easy. After all, Lukyanov *was* a Magister. He knew his business.

But now the preliminaries were out of the way.

Cinnamon was here.

Donal had been a little distracted by Edik's vomiting, and muttering about teleportation. That latter word was almost enough to suck Donal's focus out of what they were doing and make him start asking questions about how the Du Mak people traveled, and whether the Rhian people could do this as well, and whether or not this was a technique that could be taught to humans.

Donal had suspected that the fae had mastered teleportation. And that the fae were awake, and active, and interbreeding with humanity suggested that human magicians might be able to master the spells of teleportation as well.

After all, if they were similar enough to interbreed, then their magics should be able to accomplish similar feats. Even if the fae did have millennia of additional practice.

But Donal could not allow himself to lose more than a moment's distraction to such thoughts. Such possibilities. Such…

Edik jumped down through the access hatch and landed down in the room below, joined once more by Dola. The red-and-yellow bear servitor was watching Edik closely, as though expecting a trick from him…

Donal almost snickered. But that would have given away the fourth spell he'd cast, back on the deck above. The most subtle of them all, and the one he couldn't afford to spend time thinking about just then, lest he risk it collapsing.

That fourth spell — the first one he'd cast before they even approached the servitor — was a small thing that suggested Donal wasn't subtle enough for subterfuge or deception. That he could manage only straightforward efforts, and was not skilled enough to fool anyone.

Thus, the bear's focus was on Edik, when it should have been on Donal.

And Donal took the extra moment to climb down the ladder to the room below, where Fionn stood to one side. Flanking the servitor, yes, but also out of the way during the preparations.

"All right," Donal said, rubbing his hands together. "Ready, Edik?"

Edik still looked a little "green around the gills," as Donal's mother would have said. But Edik wiped his forehead on his sleeve and nodded.

"Ready, Cinnamon?" Donal said, and the leader of the Du Mak — if they had a leader, really — gave a slow, awkward nod of its serpentine head.

"Servitor? Are you ready as well?"

"*Da*," it said, looking Donal up and down as though seeing him for the first time, "but I am wondering, why is it you are the one asking?"

"Because I'm the ranking magician here, and I'm going to lead the effort to break through the anti-link ward."

"*Nyet*," it said. "This place feels like Barshai from its core to its edges. I am thinking this is his demesne, not yours. You have not challenged for it, so am thinking you are either too weak in will or power to claim it."

Donal almost argued that by reflex, and had to bite his tongue hard enough to hurt, just to keep his mouth shut while the servitor continued.

He could taste the tang of blood.

"And so, as the important spells all involve Barshai, not you, and as this is his demesne, not yours, am thinking he will direct the force here. Not you."

"Donal is a Journeyman," Edik said, and his voice still sounded a little shaky. "I'm just an Initiate. This is my demesne because it's my ship, but I'm willing to let Donal lead this effort."

"Perhaps," the servitor said in a considering voice that echoed slightly in Donal's head, "but I am not. And am thinking this is my decision, or I will believe you are trying to trick me. And this is not a thing you are wanting, *da?*"

"Yes," Edik said through gritted teeth. "But—"

"It's all right, Edik," Donal said. "Fionn and I will stand over here and—"

"*Nyet,*" the servitor said. "You and your familiar will take yourselves from this room. Wouldn't be helping us to distract during important work."

Donal swallowed a little of his blood and tried not to wince from the pain in his tongue. But he managed a smile anyway.

"All right," he said. "Fionn, translate this for our friend, won't you? No doubt he has no reason to understand our little societal foibles."

Edik's eyes darted right to Donal at that, and Donal gave the smallest nod he could manage.

Fionn would let Cinnamon know how this would go down.

Donal made his way back up the access ladder. As he climbed he said, "You know, you could have told me this in advance. Would have saved me a trip down the ladder."

The servitor didn't answer until Donal and Fionn were back on the deck above.

"*Da*," it said, "but you could have not wasted my time with your little illusions too. Journeyman."

The access hatch slammed closed.

DONAL STOOD THERE ON THE DECK. SHOCKED. HE WOULD HAVE SWORN that this servitor had not noticed his deception spells. Would have sworn that its design focus did not include levels of perceptivity necessary to penetrate Donal's stronger spells these days.

His deceptions of a year ago? Of course. Six months ago? Probably.

But today? He wouldn't have believed it.

And yet, here Donal stood. Alone with Fionn, one deck above where Edik was locked up with that bear servitor. Dola was along, which was good, and Cinnamon was with him, which might have been even better.

But Edik didn't have the skill to break that memory circle variant without killing himself in the process. Not even with the added punch that Cinnamon could provide.

And Donal couldn't do it from where he stood. There were wards woven into the deck specifically to cut it off, magically, from the deck below. Safety measures, which would, in theory, protect the crew if the lacuna got loose.

Wards strong enough that Donal couldn't slip past them without shattering them. And shattering them probably had larger consequences than Donal could easily foresee.

"Fionn," Donal said. "What do we do?"

"We trust in Edik," Fionn said. "He'll have to come up with something."

EDIK STARED AT THE CLOSED ACCESS HATCH ABOVE HIM. HIS KNEES STILL felt a little shaky, and he still had more sweat under his collar. And that was just from earlier. Magic had done so many things since Lloyd Bird brought it back, but actual, physical teleportation?

That was more than most people even dreamed of. The potential ramifications were just flat overwhelming. Edik would need time to adjust to that one.

And this latest development — kicking Donal and his familiar out of the room — that had made his breathing shallow, and made his heart rate jump up a bit.

He looked over at Dola, who shook his head.

No ideas there.

"Now," the servitor said, "now we are free of interfering busybodies, and I suggest we see about breaking through the anti-link wards."

"I can't," Edik said. "This is way beyond my skill level. I don't know the first thing about trying to punch through wards. I can barely make my way through them. If I tried to unweave a ward, maybe I could do it in an hour or so. With a simple ward, one I understood."

Edik shook his head.

"But something like this? A complex web woven by multiple Journeymen and maybe some Magisters too?" Edik shook his head again. "We need Donal for this."

The servitor looked over at Cinnamon. And Edik was amazed again at the scent of this strange member of the Du Mak people, who smelled so much like the little bits of cinnamon that Edik's mother had put on his morning toast every day of his childhood. A smell that overrode the lingering scents of alchemy past.

What were the chances that this new species of spirit would smell exactly that way?

But the servitor didn't seem to care about the smell. If it even could smell. It looked the Du Mak over, then nodded.

"You. You have much power, this is true. Much more than even my master, the great Magister Dmitiri Lukyanov, provided to me to perform my tasks. Am thinking you have the power to break through that ward."

"I sense many wards, but suspect that most of those I sense should not be broken. They seem important to Edik Barshai, and they carry his flavor to them."

"*Nyet*. This is different ward. Edik you will show."

"I can't even begin to sense that thing from here. I'm telling you, we need Donal."

"And am telling you that the tricksy magician who loves his glamours is not one we should be trusting." It tilted its head. "And I include you in that, Barshai. You should not trust that one. He is not good for a *russkiy chelovek* like you."

"I think I can pick my own friends just fine," Edik said. "Donal knows more about magic than I'll know if I live to be a hundred."

The bear servitor shook his head.

"*Nyet*. Say not such things. He is a Scottish boy. Or Irish. Something like that. Those Celts will never feel magic in their blood the way your people do. They do not have it in their bones, as your people do. My master, my maker, Magister Dmitri Lukyanov, he knows these things. And he bid me remind you of them, when we were alone."

Edik resisted the urge to spit at the servitor's paws. To remind him that it had been a Celt, not a Russian, who brought magic back to the world.

Edik did possess more than a little pride in his heritage, but every time he had to deal with a great family, that pride went straight out the window.

So instead, he stuck to the subject at hand.

Because Edik had an idea.

"Look," Edik said. "You are attached to this spell in its entirety, right?"

"Which spell?" the servitor said. "We have spoken of so many spells this day."

"The memory circle," Edik said, gnashing his teeth. "The whole point of this."

"*Da*, that. Is not true memory circle, but *da*, I am taking your meaning. And *da*, I am connected to every thread and wisp of its workings, so do not think to trick me into missing anything."

"That's not why I ask," Edik said, cursing inwardly, because he'd been hoping to find a flaw there. Still. "If you're connected to the whole thing, then you can follow the links from me through the circle and all the way to the ward barrier, yes? I mean, right?"

"I can do this," the servitor said slowly, yellowish eyes narrowed in suspicion. "What do you have in mind?"

"You follow the link up to the ward. Find the weak point, maybe even as well as Donal could, if Magister Lukyanov put enough skill into you."

"There is nothing your Celtic friend can do that I could not, as it relates to the provinces provided for me by my master."

Edik frowned as he parsed that.

"So you *can* or *can't* do it?"

"If there is a barrier, preventing this spell from reaching home — and the spell does not reach home, so I trust you are not lying about this — then I could follow the threads of this spell to the barrier that stops it. From there, I could examine the barrier. And *da*, I should be able to find its weakness."

"Excellent. Then you find the weak spot, and Cinnamon here will provide me with enough power to break through it."

Edik hoped Cinnamon would go for his true plan, which was still the same plan he and Donal had held to all along. Provided Edik could make this adjustment to the plan work.

But Edik could not tell anything about Cinnamon's attitude.

The strange creature had only watched the discussion, silently, its serpentine head moving back and forth as though following the interplay with great interest. But with no expression Edik could read.

"And you," the servitor said to Cinnamon, "you promise to aid us in this?"

"I owe my liberty to Edik Barshai. I will aid him as he needs."

The servitor nodded.

"What spell will you use to piece the ward?" the servitor asked.

"That's the part I'm not sure about," Edik admitted. "I'm not exactly a combat magician, and I don't specialize in any of the elements."

"You are of peasant blood, but still, good Russian stock," the servitor said. "What talents have you?"

"I'm good at conjuration," Edik said, gnashing his teeth again.

The servitor hummed as he considered this. "Not much good for this, no. But you have mastered the basics of fire, *da?*"

"I have," Edik said.

"Then I will guide, and this one here will provide the power. You need only provide the framework of a basic fire-calling. You can do this, *da?*"

"Long as we're not talking about manifesting that fire physically, yes."

"Bah," the servitor said, waving a dismissive paw in a gesture that reminded Edik of Alexei Lukyanov.

Edik felt his face smooth with recognition. That accent. The gestures. Dmitri had based this servitor on his father.

Edik had to stifle a chuckle as the servitor continued, "Physical fire is not needful to break wards. Only the element itself. I will find the spot where it will be the most effective."

"Look," Edik said then, taking his big gamble, "this is a big thing. And if we get it wrong, the every one of those ships is going to be coming down on our heads. I need someone to check my work for this. I can't risk a mistake."

"You have familiar."

"Dola, do you know anything about fire magic?"

"I specialize in space magic, Edik," Dola said in smooth tones, as though they'd rehearsed this whole conversation. "You know that."

It was true. It was also true that Dola knew more about every kind of magic than even Donal might. Of course, it was also true that just because Dola *knew* that magic didn't mean Edik had the training, skill or capacity to make it work.

But none of that would matter. Not if Edik played this right.

"Mmmm," the servitor said. "Am not tutor. Cannot help there." He looked at Cinnamon. "What about you?"

The Du Mak shook its head, a slow, swaying back and forth

motion that Edik suspected was an attempt to imitate what it had seen humans do.

"I do not know magic the way you do. My knowledge would not serve you."

"And what is it you want then, Barshai?" the servitor asked in a suspicious tone.

"Open the hatch, so I can discuss the spells with Donal. He'll make sure I don't screw this up."

"I open the hatch, and maybe your friend tries something he shouldn't?"

"I can personally guarantee that Donal won't do anything he shouldn't."

Edik had not spoken truer words this whole trip.

The servitor stared at Edik for a moment.

"You realize," the servitor said, "you try to break this spell and bad things will happen to you."

"And that's part of the reason I'm working with *you* instead of the locals."

The bear nodded.

"Very well," the servitor said, and with a single wave of a paw it opened the hatch again. A casual gesture that performed a greater feat of telekinesis than Edik had ever seen a human perform.

"I am going now," the servitor said, eyes focused through the open hatch and on Donal. "You behave yourself."

And then the servitor vanished.

DONAL JUMPED DOWN THROUGH THE HATCH THE MOMENT THE SERVITOR vanished.

He landed badly. Tweaked his ankle hard enough that he had to hop around on it while the spike of pain settled down.

Edik pulled a knife from his boot. Gave his arm a shallow cut. Wipe the blade in the blood and tossed the knife to Donal.

Donal caught it without thinking. Impressed himself, considering he was still hopping.

But he didn't have time to enjoy the moment.

"We … don't have long…" he said as he hopped. "You … sit."

Edik dropped to sit cross-legged in the middle of the room. Donal hopped over and popped out the memory circle variant, then sat cross-legged next to it. Took blood from the knife blade and drew a small equilateral cross between his eyebrows.

Pain made his heart beat faster, made his breaths shallow.

He had no time for that.

"Edik, make yourself as empty as you can. As fast as you can. Dola, guide him."

Dola immediately pressed his nose to Edik's forehead and began muttering.

"I presume," Cinnamon said, and Donal wondered again why Edik called him that when the creature clearly smelled like fresh-mown grass, "that you still require my assistance?"

"I do," Donal said. He almost said more, but checked his sore tongue. For all he knew, the servitor still had enough connection here to pick up on conversation.

At least it couldn't seem to just pick up on thoughts. Not that Donal had ever met a servitor that could. Thoughts, especially those of a magician, were generally sufficiently held within the magician's mind and natural, personal wards, that picking them up was difficult, even with directed effort.

So Donal's mind was safe enough. Even if Donal's body was just plain having a bad day.

Focusing on the lingering ache in his tongue helped distract him from the pain in his ankle. Provided a neutral point between the crests and valleys of the pain in his body, and Donal leapt his focus straight into that neutral point.

Donal shifted awareness, fled deep into a meditative state. Probably deeper and faster, even now, than poor Edik would accomplish before the whole thing was over one way or the other.

The pain in Donal's tongue vanished. The pain in his ankle followed suit. His heart rate plunged down from its spike, as though hesitating a beat before picking up again at a much slower pace. His breathing slowed through a single, deep inhalation and an even slower exhalation.

Donal brought his mind further and further into itself. Going just as deep as he could, as fast as he could.

Then Fionn eased into Donal's awareness. A point of emerald light right in front of Donal that formed slowly into the familiar shape of the *cú sidhe*. That meant Donal had gotten as deep as was necessary for this.

Donal felt a small thrill at the speed at which he'd attained this speed. The pace of his progress since entering grad school was not lost on him.

But this was no time for celebration. Work first. Party later.

First, Donal connected with the blood on his forehead. Sank into it. Surrounded himself with Edik. Not only Edik's magical signature, but the Edikness underneath it. As deep a link and connection as he could draw, aided by what he had learned about the man through their travels together, and the thaumaturgic work they'd already done together.

Fionn guided Donal out of his resting body and into the spellwork of Magister Dmitri Lukyanov.

Donal remembered this spell well from his first encounter with it. Intricate and clever, the truth was Donal would need a week's study to truly understand the deeper levels of what Magister Lukyanov had done here.

But Donal didn't have that kind of time. And to break the spell, he didn't need that depth of understanding.

First, Donal followed the web of spellwork to the core within Edik himself. There he found the danger zone. Wrapped around Edik's essence — the place that the core of Edik's Edikness bound itself to his physical body — was a series of spikes. And within those spikes lay waiting what seemed to be poison.

It wasn't poison in any conventional sense. But it might as well have been. It was a combination of earth and water that would corrode all the joins between Edik's self and his body. Might be enough to kill him outright. Might even be enough to damage his deeper self in the process.

Some would have called that deeper self the soul. Donal tried not to get that metaphysical about it. What mattered was that within those spikes lay the truest part of Edik, and without them lay the body it was attached to.

Alas, Edik had not managed to empty himself enough to create a gap between the spell and Edik. Wasn't even as absent as last time. Must have been having trouble getting past the pain of his cut.

So in some senses, this was the same situation Donal was in the last time he'd attempted this. Maybe even worse.

But the presence of Cinnamon was a game-changer. Donal hoped.

He began to weave his spell.

This was a difficult one. More complicated than any Donal had tried to weave on his own before. Oh, he had Fionn's immeasurable aid and guidance, but Donal knew that the closest he'd come to this sort of work before had always been following the groundwork laid out by his professors.

Donal had no such guide here.

So he followed his instincts, and his training, and his familiar.

Donal eased air-aspected, air of fire in around those spikes, and then the wiry ribbons of spell that held them in place. He spent an unknown amount of time — for deep in focus as Donal was, time was more of a suggestion than a truly appreciable factor that he could track — going over every place the Magister's spell linked into Edik and preparing his own counterstrike.

And most important, Donal used his blood-and-experience-link to Edik to subtract Edik from the effects of Donal's own spell. No matter how much power Cinnamon shunted through the final structure of Donal's spell, not a single drop would be able to harm Edik on any level.

Might even help shield Edik, if the memory circle variant's attack was swifter than Donal's counterattack.

Next, Donal followed the spell to the memory circle, and laid a fire-aspected, fire of water trap on that end of the connections. That should annihilate the connection at that end, and overwhelm it in a way that it might not trigger the rest.

Donal knew that wasn't likely. Knew that everything on the memory circle variant side of the equation would react too quickly not to trigger the rest.

But if Cinnamon could lend enough power, and Fionn could aid in Donal's speed, and if Donal had gotten his spells right, then this might work.

"Donal," Fionn warned, "it returns."

"Almost done," Donal answered.

Donal projected part of his attention at Cinnamon…

…and almost got overwhelmed.

The mind of this Du Mak. It was ancient. Powerful. It … it was like no other mind Donal had contacted. Fionn was old. Donal knew that. Centuries old. But still, it wasn't the same thing. Not remotely. Fionn, in this world, was part of Donal. So however ancient Fionn might have been, the spells and alchemy that created the familiar bond shielded Donal from direct exposure to that age.

With Cinnamon, there was no shelter.

This was a mind so vast and deep Donal almost got lost just within its orbit, not even within the mind itself.

Donal understood in that moment how ancient magicians first came to worship spirits. If Donal had had less of a sense of self, less faith in the gods of his forefathers perhaps, he would likely have fallen to his knees before so mighty a force.

And this was what those idiots wanted to *own?* To claim as their possessions, as though the Du Mak people were just so many inert rocks?

Anger flared in Donal's belly at just the thought of it. And that anger gave Donal focus. Helped bring him back to himself. To remember the purpose of reaching for that vast, ancient mind.

"Aid me now," Donal said.

"You or yours?" Cinnamon said. "Choose."

Donal didn't understand the question. Didn't have time to ask for clarity, not if the servitor was on its way back. Donal needed to break the spell before the servitor had the chance to stop him.

"Me," he said. And the moment he said it he felt a swell of power.

Power flooded through him. Buoyed him. Almost, again, enough to make him lose focus.

But Donal had been working on focus for months. And even though he now felt more power flowing through him than he had ever dreamed of before, he held to his focus and his goal.

Fionn was not here to help Donal. Must have been distracting the servitor on its way back.

Donal channeled every minute drop of that power into his spells. More than enough to trigger both at once. And with Edik shielded from the effects of Donal's spell, he had no problem over-flaring them, wiping away the Magister's work for an area around the spell itself, in case the contingencies activated separate effects.

And they did. But Donal's design had been clever, and the Du Mak's power immense.

The memory circle variant flared for a moment, and then was no more.

Donal opened his eyes.

Fionn lay bleeding citrine blood onto the white ceramic deck before him.

"Fionn!" Donal yelled, jumping to his feet. But his ankle was still twisted and swollen, and Donal fell right across his familiar.

Fionn winced in pain.

Donal began to take in more of the scene, just through the edges of his perception.

Dola lay likewise on the floor, and his blood flowed cerulean like his eyes. Edik was curled up against his familiar's back, whispering softly, eyes squeezed tight.

"No time for that," Donal said. "Bring me mugwort, chamomile, rubber tree resin and thyme."

Edik stared at Donal, unseeing.

"Now!" Donal snapped, and that impelled Edik into motion.

Meanwhile, Donal shifted awareness again. Synchronized himself with the labored breathing of his beloved familiar.

"Easy there," Donal said. "Didn't think anything could hurt you that way."

"Had … to buy … you time," Fionn said, and he sounded even weaker than he looked.

The poor *cú sidhe* couldn't have been fully healed from its efforts on the trip here. And now this. Donal shunted small amounts of power through his connection to the familiar. Just little bits, enough that even in his current state, Fionn would be able to direct to try to begin healing himself.

"Pretty bad," Fionn said.

In the corridor above him, Donal could hear Edik tearing through his alchemical supplies. Swearing as he went.

"Nothing worse than I've come back from," Donal said, though he wasn't sure it was true. "And you've always helped me heal. You know I'll do the same for you."

Fionn tried to say something else, but Donal shushed him.

Fed him more power. Then tried feeding a little to Dola, but it didn't reach. Not the way it needed to.

"Do you know anything about healing?" Donal asked Cinnamon.

"My own kind, yes. But these spirit creatures, I do not."

"Here," Edik said, jumping back down into the room with more aplomb than Donal had managed. "Can you help Dola too? I … I…"

"Stop," Donal said, going for a schoolteacher tone. "We can heal them, but we have to act fast. Do you have two mortars and pestles?"

Edik nodded. Handed Donal a white granite mortar and pestle from the box he carried. Dug a black granite version from a pop-up drawer in the wall.

Donal began instructing Edik in how to grind the herbs for this. The order was important, as was the degree of grinding. Then there was the adding of blood, and sweat, and finally tears to the mixture.

It was a slow process, but having someone else to lead through it made the whole thing more manageable for Donal. He didn't have the mental room to worry about Fionn. Not when he was leading someone else through such important alchemical work. Not to mention the spells that the alchemy would support.

It wasn't quite as involved as summoning Fionn had been in the first place. But it wasn't far off.

They got to the final spells within fifteen minutes. A testament to the focus of both men, as well as the love both men had for their familiars.

But finally, the wounds closed on both *cú sidhe* and cat. Donal immediately ordered Fionn into his silver faun pendant to rest. Edik did likewise with his own familiar.

And then the two men were alone in that room.

The lacuna in the drive bay — which Donal only now realized had been eerily silent through all of this — began to trill out a low, seven note disharmony that spoke of loss and longing.

"Fuck you," Donal muttered. "Fionn's going to live."

"You … understand that?" Edik asked.

"No," Donal admitted, "but doesn't it sound—"

"Trust me," Edik said, "the sound to us has nothing to do with whatever it's saying."

Both men sat still for a moment, listening. It still sounded to Donal like a lament.

He looked down at the white ceramics of the deck. Only minutes ago, Fionn's citrine blood had seemed to pool there. But now not so much as a tacky spot. As though the *cú sidhe's* blood were even less substantial than the emerald deerhound himself.

"Did it just vanish?" Donal asked. "Or did it fade away?"

"The bear?" Edik asked. "It vanished all at once. Same moment I felt like something let go of my heart. If that makes any sense."

"That was just when the spell broke," Donal said. "I'm talking about the blood. Fionn's blood."

"I'm not sure they really bleed," Edik said. "Not the way we do. More like a leak of their vital energies."

Donal thought about that for a moment.

"Think they'll heal up all right in their houses?" Edik asked, and his tone begged for reassurance.

"Of course," Donal said, and he was telling the truth. Or at least, what he believed was the truth. "We got to them in time with the right reagents, and the right spells."

Donal looked over at Edik.

"You weren't wrong about your specialization. Most Initiates try to boast a specialization, but most can't actually handle the requirements of one. You're good at this kind of magic. Good enough that you could make Journeyman, at least. If you wanted to."

"Screw it," Edik said, and leaned back against a bulkhead. "Flying a ship is a hell of a lot more fun than anything I've ever done that involved magicians and formal thaumaturgy."

Donal almost objected. But then he thought about how many times he'd he'd come to death just in the last two years.

"You may have a point," he said.

"Want to sign on?" Edik said with a tired smile. "Could use a first mate, I start taking longer voyages like this."

Donal only smiled back.

"Didn't think so," Edik said. "You're magician through and through."

Donal nodded, slowly.

His ankle hurt. His tongue hurt. His heart was still beating too fast with worry over Fionn, even though, if Donal knew what he was doing — and he devoutly believed he did — the *cú sidhe* should be fine in a couple of days.

Donal felt strung out and exhausted. He could have closed his eyes right there and slept for at least a week. So much intense spellwork, so very quickly. Then there was the sheer volume of power he'd shunted through himself. Power from…

Donal realized then that Cinnamon still stood there, having watched the whole thing.

"Um," Donal said.

Edik looked up. He looked as exhausted and spent as Donal felt.

"Cinnamon," Edik said with a smile, as though he'd forgotten the

Du Mak was there too. "Thank you for everything you've done for us today. You're a lifesaver. Literally."

"They fought for you," Cinnamon said. "At risk to their own lives. In more ways than I believe you understand. They spilled themselves, for you."

Donal wasn't sure about the "more ways" part, but he was so tired he could only nod anyway. Edik did the same.

"But their doing so hurt you as well. The tears you shed…"

Donal marveled that the Du Mak understood tears.

"…the desperation of your effort to save them."

Donal didn't know what to say to that. He could only stare at the serpentine head of the Du Mak leader.

"You are bound to them, but there is more. There is love."

"Of course," Donal said, as though that were the most obvious thing in the whole waking world. And it may well have been.

Edik said the same thing, in not far from the same tone.

The Du Mak nodded, albeit slowly and awkwardly.

"Good information for me to have." Cinnamon looked from Donal to Edik. "Is there more you wish of me?"

"Nothing I can think of right now. Donal?"

Donal only shook his head.

Cinnamon walked over to Edik. Brought his long tail around and dropped its tip into Edik's lap. Cinnamon then walked over to Donal and did the same thing, though Donal was ready to catch his.

A perfect oval of greenish brown shale, no longer or wider than Donal's thumb.

Donal didn't even need to shift his awareness to sense that this stone was still connected to Cinnamon as perfectly as though it yet remained the tip of his tail.

Donal's jaw dropped as Cinnamon swayed to the center of the room. Looked over a Edik.

"Call on me if you have need." Cinnamon looked over at Donal. "You as well."

And then the Du Mak simply vanished.

No flare of power. No show of light. No matrix of spell that Donal could perceive, not in the least.

And yet it was gone.

"Teleportation," Donal said, wonder in his voice.

"Scary," Edik said. "Isn't it."

Donal didn't think it was scary. He thought it was full of marvelous potential. Potential he would love to explore.

But that didn't matter now. Not compared to something else.

"Edik," Donal said, "what happened with the bear?"

"It came roaring back into the room. Charging at you. Screaming about betrayal." Edik shook his head. "Fionn interposed. Began to fight it. Dola too, before I could even tell him to do it or not."

"They knew what was at stake," Donal said.

"Damn near got themselves killed. Never seen anything claw and bite so fast as that bear."

But then Edik smiled. "Gotta say though. Fionn and Dola made a pretty damned good team, fighting together."

Donal shared that smile.

"How long you think they'll be out of it?" Edik asked.

"Couple of days, at least," Donal said. "Maybe more."

Edik blew out a slow breath.

"Well," Donal said, "I want a year of either sleep or a meditation and I don't care which."

"You don't have it," Edik said. "In fact, Nixia?"

The lemon yellow sylph manifested in front of Edik.

"Yes, Edik?"

"I told you to tell me when our hour is up. How much longer do we have?"

"You don't," she said. "I didn't want to interrupt you as you healed Dola, nor spoke to the Du Mak *Li-Shan*."

"*Li-Shan?*" Edik asked.

"Yes," Nixia said. "I didn't catch his name, but I could tell his title from his bearing."

"You've met the Du Mak before?"

"I did exist before I heard your call, Edik."

Nixia looked coy, pleased to have secrets. No real surprise to Donal there. Most air spirits had long memories and many secrets. If she had experience with these Du Mak, though, she might be able to answer a few important questions though…

Wait. Had she said their hour was up?

"Our hour's up?" Donal said. "They'll be looking for us soon then."

"Actually," Nixia said, "there are several people gathering outside the ship right now."

9

Edik glanced out the porthole of the *Third Son's* main cabin and saw exactly the group that Nixia had told him about. Three settlers — men in dull green outfits, and from what Edik had seen, the color implied that they carried slingers — and three fit young men in the red jumpsuits of Zeus Industries.

Six total. No leaders. Edik wasn't sure what to make of that, but he made sure his saber was loose in its scabbard. Just in case.

Edik risked a glance back at Donal. Donal was only now finishing up the ham-and-cheese sandwich Edik had forced on him. The kid looked even more strung out and tired than Edik felt, and Edik felt as though he'd *towed* his ship all the way to Ganymede.

He'd even wolfed down his own sandwich. And that was just this side of criminal. A waste of good Terran ham, spicy mustard, and real California cheddar, all on good wheat bread.

At least they lingered on his tongue, especially the mustard.

But Edik hadn't had time to heat any borscht. And he knew both he and Donal needed to eat. They needed all the strength they could manage on this day that wouldn't end.

How long had he and Donal been awake when they first flew past the picket lines?

Edik wasn't even sure anymore.

And the hours in between now and then had stretched with too much information and too much effort. Fatigue was starting to become a real factor for both of them. And this time, neither would have his familiar to help.

But further delays weren't a practical option.

"Ready?" Edik asked.

Donal nodded.

That too worried Edik. The kid wasn't saying any more than he absolutely had to. Hadn't since the healing ritual. And if Donal's behavior on the flight here had been any indication, the kid only ever shut up when he was meditating.

Could he have been…

No.

No way the kid could be meditating as he stood there.

Or could he?

If so, that would have explained so much about the way Jones carried himself sometimes. And the tireless way he always seemed to have all of his magic at his disposal…

"All right," Edik said though a deep breath. "Here we go."

Edik opened the passenger hatch.

"Hey boys," he said with a smile. "And it is all boys, isn't it. What, afraid to let your girls near a couple of sexy guys like us?"

"Time to go, Barshai," said a man in a red jumpsuit. He looked a little bulkier than the other two. And he had a symbol on his cuffs that the other two lacked.

A lightning bolt.

Likely an executive of some sort then.

"And you are…" Edik said, still standing inside his own ship's wards.

"Michelson," he said. "That's enough for you."

"Well, Michelson," Edik said, "a surname alone may be enough for someone like you" — Edik made a show of looking the man up and down and being unimpressed — "but I am a helioship captain, and I expect the respect my position is due."

"Right," Michelson said with a scowl. "*Captain* Barshai. Time to get a move on, *Captain*, sir. The others are waiting, but they won't wait much longer."

"Donal," Edik said, then swept a hand in a grand gesture to let Donal precede him, so Edik could seal the wards behind them.

"You don't have to bother," said one of the guys in green. "Gonza-lez-Villarreal said no one touches you or yours. At least, not until this is settled."

"Ah," Edik said through a smile he didn't feel, "but her word doesn't speak for Zeus Industries, does it?"

"It does," the man in green said, at the same time that Michelson said, "It doesn't."

They turned glares on each other.

This had real possibilities.

"Have your pissing contest later," Donal said. "I think you're here to escort us to your betters."

That got a sincere smile out of Edik.

"Right you are, Donal," he said. Then to Michelson, he added, "Let's get a move on. They won't wait forever, I hear."

Michelson grumbled something, but the group fell into an odd formation, for an escort party. Michelson and the loudmouth in green up front, then the two others in green flanked Edik and Donal, and then the two others in red took up the rear.

Edik wished Dola was here to watch his back. He had to settle for glances backward.

Donal didn't settle. He stopped ten paces into their journey.

"This won't work," he said. "The Zeus Industries men have to be where we can see them."

"Don't trust us?" Michelson said with a nasty smile.

"Not a bit," Donal said, completely deadpan.

Michelson's humor died, leaving only an even nastier look on his face. He opened his mouth, and Edik had been sure Michelson was about to say "too bad" but the leader from the settlers said, "Make the damned switch. I don't want to be late because you can't control your men."

Michelson whirled on him so fast Edik thought they'd come to blows right then.

Donal interrupted them.

"I said, 'pissing contest later,'" he said. "Weren't you listening?"

Michelson flushed bright red. The man in green only gritted his teeth, turned, and started marching.

The group fell into step behind him. Even Edik and Donal, though Edik had to fight himself not to go out-of-step just to spite them. That wasn't a fight worth having, not with those two obviously bickering among themselves.

But the Zeus Industries men were all where Edik and Donal could see them now. And that was what mattered as they made their way across the compound to the Zeus Industries building. Edik was sure that Gonzalez-Villarreal wouldn't give up her moral high ground by letting any of her people go back on her word. No matter how mad she might have been at the way Edik tricked her.

The Zeus Industries building looked just like all the other temporary constructions around here. More or less. Clearly it had been built from the same kind of system. Conical and ceramic, heavy on the alchemy.

There were differences though. This one was taller. Must have had four stories, with a ring of windows at every level. Edik guessed the layout was storage, offices, and living quarters, in that order, above the ground floor cafeteria and breakroom level.

Also, this cone was bright red. Scarlet, like the jumpsuits of its workers in this place.

The final difference: it had the Zeus Industries flag flying atop it.

More differences, as they entered the building.

This interior wasn't all white. The ceiling and floor were still that white ceramic, but the wall were muted tomato red. A much better match for Gonzalez-Villarreal's clothes than the scarlet of the jumpsuits. But then, Edik figured that bright a red might have been too much to live inside every day.

The layout wasn't all bench tables either, and it wasn't all one room outside the kitchen.

Kitchen was in the same place — the back, on the left — but there was another private room mirroring it on the right. Between the front door and those rooms, four double-length bench tables for the rank and file to eat at. Those were off to the left.

Off to the right, a few game tables. Pool. Ping pong. A large shadow play display to keep up on the latest in Terran entertainment. And finally, a holographic game table.

They lived pretty well, out here on the rim.

In the exact middle of the ground floor level, the bubble tube. No stairs or access ladders for these guys. Edik didn't like bubble tubes. Seemed unfair, to just bind a handful of undines to do nothing but carry a steel cage up and down all day, every day, for the foreseeable future.

And the poor air elemental bound in the middle there, all on its own, providing the bubble of air that kept all gear and passengers dry. Not to mention allowing the passengers to breathe.

Unfair. Too many spirits for such a simple job. Telekinesis might have been one of the most difficult things to accomplish, much less to preserve movement spells through alchemy, but there had to be a way...

Edik shook himself to bring his focus back.

Three exits from this room. The front door, the kitchen — which might have a delivery access in the back — and the bubble. He didn't count the other small room, because Edik figured it didn't have an exit.

There were windows, yes, but Edik knew from experience that they were nothing but the same grade of hull ceramic used for portholes on helioships. Not breakable into exits.

Edik already began to feel trapped here. He should never have agreed to meet in this place. Not with the Terran Navy playing a role. And the unknown people on the *Silver Streak*.

This was a bad idea.

Edik reached into his pocket for the tiny piece of Cinnamon. Just holding it made him feel better. Reminded him why he was putting himself at such risk.

"Where is everybody?" Edik said, before the party had crossed half of the cafeteria. "If we're going up, mind if we take the stairs? I object to bubbles on principle."

That got a curious look from Donal, but Edik gave a quick shake of his head, lest the kid ask one of his ill-timed questions.

Michelson stopped walking so abruptly that the loudmouth in green continued until Michelson started talking.

"See that door over there?" Michelson pointed to the room at the back. The room that likely had no other exits. "Everyone who matters is there. And for some reason, they decided to include a couple of nothings in their deliberations. So shut the fuck up and do what you're told."

Edik felt his jaw clench. His right hand longed for the hilt of his saber. Nobody had the right to talk to him that way. Certainly not some little…

Donal started laughing. Not aggressive laughter either, but whole-hearted, sincere laughter. As though this were a laugh Donal had been needing for days. It might have been the biggest, best laugh Edik had heard from Donal in the entire week-plus of their acquaintance.

Everyone stared at Donal. Well, everyone but the loudmouth in green, who stared at Michelson as though trying to shoot fireballs out of his eyes.

Michelson opened his mouth to speak, but Donal spoke first and louder, as though he'd been waiting for that.

"You know," he said, "one of the first lessons taught me by Donatello Mancuso — maybe you've heard of him, he runs all of *4M* — was that anyone who feels the need to call someone a nobody, *is* a nobody."

Michelson's mouth closed.

Donal frowned. Shook his head. Looked over at Edik. "I'll never get that man's quotes right. He has this *way* of talking that I just can't imitate, you know?"

Edik didn't know what to say. He felt just as flabbergasted as the rest of these schlubs must have that Donal was on speaking terms with the CEO of a gigantic interplanetary corporation like 4M. 4M was so big it made the Romanov Company look like a tiny, local concern.

"Come on, Edik," Donal said. "Everyone's waiting."

And then Donal did the last thing Edik expected. He looked around at all of these guards and dismissed them with a wave of his hand.

"The rest of you can go. You've done your job."

Donal started walking. Edik hopped to fall into step with him.

DONAL OPENED THE DOOR TO THE LITTLE ROOM, AND SAW PRETTY MUCH what he'd expected to see.

Rectangular room around a rectangular table. Four chairs to a side and one at each end. Executive style chairs, with extra padding and alchemical twists to their feet, so they could slide easily, but not too easily. The chairs were done in dark gray with rich, brown cushions. The style currently in vogue with movers and shakers throughout the planets.

The room itself was more eggshell white than the almost mayonnaise white of typical ceramics. And the reds in here had a little more depth and character. Closer to cardinal.

After all, this was a room for executives.

Private bubble in the back corner, only big enough for two to stand in comfortably.

And seated at the rich, varnished oak table? Just about the mix of people Donal expected to be at an executive gathering, now that he thought about it.

Thinking of Donatello Mancuso — and Donal had worked hard in his own head to stop calling him *Mr.* Mancuso, at the man's own insistence — back in the cafeteria room had done wonders to settle Donal. Donal'd had quiet chats with him at least a dozen times since Donal helped free him from Li Hua's intricate mental control. Chats about people, about leadership, about Donal's own future. Donal'd been to the man's chateau in the south of France, his estate in Mazatlán, his mansion in Kennedy.

And Donal had watched as Donatello Mancuso casually handled dozens of dignitaries and spontaneous business emergencies.

Donal might not have had the man's experience nor his apparent natural flare for leadership, but Donal had been learning all he could.

So Donal expected to see a Terran Navy captain, seated at one end of the table, flanked by a pair of commanders. The captain had the smooth look of a man who had never done his fighting hand-to-hand. He lacked the set to his eye and jaw, or any visible scarring, that Donal had seen in other men of action. His commanders were a different matter. They were hard men, both older than their captain — graying and lined, while his hair was as smooth and his skin youthful.

Seated at the other end of the table — which was the head of the table and which the foot not doubt depended on which man you asked — was Nicholson. And he was flanked by two, standing, flunkies.

A show of guards instead of advisors. Donatello Mancuso said that meant the man was small on the inside. Someone to push around when you were in a position of strength. From an apparently inferior position, though, he could be agitated into making a critical mistake.

Sitting alone on one long side of the table, just the Zeus Industries side of the exact center, was Gonzalez-Villarreal.

No aides or guards for her. That was probably Nicholson's doing. Likely set her up by claiming that he wasn't going to have aides, so neither should she, and then bringing guards to give him backing while holding to literal truth.

Donal could almost hear the man thinking that he was reminding Gonzalez-Villarreal who was *really* in charge here.

But Gonzalez-Villarreal sat with quiet confidence all the same. Yes, there was still that fire in her eyes, but it held a background position now. She didn't need it in the foreground, and she was clever enough not to bring it out until she needed it.

Of all the local power players here, Donatello Mancuso would probably say that she was the most dangerous. Nicholson was too small inside, and the captain would be too guided by regulations and orders to have real flexibility.

Of course, Donal could imagine Captain John Jacobs — the only helioship captain Donal had known before Edik, and a man with more years in the navy than the three men in this room combined — disagreeing with Donatello Mancuso on that point.

Donal would try to keep both perspectives in mind here.

He needed allies in this room. Or at least, he needed to figure out who the enemies were, and set them against each other.

Donal knew that Edik would call all of these people enemies. Donal didn't want to do that. Not if he didn't absolutely have to.

There had to be some better way here than pure opposition.

Of course, the answer might be in whoever had flown in aboard the *Silver Streak*. That person was still not present.

"About time you got here," Nicholson said. "Grab a seat and let's get started."

The captain placed a call disc on the table and slapped it. It glowed bright red. Wherever its twin was, it would glow bright red as well — and likely a little warm — informing whoever had it that they were being summoned.

Donal didn't wait. He took a seat opposite Gonzalez-Villarreal. Edik sat beside him, sliding his chair just enough to let him draw his sword, if he had to.

The movement drew the captain's eyes to Edik's weapon.

"I object to the presence of a weapon at these proceedings," the captain said.

"Then we should ask those two to leave as well," Gonzalez-Villarreal said, gesturing blandly at the two men standing behind Nicholson. "For that matter, as the three of you gentlemen are combat-trained, I could object to your presence for the same reason."

Nicholson and the captain both started to speak. Gonzalez-Villarreal spoke over them.

"By the same logic, I could object to the presence of Donal Cuthbert, as a magician, and you could both object to my presence for the selfsame reason."

She faked a smile at Nicholson, the captain, and then Donal and Edik.

"What say we just accept the situation and move on. Captain Barshai here has reason to feel uncomfortable after the reception he just got, and I bet that letting him keep his sword will ease his mind, and make this whole discussion a little better."

Edik nodded.

Donal fought not to smile. Battle lines drawn then, apparently.

Donal noted, during that little exchange, that no one present was carrying anything that could be construed as a combat enchantment. In fact, apart from familiar houses, the only spelled object in the room at all was in the closed hand of the captain.

The bubble arrived, its cage opened, and out stepped Natalia Romanova.

DONAL HADN'T SEEN NATALIA ROMANOVA SINCE THAT VOYAGE TO Venus, and she didn't appear to have changed a bit. Perhaps a decade older than Donal, she was, and tall — maybe a centimeter or two taller than Donal — with her pale blonde hair flowing loose down below her shoulders. Her features were sharp as a raptor. On another woman they might be too severe, but her poise made her beautiful.

Though her eyes were cold and blue as ice chips.

She wore a dress of deep, forest green, trimmed in gold, with a gold sash at her waist that bore her family crest. No other jewelry for her though.

Donal wasn't sure whether or not to be surprised she was here. Or that she was the one in the *Silver Streak*. Edik didn't look surprised. And Donal, well, once he'd heard that one great family of Luna was involved in this, how surprised could he be that another got involved as well.

"Natalia," Donal said, with a nod that got him a glare from Edik.

"Donal," she said with a broad smile as she strode to the chair on the navy side of Gonzalez-Villarreal and took it. "Good to see you again. I trust Donatello is doing right by you? I understand he makes time to see you whenever he is on Earth."

"I don't know that I'd go that far," Donal said, "but he's been as generous with his time as he has been with his money."

"I should think so. If you ever performed a service so great for the Romanov family, your future would be guaranteed." She smiled broadly. "I am so pleased to see that you are the Cuthbert who is present, and not your brother."

Donal ignored the open-mouth gaze of Nicholson, the calculating looks of the captain and his commanders, and Edik's outright hostile glare.

"Oh," Donal said, forcing his tone to stay light. Donatello Mancuso had always told him that looking in control of any situation was almost as important as *being* in control of any situation. And the one often led to the other. "Do you know Bran?"

"I have not yet had the pleasure of his acquaintance," she said, "and please do not take my words as a dismissal of your brother. By his reputation, he is as skilled and honest as you are. But given a choice, I always prefer to deal with someone I've met before."

"Even someone you've tried to kill in the past?" Probably not Donal's most politically astute line, but he was getting tired of Edik's glare.

"Fah," Natalia Romanova said, waving a dismissive hand. "That is past and forgotten."

Donal couldn't help smiling at that.

"The incident on Luna, yes. But it hasn't been two weeks since your *Silver Streak* tried to blow us out of the sky."

"A simple misunderstanding," she said, waving her hand again. "Had I known you were aboard the *Third Son* I would never have permitted my men to open fire."

"So you *were* trying to kill *me*," Edik said, anger rumbling through his voice.

"Not at all," Natalia Romanova said, blinking as though shocked at such a proposal. "I merely wished to see your ship disabled. I do grow tired of your feeble attempts to interfere in Romanov family business."

"Why you—"

"Now, speaking of people I know," she continued, and Donal marveled at the way she both ignored Edik's attempt at a threat *and* seized control of the meeting at the same time, "Commodore Sarandon I know, of course." She favored him with a smile, but never cast her eyes at his commanders. "And Mr. Nicholson who does not like to give his first name, I know you from our conversation earlier."

If she expected Nicholson to provide his first name there, she was mistaken. Donal wondered if he was concerned about the potential magical uses of his name. Donal could have told him that the name alone was not enough, not in any current system Donal knew of.

"But you," Natalia Romanova said, turning to Gonzalez-Villarreal right next to her, "you I do not know, but I presume you are in charge of this settlement?"

"I am," Gonzalez-Villarreal said. "And my name is Rosita Gonzalez-Villarreal."

"A pleasure," Natalia Romanova said, shaking hands with her briefly. "Now, I believe we are ready to start, yes?"

"What," Edik said, and Donal was impressed at how clearly his words came out, considering that Edik was grinding his teeth so loudly, "insults for me, but no greeting?"

"Oh, Barshai," Natalia Romanova said through a laugh, "I do not waste words on advisors or thugs."

Edik looked ready to go for his sword, but Donal nudged him and said, "*Captain* Barshai is here as the man currently in charge of the first contact protocols in this matter. He's claimed the right of oversight. So he is at least as important to these proceedings as you are."

"Doubtful," Natalia Romanova said, "but as you would have it."

"Now," said Captain Sarandon — or rather, Commodore Sarandon — "shall we begin?"

"Of course," Gonzalez-Villarreal said before Natalia Romanova could.

These two might be something to watch. But Donal couldn't afford to let either one of them take control here. He needed it hold it as long as he could. Or at least, to seize control when it mattered most.

"So," Nicholson said. "I think the question before us is why the military, some corporation from Luna, and uninvolved civilians seem to think they have the right to stick their noses in our business."

He pulled out a memopad and slapped it on the table. It displayed some official-looking document.

"Here's our license to be here, and you'll find it confirms that we own all mineral rights to this moon."

"You don't," Gonzalez-Villarreal countered. "You bought that permission from Mars, and Mars has no legitimate claim to Ganymede."

"Mars is a free and independent planet," Nicholson said, with a nasty smile. "Their claim to Ganymede is every bit as legitimate as Earth's. And they have just as much right to sell us the mineral rights, as Earth has to let you settle here."

"One difference," Commodore Sarandon said in a smooth baritone and raising a single finger. "Earth *is* a free and independent planet. Mars is a *colony*."

"Mars says they're free," Nicholson countered.

"Earth says they aren't," Commodore Sarandon said, "and Earth has ships there right now, reminding Mars who's in charge."

"But this needn't be a question of governmental rights," Natalia Romanova said in a soothing tone. "Surely you can all see how much there is here for all to benefit from."

"What is she doing here?" Nicholson asked. "Zeus Industries does not recognize the Romanov Group's right to interfere in this matter."

"Interfere?" Natalia Romanova said, waving a hand to still the protest of Commodore Sarandon. "Why, I was invited by Earth to come facilitate negotiations."

"Is that why you tried to shoot your way down to the planet?" Gonzalez-Villarreal said.

"Oh, that little display?" Natalia Romanova said though a laugh.

"Nothing worth mentioning. Once Admiral Fulbush's communique came in, all was settled."

"It's true," Commodore Sarandon said, and Donal thought that the man's tone meant that he didn't believe it either. "She's officially here as an envoy of Earth."

"She's not even *from* Earth," Edik said. "She's from Luna."

"Oh, Barshai," she said, laughter still in her voice, "you can't be so naïve that you believe I don't have holdings and ties on Earth."

"*You* don't have anything," Edik said. "Your *family* does." He smiled evilly. "That's right. Lukyanov spilled the beans. Your father is still alive and still has the official say-so on all your family business."

"My dear father is resting comfortably, and I thank you for asking after his health," Natalia Romanova said, though Donal didn't think that's what Edik had done. "As for my role, you'll find that dear Alexei's information is sadly out of date. Or, perhaps, he was fooling with you. I am officially in charge of the Romanov Group now."

"But—" Nicholson tried to interrupt, but Natalia Romanova spoke over him.

"But," she said, "I am not here in that capacity. I'm here as a facilitator only."

"I find that hard to believe," Edik grumbled.

"*Captain Barshai*," Commodore Sarandon barked, and Donal was impressed by the steel in the man's voice. Perhaps there was a reason he was the ranking captain on Ganymede. "She's already said why she's here, and *I've* confirmed it. Believe me if you won't believe her."

"It doesn't matter," Donal said quietly.

His heart was pounding. He was trying a trick he'd learned from his leadership mentor, and he'd never done it before. He almost pushed out more words. Almost tried to make everyone look at him by explaining and explaining until they all surrendered.

But no, his quiet words had done just what Donatello Mancuso had told him they would.

Everyone was looking at him.

Including Edik, though Edik looked more surprised than curious.

"It doesn't matter why she's here," Donal said. "She *is* here. Just as you're here" — Donal gestured to Nicholson and then to Gonzalez-Villarreal — "and you're here" — Donal gestured to the naval officers — "and most important of all, *I'm* here."

"You're here as a courtesy," Commodore Sarandon said, "to Hierophant Nicholas Mason, who managed to get your name on a list controlled by the no less than the Magician of the United North American States. And I'd like to know how you managed that, but what matters is that you are here as an observer. Nothing more."

"No," Donal said, struggling to keep his tone quiet. "I am here as the official representative of the Fae Courts. And the Fae Courts officially recognize the Du Mak people as cousins of the court and claim jurisdiction over their welfare."

The room grew so silent Donal could hear not just his own heartbeat, but Edik's, and quite possibly Gonzalez-Villarreal's.

"Ridiculous," Nicholson said. But he was the only one who said it.

Gonzalez-Villarreal narrowed her eyes at Donal. Natalia Romanova tilted her head, thoughtfully, a smile playing around her lips that never approached her eyes. No doubt trying to decide how to factor this information into her own plans.

But Commodore Sarandon shook his head.

"I must agree with the representative of Zeus Industries," Commodore Sarandon said, but his tone was careful. "We have no reason to believe that the Fae Courts are anything but folklore."

Donal's eyebrows rose at the phrasing of that denial. That sounded to him like an *official* denial of something the Commodore believed was a secret.

Donal drew a deep breath, and tugged on the power he held coiled within himself at all times these days. When he did, he saw Gonzalez-Villarreal's eyes widen.

"I, Donal Cuthbert, certified and licensed Journeyman and certified Doctoral candidate, swear upon my power that I was met in the San Luis Obispo spaceport by a representative of the Fae Courts, whose identity and role were vouched for by no lesser witness than my own familiar, a registered *cú sidhe*, or fae hound. I further swear that this representative offered me the position of official emissary for the Fae Courts in this matter. A position I accepted. By twig and by stone, by blood and by bone, I am their eyes, their ears, and their voice in this place."

Donal heard at least three breaths drawn in to interrupt, but he spoke louder and finished what he started.

"These things I swear by the Dagda, by the Morrigan, and by Lugh."

His words gained the echo of his power as he released the oath.

"Do something," Gonzalez-Villarreal said into the sudden silence. "Anything. I can swear that I just witnessed an oath of true magic, but right now you need to prove its worth in front of non-magicians."

Donal drew again on his power, centered it through a breath, and called on the element of fire. He gathered together his sense of fire. Channeled it onto the palm of his right hand. Used the power he'd gathered to open a connection to pure elemental fire.

Muttering to himself in Gaelic, Donal channeled that pure element, and released its power as visible light, pure and blue as the heart of a flame.

The heatless fire crackled on Donal's palm.

Gonzalez-Villarreal whistled. The others at the table — except Edik, who was watching them the way Donal did — all sat back in their chairs in shock.

"You're all witnesses," Gonzalez-Villarreal said. "As a licensed Journeyman I confirm and verify that I witnessed his oath on his power. And all of you are witnesses that he still has power."

She drew a deep breath and said, "Now we need to figure out what it means."

EDIK WANTED TO LAUGH OUT LOUD. HE WANTED TO SING AND DANCE around. He knew that Donal was here as a fae emissary, but he hadn't realized what exactly that meant, or what Donal would do with his position.

Edik half-chided himself that he should have known.

Still, Edik reveled in the chaos Donal had wrought.

At one end of the table, Nicholson was ranting so hard spittle flew from his mouth. Enough to make Edik glad there were several seats between him and the spit master.

At the other end of the table, Sarandon was speaking firmly and certainly, the way officers did when they were sure they were in charge, whether or not they really were.

That sort of attitude is one of the reasons Edik never signed up for naval service.

In the middle, Gonzalez-Villarreal was staring at Donal as though she'd never seen him before. Or maybe wondering what it meant that she'd given an oath on her own magic to a fae emissary.

After all, even Edik had heard the old Irish fairy tales about people in debt to the fairies. Did that count for their emissaries as well?

Edik didn't know. And he was betting she didn't know either.

Worst of all, though, was Romanova. Sitting there, ready to pounce, like the big fat cat she was. And no matter how lean she was — or how quick with a sword — to Edik she would always be just another fat cat. Same as all the people from those great families, save one.

Save Anna.

Donal either didn't know what to do next, or he was letting them yell themselves out. Which Edik was more than happy to do as well.

Finally Commodore Sarandon began banging his fist on the table like a gavel, and either Nicholson was done, or he yielded to Sarandon's authority, because he finally shut up.

"All right," Sarandon said. "Let's start with this new information."

"I would advise," Romanova said, "that we recess for an hour while we *absorb* this new information. No one here can deny its significance."

"I can," Nicholson said, surprising no one. "He represents the Fae Courts *of Earth*. The Fae Courts of Mars have sent no emissaries, and Mars claims Ganymede as its lawful territory."

"As I've already told you, Mr. Nicholson," Sarandon said with an admirable amount of condescension, "Earth does not recognize the independence of Mars. So Mars' opinion in this matter has less significance than yours does."

Nicholson tried to object. Sarandon spoke over him.

"That's right. You heard me." Sarandon drew a slow breath through his nose. "The navy holds final jurisdiction here—"

"No," Gonzalez-Villarreal said quickly, "it does not. You guys are here to protect this settlement, and, I expect, to keep us from declaring independence as every other colony has. But" — she held up a hand to forestall Sarandon's objection — "this is still a civilian settlement, and we're the ones who found the Du Mak."

"And your settlement is under Earth's jurisdiction," Romanova said, ticking off points on her unpainted fingernails, "which makes you subject to Earth law, which raises questions of planetary security and perhaps even eminent domain. Which brings the Terran Navy in. Which makes this their call."

"There's no call to make," Donal said in that spooky quiet tone of his. Edik hadn't heard that tone before this meeting, and he had to admit he hoped it vanished when the meeting ended. "I do not represent the Fae Courts of Earth or the Fae Courts of Mars, but *the Fae Courts*. There are exactly two, and I think you'd prefer me not to have to name them here."

Donal looked up and down the table, significantly. Edik wasn't sure why that was a big deal. Seelie and Inseelie or something like that?

"The *Fae Courts* have declared," Donal continued. "If Earth wants to make a political issue out of this, they can, but I don't think that's a call you want to make, Commodore. I suggest you call home and get someone of a higher pay grade to make the decision."

"I can make the call," Sarandon said in an irritated tone, "for an obvious reason. The Fae Courts have no official presence on Earth—"

"Don't they, Commodore?" Donal asked, turning to look the man square in the eye. "Or is it that their official presence is simply not known to the public at large. There's a crucial difference between the two, and I suggest you make sure you know which it is before you make this call."

Donal let those words fall, while Sarandon's eyebrow rose.

"Earth doesn't want to make enemies of the fae," Donal said, holding that spooky quiet tone of his. "Think of the consequences just among the familiars of the worlds. How many were bound after answering calls issued into the realms of Faerie?"

Sarandon hesitated.

"Mars—" Nicholson started, but Romanova spoke over him.

"Is not here." She looked up and down the table. "I see no diplomat. No member of the Mars military. I do not even see a Martian corporation like Red Sun. I see only a petty man from an Earth corporation that tried to game the system by giving Mars money to purchase something Mars doesn't care about in the slightest."

"She's right," Gonzalez-Villarreal said, smiling wider than Edik had seen before. It looked good on her. "And in light of this information, as leader of this settlement, I officially reject your presence within our Barrier. You have until morning to vacate the moon."

"A decision the Terran Navy agrees with," Sarandon said. "And if you resist we will not hesitate to use deadly force. After all, your claims could be considered supporting Mars."

"True," Romanova said, "and didn't I read last week that Earth has declared such support treasonous?"

"You did," Sarandon said. "Now, Mr. Nicholson, as an executive of Zeus Industries, an Earth corporation, if you officially support a free and independent Mars this way, then your support will be taken as official support from Zeus Industries, and the government of Earth will act accordingly."

Nicholson ground his teeth. Banged his fists on the table. But said nothing.

Everyone waited and watched. Edik wished he had some popcorn. Or at least that Dola was here to enjoy the show.

Finally, Nicholson heaved a sigh that made him look deflated to half his original size.

"All right," he said, finally. "You win. Zeus Industries rescinds their claim. Now all of you get out."

"No," Sarandon said. "We won't be doing that. The Terran Navy is officially commandeering this building for our needs here on Ganymede." He looked over at Gonzalez-Villarreal. "If you don't object."

"To having your people where I can see you, in a big, red building?" She smiled. "I don't object at all."

"You and your people may take your ship, though," Sarandon said. "The navy has no need for it."

"But you must leave this meeting," Donal said, still in that quiet tone. "With no claim, and no official position, you have no reason to be here."

Agreement all around.

Nicholson stormed out of the room, his lickspittles right behind him.

———

EDIK, ALONG WITH DONAL, ROMANOVA, GONZALEZ-VILLARREAL, AND Sarandon watched Nicholson and his people leave the conference room. Only the two unnamed commanders kept their eyes on the people at the table.

Donal spoke as soon as the door closed behind the last thug from Zeus Industries.

"That's one," Donal said, turning now to Sarandon. "What about you, Commodore? Do you wish to dispute the united decision of *both* Fae Courts in this matter?"

"When he puts it that way," Romanova said, "I advise you to answer 'no.'"

"I cannot accept any official position from the Fae Courts without confirmation back home."

"Smart," Donal said. He turned to Gonzalez-Villarreal. "And you?"

"The Fae Courts have never approached us. Earth has given us no instruction. And we were the first to make contact with the Du Mak. Following the tradition of explorers for as long as there have been countries, we claim we were settling officially unsettled land, which makes anything we find, ours. The Fae Courts made no claims when we filed our paperwork, and issued no counterclaims when we settled. We've registered three new types of rock, and two new types of creature. The Fae Courts said nothing."

She flared a deep breath through her nose. "The Fae Courts claim the Du Mak people as cousins. But I have met no fae here on Ganymede. I have met only a human emissary, who failed to disclose his position on our first official meeting. As such, I dispute the claim that the Du Mak are kin to the Fae Courts. And I shall stand in dispute until this claim can be proven through thaumaturgy."

"I—" Donal started, but Gonzalez-Villarreal cut him off with a sharp gesture and sharper words.

"You are an involved party. I require an independent observer, of at least the rank of Magister, to certify this claim."

"There's no reason we need a Magister," Sarandon said.

"The fae are noted for their mastery of glamour. I see no reason to believe that any magician without at least the training and experience of a Magister could be trusted to maintain clarity. In fact, it seems to me that Donal Cuthbert may not be an emissary at all. Especially since the Fae Courts are not noted for working together, or issuing unified statements. Donal Cuthbert might be laboring under the glamour of a single fae. His oath may be sincere, but it does not mean that he truly represents the Fae Courts, or is empowered to negotiate on their behalf, nor make claims of kinship."

"The identity of the fae representative was certified by my familiar."

"Perhaps that was part of the glamour," Romanova said. "Perhaps your familiar was not even present." She smiled. "Call him forth. Resolve that part right now."

Edik felt himself go pale, and felt his stomach fighting the urge to get rid of that ham-and-cheese sandwich.

"I … can't," Donal said. "Not now. Not for a few days."

"Why not?" Romanova said, and Edik didn't like the implications in her tone. How could she have known about this?

"My familiar suffered injuries in battle with a servitor. He must remain housed until he heals, and that will take several days."

"Why was your familiar battling a servitor?" Sarandon asked.

"Yes, Donal," Romanova said. "Where did this servitor come from?"

Everyone was staring at Donal. Edik answered for him.

"It was the work of Magister Dmitri Lukyanov, who had placed me under an information spell and guarded that spell with a servitor. Donal freed me from the spell, but the cost was a battle between the servitor and our familiars. Both were injured."

"Lukyanov?" Romanova asked, fake shocked tones all through her voice. She turned to Sarandon. "You see? As I told you. The Lukyanov family is working against Earth."

"No," Edik said, and all he could think about was how poor Anna would suffer if anything happened to her father. "Lukyanov wanted to know what I found here. That was all."

"Of course it was," Romanova said, tone dripping with sarcasm. "And I'm sure you fought so hard not to tell him that you allowed Dmitri to enchant you." She fluttered her eyes. "Or did you fight it? Tell me, Captain Barshai, did Dmitri cast this against your will?"

"No," Edik said, grinding his teeth at the technicality he had to abide by. But if he'd said anything else, he'd have to proceed with a claim of illegal thaumaturgy, in the first degree, against Dmitri Lukyanov. A claim he'd lose, as the pressure he'd been under had not been magical.

"This," Gonzalez-Villarreal said, "is not the issue here. This settlement doesn't care about Luna's great families, or their relationships with Earth. We care about our people, and the sanctity of our discoveries. So." Gonzalez-Villarreal turned a piercing stare on Donal. "Have you any paperwork to testify to your position?"

Even Edik knew the answer to that one had to be no. If the Fae Courts hadn't made a big official splash about their existence, no way they had any paperwork that any court of law would acknowledge.

"You're playing a dangerous game," Donal said, and if anything his voice got even quieter. Almost a whisper now. "Are you sure you want to risk making enemies of the fae?"

"I have no desire to make enemies of the fae," Gonzalez-Villarreal said in a firm tone. "I'm a magician too, after all. And I swear that if your role is proven to reasonable satisfaction, then my settlement will acknowledge the Fae Courts' claim as verified, and report it to Earth as such."

That last bit narrowed Sarandon's eyes.

"But until then," she continued, "I stand by our claim." She let her tone get a little more conversational. "I'm sorry, Donal. And if you're truly here representing the fae, then I apologize to them as well. But I have to do what's right here."

Donal turned to Sarandon.

"What do you say, Commodore?"

Sarandon looked at Gonzalez-Villarreal, then at Romanova, then back at Donal.

"Their points are valid, Mr. Cuthbert. Prove your claim. When you do, I'll call home and get official orders. Until then, this is Earth jurisdiction. And Ms. Gonzalez-Villarreal will continue to research and exploit it under the strict guidelines and supervision of the Terran Navy."

Gonzalez-Villarreal glared at Sarandon.

He glowered right back at her.

Romanova, on the other hand, looked as though she'd accomplished everything she wanted to do, and was ready to call it a day.

Donal, however, was not.

"All right," he said, voice still quiet. "How about this, then? Edik and I will return to Earth and retrieve the proof you require."

Edik almost — *almost* — asked Donal just what the hell he thought he was doing. Tactically, this sounded like the stupidest thing ever. Financially, it sounded even worse. Who would pay for a whole second round trip to Ganymede?

"Sounds like the smart way to go," Sarandon said, in placating tones.

"I'll want certifications from you," Donal said, tone growing a little louder now. A little more conversational, if a bit defeated. "Written orders that will get us past your picket line when we leave, when we return, and when we leave again."

"Of course," Sarandon said. "I'll get you copies before you leave, and you can watch me transmit them to the picket line."

"And because the Terran Navy is requiring this, I'd like the navy to pay Edik's costs for that return trip, as a gesture of goodwill to the Fae Courts."

"Well—"

"Remember," Donal said, "there'll only be a return trip if I have *incontrovertible* proof. Consider it a gesture of goodwill to a new power."

"Fair enough," Sarandon said, and Edik felt better about half of this lame-brained idea.

"Finally," Donal said, "I want written certification from both you, Commodore Sarandon, in your capacity as the commander of the Terran Navy presence in this part of space, and from you, Rosita Gonzalez-Villarreal, in your capacity as leader of this settlement, that you will only observe the Du Mak people, and in no way ensorcel, enchant, or otherwise pressure, bind, or compel them for a period of no less than six months. To allow me time to gather the proof I need, and return."

Gonzalez-Villarreal frowned, but nodded. "You'll have it."

"From me too," Commodore Sarandon said.

"I also require written certification from both of you that, at this time, no members of the Du Mak people are *currently* ensorceled, enchanted, bound, compelled, or otherwise pressured by this settlement or the Terran navy."

"No problem there," Gonzalez-Villarreal said, her tone a little bitter. "You've already released the only ones we had."

Commodore Sarandon nodded agreement.

"Finally," Donal added, looking over at Edik, "I want acknowledgment from both of you that Captain Edik Barshai properly claimed oversight of the first contact protocols here. That may become important when I return with proof."

Gonzalez-Villarreal looked as though she wanted to object, but Natalia Romanova held up a hand and said, "A moment."

She leaned in to Gonzalez-Villarreal and whispered something, then did the same to Commodore Sarandon. Gonzalez-Villarreal looked as though she's swallowed raw beets and cabbage slurry when she'd been expecting chocolate pudding.

Commodore Sarandon only narrowed his eyes and tightened his jaw. But he nodded.

After a moment, Gonzalez-Villarreal did the same.

Edik felt an urge swell to object. Anything Romanova would have said could only have been bad for him and Donal, not to mention the Du Mak. This was a bad idea.

But before Edik could object, Donal smiled said, "Then let's get those forms started, shall we?"

The various orders and certifications were processed in less time than Edik would have believed. Apparently there were standard forms for these sorts of things.

Edik wasn't sure how he felt about that either.

Finally, Donal checked the forms twice on his zephyrpad. Then he furrowed his brow for a moment, probably trying to make sure he didn't miss anything.

Finally, he said, "That's it then. Edik?"

Edik hesitated. This was a mistake. All a terrible mistake. But how could he call Donal out on that fact in front of these jackals?

"Edik?" Donal said again, and Edik heard a thread of either warning or pleading in the kid's voice.

Edik stood, bowed ironically to the room, and turned to leave.

Donal followed, a step behind.

10

Once Edik and Donal were back in the main cabin of the *Third Son* and the hatch was securely closed behind them, Edik whirled on Donal.

"What the hell are you thinking? Six months? Do you know how much can go wrong in *two days* if we leave the Du Mak people here?"

"Why, nothing can go wrong," Donal said, and he was smiling broader than Edik had ever seen him smile before. "I'll explain once we're in space."

"Those forms won't mean *anything*," Edik insisted. Why didn't Donal get this? "The minute we're off this moon, they'll countermand them. Or 'new information' will come in that overrides them."

Donal was still smiling.

Edik stepped closer. Put his hands on Donal's shoulders. Lowered his voice.

"Donal, you didn't get any kind of magical oath on this one. They'll break their word the second we leave orbit."

"Edik," Donal said, *still* smiling, even though he looked tired enough to fall asleep right there. And honestly, Edik could have joined him. But Donal was still talking. "You have to trust me here. Let's get moving. I want to clear that picket line as soon as possible."

"Uh uh," Edik said through a yawn. He must have been running on adrenaline and not realized it. He was starting to get shaky. "I need at least eight hours in my hammock, and you clearly need the sleep yourself. Making an offer like that. When you wake up—"

"When I wake up I want to be decans from here. Seriously, Edik, let's move."

And Donal did look serious now. But maybe he was pulling some Journeyman trick to avoid noticing just how tired he really was. Costly, in the long run, but Jones had talked about having to use tricks like those himself, and Edik wouldn't put it beyond Donal.

Edik needed to make him understand.

"Donal, we need sleep."

"Edik, the Du Mak people desperately need us past that picket line. Right now."

Edik blinked at him.

"If these people are as likely to go back on their word as you think — and I agree with you — then you have to let me pull the final step of my plan. And I can't do it until we're past that picket line, or we might as well just cut our throats *right now.*"

Edik had to admit. The kid looked sincere.

And Donal seemed to know what he was about more than he didn't.

"All right," Edik said through a yawn. "I hope you're right."

Edik turned and hustled onto the bridge, Donal a step behind him.

"Nixia," Edik said while still en route, "take us up. Fastest route past that picket line. Donal, upload that order ASAP. I want it going out on every link channel until we're past that picket."

"Aye aye," Donal said, and Edik resisted the urge to turn and throttle the kid. Probably had no idea just how stupid he sounded or how much Edik hated that expression.

Besides, Edik didn't really have time to throttle Donal. Not if he was going to get past that picket line. Plus, Edik needed to see what Donal had up his sleeve.

Edik settled into his captain's chair. Strapped in and took charge of the golden holographic controls as soon as he could.

Donal transferred copies of all the forms into the ship's holographic workspace, and immediately send the Commodore's orders out on the link, along with his spoken message: "This is Donal Cuthbert, of the *Third Son*. We are leaving Ganymede and returning to Earth, as discussed with Commodore Sarandon. This is his confirmation of his orders to allow us past the picket line unchallenged."

Donal kept linking the information out, and repeating what he said, while Edik got the ship underway.

Well, Nixia was getting the ship underway, now that Edik had made a few adjustments to the controls. Edik was now plotting his course for Earth on the quickest route he could manage, using the charts their two familiars had so strained themselves to produce.

As he plotted, Edik said to Nixia, "Also, wake up Xincapph. We'll need him ready to fly as soon as possible."

Nixia vanished to do so, and returned only a moment later.

"Xincapph has been resting deeply," Nixia said. "He may not be ready for any swift travel."

"How fast can he manage?"

"Unknown."

Edik hated that word, just in general, but he hated it most when it came from an elemental. Because he knew when a member of his elemental crew used that word, not only was it correct and appropriate, it had the drawback that it could be that Edik asked the wrong question.

And Edik wasn't sure he could spend time on finding the right question.

And he *really* needed Xincapph.

"Best estimate?" he asked, hope silently crying out from his toes on up.

"Half speed, at best, for at least three days."

Edik whistled. "If that's what he's got, it'll have to do."

"Won't be enough," Donal said. "Not if they react the way I expect them to."

"Mind sharing what you have in mind?" Edik said.

"You'll see in a moment."

Donal went back to linking out the Commodore's orders, and repeating his statement with each link. Meanwhile, Edik watched those navy ships getting closer and closer.

He had his route set now — such as it was. He couldn't vary greatly from the route he'd taken in, after all, and that meant returning to the Mars-Earth routes before he could make any adjustments, instead of going straight to Earth.

True, they had six months, according to Donal's deal — if the navy and the settlers stuck to it, which Edik doubted — but wasn't time supposed to run oddly for the fae? What if Donal went to talk to them and a decade passed before he returned?

Thoughts like that one did nothing for Edik's digestion — although only having had a single ham-and-cheese sandwich in the last several hours meant that he didn't have much to digest anyway — but they did help resurrect what remained of his adrenaline.

Edik could feel how shaky his hands got as his ship got closer and closer to the picket line...

...then flew right through.

Relief. Sweet, sweet relief flooded through Edik. He sighed so hard he almost fell asleep in his chair.

"Good," Edik said. He reached for the red lever that would take them away from this place as fast as Xincapph could manage.

"Not yet," Donal said with a tired smile. "One last thing before we go."

Donal stepped back from the web of strands of blue light that represented the communications station of the *Third Son*. No point in sending that message again. That the ship had passed the picket line meant they'd gotten the message.

Donal could only hope they stuck to those orders after Donal pulled his final trick.

He also hoped it wouldn't take much in the way of thaumaturgy to pull off. He'd never tried anything like this before, and tired as he was, if he did too much he'd collapse right there on the deck of the cockpit.

Bridge, Donal reminded himself sleepily. *Edik calls it a bridge.*

Donal smiled over at Edik, who sat in the pilot's chair, one hand on the red speed lever. Half his attention on Nixia's flying, and the other half staring at Donal. Curiosity and exhaustion all over Edik's face.

Donal smiled.

Reached into his pocket and pulled out the stone that Cinnamon had given him.

Edik's eyes grew wide.

Donal reached into that stone, projected a tiny bit of himself into it, willing contact to come with Cinnamon.

Cinnamon did him one better.

The moment Donal felt the contact take hold, Cinnamon appeared right there on the bridge, standing in the space between the pilot's station and the spare seat that Donal normally used, whenever he joined Edik on the bridge.

Cinnamon craned his long neck and looked to Donal with a curious expression.

"How may I aid you, Donal Cuthbert?"

"Get your people off of the moon we call Ganymede. Right now. You guys can teleport, and you can travel through space on your own. Do it now. Get all your people away."

"That would be ... difficult," Cinnamon said. "All have incarnated currently, and the limits of our teleportation would not take us farther than..." He looked over at the star charts. Pointed with his tail at Io. "There."

"Good enough," Donal said.

Edik immediately leapt on the idea. "He's right. Do it. Get your people out of there."

"There is one other complication."

"What?" Donal and Edik asked at the same time.

"Your people. They have finally proven their ability to travel from planet to planet. To settle into a strange world, and make it their own.

That means that we are not the only incarnating race to travel the worlds around this sun. We will meet you all again. We must achieve some kind of understanding between your people and ours. If we can get yours to listen."

Donal wasn't quite sure what happened in the next moment.

One second he'd been standing there, trying desperately to think of an argument that would take root in Cinnamon's consciousness and persuade him to move his people before the settlers, the navy, or hell, maybe even Zeus Industries or Natalia Romanova found some means or excuse to begin binding them all over.

The next second, Donal felt his consciousness receding. It was as though he were deep in meditation, retreating far inside his own mind to contemplate some pressing concern. Except that he was doing no such thing.

And worse than that, Donal realized he wasn't alone in his own head.

Donal had felt the presence of other consciousnesses before. Other spirits he had conjured, not to mention the countless contacts he'd made with Fionn and other familiars.

But this, this was unexpected. Troubling on its own. But worse than that, this presence was powerful. On a level of power and age that might even match with Cinnamon.

And this presence spoke with Donal's mouth.

"Hail to you, who are called Cinnamon," Donal's mouth said in a hollow voice. "I greet you from your kin and cousins in the Courts of both Winter and Summer. We have looked upon your essence. Touched it with our own, and found within you a most unexpected kinship."

Donal felt his lips smile, and he didn't need to see Edik's shock to know that the smile wasn't one that belonged on Donal's face.

"You are new," the voice continued, "and we have not met anything new in millennia. But you are also old, perhaps as old as we are." Donal's body bowed. "Do as this one bids you. Transport yourself to that other moon. And there we will hide you, until we send true emissaries to greet you and treat with you."

Donal's face smiled once more. "It remains to be seen if you belong with the Summer Court, the Winter Court, or perhaps deserve a Court of your own. But the prospect of discovering this excites us as little else could. Will you do as we bid?"

"There is … something familiar to you," Cinnamon said, showing the first hesitation in his voice that Donal could remember. "I cannot place it, though perhaps an elder can."

Cinnamon did that slow, awkward nod. "I shall guide our people to this place" — and the image of a location flitted through Donal's mind so fast he could barely glimpse more than a reddish dirt landscape — "and await your emissary. If your magics will hide us, we will not interfere with them."

"Then we are agreed."

Cinnamon vanished in the same moment that the presence vanished from Donal's mind.

He realized in that instant that his body's muscles had locked up rigid that whole time. All it once they came loose, and he collapsed down on the floor.

"Donal?" Edik cried out, but didn't leave his post. "You all right?"

"No," Donal said, wriggling himself to a sitting position. "A thousand-plus year old *sidhe* just used me as a fucking *link*."

Edik didn't have an answer to that, though Nixia, floating in the air beside him, nodded.

"An apt description," she said. As though this happened every day.

"Did you know that was going to happen?" Edik asked.

"I didn't even know it *could* happen," Donal said. "I'm going to have some words for Rowan MacPherson when I get home."

"Well, you *did* make a deal with the fae," Edik said, in entirely too reasonable a voice.

"Yeah," Donal said with a sigh as he hauled himself to his seat and strapped in. "My mom's going to be pissed."

"Can we go now?" Edik said in a plaintive voice. No doubt realizing why Donal felt urgent to get away.

"Punch it," Donal said.

EDIK *KNEW* HE WAS TIRED NOW.

Oh, he'd had a pretty good idea. He knew how long it had been since he'd slept. He knew how hard he'd been working and how stressful the last several hours had been.

But it wasn't until he watched some ancient goddamn fairy *possess* Donal right there on Edik's bridge, that he realized just exactly how tired he was.

Because Edik should have been terrified by this. The fae were dozens of decans away, on Earth. Farther, according to reports, than even a link could connect without relays. In fact, there were at least a half-dozen reasons Edik could think of to explain why this possession shouldn't have been possible.

Not the least of which was that Journeyman are trained specifically to prevent possession. And Donal had most likely had even more advanced training in such techniques as he started grad school.

And yet Donal, right here on Edik's own bridge, had been possessed by a fairy.

Edik should have been terrified. Shaking. Maybe even throwing up again.

But all Edik could feel was a slight, dull fear, and over that relief that the Du Mak were going to get away.

In fact, had gotten away now.

Donal had given Edik the go-ahead, and at this point Edik was ready to believe that Donal could identify every single one of the Du Mak people and their positions on Io right this second.

At this point, Edik would believe just about anything Donal said.

And Donal said, "punch it."

So punch it Edik did. Or tried to do. He shoved the speed lever forward, hoping for Full Ahead, but it fought him and locked stock still at Half Ahead.

It would have to do.

"Nixia," Edik said.

One of the links flared bright blue, and the slap pad underneath it glowed bright red. An alarm bell chimed. A three-note trill, high pitched. A warning from the system that the call was coming in with full military priority. That Edik had approximately ten seconds to answer before the link connected without any effort on his part.

Well, if it was going to happen anyway, Edik didn't intend to waste any effort on it.

"Nixia," he said again, "get the sylphs to back our speed as much as they can until we're all space around us."

"We have already," she said. "Once you were past the picket line, we could do no more."

The link connected.

Commodore Sarandon's angry face appeared above it.

"Cuthbert!" He yelled. "Get me Cuthbert right now before I blow the both of you traitors out of space."

Behind Edik he could hear Donal start unstrapping himself from his chair.

That struck Edik as a singularly bad idea. He waved a hand back at Donal to keep him where he was.

"Sorry, Commodore," Edik said, turning enough that he knew he'd be visible. "Donal's on the bridge, and he can hear you, but he's strapped into his seat, in accordance with General Space Regulation Fifteen, Section Cee—"

"Don't quote space regs at me," Commodore Sarandon growled. "If he can hear me, he can goddamn answer me."

"I can hear you," Donal said, and Edik thought the kid sounded half-asleep.

"What the hell did you just do, boy? I'm getting reports of the Du Mak—"

Suddenly that voice was back. Oh, it used Donal's throat, lips and tongue, but it sounded nothing like Donal. This voice that spoke through him sounded high, and clear, like a natural soprano. And there was a sense of tinkling bells to it. And Edik would have sworn that the voice carried the warmth of a cozy fireplace, like the one where Edik's father lit wintertime fires when Edik was a boy.

"You, Commodore Phillip Sarandon, will not address our emissary in that tone."

That made the Commodore hesitate. "Who am I speaking with? I demand your full name and—"

"Names?" Laughter, and that *definitely* tinkled like bells made from pure crystal. "You ask for names? Oh, you cannot be so foolish, and I will not grace such a question with an answer."

"I damned well expect to know whom—"

"Call me Puck," the voice said, then laughed again. "It's name enough for you."

Commodore Sarandon blinked at that. "You telling me you're..." — and he grumbled the rest through gritted teeth — "one of the good neighbors?"

"Marvelous," the voice said, and Donal's hands applauded. "I see someone has required you to do your homework. But you've trapped yourself, I'm afraid. You've acknowledged who and what I am, and that means acknowledging that Donal Cuthbert here is exactly who and what he says he is."

"Not at all," Commodore Sarandon returned swiftly, his voice smooth again. "It only means that I acknowledge a possibility, and that I refuse to accidentally give offense on behalf of my government. Now, if you were to return here and confirm your identity..."

The voice got so cold that Edik started shivering.

"That will not happen. You have already given offense. You and yours have defied the Courts, denied our emissary, and attempted to imprison those we consider cousins. Your betters shall hear about this."

And just like that, the voice was gone. Edik wasn't even looking back at Donal, but he didn't need to. That feeling of cold was gone. And Edik hadn't realized it, but there'd been a different quality to the air while Donal was possessed. Having perceived it twice in quick succession, Edik was quite certain of it now. While Donal was possessed, the air of the bridge felt more like ... like a spring breeze.

"Now just one damned minute," Commodore Sarandon said. "We

made perfectly reasonable concessions, under the circumstances, and—"

"Forget it Commodore," Donal croaked out. His throat sounded as though Donal had spent the day shouting at the top of his lungs. "He's gone. And, for the record, he disagrees with you."

"What did you do?" Commodore Sarandon asked again.

"Simple," Donal said, and his voice now sounded absolutely painful. Like rocks were grating in Donal's throat with every word. "I told the Du Mak to flee Ganymede."

"Impossible. You were on the other side of the anti-link ward. No way you contacted the surface."

"Then I did nothing," Donal said through a yawn. "Don't know what to tell you."

"All right," Commodore Sarandon said, as though he were thinking of something else.

"All right," he said again. "You've admitted, on the record, that you advised the Du Mak people to flee Ganymede—"

"You just said that was impossible," Edik reminded him, one hand still trying to force the speed lever past Half Ahead.

"Clearly he found a way past the anti-link ward," Commodore Sarandon said, and Edik didn't like the distracted quality in the man's voice. As though he were trying to convince himself of something. "Made contact anyway, and did just what he said."

"And?" Donal said, and Edik wished he hadn't.

"You've taken diplomatic action against Earth without confirming your credentials—"

"*He just confirmed his credentials,*" Edik said.

"Apparently," Commodore Sarandon said, raising one finger to make his point. "But his registered specialization is deception magic, and he's fooled the scanners of our ships once in the last forty-eight hours. No reason to believe he couldn't do it again."

"That's the biggest load of—"

"Thus," Commodore Sarandon continued, "this action is tantamount to treason. And as the highest authority in this part of space, I sentence you both to death."

Edik screamed obscene rejections to the Commodore's decision, but the man had already cut the link.

"Nixia," Edik said, "log that whole conversation, and start transmitting it on the special link back to the office. Keep trying until it gets through. Donal?" Edik glanced back over his shoulder. "Up for a fight?"

Donal lay half-draped over his seat. He blinked back at Edik, as though not sure where he even was.

"What?"

On the scanners, Edik saw two destroyers leave the picket line.

They struck an intercept course with the *Third Son*.

11

Edik felt his stomach try to drop straight through the deck and try its own escape route through space. Sweat began pouring down his face, stinging his eyes.

Donal wasn't more than half-awake, if that. Might have been nodding off even now.

Edik had a ship only capable of half its top speed. In an unknown part of space.

Two destroyers were moving on an intercept course, and already gaining on him.

And nowhere to turn for help.

He could call the Du Mak, but at the same time, he couldn't. Yes, he had the stone, but what was its range? And if Cinnamon even answered the call, he might not be able to return to his people. And he needed to be there when the fae made contact...

No one around this time.

Even the sight of the *Silver Streak* would have been welcome. But Baba Yaga never rides to the rescue.

What would Ivan Tsarevitch do?

Edik gritted his teeth and tightened his grip on the controls. Maybe he could feint as though he were heading for a different moon.

Or maybe for a nebula, there was a red one not far away. Maybe the navy ships would hesitate to follow.

Suddenly, Dola manifested beside Edik. His fur looked matted, and scarred, and his tail and whiskers drooped.

"What are you doing here?" Edik asked. "Go back and heal."

"I felt your need, Edik," Dola said, sounding at least as tired as Edik felt. Maybe as tired as Donal was. "How can I help?"

"Um…" Edik said, thinking quickly and trying not to dwell on the sight of those approaching destroyers. They'd be within firing range all too soon. "Donal! Wake up Donal. We need one of his miracles."

"Right," Dola said, then loped across the bridge.

"I'm awake! I'm awake!" Donal said a moment later, which made Edik wonder exactly what Dola had done. "What's going on?"

"Destroyers. Incoming." Edik shook his head. "No way we can outrun them, not with Xincapph up to only half-speed. Any way you can shake them off our tail? Maybe try that illusionary fireball thing you did against the *Silver Streak?*"

"It'd never fool the scanners of a military ship," Donal said, yawning again. "They have a separate lacuna just for … just for … scanning…"

"What?" Edik said.

"Just a thread of hope," Donal said, and his voice sounded a little stronger. "Get me a side view of those ships. I'll do what I can."

"If you don't act fast, you'll get a side view all right," Edik said. "For the moment it takes them to burn us down."

"I need this, Edik."

"Fine."

He heard Donal head off of the bridge and into the main cabin.

Edik started working the controls. Figuring how he could try to maintain maximum distance while giving Donal a naked-eye view of the approaching destroyers.

Didn't make sense to Edik though. By the time those ships were close enough that Donal could see them with the naked eye, they'd long since have opened fire.

But right now, Edik had to put his trust in Donal.

At least the gravity in the main cabin didn't require the kind of straps that the bridge did.

Edik sent his ship into a spiraling dive.

———

DONAL STOPPED IN THE MIDDLE OF THE MAIN CABIN. TOO MANY IDEAS running through his brain at once. He needed to slow down. But he had a spike of adrenaline, and he knew it wouldn't last long. And once it was gone, Donal knew that was it for him.

He already pushed himself further than he should have. And that didn't even count getting possessed *twice*.

Yes, he was definitely going to have words with Rowan MacPherson about this.

But first, he had to survive to make the trip home.

Donal began regulating his breathing. Getting his heart rate under control, as well as calming the fatigue shakes in his knees and arms.

Fionn appeared beside Donal in a burst of emerald light.

Fionn himself looked a little less emerald than usual. The fae deer-hound's fur looked pale, and still bore wicked scars from his battle with the bear servitor. His tail hung down, and his ears had no perk to them.

Still, the courage in Fionn's eyes blazed out, undimmed by damage or exhaustion.

"Fionn?" Donal asked. "What are you doing here? Get back in your house and heal."

"Your need is greater, Master, if you are still to live by the time I fully recover."

Donal shook his head, but couldn't deny that, once again, his familiar knew better than he did.

"What do you think, Fionn?" Donal crouched to look the deer-hound in the eye. "I'm thinking of going after their lacunas directly. The ones they use for scanners. If I can blind them, they can't track us."

"Dangerous," Fionn said. "It takes more power than you can call right now to hurt a lacuna. And if you fail, they will double their efforts to aid our pursuers."

Donal blinked at that.

"Wait," Donal said. "Do lacunas have opinions about what their ships do?"

"Of course," Fionn said, as though it were the most obvious thing in the world. But he held Donal's gaze, as though begging him to follow that line of logic. To ask questions...

...to ask questions Fionn couldn't answer unless asked directly.

Hope swelled in Donal's chest.

"That's why Xincapph works so hard for Edik, isn't it? He approves of Edik?"

"That's right," Fionn said, nodding.

"The lacunas aboard the naval ships though, how would I know if they approve of how those ships behave?"

"How do the main engines work, in most helioships?" Fionn looked as though he wanted to grab Donal by the collar and worry the right answer out of him. "A Deception Drive, for example."

"It tricks a lacuna into..." Donal smiled. "It tricks a lacuna into believing it *wants* to go where the captain wants to go."

"And what does that tell you?"

"That it's all about what the lacuna wants."

"And..."

"And I need to know what lacunas *don't* want. What would make them stop."

If only Donal could think of what that could be.

The link opened up again. Third time since Edik had begun his flying maneuvers.

"I've cut you off twice already," Edik said, twisting through another roll and hoping that Donal knew what he was doing back there. Those ships were no more than a minute from firing range.

"And I hope you'll listen to reason this time," said the woman who'd been linking through using military priority. Edik hadn't bothered catching her name. Captain Somebody, he knew that much. Looked too much like Romanova for Edik's tastes. Too pale, blonde and severe.

"Why should I?" Edik asked.

"Because I don't want to shoot you down."

"Bullshit," Edik said, voice conversational. "All you people like to follow orders, and your orders call me a traitor and say to burn me down. Don't they?"

"They do," she conceded, which was further than Edik had gotten with her yet. "But I don't want to follow orders that might be illegal. Work with me. Surrender. Come aboard my ship. Yes, you'll be in custody, but you'll live while we work this through…"

Her words petered out, no doubt because Edik was laughing on the edge of mania.

And he kept laughing.

He didn't cut her off this time. He just kept laughing until his sides ached, and his empty stomach ached, and even the muscles of his face ached.

But finally the laughter died down in him.

"So that's a no?" Captain Somebody asked.

"Die aboard my ship fighting to avoid illegal orders, or die by firing squad and let you bastards impound my wonderful ship? Gee, I know which option I'll take."

"You're being—"

Edik cut her off. No point in continuing the conversation. Edik wasn't long on trust for the military anyway, and something about that woman rubbed him the wrong way.

The image of Natalia Romanova's sneering face came to mind.

Edik shoved the foul image away. How Donal could even be civil with her was beyond Edik's understanding. But he'd spoken to her as though they were colleagues. Even though Donal seemed like an all right guy…

Hey, wasn't Donal supposed to be doing something right now?

Finding some way to get him out of this mess? He was supposed to pull off another one of his miracles, wasn't he?

Wasn't…

Dola shoved his cold, wet nose against Edik's cheek.

Edik had slumped, asleep in his chair.

"Coffee," Edik said, shaking himself and seizing the controls again. "And bring it by the gallon."

And just before Dola left the bridge, Edik added, "And thanks. You're the best, and you know it."

Edik thought he heard the great cat purr as he left the bridge.

And Edik continued trying to figure out what moves those destroyers were about to do, so he could counter them first.

Whatever Donal was going to do, he better do it soon…

"Maybe there's a way to help Xincapph?" Donal said. "Get him back to full strength right now, so he can pull one of those uber-fast flights?"

"I saw Edik's alchemical reserves after last time," Fionn said. "Do it and there won't be enough to get you guys home."

"All right then," Donal said, sinking down to sit cross-legged in the middle of the thick, red runner rug in the main cabin. "I've got to find some way to warn off those lacunas then. Get them to make their ships leave us alone."

"Why don't you sit in a chair?" Dola said, as he limped through the cabin.

"He'd fall asleep in a second," Fionn said, then returned his attention to Donal. "What's our plan?"

Donal sighed through a breath, then eased his breathing deep and regular. Slow and steady.

"I can't reach the engine lacunas, can I?" Donal asked.

"No," Fionn confirmed, expectation in his voice.

"But I can reach the lacunas in their scanners."

"Exactly. And what will you tell them?"

"Wait!" Donal smiled. Opened his eyes, and only then realized he'd closed them. "How old is Xincapph?"

Fionn smiled. "Very good. Xincapph is young, for a lacuna."

"And do lacunas care about their young?"

"Why yes, Donal," Fionn said, and Donal heard satisfaction in his familiar's voice. "Yes they do."

"Then I have a plan."

⸻

THOSE SHIPS WERE GETTING TOO DAMNED CLOSE. EDIK HAD TRIED EVERY trick he was willing to pull right now, taking slight advantage of the superior maneuverability of the *Third Son*.

But the problem was that, with Xincapph in bad shape, the destroyers were faster than he was. And they didn't have to catch him. They just had to get close enough fire.

Those great balls of fire flew much faster than the *Third Son* could. Especially right now.

"How long until firing range?" Edik asked Dola.

"Maybe a minute?" Edik could hear the shrug in Dola's voice. "We might be within range now, but maybe at the edges of their range. They might be waiting for a better shot."

"They can wait forever, for all I care," Edik said, then slugged down more coffee. Hot and strong, just the way he needed it right now. Even if the acid was trying to burn a hole in his empty stomach and he was so strung out his legs jounced nonstop.

If he lived, he'd eat later. Sleep too. If he didn't, he wouldn't care.

Then it happened.

The first ball of fire shot out.

Green it was, burning with acid and alchemy. And headed straight for the *Third Son*.

Only a test shot. A warning shot. A range finder.

Edik knew they didn't care if this shot hit or not. They were testing Edik. Seeing how he'd respond, so they could make the next shot that much better. That much more accurate.

But God, it looked big. And fatal.

Edik's nerves jangled at the sight of it. Could already feel the heat burning away at him as it approached. Bigger and bigger.

Edik pulled out the last of his stops. He'd been holding back a bit. Trying to give them a false sense of the capabilities of the *Third Son* so their gunners would have a hard time targeting.

But the time for that was past.

They were shooting. And Edik needed to survive. Needed to buy time for the trick Donal had up his sleeve.

And Edik was praying that Donal had one more trick up his sleeve.

Edik waited until the bulk of the great, green ball of flame was between his ship and the oncoming destroyers, then dove hard and banked to starboard.

Evaded the shot, and kept it between him and their scanners as long as possible. Showed as little of what he could do as he could manage, while still getting out of the way cleanly.

The dance had begun.

Two more shots came now. One from each ship.

One thing was for sure. Edik was awake now.

GETTING UP OFF OF THE RUG IN THE MAIN CABIN FELT LIKE THE MOST difficult thing Donal had done that day, and that was saying something. Of course, now was when his ankle started reminding him of how sore it was.

He had no time for that. He shunted the pain away. He shunted his exhaustion away too. He had no time for it.

He might die if he failed this trick, but if he died he was going to die as a magician — transcending the limits of his body to work the greatest magic he could manage.

"Come on," he said to Fionn, then hustled down the cabin, down the access ladder, across the deck below, and finally into the room where Fionn had almost died.

Yes, this was the room where Edik did most of his alchemy. Yes, it was next to the drive room, which was why Donal needed to be here. But forevermore he would think of it as the room where he almost got his familiar killed.

He hoped he forgave himself for that someday.

But right now, he needed to focus on the present.

Xincapph was awake, and singing some kind of ringing song in five discordant simultaneous notes. Something that sounded almost like chords, but wrong somehow.

That didn't matter. What mattered was that Xincapph was present. And visible as a swirling column of green and blue mist, with a pair of pale orange globes in the center, like eyes staring out. Even though lacunas had no eyes. Not that Donal had ever seen.

Donal sat cross-legged on the floor. Shifted his awareness hard and deep. Shifted his breathing as well, taking his heart rate with it.

In moments, Donal was deeper than he could have gone even a few weeks ago.

And Donal stretched forth his perceptions to feel the lacuna.

Once before, Donal had stretched his feelings into space, to encounter a spirit native to space. That had been his first, disastrous encounter with a zuglodon.

This was different though. Xincapph had nowhere near the power of that zuglodon. And Xincapph was bound happily — or at least, apparently happily — in the engines of this ship. And Xincapph had seemed to approve of Donal's presence.

So Donal stretched out his senses. Developed a good feel for Xincapph. A feel that he understood deeper now, because of his Enochian studies. If he were to try to describe it in those terms, Xincapph was, perhaps, space-aspected air of space. That was the closest Donal could come to a description.

The lacuna felt to him as a nebula might. As a dry mist high above a mountain peak, right at the place where the blue of sky met the black of space. With a scent like the memory of shamrocks.

Just as Donal thought that, Xincapph's colors shifted to blue and black, with a bare hint of green. His song shifted as well, six and seventh notes joining the song to form a deeper harmony. A pleasant, soothing song now. Almost a greeting…

Donal grasped that feeling. That sense of greeting. Completed his understanding of this strange space elemental. At least as well as he'd be able to without weeks more of study.

He nodded to Fionn. Not with his chin, but with his mind. And Fionn answered, led Donal out past the wards, past the twisting hull of the dipping and diving *Third Son* and into the black of space. Closer and closer now to those huge destroyers. So anachronistic with their look of steel seaships. Their shots of great green fire that could not touch Donal. Not as he was right now, merely consciousness floating through space, guided by an even less substantial aspect of his familiar than the translucent companion who walked beside Donal through his daily life.

Fionn led Donal close to both of the destroyers, easily done because they flew in formation. Perhaps two hundred meters between them at all times, their noses always pointing the same direction.

Donal knew he was well inside their scanners now.

And Donal projected that sense he had of Xincapph. He projected it with all the honest clarity he could manage. Drove home the point that the little red bird ship that these great destroyers chased contained a young lacuna. A tired, vulnerable lacuna. A lacuna who loved the man he took orders from.

Donal blinked at his realization of the truth of that statement. He hadn't realized that lacunas felt love, as he understood it.

Honestly, in that moment, Donal wasn't sure what Xincapph felt *was* love as Donal understood it. But love came out in his own mind as the translation. And the original sense of the information would be conveyed without judgment or opinion.

Donal could do nothing but inform the lacunas that scanned space on behalf of those destroyers.

He had to hope the lacunas would show mercy for one of their own.

"THEY'RE FALLING BACK!" EDIK CRIED OUT, THRUSTING HIS FIST IN the air.

He immediately got that hand back on the controls. Those destroyers were still firing, even if their range was growing greater and greater with every passing second.

Edik timed every evasion to put more and more space between himself and those destroyers.

And the destroyers were falling behind as though … as though they stood still…

"Donal," Edik said, with an amazed and relieved smile. "I don't know what he did, Dola, but he really saved our bacon here."

"And I suppose you've just been sitting there," Dola said, both tired and wry in equal measures, "twiddling your thumbs while the navy tried to murder us?"

"Well, no," Edik admitted, "but—"

"Then let us say you *both* did it, thank you very much."

Edik chuckled and smiled back at Dola, whose whiskers were no longer drooping, and whose tail had the distinct lift of pride to it.

"All right," Edik said. "We both did it. We all did it, including you, and Fionn, and Nixia and Xincapph and the rest of my crew."

"Much better," Dola said.

"Did it work?" Donal asked, rushing onto the bridge with Fionn hot on his heels.

"It did," Edik said. "I don't know how you did it, but those ships are hanging dead in space. We're outside their range now, and getting farther away every second."

"They'll send more," Donal said. "And I'm not sure I can handle doing that again."

Edik looked back at Donal. The poor kid looked dead on his feet. Every part of him was drooping.

"How are you still conscious?" Edik asked.

"He shouldn't be," Fionn said, "and he will pay the price for it later."

"Only if we survive," Donal said.

"Well, I'm…" Edik started, but his words trailed off as he shoved the speed lever again out of habit.

It went all the way to ahead full. The ship lurched forward and Edik cried out again in triumph.

But Donal cried out something that didn't sound like triumph, and Edik glanced back to see Donal, half-fallen and being supported by Magom.

"Edik," Nixia said, appearing before him and cutting off Edik's comment, "Xincapph reports that he is fully healed, and would be more than happy to handle flying for a time, if you wish more speed."

"How?" Edik said.

"The lacunas?" Donal asked, getting helped to the bridge's guest chair by Magom.

Fionn nodded.

"Had to be," Dola said.

"From the destroyers?" Edik said. "Wouldn't we have picked up something on the scanners?"

"Scanners provided by Xincapph?" Dola said.

"Shouldn't we have felt something?" Donal asked. "Sensed the flow of power?"

"Lacunae," Fionn said, "do not interact with this universe the way the rest of us do. I suspect they did not want their own humans sensing what they did, and simply shifted the flow of power outside the range of your senses."

Edik sighed and smiled.

"Nixia, please tell Xincapph that I would be more than happy to let him handle the flying for a time. And please, Nixia, keep him within safe limits."

"You won't be on the bridge?" she asked.

"No, I have an overdue date with my hammock. And Donal, you need sack time too," Edik said, turning to look at Donal.

But Donal was already fast asleep.

12

Edik didn't make it back to the bridge for at least eighteen hours. It might have been twenty. He wasn't sure, and during long flights, he didn't really care all that much. Not when things weren't blowing up in his face.

And for the first time in what felt like years, things weren't blowing up in his face.

He'd slept well and he slept hard in his hammock. Then he'd gotten up, fortified himself with borscht, and slept again.

Then he repeated this until he felt almost human.

Then he showered and put on fresh clothes, and he *actually* felt human. Yes, the trousers were indistinguishable to the naked eye, but this pair of black pants with the stripes on the sides were older, better broken in, and comfortable enough that Edik felt as though he could have done the splits in them.

The image made him smile. Dola would love to see that.

Dola was still back in his house, resting. Probably popped out once or twice to check on Edik, but Edik hoped he hadn't. The cat needed the rest even more than he did.

Only one of them was recovering from being mauled by a bear, after all.

Donal, so far as Edik could tell, was either fast asleep or meditating in the forward port side chair in the main cabin. He had it tilted back as far as he could go — which probably meant sleeping.

For the best. The kid wore himself down even harder than Edik had. Especially with those two possessions.

Edik shivered just remembering those.

Before he continued on to the bridge, he left Donal another sandwich. Roast turkey and muenster, with lettuce, cucumber, and only a little spicy mustard. Best not to be too hard on Donal's stomach until he was up and about.

This was the third sandwich Edik had left for him. Donal must have been waking up every so often, because the sandwiches vanished, but not too often, because by the smell of him, Donal had not yet hit the shower.

Edik shook his head, and finally went to the bridge, sat in his captain's chair, and said, "Nixia, how we doing?"

"Perfectly on course, Edik. I think."

Uncertainty? From Nixia?

Edik sat forward. Looked into those tiny orange eyes.

"Why aren't you sure?"

"Xincapph has been … taking liberties with your route. I haven't understood his explanations, but he seems confident in them."

"He knows where we're going, right?" Edik asked as he called up the charts…

…and felt his jaw go slack.

They were three days ahead of schedule.

"How fast has he been flying us?"

"Actually," she said with a smile, "he's barely taken us faster than you do. Only a little, and only at first. But then he deviated from the course, and, well, I wasn't sure if I should wake you up or trust in Xincapph."

"I'm sure you made the right call," Edik said, then whistled. The route Xincapph had taken.

First of all, Xincapph had flown nearer the nebulas than Edik ever would have, and nothing bad had happened. That was good to know.

Better to know was that Edik's charts contained data now that they hadn't had before.

"Did you do that?" Edik said, pointing to the charts. Specifically at a small cluster of what might have been meteors.

"The charts?" Nixia asked. "No, that was Xincapph. I think he saw what Fionn and Dola were doing on the flight here, and continued the process for them."

"You mean he could have..." Edik drew a slow, long breath through his nose. Then another.

It wasn't Xincapph's fault. He couldn't have known. Hell, Edik could barely communicate with him. Not his fault that Fionn and Dola were so exhausted from charting when they had to fight that servitor.

No. Xincapph was helping. That was what mattered here.

"All right," Edik said. "All right."

Edik nodded, until he felt more sure that he could agree with that.

"Have you been checking on sleeping beauty back there?"

"Yes," Nixia said. "He has arisen four times. Once to use the head. Three times to eat. Once just to stare into space before he began meditating."

"Has he been meditating a lot?"

"When he has not been sleeping, he has been meditating. In equal portions, I think."

Edik shook his head. No, he definitely did not want to live the life of a Journeyman. All that sitting still would drive him crazy.

"Have you been sending that conversation home?"

"Yes, it reached Carl Jones six hours ago. He bids you contact him as soon as you are able."

Edik laughed softly through a single exhalation. Of course the air elemental wouldn't mention that until all of Edik's usual priorities were sorted out.

All except one...

"Has there been any sign of pursuit?"

Nixia spun coquettishly in the air and gave him a shy smile.

"Edik," she said in an admonishing tone. "If there had been, wouldn't I have mentioned that first?"

Edik bowed his head. "You're quite right. I'm sorry, dear Nixia."

She smirked, then twirled in the air until she dissolved into nothing.

Edik turned and grabbed the special link, at the bottom of the snarl of blue strands at his communication station.

Almost immediately Edmund's smooth, young features appeared above the snarl.

Edik felt something loosen in his guts, just to see Edmund smiling. Like a little piece of home out here.

"Edik!" Edmund said. "I'm so glad you called. The last day or so has been the strangest—"

"Is that Edik?" Jones' voice. From somewhere in the background.

Then Jones' sober features replaced Edmund, only the one head floating there, thankfully.

"Edik," Jones said, tone urgent. "What have you gotten into out there?"

"What do you mean?"

"I've been picking up chatter on a few official channels. Nothing I'm supposed to know, these days, but I still have friends in the military, and they know I've been hanging out with you."

"Oh, boy," Edik said. He could see where this was going.

"They're waiting for you on Earth. They're going to burn you down before you get there."

"Then we're not going to Earth," Donal said, standing in the doorway of the bridge. "We're going to Luna."

"Who's that?" Jones asked.

"Donal Cuthbert," Edik said, "I'll introduce you."

"Well tell him that here's no safer for you. Earth's got ships in orbit." Jones shook his head. "I think they got wind of Luna trying to establish its own navy, and they didn't care for it."

"Luna's going for independence?" Donal asked, strapping himself into his seat.

"No," Jones said. "That's what's got most people confused. Luna just wants—"

"Later for the politics," Edik said. "Let's talk about where we can set down without getting burned down."

"I'll handle that," said the strong young voice of Anna Lukyanova.

A moment later, her all-too-beautiful features wedged themselves in next to Jones'.

On the one hand, this meant that neither head was cut off, which Edik greatly appreciated. On the other, it might imply that Jones and Anna had gotten … closer. Edik didn't like that at all. He'd come to think of Anna as the younger sister he'd never had, and he would do anything to keep her from getting hurt.

Jones wouldn't mean to hurt her. But he was a man of violence. In a way Edik had never seen in anyone else, and hoped he never saw again. Jones might hurt her to keep from hurting her worse.

But she'd still be hurt.

Edik shook himself. Anna was fussing over the state of him, even though he'd had a shower.

"And you've clearly not been eating enough," she finished.

"What were you saying about handling the Terran navy?" Edik said.

"I am a Lukyanova, and this is Luna. They will not dare harm you here."

"The space between here and there," Edik started, but Anna cut him off.

"*Nyet*," she said, which only showed how angry she was, because Anna rarely spoke Russian except to her family. "I will make them all understand. And I will make sure Hierophant Mason helps me. Between us we have considerable resources."

"You can say that again," Donal said, and Edik didn't like the slightly distant tone in his voice.

Edik raised an eyebrow at him, but Donal was looking at Anna.

Worse and worse.

"Well, you try to get that sorted out," Edik said, eager to cut the conversation short, "and let me know if it's safe or if we should hide out on Mars—"

Edik had only meant that as a joke, but if anything, Jones had gotten even *more* serious.

"Do not go to Mars," Jones said. "Either of you. It's a free-fire zone right now. Earth is shooting it out with Mars, and there are corporations on both sides."

"Right," Edik said, swallowing hard. "Mars is out."

"I know a good place on Venus," Donal said. "Be a chance to study the wild magic. I barely got to touch it on Ganymede."

"Better Venus than Mars," Jones said.

"You will come to Luna," Anna said, "and you will land in your usual bay at Kennedy. I will see to it."

"Anna—"

"I have spoken," she said, cocking an eyebrow with more authority than someone with her few years should have been able to muster.

Maybe the great families got where they were for a reason.

"All right," Edik said. "Call me when you know more."

He cut the link.

Donal whistled.

"She's not twenty yet," Edik said. "Too young for you. *And* she's seeing Edmund."

Donal looked at Edik, then snorted and shook his head.

"She's from a great family of Luna." He raised his hands. "That's more than enough to keep me away."

Edik thought about throwing Donal's comfort around Natalia Romanova in his face, but decided to quit while he was ahead.

DONAL PASSED THE NEXT FEW DAYS AS HE OFTEN DID WHILE TRAVELING. Meditating, reading, and chatting. In the latter case, his options were limited to Edik at first, but Fionn and Dola were back to their normal selves only a day ago.

Edik seemed thrilled at their speed. Even if he hadn't heard back from Anna about whether or not Luna was safe for them.

Just what Donal needed. To be hunted by the entire Terran navy.

Hierophant Mason had seriously undersold the risks of this job. And Rowan MacPherson, she had things to answer for as well.

But dwelling on either of those things wouldn't help Donal in the slightest. So instead he dedicated his time and focus to figuring out a deception that would get them past naval ships that would be looking for it, past Port Authority, who would be watching for smugglers who might use similar methods to anything Donal came up with, and probably the great families as well.

They seemed like the type to watch for hidden ships. Certainly Natalia Romanova seemed the type.

Donal wondered briefly if Anna Lukyanova ever watched for hidden ships.

Then he shook his head. However pretty she might be, the last thing he needed right now was a romantic complication.

And anyway, he wasn't convinced she was either prettier or more interesting than Esmeralda Villaseñor. This Anna Lukyanova just had what all the women of great families seemed to have: charisma. And Donal hadn't been ready for it.

Edik did seem upset about the notion of Donal coming on to Anna. And not because Edik was interested in her himself. That much was apparent.

A small part of Donal toyed with the idea of showing interest in her, just to tease Edik. But no, that wasn't something he had the time or inclination for. Being back in college, where students played those sorts of games, had temporarily made Donal forget just how dangerous the real world could be.

And Donal had to find a way around this danger. Just in case Anna Lukyanova was not quite so resourceful as she thought, or Hierophant Mason found that he had played one card too many.

And Xincapph might have given Donal the answer.

Lacunas appeared to work along the lines of space-aspected air of space. Space and spirit were one. The same element, in both classical and Enochian terms.

If lacunas were pure space-aspected space of space, then that would mean one thing. But the presence of air in the mix, that might be the lead Donal needed to puzzle through this.

Lacunas had transmitted power through the wards of their own ships, through the wards of Edik's ship, and straight to another lacuna.

Despite the fact that all three space elementals were bound within constraints of their own.

Those two lacunas that sent power, they should not have been able to do so. Not within all those wards and bindings.

Which meant that the usual bindings for lacunas were missing something, something that the elementals could exploit, when properly motivated.

Was it enough for them to be able to abandon ship?

That was a question Donal had not considered, but he considered it now as he sat in his usual seat in the main cabin. His belly full of borscht and good iced tea, and Fionn sitting beside him, their minds in light contact.

Fionn wasn't leading this time. He merely seemed to watch Donal's contemplation.

That was fine with Donal.

Donal sank deeper into meditation.

Those two naval destroyers had been left floating, apparently dead in space. But not necessarily *actually* dead in space. It might have been that their lacunas refused to behave until the *Third Son* was well away.

But what if they were *actually* dead in space? What if Donal had just discovered a means of shutting down any ship?

If this were true, then the navy would hesitate to burn down the *Third Son*. They'd want that ability for themselves. A hammer to wield against Mars, against the corporations, to keep Venus and Luna in line...

Donal wasn't sure about this.

And for this first time in recent history, he didn't seek the answer alone.

Donal ascended from his meditation to a normal state of mind. He strolled onto the bridge, Fionn at his side, where Edik savored a bowl of borscht and a wheat beer.

"Donal," Edik said with a smile. "What brings you out of your meditations. Want a brew? Might as well drink them now. We might get burned down any day now."

"He's been like this all day," Dola said. "He won't listen to reason."

"Have you heard from Anna?" Donal said.

"Yep," he said. "No dice. Not for her, and not for the all-powerful Hierophant Mason." Edik laughed. "So much for the man being able to do anything."

"There may be a good reason for that," Donal said, and that got Edik to hesitate with his beer halfway to his mouth.

Donal waited until Edik set the beer down to continue.

"Have you been able to get a report of the charges?" Donal said.

"Treason wasn't enough for you?"

"Humor me."

Edik turned to his communications station. Frowned at it. Shrugged. Linked his office.

North answered. His big, blocky head covered in scraggly black hair and beard overfilled the space above the blue spaghetti.

"Barshai," he grunted. "They ain't killed you yet?"

"Sorry," Edik said, not sounding sorry at all. "You're going to have to wait on that insurance."

"No good," North said through a grimace. "They won't pay for treason."

"Excuse me," Donal interrupted, getting North to look his direction.

"That your passenger?" North asked, sounding offended. "On your *bridge?*"

"He crews better than you do," Edik said. "Don't insult him."

"Well what is it, your high-and-mighty Journeymanship?"

"Have you seen an actual list of charges?"

"Nah," North scoffed. "Jones won't let me see it. Says it's bad."

Edik cut the link.

Donal blinked at him.

"That was all you wanted to know, right?" Edik said.

"Well, yes, but—"

"Then the less I have to talk to that idiot, the better. I don't want to waste any of my last few hours on that arrogant…"

Edik let his words trail off. Shook his head.

"Swearing about him's almost as bad as talking to him."

"I think I know what the problem is," Donal said.

"He's a stupid, lazy ingrate who isn't half the flier, a third the swordsman, or a fourth the magician he thinks he is?"

Donal blinked, then shook his head. "No, I mean why the navy's after us."

"What part of treason is hard for you to grasp?"

Donal explained his theory about the destroyers.

"Well," Edik said, toasting Donal with his beer. "If I have to die for this, at least it's for a good cause."

"Good cause?" Donal asked.

"Yeah. Those sons of bitches have been abusing their lacunas for far too long. I say, let them *all* go."

"No," Donal said through a sigh. "When we get closer to Luna, we're going to need your friend with the navy connections to get us someone high-powered on the link."

"You have an idea, don't you?"

Donal nodded.

<hr>

EDIK STOPPED DRINKING AFTER THAT. DONAL HAD A PLAN, AND SO FAR Donal's plans had been good ones.

True, the kid only needed to be wrong once for this all to go horribly awry, but Edik reasoned that if he was wrong *this* time, at least there wouldn't be much opportunity to lament the failure.

So Edik focused on getting them to Luna as fast as he could

reasonably go, given his limited alchemical resources for replenishing his lacuna. But then, Xincapph had seemed fresher than ever after that encounter with the two destroyers.

Edik had tried to get answers about that out of Nixia. To find out as much as he could. But either Nixia couldn't get the answers out of Xincapph, or she refused to disclose them.

No real difference between the two.

And flying gave Edik good things to focus on. Positive things. Flying cheered him up as much as anything, even to the point that he shocked Dola by trying to continue something like a meditation schedule.

Edik had no idea how well that schedule would survive running into his regular life, but for now, it would do.

And Xincapph was making great time. They were going to reach Luna almost a week ahead of schedule. And that pleased Edik for one special reason. A reason he refused to give voice to, if only because a part of Edik was still the six-year-old boy who believed in Baba Yaga and Koschei the Deathless.

And if Edik gave voice to his reason, then it might collapse, and Natalia Romanova might beat them back to Luna anyway.

Of course, Edik wasn't flying directly to Luna. Jones had arranged a rendezvous point a few hundred klicks outside of the Luna-Earth patrol routes. Just far enough for their ship to be detected by a naval vessel that left those routes at the right spot, and looked for them in the right place.

In theory, this would be the only person Jones could find with enough clout to make a difference.

If Donal could talk them into not burning the *Third Son* out of the sky.

Edik almost wished he had some wood to knock over that one.

So Edik flew and meditated, and Donal meditated and ... did whatever the hell else he did when he wasn't on the bridge. Reading maybe? Preparing for his big moment?

Edik tried not to worry about it.

So Edik focused on flying.

And it almost seemed too soon that they reached the rendezvous point. An empty spot of space, far away from any local traffic to make Edik feel either at ease or concerned, depending on his mood.

Right now, he felt a mixture of both. Happy that no squadron of ships was waiting for him. Nervous, because this could all go horribly, horribly wrong.

For better or worse, Edik couldn't decide which, Luna sat so temptingly near that Edik could almost reach out and touch it.

"It looks like a giant ball of crinkled up paper," Dola said, beside Edik, and got a raised eyebrow from Edik for his trouble.

"What?" Dola said in mock innocence. "Tell me it wouldn't be fun to watch me bat that thing all around the system."

Edik chuckled despite himself, and a pleased ripple worked its way down Dola's fur.

Donal stepped onto the bridge.

"No Fionn?" Edik asked in unfeigned surprise.

"He's running a little errand for me," Donal said as he strapped himself into his chair.

"No need for that this time," Edik said. "We're sitting still until they—"

A strand glowed blue, and underneath it the slap pad glowed red.

Just at that moment, a gunboat showed up on the scanners. Smaller than a destroyer. Maybe only twice the size of the *Third Son*. But it carried more than enough firepower to take out the *Third Son*, and maybe three or four other ships, as long as it was in the area.

But the military priority alarm didn't go off…

Edik looked over at Donal. Donal nodded.

Edik activated the link.

The head of an old Japanese man appeared. He had more gray than black in his short hair, and more wrinkles than smooth skin on his face. His eyes looked out with suspicion, but his head was held high, straight and true.

"I am Rear Admiral Saito. I wish to speak to Donal Cuthbert."

"Here," Donal said, and stepped up so he would be visible.

Edik shifted a little in his chair so he would *not* be visible. He didn't wish to risk spoiling this conversation by giving anyone else the disquieting feeling *he* got when he had two heads, or a head-and-a-half, appear at a communications station.

"Mr. Cuthbert, I am only making this connection for three reasons. One, Carl Jones has vouched for your pilot, Captain Edik Barshai, and Carl Jones does not vouch for many. He is a man well known to me, and his word impresses me. Two, I have met your brother, and would not wish to take the life of Bran Cuthbert's brother unless I must. I have no wish to cause him sorrow."

Donal's expression barely changed, but Edik thought the kid's lips puckered a little at hearing his brother's name thrown around even here and now.

"And the third reason. I am acquainted with Donatello Mancuso, and he speaks very highly of both your thaumaturgy and your character. I wish to hear what you have to say."

"Thank you very much, Admiral," Donal said, and Edik was surprised he didn't bow.

"Now," the Rear Admiral continued, "you understand the charges against you?"

"They were only made to justify Commodore Sarandon's intended betrayal of his own word," Donal said. "Have you seen the communique?"

"I am entirely up-to-date on the situation," the Rear Admiral said, and Edik hoped Donal could read something in the man's expression, because Edik certainly couldn't.

"Now I will swear to you on my power that I did indeed fly to Ganymede as the emissary of the Fae Courts, and that I never intended to act against Earth in any way, shape or form."

"I cannot accept such an oath," the Rear Admiral said. "Not over a link. There would be no way to verify it."

The Rear Admiral shook his head.

"Also, your oath would only address one charge, and, to be frank, not the most important."

"You're concerned about the charge that I disabled two ships at space?" Donal asked.

The Rear Admiral nodded.

"Tell me," Donal said, "were the ships truly dead in space?"

There was something in Donal's tone there. Almost regret. Edik almost snorted. He wouldn't have had any regrets, not if *he'd* pulled off something like that.

"For *twenty minutes*," the Rear Admiral said. "We have never seen anything like that. No spells penetrated the ships' wards. No alchemy either. You have displayed some untraceable power, perhaps because of your connection with the fae. We cannot permit you to roam free with this power."

"I don't have such a power," Donal said, and Edik could hear the relief in his voice. "I swear. I'll explain what happened. It was a fluke occurrence."

The Rear Admiral stroked his chin, then gave a single nod.

Donal explained. Far too much, for Edik's liking. About how young Xincapph was. About how the lacunas looked after their own. About how he had informed the lacunas about the situation, and they, not Donal, had chosen to act to save Xincapph, and through him, the *Third Son*.

When Donal finished, the Rear Admiral said nothing for a moment. Then he cast his gaze away, as though … as though listening to others who had been in on the conversation.

Edik could have reached through the link and throttled the man. Jones had promised a *private* chat.

"I would ask," the Rear Admiral said, "how you knew the youth of your lacuna, but it seems to me that a man who learns his lacuna by name, might have the means to determine such a thing."

"We can prove it. If you want to bring your ship's mage aboard," Donal said, and Edik could have kicked him. The last thing he wanted was some strange magician poking around in his engine, or messing about with Xincapph.

"I don't believe," the Rear Admiral said, one eyebrow raised, "that your runabout has a hatch that is spaceworthy."

"Nope," Edik said, staying out of view.

"Stay where you are," the Rear Admiral said. "I will connect again in five minutes."

The link cut.

"What were you thinking?" Edik said. "I don't want these bastards messing with Xincapph."

"Would you rather let them look at your setup, or burn us out of the sky?" Donal raised a hand. "Before you answer, remember that Anna needs you."

Edik grumbled and let out a slow breath through his nose.

With Donal saying things like that, the five minutes passed before Edik realized it. Suddenly the link was glowing again.

Edik slapped the slap pad.

The Rear Admiral's head appeared again.

"Mr. Cuthbert," the Rear Admiral said. "Do you swear to me on your place at California Thaumaturgic Academy at San Luis Obispo that you truly flew to Ganymede representing the Fae Courts?"

"I swear it. I can even introduce you to the person who gave me the position."

"That ... may not be necessary," the Rear Admiral said, which made both Edik's and Donal's eyebrows shoot up. "I believe independent verification can be acquired."

"Now," the Rear Admiral continued, "about that little trick you pulled to disable two destroyers at space. Are you willing to give a seminar to a group of military magicians about the technique? You'd have to be thorough."

"I..."

Donal looked over at Edik. Edik shook his head frantically.

"Mr. Cuthbert," the Rear Admiral said in a heavy voice, "I'm afraid that this is not a negotiation. If you are willing to do this, then I can have the order to terminate your life rescinded, and include Captain Barshai and his ship in the bargain. It would be worth these things to the Terran navy to learn what you have to teach about this."

"It won't work the same way again," Donal said in a warning tone. "I can only show you what I did and explain how I came to my conclusions. I can't guarantee results."

"Nothing is guaranteed where thaumaturgy is concerned," the Rear Admiral said. "Very well, I am transmitting two forms to you. The first, a written testament to your status as emissary to the Fae Courts. The second, your affirmation that you will teach this seminar, at a time and place of the Navy's choosing, albeit with allowances for your school schedule. Sign and return these to me, and you will be free to go."

"We have a deal," Donal said.

***

SEEMED LIKE ONLY TWO HOURS LATER, DONAL WAS DISEMBARKING THE *Third Son* and stepping down onto the blue white stone of a Kennedy Spaceport landing bay. A round landing bay, with matching blue-white walls far enough back that the bay could have held at least two other ships the size of the *Third Son*. Overhead, the pale green sky of Kennedy.

Donal drew a deep lungful of licorice-scented air. He could have dropped and kissed that blue-white stone, but he felt the need for a certain amount of decorum.

After all, this landing bay already had people in it.

Some of them he hadn't met, not in person, but he'd already seen over the link during his flight.

Others, of course, he knew well or all too well.

The first of these was Fionn, standing over by Hierophant Mason, and looking just about as pleased as the deerhound could possibly look. He immediately trotted over to Donal's side, beaming up at him.

Hierophant Mason looked as he always did — as though he'd walked right out of some shadow play, with an aura of power that would be the envy of just about any other magician alive. Slender and fit as the rapier at his side, clad in shades of blue airsilk that managed to look even better here in the spaceport among all the blue-white stone. His flowing brown hair hung loose about his shoulders.

And just like that, Donal felt like he was still a gawky teenager, unsure how to dress or comport himself. Right now, Donal wore a good, green airsilk shirt (that matched his familiar) with gray airsilk slacks and soft calfskin shoes. He should have felt like a million bucks. But compared to Hierophant Mason...

Next to them stood a blonde woman of almost staggering beauty and youth, dressed in a dark red airsilk dress that managed to contain her modestly while still leaving no doubts about her figure. She wore it the way royalty wore clothing — as though the effect of the clothing were only an aspect of their personage.

This had to be Anna Lukyanova.

Her hair was bound into a tight and complicated series of braids that hung down low past her neck.

Standing close enough to this woman to imply that they were more than friends stood Edmund, looking sharp in a black silk suit. Not airsilk, but then, he might not have had the money for it.

On the other side of Mason stood Carl Jones. The man looked like some god had reached down and packed thunder into a human body. Strong, scarred, with his hair cropped down almost to his ebon skin.

Edik had said something about Carl Jones being an Initiate, but he had a Journeyman's aura of power.

No familiar, though. Odd that.

Stomping forward from the group was the scraggly force of nature that was Captain North. And he was charging right for Edik.

North dressed in an imitation of a military uniform — navy blue, faux wool material and complete with little gold symbols of rank at his collar — but he wore it like a pirate instead of a captain.

Of course, that might have been the effect of the big freaking cutlass at his side.

"Barshai!" North bellowed. "What the hell are you doing running us afoul of the fucking TERRAN NAVY?"

"A little louder, North," Edik said, one eyebrow high, "I think some of the potential customers in King didn't hear you."

That got North to lower his voice, and Donal didn't stick around to hear this argument. He strode past them over to the group. Though Carl Jones had a grimace on his face and was moving over as though he wanted to break up North and Edik before swords were drawn.

And Donal had the feeling that those two had drawn steel on each other before.

"Anna, Edmund, I feel I know you two already, the way Edik talks about you," Donal said as he stopped in easy conversation range, though they all had to speak a little louder to hear each other over Edik and North.

"He speaks very highly of you too," Anna said, bowing her head slightly, "and I understand you know Natalia Romanova as well."

"RIPPING AWAY OUR BUSINESS ON SOME DAMNED FOOL ERRAND," North screamed.

"Probably better than he'd like to, if I know Donal," Hierophant Mason said, louder still, and stepped forward to shake hands. His grip was strong, but not challenging. "Good to see you again."

"I MADE THE RIGHT CALL AND YOU KNOW IT!" That was Edik.

Donal tried to ignore them.

"You too," Donal said, "though it was a near thing."

"I never doubted you for a moment," Hierophant Mason said, his smile broad.

There were a half-dozen things Donal wanted to say to that. Whether they were digs or doubts or just complaints that he hadn't been prepared well enough for this. That Hierophant Mason had kept too much from him. That holding back too much information had almost gotten him and Edik killed.

But there were non-magicians watching, and Donal found himself thinking about the admonishments he got from Magister Ronaldo Machado aboard the *Horizon Cusp*. Mystery. Magicians needed to maintain an air of mystery.

So Donal decided the complaints could wait until Donal had a moment alone with Hierophant Mason. He had the feeling he'd be getting that before he knew it.

"Of course not," Donal said with a smile. "If you'd had doubts, you'd have sent my brother."

Donal turned away then, and toward the rest of the group. Edik sounded as though he was done with his argument with North, and was coming over to greet everyone else.

Anna got a hug from Edik, while Edmund got a handshake and Hierophant Mason got a handshake that Edik held a little long.

Long enough to still be shaking hands as he said, "I got underpaid for this job."

"Nonsense," Hierophant Mason said, still smiling. "You were paid for a month. Here, you were barely gone half of that. Keep the rest though," he said, reclaiming his hand and turning to leave. "Consider it a tip."

Hierophant Mason barely made it three steps before he turned back, snapped his fingers, and said, "Oh, and Donal. Good move sending Fionn to me with that information."

"Well," Donal said, "I couldn't let it die with me. Doesn't matter though. The navy's going to make me teach it to them."

"It matters a great deal," Hierophant Mason said. "Now they can't just declare it secret."

He winked, and turned to leave.

Edik looked as though he intended to pursue, but Anna stopped him with a hand on his chest.

"Not now," she said. "He'll be around. He's still helping with the Rhian."

"How's that going?"

"Very well," Anna said, and happiness seemed to make her glow. If it were possible for a person to smile from the core of her being on out through the farthest reaches of her aura, then that was how Anna Lukyanova smiled just then. "There's been a development that's made them postpone any further actions for six months, while everyone adjusts to it."

"What development?" Donal said, with a sinking feeling in his stomach.

"*Oh,* it's the most exciting thing," she said. "*The Fairy Courts sent a diplomat.* They claim the Rhian are a lost tribe, and as such, the Fairy Courts are claiming—"

"Jurisdiction over their welfare," Donal and Edik said at the same time.

"Exactly." She turned to North, who was only just rejoining the group. "See, Roger, I told you they would know. Probably the same exact thing as they were talking about out on Ganymede."

"I bet," Donal said, and by now his stomach was sinking down to his knees.

"Oh, and *Donal.*" Anna turned a different smile on him then. It was a smile Donal had seen from time to time, on the faces of female friends.

It was the smile of a matchmaker.

"That diplomat, she says she knows you. In fact," — Anna leaned a little closer, spoke a little quieter — "she's got the top room at the Kennedy Pyramid. She's waiting for you there. She said you'd have a lot to 'talk' about."

Donal snickered at the same implications that made Edmund and Edik raise their eyebrows, and North leer.

He didn't bother to disabuse them of the notion. If he spent much time with them, they'd learn the truth soon enough.

And now, Donal very much wanted to go to the top of the Kennedy Pyramid and talk with Rowan MacPherson.

13

Much as Edik wanted to enjoy his homecoming, his need to talk to Mason weighed too heavily on his mind. So he pried himself from a much-desired conversation with Anna, Edmund, Jones and North and set his boots ringing out on the blue-white stone of the Kennedy Spaceport.

He was still walking between landing bays, in the area that isn't barred to the public, but isn't advertised as open to the public either, when he turned to Dola beside him to brainstorm where the Hierophant most likely wandered off to.

"I bet he's gone to eat," Edik said without breaking stride. "Guy like him probably has dinner dates. Business ones. We can—"

"I know where he is," Dola said, tone so casual that Edik stopped right there. So abruptly that Dola continued to pad along for a few steps before turning back to Edik.

Dola blinked innocently, whiskers almost quivering with amusement.

"What?" he said.

"First of all, where?"

"Bar in the spaceport. That one all the magicians go to, but I can't get you to set foot inside."

"Archimedes," Edik said, and he knew he made the word sound foul. "Fine. And just how, dear Dola, did you know this?"

"He told me."

Edik crossed his arms over his chest and waited for his familiar to tell the rest of the story.

He didn't have to wait long.

"All right," Dola said with a slight chuckle. "As he left the bay, he sent a servitor over to tell me where he'd be, and that he'd be waiting for you when you were ready."

"I didn't detect a servitor."

"I'm not sure Donal did either," Dola said, ears folding back slightly. "It was a little, wispy thing. I'm not even sure *I'd* have noticed it, if it hadn't approached me."

Edik let his head hang forward.

"Great," he said through a sigh. "Just great. So he can make servitors that we…"

Edik let the thought fall. He didn't want to pick it up anyway.

He drew a deep breath, and pushed on ahead into the spaceport.

Scant minutes later Edik stood outside Archimedes.

No missing this bar. It looked like a giant oak tree. A single, lone growth inside all the blue-white stone of the Kennedy spaceport. And it was a *giant*. Easily twenty meters across, and visible almost anywhere inside the port proper.

Almost, because Edik went well out of his way to not notice Archimedes. It just seemed like the most pretentious, over-the-top idea a magician could have. To set up a bar for magicians only, and to make it look like a giant tree, standing in the middle of a place where no tree would ever grow.

But then, humans were only on the moon because magicians made things grow where they would never grow without magic. So maybe it was just a reminder to all those people without enough talent to study magic beyond the most basic of high school skills. Or maybe it was "a respite from the cares of mundane life."

Or some other bullshit like that.

And now Edik stood just outside it. And he had to go in.

He wanted to pinch his nose and hold his breath, but that would have been a terrible way to try to hold a conversation.

The front door was a giant knothole without a knob.

Edik sighed and looked at Dola, and Edik would have sworn that Dola suppressed a sigh. Good thing too. Edik would never have let his familiar live that one down. Dola was always after Edik to socialize more with other magicians. To accept and embrace his talents and skills, instead of always sublimating their importance to his piloting.

No way Dola could get away with a sigh right now.

Edik drew back a fist to knock.

A male air elemental wisped into view right before Edik. The little thing stood only maybe as tall as Edik's head. He looked slender and arrogant, with a cruel twist to his sun-yellow mouth.

"Oh, hello," Edik said. "I'm Edik Barshai, this is my familiar Dola."

"A familiar, eh," the air elemental said, one eyebrow high in disbelief. "Am I to understand that *you* summoned and bound a *familiar?*" The air elemental looked Edik up and down. "Doesn't seem very likely, does it?"

Dola spat out words that Edik couldn't understand.

The male sylph's orange eyes widened in shock. He looked closer at Edik.

"I don't believe it," he said, but his tone was amazement, not derision.

"I didn't catch your name," Edik said, trying to keep his tone steady and light, even though anger boiled in his stomach.

"I'm not allowed to give it," the male sylph said. "But your familiar is right. You are certainly a magician and thus, admitted."

The male sylph bowed, then vanished in a swirl of yellow.

Now Edik could see a knob on the door.

Edik sighed and opened the door.

Inside, Archimedes looked much like any other bar, albeit done in dark woods, in contrast to all the blue-white stone outside. A long, mahogany bar ran along one wall. Small booths ran around the edges, and small, round tables filled the center.

Edik could hear the bubble of conversation, but he couldn't pick out any words. He could see booths and tables, but he couldn't see any faces.

Edik had heard of this effect. Privacy enchantments, and thorough ones, clouding all conversations as well as even the appearances of those at those tables.

Each table was effectively a bar unto itself.

The bar appeared to be the exception. Edik could see three magicians, two men and a woman, all about Donal's age. The men looked to be vying for the woman's attention, and the bartender, a middle-aged Israeli man by the look of him, amused himself by paying casual attention in between filling drink orders.

Now that Edik thought about drink orders, he could see the wait staff. Fit young men and women, dressed in somber earth tones, their clothing enchanted to make them fade into the background.

Apparently, unless one thought about drink orders.

"Good evening, sir," a voice said, and Edik realized a host was standing beside him, dressed in a sharp black outfit that contrasted sharply with his pale white skin. "Do you wish to sit at the bar? Or are you meeting someone?"

"I'm here to meet—"

"Ah ah," the host said quickly, albeit with a smile. "I need your name before we can proceed."

Edik sighed and gave it.

"Oh," the host said, eyebrows coming up. "Excuse me, sir. I didn't recognize you. This way, please."

The host led Edik through the tables and toward a stairwell at the back. Walking between the tables was disconcerting. No matter which table Edik looked at, the effect was the same: a bubble of voices without words or character, and every table looked empty when he looked right at it, but out of the corner of his eye every table looked full. And he couldn't tell anything about the people sitting at those tables.

He focused his attention elsewhere.

"How," Edik asked Dola in words only Dola could understand, "could the host possibly be impressed by me?"

"I could answer that a hundred ways," Dola said, in the same manner, "but it's probably that you're here to meet Mason."

And two floors later, Edik found himself in a small room that smelled of rich woods and comforting old smoke. The room was no larger than the bridge of his ship. Inside the room, a single round table, oak maybe, with two comfortable-looking padded chairs.

Hierophant Nicholas Mason sat in one of those chairs, smiling up at Edik. On the table waited two bottles: one of scotch in front of Mason, and one of cognac in front of Edik's chair. Both glasses had three fingers of brown liquid in them.

Somewhere in Edik's quick assessment of the room, the host had vanished.

"Welcome," Mason said, gesturing to the empty seat. "I hope cognac was the right choice."

"It was," Edik said, taking his seat and trying a sip. Rich, full-bodied cognac. Well-aged, with hints of cherry. Just the way Edik liked it.

Pleased, he nodded to Mason, who took a sip of his scotch.

"Now if I had a guess," Mason said, "you're not here for money — which I've already transferred — but for answers."

"Will I get them?"

Mason laughed, and damn the man but his laugh was infectious. Edik didn't want to smile, but couldn't stop himself.

He tried to reassert himself.

"Forgive me, Hierophant—"

"Not here," Mason said sharply. He leaned forward in his seat. "Ranks are a game we must play these days. I accept that. But here, this room, is the most private place we will find outside of the Pyramid. In here, I want the old ways. In here," — he smiled — "please call me Nicholas."

"All right … Nicholas…"

"Yes, Edik?"

Edik tried to find the best way to ask his question, but what came out was, "Why?"

"Which why are you asking?" Mason said, no judgment in his tone. "Why did I send you? Why did I send Donal? Why did—"

"No," Edik said. "My question about Donal is did you know? Did you know he was going to be the emissary of the Fae Courts? Did you know they'd possess him?"

"I'm afraid," Mason said with a sigh, "that on the subject of the fae I can't give you answers right now. Someday, yes, but not right now."

"Well, then why me? And don't give me that crap about first contact protocols. You must have known that wouldn't work."

"There was always a chance," Mason said with a shrug. "I like to employ the simplest approaches first. But if it didn't work, of course I wanted you there. And if you're not sure why, ask your familiar." Mason leaned forward a little, clearly enjoying himself. "And if you're *still* not sure, ask your *crew*."

Edik blinked. "This was about my relationship with spirits?"

"Seems obvious, once you say it that way, doesn't it?" Mason tossed back the rest of his drink and stood. "And now, I'm afraid, I really must be going. I have to get back to Earth, before this Fae Court problem blows up system-wide. Feel free to finish the cognac. Keep the bottle, if you wish."

"Wait," Edik said. "I—"

"Oh," Mason said, and the devil glinted in his eyes. "I should tell you. I've had words with Magister Dmitri Lukyanov about attempting to spy on *my* mission. I doubt the Lukyanov family will say anything more about it. Publicly, at least."

"Well…" Edik started. He hadn't even thought about that memory circle thing recently. Hearing it mentioned now almost drove the next questions out of Edik's head.

Almost.

"But what about—"

"Sorry," Mason said, and Edik doubted he felt sorry, "maybe next time."

A puff of smoke, and Hierophant Nicholas Mason was gone.

"Tell me he didn't just—"

"Illusion," Dola said. "Covering his exit. Damned impressive illusion, but illusion." He put a paw on Edik's wrist. "*Not* teleportation."

"Good," Edik said, and slugged down the rest of his cognac. It burned on the way down, but it tasted good, and the burn was solid. Real. Comforting, in a moment where a little comfort was needed.

Edik left then. And he took the bottle with him. After all, it was good cognac.

SOME OF THE FANCY HOTELS IN BIG CITIES WENT FOR OLD WORLD charm. They tried to replicate the look of things from the few decades — or sometimes centuries — before the rise of magic, and work in little bits of magic to make everything seem a little more wondrous.

That wasn't how the Kennedy Pyramid did things.

First of all, it didn't try to look like an ancient pyramid. It had the shape, but that was where the similarity ended. The entire exterior was done shades of green that could be found on Luna's surface. The dark sections lined the edges, windows, doors, balconies and so forth. The paler sections covered most of the walls, done in a stucco style to make it resemble the actual terrain outside the Barrier, complete with crests and ridges to fake the appearance of craters.

The front doors appeared to be more dark green rock, and the man who opened them — a doorman made up through alchemy and illusion to have a greenish cast to his face and too long a nose, as though he were alien — said nothing in the way of greeting as Donal entered, Fionn beside him.

Entered into darkness. Darkness that lit immediately, but only along a trail ahead of them. A trail of blue-white, just like the spaceport itself.

The air was still in here, and they'd cleansed the slightly licorice scent that perpetually haunted the air in Kennedy. Donal was willing to bet that the water here didn't taste of lemons, either.

No subtlety here. This place was *thick* with magic. Donal could sense scores of spells operating just within a dozen meters of where he stood. Most of them involved communication, scrying, deception, and … different elements.

Ten steps down that lit pathway, a glowing red word appeared in the air.

DESTINATION?

"I'm heading for the top of the pyramid," Donal said, feeling slightly foolish, talking to a sign. "I'm Donal Cuthbert. I've an appointment with Rowan MacPherson."

After a hesitation only just long enough for Donal to notice, the light path changed and led to a bubble.

"A bit much, isn't it?" Donal said. "The cost to maintain just the spells on the lobby for a month must be more than a year of my graduate studies."

"It's a place for those who value privacy," Fionn said. "The tourist guide said that a guest could stay here for a year and never see another human being, if they so wished. They promise perfect security and privacy."

"What about people who want company?"

"I presume they stay elsewhere."

Donal nodded.

They reached the bubble. But the cage didn't open.

"Hello?" Donal said.

"There is a passphrase. In San Luis Obispo, Donal Cuthbert speculated about the job Rowan MacPherson held. What did Donal Cuthbert guess?"

Donal chuckled. "Corporate spymaster."

"Welcome, Donal Cuthbert and familiar."

The cage opened.

"His name is Fionn," Donal said as they entered the cage. To the water elementals, he said, "Top of the pyramid, please."

Moments later the bubble stopped. Donal hadn't seen anything between the first floor and, he presumed, the top. Nothing but the tube of water outside the cage. The bubble was even scry-warded, to keep Donal from casually picking up any spells outside the cage he stood on.

The cage opened at that top floor, and a lit blue-white path led to a door. A good old fashioned solid oak door. Very solid, by the look of it. Donal half wondered if he could knock loudly enough on it for his knock to carry. Especially since Donal could tell as he approached that this door, too, was warded for privacy.

He needn't have worried. The moment he and Fionn reached the door, it opened.

There stood Rowan MacPherson, redheaded and glorious in a cream dress that showed off her figure, and fell short enough to show off her legs and bare feet.

Her hair was down, and she looked more casual and relaxed than Donal had ever seen her.

That alone put him on edge.

"Donal," She said, arms wide for a hug.

"Ah," Donal said, raising a hand to interpose. "I'm not sure we're on hugging terms."

"So paranoid," she said and shook her head as she invited Donal inside.

The room looked plush. Donal had stayed in some *nice* places, and this, well, it didn't *bury* them, but it certainly stood in the running.

Thick, pale blue shag carpet all the way around that radiated comforting earth magic. The interior walls were off-white and soothing, and held landscape paintings from across Luna that freshened the air on a constant basis. The lighting was sourceless, and comfortable. Like the half-hour before twilight — not dimming quite yet, but not bright either.

The freshened air smelled subtly like vanilla, and the furniture all looked heavy and comfortable, not just by design, but through enchantment as well.

Donal was willing to bet that the toilets in this place were enchanted against constipation. Just seemed like that type of place.

Rowan started for the couches. Donal detoured her to an unenchanted dining room table set. Dark woods and upright chairs, and no possibility of mixed signals.

Rowan shook her head with a slight bemused smile, but let Donal sit at the head of the table, and then pointed to the seat at his right hand.

"Too close?" she asked, one eyebrow raised. "Shall I sit at the other end?"

"There's fine," Donal said, and she sat at his right hand.

"All right," she said. "You're not giving a centimeter, and you're not greeting me the way I'd hoped. What's wrong?"

"I was possessed by the fae. Twice."

"Yes," she said, and she looked entirely too comfortable with what Donal just told her. He'd expected a little surprise, at least.

But no, she didn't even bat her green, green eyes.

"I'd worried that something like that might happen," she said, "but I'd hoped it wouldn't be necessary. Was it hard on you?"

"I. Was *possessed*. By *sidhe*." Donal held up two fingers. "Twice."

Rowan frowned. "Is it the possession you object to, or the fact that it happened twice?"

"Rowan."

"All right," she said, raising her hands in surrender. Then she sighed. Then she shook her head. In fact, she seemed to be doing just about everything she could think of, in terms of gestures, to not say what she had to say next.

"You are getting to the point, right?" Donal asked, pleased with how … conversational he'd kept his tone. Even Fionn, seated on the floor beside him, looked impressed.

"Donal," she said through another sigh, "what did you expect? You agreed to be their eyes, their ears, and their mouth."

"I *expected* that I was there to see for them, to listen for them, and to speak for them."

"Donal," she said, tone admonishing. "You agreed *to be their eyes, their ears and their mouth.* You, of all people, should have known what that meant. Speaking for the fae sometimes means speaking for the fae."

"I…" Donal let the word trail off. He grimaced and sat back in his chair. He looked down at Fionn, who looked sympathetic around the eyes, but his ears and tail both clearly said *you should have known what you were getting into.*

"Look at it this way," Rowan said. "By allowing that, you've given the fae better service than they could have dreamed. You accomplished more on this trip than they expected. More even than they hoped. Both Courts are quite pleased with you."

"I'm not so sure that's a good thing," Donal grumbled.

"Bit late to worry about that now."

"True." Donal sighed, then sat up straight, smiling. "But I only agreed to it for that trip to Ganymede."

"That's correct," Rowan said. "But, Donal, think about it. You're the first pure mortal to perform such a service for the fae in hundreds of years. Perhaps since True Thomas. They're better disposed toward you and yours than you could possibly guess."

"… and mine?" Donal said, then leaned forward, elbows on the table, face in his hands. "My mom is going to *kill* me."

"Not at all," Rowan said. "Your mother is a delightful woman. I'm sure she'll understand."

That brought Donal's head up out of his hands.

"You've met my mother?"

"Of course." Rowan laughed, and in her laughter Donal now heard a faint echo of that *sidhe's* laughter. "Years ago, of course, and she had no idea who I was, or why we met when we did."

Donal blinked. "How long have you been working for the fae?"

"My whole life, of course." She smiled a warm smile. "And you, my dear Donal, are the first full mortal who has a chance to do the same. We could work closely together, you and I. Bring the two worlds together in a way that no one has, perhaps not since the invasions of Ireland."

The invasions of Ireland? Donal thought those were pure myth, the stories of Fintan, and the Fir Bolg, the Tuatha De Dannan and the Fomorians…

But then, Donal had also thought that most of the stories about the fae had been metaphorical…

"I don't know," Donal said, and just as fast added, "I'm not committing to anything here and now. Nothing. I've completed that task, and my obligations are finished with it. I quitclaim any obligations I have imposed through my service, that have not already been fulfilled."

Rowan tilted her head. "You're good. I knew there was a reason I liked you."

Donal almost responded to that, but responding to flattery didn't seem like his best course right now.

"So what happens now?" he asked.

"Well, we both know you have to return to grad school. And I understand you've incurred a new obligation to the military that you'll have to fulfill."

"You know about that?"

"Donal," she said, in an admonishing tone. "Tell me that doesn't surprise you."

"It doesn't," Donal said, wishing it surprised him more than it did. Even now, he could remember Rear Admiral Saito saying he had his own way of independently verifying Donal's position...

Wait.

"The military," Donal said. "They don't know my job is done, do they?"

"On the contrary," Rowan said, looking pleased. "They're quite under the impression that it's ongoing. After all, you never told them it was a one-trip gig. And what's more, you told them you'd return with proof in six months."

"I don't need to do that now. Rear Admiral Saito took care of it."

"Yes," she said, rubbing her hands together, "he did, didn't he? But the point is that you implied to them that it was ongoing, and said and did nothing to contradict that."

"So you're saying that the military..." — Donal's eyes widened as his understanding deepened — "and through them the governments, and maybe even through them the media..."

Donal gave Rowan a hopeful look, praying she'd deny that.

"They had marvelous images of you on the shadow news, when they announced you as the first human ambassador to the Fae Courts."

"My mom is going to *kill* me. My grandmothers too. All three of them are going to—"

"To what, Donal?" Rowan said, leaning a little closer. Voice a little more intimate. "To rail at you for doing what people of our shared heritage have been doing for centuries? Mortals have a long tradition of working with the fae."

"Getting tricked by them is more like it. I'm in way deeper now than I agreed to get."

"Do you want out, Donal? Do you really?" She leaned a little closer yet. "You called a *cú sidhe* to be your familiar. After telling all your friends at college that you were going to wait and bind an elemental from the Enochian approach."

"But—"

"And Donal, you could have said no to my offer in San Luis Obispo. We both know it. But you didn't *want* to. The truth is, you *want* to work with the fae. You *want* to be their emissary. To learn some of their magics perhaps."

"Not to be possessed by them."

"We can work that out," she said, smoothly, her voice almost hypnotic in its lulling tones now. "There's no need for it to ever happen again. They needed to save the Du Mak people and send a message at the same time. But now they've done that, and they've spoken for the Rhian people as well."

Donal smiled. No irony to that smile now, save maybe a hint of superiority that he didn't mind feeling at the moment, all things considered.

"You don't really think shifting your voice that way is going to do anything to persuade me, do you?"

"No, Donal," she said never looking away from his eyes. "That's not what I want here."

"What do you mean?"

"We've been talking about what you want. And what the Courts want. But haven't you wondered what *I* want? Right here and right now?"

Donal narrowed his eyes in suspicion. "What?"

"You."

"Seriously," Donal said. "What?"

"I'm being serious," she said, through a soft chuckle. "You're handsome, you're an impressive magician, and you've been touched by the fae without being burnt. A girl could do much worse."

Donal's first response was to snap back a denial of any possibility along those lines.

But he checked that. There was more to this woman than met the eye. He'd learned that much over the past few weeks. Denying her outright might not be his smartest move.

He almost shook his head when he heard himself think that. Only a couple of weeks of involvement with the fae, and he was starting to think like one.

"Not today," Donal said finally, in a tone that brooked no debate. "You're beautiful, there's no denying it. And maybe we have more in common than I would have believed only a few weeks ago. But I need to keep a clear head if I'm going to even consider working with the fae. And I can't do that if you and I..."

Rowan's laugh then almost felt like foreplay. It was low and intimate and Donal would have sworn he felt it rubbing along his spine. But then she sat back and smiled a more professional smile, her tone all business.

"Right then," she said. "Until you feel more comfortable on the fae front, let us be business allies. Anything else can wait."

"Right," Donal said slowly. "But if you're with the Courts—"

"So are you, Donal. At least, in the eyes of the public, the governments, and the military."

"That's right," Donal said, feeling a slow smile cross his face. "So if I came forward now, say, at a press conference, and said that I left that position..."

"You wouldn't."

"Well, that would weaken the way the Courts look, in the eyes of the human governments."

Rowan paled, which was quite a feat, given her creamy complexion.

"Dangerous game to play, Donal. Please don't."

"Donal," Fionn started, in words only Donal could understand.

But Donal cut Fionn off with a quick gesture.

"What?" Donal blinked in faked innocence and raised a hand to his chest. "Would I do that?"

Rowan narrowed her eyes.

"You don't know," Donal said. "And that's the point."

"What are you saying?" she said.

"I'm saying that I have a better position to negotiate my role than you were giving me credit for."

That got a broad smile out of Rowan. So broad and sincere Donal felt it give him a lift, despite himself.

"Very good, Donal. *Very* good. Oh, it's going to be fun working with you."

"We haven't worked out terms yet…"

But Donal knew they would. He knew he wouldn't leave that room without agreeing to continue on as an emissary for the Fae Courts. But he was damned sure going to negotiate better terms, and a no-possession clause. He was going to show them just how much he'd learned from Donatello Mancuso.

Still. His mom was going to *kill* him for this.

SIGN UP FOR STEFON'S NEWSLETTER

Stefon loves to keep in touch with his readers, and loves to keep you reading. The best way for him to do both is for you to sign up for his newsletter.

Sign up at http://www.stefonmears.com/join

If you sign up for Stefon's newsletter, you get...

- Monthly updates about his publishing and travel schedules
- His latest news, in brief, and answers to reader questions
- A free short story for signing up
- List-only offers and occasional specials
- Plus a free short story every month!

ABOUT THE AUTHOR

Stefon Mears has the birthmark of a changeling. Stefon has more than thirty books to his credit, and he never stops writing. He earned his M.F.A. in Creative Writing from N.I.L.A., and his B.A. in Religious Studies (double emphasis in Ritual and Mythology) from U.C. Berkeley. He's a lifelong gamer and fantasy fan. Stefon lives in Portland, Oregon, with his wife and three cats.

Look for Stefon online:
www.stefonmears.com
himself@stefonmears.com